TO REFRAIN FROM EMBRACING

copyright © 2023 by Jeffrey Luscombe.
All rights reserved.

No part of this book may be reproduced in any form without written permission from the publisher, except by a reviewer, who may quote brief passages in a review where appropriate credit is given; nor may any part of this book be reproduced, stored in a retrieval system, or transmitted in any form or by any means—electronic, photocopying, recording, or other—without specific written permission from the publisher.

All of the names, characters, places, and incidents in this book are the product of the author's imagination or are used fictitiously, and any resemblance to actual persons, living or dead, events, or locales is entirely coincidental.

Interior book design by Ryan Vance.
Cover design by Ryan Vance.
Author photo by John Burridge Photography

Published by Lethe Press
www.lethepressbooks.com
lethepress@aol.com
ISBN: 978-1-59021-748-1

TO REFRAIN FROM EMBRACING

JEFFREY LUSCOMBE

For Mom

A time to weep, and a time to laugh; a time to mourn, and a time to dance; A time to cast away stones, and a time to gather stones together; a time to embrace and a time to refrain from embracing.

Ecclesiastes 3:4-5

May 1977

One

"I can't believe they actually have goddamn basket weaving here," Ted said. The corners of his mouth slid into a half-smile as he lit a cigarette and exhaled bluish smoke into the air with a sigh of pleasure, pushing a greasy strand of his shoulder-length hair behind his ear. Ted wasn't supposed to smoke in his hospital bed. They had been told to either go to the smoking lounge at the end of the corridor or, if a walk down the hall seemed exceedingly difficult, to stand outside their room where cylindrical ashtrays lined the hallway. Still, cigarette butts would pepper the hospital corridor until someone on the cleaning staff swept them up with a broom periodically during the day.

For the most part, hospital staff turned a blind eye to patients smoking in their rooms as long as they were not over-medicated or had not just returned from their latest round of ECT. Now, after five weeks, Ted was finally free of the haze he had been in his first month here. During those first few weeks, he had been so groggy from the medication pumped into him that he'd nod off every time he sat down. He had fallen asleep at meals, sitting in the hospital garden, and while watching television in the lounge. One night he had even fallen asleep on the toilet, to be woken up by an orderly in the morning.

"I always thought that basket weaving in the nuthouse was just a gag until I got here."

Stretched out on his bed across from Ted with his hands clasped behind his head, Jonathan, Ted's roommate in room 215W of the Hamilton Psychiatric Hospital, grinned and continued staring up at the nicotine-stained tiled ceiling.

Ted parked his cigarette in his mouth, sat up with his legs hanging off the side of the bed, and looked down at the scuffed brown loafers he wore without any socks. He had to change his clothes sometime today. He had been wearing the same light blue button-up shirt and brown corduroy pants for three days in a row now, and if he didn't get into the shower and put on a change of clothes, then he would hear about it from Dr. Shackelford. Ted had learned that if you didn't change your goddamn pants and underwear every day in this joint, you were labeled 'clinically depressed.' Or worse. He poked the tip of his finger into the cigarette burn in the front of his corduroys, a souvenir from his first few doped-up weeks here. And that, Ted said to himself, is why they don't want you smoking in bed.

"What exactly are the therapeutic benefits of weaving baskets, anyway?" Ted asked.

He turned his head and blew a lungful of smoke over Jonathan's stretched-out legs toward the door leading to the hallway. Ted had refused to do any of the basket weaving, leather crafts, or other make-work bullshit most patients did in the large 'art room' adjacent to the cafeteria every day.

"Basket weaving is for relaxation." Jonathan wore a slight smile. He pushed himself into a sitting position leaning back on his hospital pillow. "Over and under and over and under. See how relaxing that is?"

"If you say so," Ted replied.

"And we get a stylish basket to take home to our loved ones when they finally let us loose on the world again. Just look at that..." Jonathan motioned to the empty perfectly made hospital bed on the other side of the small room, where a dozen or so woven reed baskets were stacked neatly inside one another under the bed. "And speaking of basket cases, Carl will have enough to open his own basket boutique when he gets out. He could sell them at the farmer's market."

"Yeah, maybe put up a sign that says something like—" Ted lifted his hand and motioned from left to right. "Baskets... from... the Nuthouse." He laughed until his smoker's cough set in.

"But even after all that basket weaving, old Carl doesn't seem all that relaxed, does he?" Jonathan said, smirking.

"Carl, relaxed? No, I can't say he is."

"So much for its therapeutic benefits," Jonathan said, flicking ash into a Styrofoam cup, half full of cold breakfast coffee, sitting on the brown bedside table between the two beds.

Besides the coffee cup, on Ted's side of the table, laid a biography of Che Guevara that Ted's wife, Gloria, had brought up to the hospital the previous week, along with the brown corduroy pants he was now wearing and a few pairs of clean underwear. On the only shelf at the bottom of the bedside table was an empty canister of caramel corn. Ted glanced at the canister and smiled.

Ted Moore had a round, jovial face, striking light green eyes, thick lips, and a slightly bulbous nose that could be attributed to not only his Norwegian mother but also an early acquired taste for Canadian Club Whiskey. He had grown a new light brown beard in the hospital, slightly darker than the long sandy-coloured hair on his head. Ted wore round silver-framed eyeglasses that had, by that time, gone out of style, but he could not bring himself to buy the brightly coloured larger plastic frames that everyone seemed to be wearing. He found them decadent and ridiculous, like much of what he saw around him. Ted was thin, even thinner since he'd entered the hospital, and had the pale complexion of his English and Scandinavian forefathers, making him susceptible to sunburns and, during summer months, constant peeling of his nose and shoulders. On his left forearm, an orange and black full-length tiger, a cheap and poorly executed tattoo he had gotten while in the army, crawled toward his elbow. And with lines growing seemingly by the day around his eyes and forehead, Ted knew he looked every year of his thirty-three years. He even sported both upper and lower dentures before he turned thirty. He had celebrated his thirty-third birthday in the hospital a month earlier, but there hadn't been much actual celebrating since the only birthday gift he had received that day was 150 volts to his head. Still, Ted liked to believe that a casual observer who saw him sitting in the hospital garden or lounge wouldn't think Ted was a patient at all, just a visitor dropping by to see some poor crazy friend for the afternoon... that is until that casual observer came closer and noticed the jagged black and red scar that ran across Ted's throat.

Ted scratched at the whiskers on his neck above the scar. Because razor blades were not permitted in the hospital, patients had to use a communal electric razor kept at the nurse's station if they attempted to keep a well-groomed appearance. The problem was that the electric razor was dull, often clogged with whiskers, and left as much stubble on their faces as it took off. So, a few male patients, like Ted, had decided it was easier to grow a beard, while others, like Jonathan, still did their best to keep themselves neat and trim during their sojourn at the nuthouse.

A young nurse with strawberry-blonde hair tied up in a bun and glossy red lips walked past the doorway and then, taking a step back, poked her head into the room. She was dressed all in white, from the starched collar of her white nurse's uniform to her polished white shoes, except for the black nametag over her ample left breast that read *Debbie*. She had a pretty-enough face and an early summer tan. Probably, Ted had thought, from weekend trips to the beach with some handsome and equally young guy who tanned and never peeled. She peered through the doorway with her brows furrowed and hands fixed on her hips.

"Shame on you two boys! Smoking in bed!"

Ted blew smoke out of his nose. "I guess the jig is up."

"Oh, don't worry, Mr. Moore. I won't tell on you or Mr. Pressman... this time!"

Her wide, toothpaste-perfect smile both irritated and turned Ted on. It was a smile that nurses use for invalids and lunatics. Nevertheless, he imagined what Nurse Debbie's body looked like under her white nurse's uniform. Half the porno movies Ted had seen, and he had seen a lot, had started with a girl in a uniform peeping in on some guy in a hospital room. *Her panties are white too.*

And then, with a cheery wave, Nurse Debbie turned her strawberry-blond head and continued down the hallway toward the lounge.

"I'd love to ball her," Ted said. "I mean, if I wasn't married. I don't think I've ever fucked a nurse."

Much of Ted's knowledge of nurses came from movies or television since there weren't many nurses in his neighborhood. A couple of years earlier, he had seen *One Flew Over the Cuckoo's Nest* at the Odeon Theatre on King Street. But, when Ted had found himself locked up here, he discovered that, unlike in that movie, the nursing staff at The Hamilton Psychiatric Hospital was mainly made up of overly cheerful women who, like Nurse Debbie, smiled a lot and called him Mr. Moore whenever they happened to walk by. The nurses did occasionally lay down the law and take control of some of the more challenging patients when needed, but Ted couldn't fault them for that. No, there was not a Nurse Ratched among them.

"Yeah, I'd probably ball her too," Jonathan finally said, looking straight ahead. "If, like you, I wasn't married."

"Christ, it took you that long to decide?" Ted said.

"Well, I was weighing the pros and cons. There are always cons with balling, my friend. Always!"

"Maybe you should take up basket weaving." Ted picked a fleck of tobacco off the tip of his tongue. "You ever screw a nurse?"

"I screwed a dental receptionist once. It wasn't anything to write home about."

"She probably had nice teeth, though," Ted said.

Jonathan scratched one of his long, black sideburns. "I think she had dentures."

Jonathan was a few years older than Ted, in his late thirties. He was good-looking, at least by Hamilton standards, and had a thick black moustache, a pair of shaggy sideburns, and a perpetual five o'clock shadow. He had big hands with dark wiry hair on his knuckles that ran up his arms and covered most of his body. He had a slim athletic build and wore a Montreal Expos baseball cap most of the time, taking it off only to shower and sleep. Jonathan had arrived two weeks after Ted was admitted. Ted didn't know many details but did know that Jonathan had walked into the hospital of his own accord. There were no ambulances or cops, which was the way many people arrived here. Jonathan had driven to the hospital one

Monday morning with his toothbrush in his breast pocket, walked up to the reception desk, and told them he wanted to be admitted.

Now *that* really did seem nuts, Ted thought.

The afternoon sun was shining through the window. It grew warm on Ted's back and made the white sheets on the four beds in the room glow incandescently. Ted gently touched the scar on his throat. It still had not healed. Not even close. Dr. Shackelford had said that would take months more. He ran his finger along the thick crusty scab below his Adam's apple. Though the stitches were out, Ted knew he would always have a hell of a scar there, like a cryptogram that even a child could decipher: DAMAGED. But the nuthouse was full of scars. *My scar isn't even the most interesting one in the room!*

"Still hurt?" Jonathan asked.

"No, not really." Ted took his fingers away from his throat and put his hand down on his lap.

Ted took a last drag on his cigarette before adding it to the soggy butts in the Styrofoam cup.

"Your wife coming up today?" Jonathan asked.

"No, not today. Is yours?"

"Nah, my shock treatments freak Lola out."

"Shock freaks everyone out. The funny thing is the treatments don't freak me out nearly as much as everyone else."

For Ted, the shock treatments weren't so bad. It worked faster than the antidepressants he had been taking. Before each treatment, Ted was given a muscle relaxer and some anaesthesia, so there were no convulsions. It was like going into an operation. And, in a way, shock was like surgery, slicing out painful pieces of Ted's memory. When he woke up, it was as if there was a hole in his brain, like the one in his corduroys, a beautiful dime-sized hole somewhere deep in his head where all the hurt had been. *By now, my brain must look like Swiss cheese.*

"Lola refuses to bring Max up to see me. He's only two, so he doesn't know where the hell I am. She just told the kid I went away and that I'll be back soon," Jonathan continued.

"Two years old is way too young to understand all this," Ted said.

"Dr. Shackelford said that Lola could bring Max to the garden some weekend. I'd like that. Max wouldn't even have to come into the hospital; he could meet me outside. But Lola said no. She doesn't want him anywhere near this place. As if he'd catch something."

"Josh is ten. He knows I'm here, but I won't let Gloria bring him up to visit me. Not with me being so fucked up the first month with my fried brain and throat ripped up. I'll try to explain it when I get home. I've spoken to him a few times on the phone, but when I do, he sounds so... so fucking *resigned*. It kills me," Ted said.

"Maybe we need more shock and not less," Jonathan said.

"Do you think the shock is working?"

"I guess so. It makes me forget. So, if that's what you mean by *working*, then, yeah, it works. How about you?"

"Absolutely!" Ted said. "Since they started giving me shock therapy, I haven't *once* tried to slice my throat open with a broken piece of glass again. Not once!"

Suddenly Ted heard a clang like someone had kicked something metal down the hallway outside their door, followed by Nurse Debbie yelling down the corridor.

"Rick! Your mother wants to say goodbye to you before she leaves!" Debbie shouted. "Could you please come back and at least say goodbye to her?"

"Enter Nut Number Three," Jonathan said.

A deep voice with a strong north-end Hamilton accent yelled, "Tell her to fuck off!"

"My stupid mother still thinks I'm five," Rick said, stomping into the room. He wore only Y-front navy-blue briefs and a white T-shirt under his blue and white striped hospital robe that, having come undone, hung down at his sides. He held a white teddy bear with amber plastic eyes and a red velvet bow tie in his left hand. He swung the bear around twice in the air, threw it against the wall, and then sat beside Ted; the bed creaked and dipped with the extra weight, and Ted struggled not to fall into Rick's side. Rick needed a shower, too, Ted thought. He smelled like dirty teenage boy.

"I'm guessing you didn't have a good visit with your mom, Rick," Jonathan said.

"I told her to bring me up cigarettes and candy. So, tell me how she heard me say, bring a fucking stupid-ass stuffed bear."

Rick stretched out his long muscular legs across the gap between Ted and Jonathan's beds.

"You've got stains on the front of your underwear, you dirty, bugger," Jonathan said.

Rick looked down at the front of his underwear and shrugged.

"I hope your robe was closed when you were in the lounge with your mom," Jonathan added.

"Who the fuck cares?"

"I have two teenage sons," Ted said. "You should see the mess they make of their underwear… and sheets. Sometimes the wife needs a chisel on laundry day. I can give you a clean pair if you want,"

"Fuck it," Rick said.

Rick was the youngest by almost fifteen years of the four men occupying room 215W in The Hamilton Psychiatric Hospital. The son of an Italian immigrant bricklayer from the Industrial north end of the city, Rick had played hockey all through his youth and, Ted thought, could probably kick the shit out of everyone in the room if he had a mind to. Rick had a large round face, Roman nose, dark, sad eyes, and, at nineteen, still had braces on his teeth. When he arrived, his curly black hair had been clipped short by hospital staff but now had grown out about an inch and a half. He had a thick neck, strong brawny arms, and the big hands of a bricklayer, though he hadn't gone into his father's profession. Rick had not yet grown a full chest of hair, but a reasonable amount of callow light-brown fur grew over his olive skin running down to his still baby-smooth belly where a large white starburst-shaped scar now occupied the area where Rick's navel had once been.

Rick had tried to kill himself twice.

The first attempt happened when Rick was only sixteen. He'd shot himself in the stomach with one of his father's guns. "I did it right in front of my parents while they were watching *Happy Days*," Rick had told Ted and Jonathan one day in the hospital garden. "I decided that if I was going out, I was going to leave a mess behind. But except for a big stain on the carpet by the sofa, I didn't do all that much damage to myself. They cut out a hunk of my gut, stitched me up, and sent me here, to this fucking dump for five months then sent me home. I was in the same room too—just with three different fruitcakes. No offense."

"None taken," Ted had said.

Six weeks ago, he had strung himself up in the bathroom with an extension cord but lucky for him (or unlucky by Rick's own account) his mother had come home early from grocery shopping and found him unconscious. Just in time, the doctors had said.

"Do you know she now goes to church and thanks St. Francis for that?" Rick had said. "He must be the patron saint of perpetual fuckups. Who knew it took so long to hang yourself? I sure didn't. If I was smart, I would have blown my head off the first time. But I wanted to feel, you know, what it was like as I checked out. When I go, I want to experience everything turning black. You know what I mean? When I was hanging there with the cord tight over my windpipe, I could feel it all slipping away, bit by bit. It was fucking beautiful! And it was so *easy*, you know? No one ever tells you how easy it is. Anyway, I might be locked in here even longer this time. Maybe a year, they said. So, I might see 1978 roll around after all. Lucky me."

Ted feared that one day he would walk into the washroom to take his morning piss and see that big Italian kid sitting on the toilet with his wrists slashed. But what, Ted asked himself, could be so wrong at nineteen years old? When Ted was nineteen, he had already returned home from two years in the army. Things weren't great, but...

"How's your mom, Rick?" Jonathan asked. "Besides having the temerity to bring you a teddy bear."

"She's fucked."

"Ah, come on," Ted said, slapping Rick's hairy knee. "It doesn't look like she starved you or anything. How bad can she possibly be?" Ted had seen Rick and his mother in the lounge earlier that morning, sitting at a table alone. Rick's mother had the same dark, sad eyes as Rick. If Rick's father had given Rick the hands of a bricklayer, Ted thought, his mother had given Rick the eyes of a saint.

"Jesus fucking Christ! That's the problem with your generation. You all think that as long as your parents didn't starve you or lock you in a closet for ten years, then they're golden. Sorry, that may be how it worked in the old days, but it don't work that way anymore," Rick said.

My generation? Ted thought. He makes me sound like I'm Carl's age.

"You're going to miss your mom when she's gone," Jonathan said.

"Probably not." Rick kicked off his slippers. His feet needed a good scrubbing, too, Ted thought. And his toenails should be trimmed. Nail clippers were another forbidden item in this place, though the damage nail clippers could do to a person seemed questionable.

"She'd miss you if you were gone," Ted said.

Rick yawned and fell backwards across Ted's bed. "What do I care?"

Rick was kept medicated to within an inch of his life because of his size and because he once pushed a nurse across the room who berated him for not showering. After that, they increased his meds. Despite all that medication, Rick was still horny as hell, jerking off once or twice every night under his hospital blanket. Ted didn't care; he had been in the army at seventeen and knew what young guys did in their beds in the dark. It was normal, maybe the most normal thing about Rick. The orderlies would grunt when they saw Rick's sheets on sheet-changing day, but Rick was a young and healthy guy—except for his head. No, the head wasn't too healthy, but the rest of Rick seemed to be in the pink, even minus that hunk of gut. And just maybe he wasn't a hopeless case. The kid could come around with a few more shock treatments and the right medication. Sometimes people did. Then he could go out and find himself some nice Italian girl, start laying bricks like his father, and settle down like Ted and Jonathan had. Ted shook his head. *Sure, and end up right back here in ten or fifteen years.*

"Did your dad come up today too, Rick?" Jonathan asked.

Rick had never introduced either Ted or Jonathan to his family when they visited, usually taking his folks to an empty side of the lounge or outside in the garden.

"No," Rick said. "Thank God I only have to see him once a week. He only comes up Saturdays with my big sister Claudia. She's the only person I can stand seeing. At least Claudia brings me big bags of candy and smokes." He slowly sat back up. "Hey, can I bum a cigarette, Ted? I promise I'll give it back on Saturday when Claudia comes."

"Help yourself." Ted wondered if Claudia had been in the living room along with Rick's parents the night he shot himself. Ted knew that when you're in a state like that you don't care who is around. "And you know you don't need to pay me back." Ted handed Rick a cigarette and placed the pack back on the back cover of Che Guevara.

"Hey, you got any of that caramel corn left, Ted?" Rick lit his cigarette.

"Sorry, kid, you cleaned me out."

"Are you gonna get more?"

"Without a doubt."

Ted would easily have given Rick anything he had on his bedside table: junk food, cigarettes, *Playboy* magazines, whatever the kid wanted. If one of Gloria's kids was ever in the same spot, Ted hoped someone would be around to keep an eye out for them too since Rick was around the same age as Gloria's oldest son, Kevin.

"Have you told that lady who brings it up for you that I'm the one who eats all the caramel corn?" Rick asked, dropping ashes on the floor.

"She wouldn't mind," Ted said.

"They don't give prizes away in that kind of caramel corn, do they, Ted?" Jonathan cocked his head with a knowing glace toward Ted.

"Um… no," Ted said.

Ted heard footsteps coming down the hall towards them, briefly stopping and starting again.

"Afternoon pill time," Jonathan said.

Rick groaned. They seemed determined to drug him back into semi-consciousness as soon as he gained some coherence.

"All I want is for my mom to come up once a week for five minutes to drop off a carton of cigarettes and candy and then fuck off until next week. That's all I fucking need to be happy," Rick said.

"Are you sure that's all you need?" Ted asked. "Just cigarettes and candy to make you happy?"

"Maybe some caramel corn, too," Rick said.

"What about a girl?" Jonathan asked.

"Yeah, what about some nice Italian girl from the north end with a name like Maria or Rosa," Ted said.

"You're both married. How happy are you?"

"I'm pretty happy being married," Ted said.

Rick flicked more ashes on the floor. "Not happy enough to keep you out of this place."

The kid had him there. Ted took off his glasses, placed them on his lap, and rubbed the sensitive indentations that thirty years of wearing eyeglasses had made on the bridge of his nose.

The sound of footsteps grew louder, and Nurse Debbie entered their room again, this time carrying a tray of small paper cups filled with pills and a cup of water. Ted knew the drugs weren't for him or Jonathan. Ted's next little paper cup of Thorazine and whatever other *pills du jour* they were doling out would not be until that evening, like some depressing after-dinner mints.

"Time for your afternoon pills, Rick," Debbie said.

Rick sighed and rolled his eyes.

"What's this, Mr. Moore? Mr. Pressman?" She said, turning, first to Ted and then to Jonathan. "Are you two men letting this boy smoke in bed?" She offered her big toothpaste-commercial grin again.

"I'm nineteen, lady. Old enough to finger-bang my high school art teacher in the supply closet. I'm no boy."

"Well then, here's your pills, old man," she said without looking shocked and handed Rick the small cup containing two pills, one small white one and a larger peach-coloured one.

He picked out the pills from the cup, dropped them into his mouth, and swallowed them without the water as Debbie watched. He crushed the paper cup and tossed it onto the tray.

She held out the cup to Rick. "No water?"

"No."

Debbie turned to Ted. "You know you look more and more like Jesus every day, Mr. Moore."

"Hey, Ted, turn that cup of water into wine," Jonathan said jokingly.

Ted put his glasses on again. "I wish I could… but there isn't a lot that's holy about me."

"Oh, I'm just fooling with you," Debbie said. "And you only look like Jesus when you're not wearing your glasses. When you have them on you look more like John Denver."

"Ted is nothing like Jesus," Jonathan said. "Jesus didn't have a tattoo. And Jesus wasn't a communist like Ted. Or wait… was he? Being Jewish I don't have to know that shit."

"I'm a socialist, not a communist," Ted said.

"What?" Rick said, apparently lost in the conversation.

"Someday, if they ever let us out of here," Jonathan said, "we can go to a bar, and you can explain the difference between socialism and communism to Rick and me over a beer and a Thorazine or two. That is if the politburo lets you, I mean."

Ted liked his and Jonathan's banter. It was like Abbott and Costello if they had made a movie called *Abbott and Costello Meet in A Psych Ward* or something. And he and Jonathan had more in common than one would initially think. Besides being crazy, they were both married, both had young sons, and both had been in the army: Ted as a UN Peacekeeper in the Congo and Jonathan in Vietnam.

"You men really should be in the hall or the lounge if you're going to smoke," Debbie said just as Carl Gruber, the fourth and final man staying in Room 215W walked into the room carrying yet another new basket.

"And there's Nut Number Four," Jonathan said. "The gangs all here!"

"Since that Mary Hartman had that nervous breakdown of hers on the TV last year everyone wants to have one too," Ted said.

"Well, hello, hello, pretty lady," Carl said in his high-pitched matronly schoolteacher voice, bowing his head slightly to the nurse.

"Hello, Mr. Gruber," Debbie replied without looking at him.

"And I'm not nuts, thank you very much, Mr. *Pressman*," Carl said, turning to Jonathan.

Carl placed his new basket on his bed, walked to the foot of Ted's bed, and folded his hands over his stomach as beads of sweat dripped down his red face. His fingers were perpetually orange and greasy from eating bag after bag of cheese puffs from the hospital vending machine. The smell of powdered cheese and sweat always hovered around Carl.

"Now you all make sure that boy doesn't doze off in bed with that cigarette," Debbie said before walking out of the room.

"And here I thought Carl was talking to you when he said 'hello, pretty lady.'" Ted nudged Rick, who ignored the bad joke and tossed his cigarette on the floor between the beds.

"Jesus! You are impossible to get a laugh out of, Rick, you know that?" Ted said, stretching out one leg to crush Rick's still-lit butt under the heel of his brown loafer.

"Nothing to laugh about," Rick said. "In fact, I could give you a whole fucking list of things that aren't funny right now."

"Try to be like Carl," Jonathan said. "Carl smiles through everything wrong with the world. Carl smiles all the time. Let's all try and be more like Carl."

"I just decide to make the best of things." Carl pulled a handkerchief from the front pocket of his hospital robe with his orange fingers and wiped the sweat from his face and neck.

"That's all we need to do? Just make the best of things. Why the hell didn't I think of that?" Ted asked.

"Nuclear war, famine, over-population, inflation… let's all just keep grinning like idiots like good old Carl here," Jonathan said.

Carl Gruber was a fourth-grade teacher in his forties. Short, round, and balding, Carl moved with the agility of a medicine ball rolling through the mud. Always out of breath and sweating, he carried a clownish yellow handkerchief with white polka dots, soiled from snot and sweat, in his robe pocket to wipe away the perspiration that seemed to constantly drip down his forehead, upper lip, and neck, though never using it to wipe the oily cheese puff gunk from his lips, which was permanently encrusted in the corners of his mouth and fingernails. Ted wasn't sure if it was Carl's medication or his large size that made him sweat all the time, but he must have terrorized the kids in his class.

"Did you enjoy your visit with your mother today, Rick?" Carl asked in a manner that Ted thought he saved for his fourth-grade students.

"No, I did not enjoy the visit with my mother today." Rick yawned loudly without covering his mouth.

"I wish my mother was still alive," Carl said. "You only get one mother, my boy. You should remember that."

"Oh, fuck off, you freak." Rick slipped his slippers back on his dirty feet. "I'm gonna go out in the garden to smoke a joint before these pills knock me out."

Rick fumbled with the small ties on his hospital robe and, unable to tie them with his big clumsy fingers, finally just left the robe open and walked across the room toward his bed. With a look of annoyance, he grabbed the newly weaved basket on Carl's bed and threw it against the wall in the same spot he had tossed the stuffed bear.

"Why'd you go and do that?" Carl said.

Ignoring Carl, Rick picked up a book from the bedside table between his and Carl's bed and pulled out a joint he had hidden in the spine.

"Reefer! Count me in." Jonathan rolled out of bed, straightening his Expos ball cap over his shaggy black hair.

Rick frowned. "Just how old are you, Pressman? A hundred and fifty-two? Who the fuck says *reefer* anymore?"

"Yeah, Jonathan," Ted said chucking. "Did you sit in the Vietnam jungle waiting to shoot the big bad Viet Cong communists and say to the guy next to you, 'Hey, doughboy, don't bogart that reefer'?"

"As a matter of fact, I did." Jonathan said.

"I bet you did," Ted said.

"So, how did you get your hands on that anyway? Did your mom smuggle it in up the teddy bear?" Jonathan asked.

"I got my ways. But this shit isn't cheap, so you'll have to give me a few bucks later if you want a toke."

Ted knew exactly where Rick was getting his pot. Ted had learned that you could get pretty much anything you wanted if you knew the ropes in the nuthouse. This wasn't a prison, as they liked to say. You either had a visitor bring it up or you knew someone on the inside, an orderly probably, who could get you what you wanted. Rick was probably paying through the nose for it.

"Sheesh! You guys and your dope. It's darn sad if you ask me." Carl shook his head as he walked across to the room, bent over with a grunt, picked up the basket and sat down with a thump on his own bed, carefully turning the basket over, searching for damage.

"Nobody did ask you, fuck-face," Rick said. "And just keep your mouth shut about it too. I'm Italian. I know people."

Jonathan grinned. "Who do you know?"

"And, while we're at it," Rick said, "I'm not sure what's a more fucking stupid word for it, *dope* or *reefer*. Another thing about your guys' generation—"

"Us guys?" Ted doused another cigarette in the Styrofoam cup. "I'm not Carl's generation. He's like twenty years older than I am for Christ's sake."

"I'm forty-one," Carl said.

"Forty-one? Really? Only forty-one?" Ted said, genuinely surprised.

"And you're, what, Ted? Thirty-five?"

"I'm thirty-three."

"Same difference." Carl refused to turn his gaze away from the basket he was inspecting.

Jesus Christ! I'm only eight years younger than old Carl? Christ, now I need a fucking Thorazine too. Ted hopped off the bed. "I'm coming too. Then I got to take a shower. I'm starting to smell like Carl."

"Well, if you're coming hurry up before they wise up," Rick said. "Not that they care much. They just want us comatose until they throw us back on the streets of Hamilton to hang ourselves or shoot ourselves or… slice our throats open, eh, Ted?" He smiled. Not much of a smile but enough to see.

Ted smirked. "You really are a little prick." He was just happy the kid finally smiled.

"Maybe I'll try cutting my throat next time. If nothing else I'll have another cool scar," Rick said.

"Don't use a broken beer bottle. It doesn't work too well."

"You guys aren't funny," Carl said.

"Want to hear something really fucking funny?" Rick said. "It's the crazy guy who took his entire fourth-grade class hostage and fucking scared the shit out of them until the police came and hauled his fat ass away. The same guy who wants to tell the rest of us what's funny and what's not. Now that's fucking hysterical. Though it probably wasn't so funny to those kids, was it, Carl?"

Carl ignored the remark and the three men walked out of 215W and down the ashtray-lined corridor toward the hospital garden.

"This stuff any good, Rick?" Ted asked.

"As good as you can expect."

"Luckily," Ted replied. "I never expect much."

Ted had heard stories about the infamous Hamilton Psychiatric Hospital all his life, just as everyone else born and raised in Hamilton had, but he'd never been inside it. Not until the night they brought him in.

Unremarkable from the outside, the sprawling one-storey structure had been built only ten years earlier. It was a tawny beige brick building with faded olive-green aluminum siding around its many windows and large wooden double doors at the front entrance. It could easily have been mistaken for a high school. Architects seemed to have gone out of their way to ensure the new hospital looked nothing like its predecessor, the old Hamilton Lunatic Asylum, that had once been on the same parcel of land on the edge of the mountain on West Fifth Street. The original asylum, built in the late 1880s, was an enormous red brick gothic building built to hold the growing number of hopeless inebriates that had plagued the growing industrial city. Later, the asylum would expand its mission, accepting those suffering from wet-brain psychosis, syphilitic insanity, and other such unfortunates.

Even today, Ted would hear old-time residents of Hamilton speak about the days when they would occasionally hear the asylum siren, signalling to the city below that another lunatic had escaped. As a child, Ted always felt unsafe whenever he looked up and saw the old Asylum on the mountain brow. The Hamilton Lunatic Asylum stood for generations but now the only relic left over from the old asylum days was the Manor House. Built in the same gothic style as the old asylum, it was a decaying three-story ruddy brick box with a yellowing white porch and matching two-story wings on either side. The Manor House sat directly across a well-kept garden behind the new hospital connected by a garden path, and still housed some doctor's offices, an employee lunchroom, and held, Ted was told, a century's worth of fading and molding medical files that Ted imagined to be full of botched lobotomies and suspicious deaths.

Ted shuffled down the corridor to the hospital lounge in a clean pair of jeans, a harvest-gold polyester short-sleeved shirt and matching yellow wool socks that Gloria had brought up earlier that week, and brown loafers that he had cleaned up as best he could with some water and paper towel from the men's room. He shuffled a lot these days. It was quite different from how he'd strutted like the cock-of-the-walk down the streets of east Hamilton not too long ago. It was the drugs they gave him that slowed him down, mostly. Ted had not kept track of the concoction of drugs that he was on now. They had started him on some, stopped them, tried others, and then put him back on the ones they had taken him off. Then they took him off them again. It was too exhausting to keep up.

"This is for anxiety."

"This is to help you sleep."

"This is for depression."

"This is for pain."

Chewing a fresh stick of Doublemint gum, Ted entered the cool fluorescent white lights of the hospital lounge into a fog of cigarette smoke that constantly hung in the air. He knew that if he was ever going to get out of this place, he would have to try, but he wasn't ready to get out of the hospital quite yet. For the moment, it was the safest place to be.

The hospital lounge was built for patient comradery and cheerful family visits, and they had done their best to make it look pleasant and inviting with colourful furniture and a large Zenith colour television, nevertheless it was, perhaps, the saddest room in the hospital. Its enormity, heavy with an overall mood of sadness, failure, and shame hung in the air like the cigarette smoke. Most difficulties that arose with patients happened in the lounge and usually when family was visiting. To keep any major altercations at bay, large orderlies, dressed in white, were always standing by, like sentinels, near entrances and exits. Nothing could upset patients as quickly or as thoroughly as family.

The lounge was almost empty except for a few patients scattered around the large room, and the odd visitor. Ted could always make out the visitors; they were pink and plump and always looked so concerned. Patients, on the other hand, seemed far less concerned with being where they were. And everyone in the hospital, everyone but Carl, seemed to lose weight in here. Not that Ted and the others weren't fed well; they shoved food, and big helpings of it, at them three times a day in the hospital cafeteria, but most of it went in the garbage at the end of the meals.

I should write a diet book, Ted thought. Something along the lines of *The Drinking Man's Diet* except I'd call it *The Crazy Man's Diet*. I could take photos of the patients when they came in and again when they left the hospital. *Yes! You too could lose twenty-five pounds in a month! All it takes is a bit of high voltage to the head!* I could make a fortune.

Ted looked around the lounge for Jonathan. Maybe he was in the garden or with Dr. Shackelford. Well, he can't be far, Ted thought. He sat down on a teal-coloured vinyl sofa across from the television showing an old black and white movie. He crossed his legs and grabbed the front section of *The Hamilton Spectator*. The front page was mostly taken up with the Ragno murder case again. Every day they would report the latest news and gossip but would always start by rehashing the lurid events of last fall's murder of a local woman, Linda Ragno, and her kids, eight-year-old Jennifer and four-year-old Alan. Linda and Jennifer had washed up wrapped in wool Hudson Bay point blankets on different areas of the Lake Ontario shoreline a few days apart. The search for the boy continued by dragging mouths of rivers near the lake. Today's main story was how the husband, Jake Ragno, despite being charged with their murders, was inexplicably out on bail until his November trial. Incredible, Ted thought. Jake Ragno was out there going for coffee at Tim Horton's and picking up lawn fertilizer at Canadian Tire, and I'm in here. Rick was right; you *could* write a whole fucking list of things that aren't funny in this goddam world.

Shaking his head, Ted turned to the daily horse racing results at the back of the sports section. Ted's heart beat faster under his gold shirt. There were some huge payouts yesterday. *I could have made a fucking killing with these long shots!* He lowered the newspaper to his lap and looked around the lounge again. Maybe Jonathan and Rick would stroll in stoned. Ted didn't mind being excluded; he had something of his own hidden away to take the edge off. It was also possible that Jonathan was hooking up with one of the women here. It wouldn't be the first time. After all, Jonathan was a handsome guy, and Ted certainly wasn't naive about the goings on in this place, having had to push away more than a few groping female hands under lounge tables himself during a game of cards or in the cafeteria during a breakfast of toast, bacon, and powdered eggs. Ted had also seen the glances between Jonathan and a few of the east-wing women and a bit of flirting in the garden.

At the Hamilton Psychiatric Hospital, there were more women than men, and all the men (even sad sack Carl) had been warned numerous times about messing around with the women patients in the hospital.

"That is one thing that is not tolerated," Dr. Shackelford had said to Ted early in his stay. "Our patients are at an extremely vulnerable point in their lives and taking advantage of someone sexually when they are vulnerable would be..."

Now, what was the word he had used? Ted tried to remember. *Damned ECT Swiss cheese brain!* Well, whatever the word was it wasn't good. So, they locked the men up tight in the west wing at night while the women were locked up in the east wing with a nurse and orderly on duty between them. During the day the sexes only commingled in the cafeteria, garden, lounge, and the basket-weaving art room.

Ted finally remembered the word they used. *Immoral!* Dr. Shackelford had said that taking advantage of someone sexually when they are vulnerable would be *immoral*. Christ, I really should have remembered that word, Ted thought, amused.

Even so, Dr. Shackelford had also stressed that this was a hospital, not a jail or asylum. The doctors and nurses were there to help and he promised Ted would not be constantly watched or stalked by the staff.

"This isn't the dark ages; it's 1977," Dr. Shackelford had said. "You may have come in as an involuntary patient but now, like most patients here, you are a voluntary one. You're capable of making your own decisions on treatment and you could even refuse treatment if you wished. However, Ted, I think you know that, right now, refusing treatment would be a very poor decision for you and your family."

Ted tossed the newspaper on the coffee table. He had nothing left to read after he finished rereading the Che Guevara biography last week and had read the entire collection of magazines in the hospital lounge except the ladies' magazines like *Family Circle* and *Canadian Living*. On the Zenith television, Lana Turner and John Garfield were hatching a plan to kill her husband. It was the afternoon movie on CBC. Ted has seen *The Postman Always Rings Twice* at least three or four times on the late movie over the years, and each time he saw it he thought Garfield was a bigger sap.

Ted had no problem telling when a woman was bad news. He never did. An alarm went off in his gut. And that was one thing about Gloria; she never once set off that alarm. He knew from the start that she was a good woman. That's what Garfield needed, an alarm in his gut. Ted tried to remember how the movie ended as he absentmindedly ran his hands slowly down his chest to his shrinking stomach. When he was a boy, he'd always been thin. Having grown up the sixth of ten kids (eleven if you counted poor Ruth) with a father who wasn't always around meant that there were times food had to be stretched and with all those kids, food could only stretch so far. But privation aside, all but one of them had lived to adulthood so he really couldn't fault his parents. Yeah, Ted thought, they fed you enough to keep you alive so they're *golden*. At least Ted didn't have it as bad as Gloria did growing up. She didn't like to talk about it much, but she had told him a few things. Since Gloria never had a father around at all, she and her sister, Doris, would often resort to scavenging through the garbage at the back of city bakeries for food or raid the gardens of Italians in their east end neighbourhood for tomatoes and cucumbers. Now that was real poverty! And Hamilton's penury was the worst kind of penury.

Lana Turner was looking a bit grubby behind Ted's eyeglasses, so he took them off and held them up to the humming fluorescent light above him.

"Christ. They're filthy." He pulled up the tail of his polyester shirt and cleaned each thick lens.

Ted had worn glasses since he was six years old. He could still remember the doctor putting his first pair on his face and how his mother had burst into tears the first time she saw him wearing them. They were those enormous heavy black frames that people wore back then, too large and heavy for his small head. They kept slipping down his nose, creating a nervous tick of pushing his glasses up the bridge of his nose, which he had to this day. Ted had been so proud of that first pair of glasses until he went to school, and the other kids laughed and called him Teddy Four-Eyes. Over the years, other kids in school would also get glasses, but Ted, being the first, would continue to be called Four-Eyes until he went into the army at seventeen. Now there's a sob story to tell Shackelford next time, he thought. Shackelford loved a good sob story.

Ted put the round wire frames back on his face, and Lana Turner looked even grubbier. "Jesus, that just made them worse," he said aloud.

"Quiet around here today, isn't it?" said Carl, coming up behind him.

"Christ, Carl! Don't sneak up on me like that!"

Carl moved along the back of the sofa and grunted as he sat on one of the matching teal armchairs near the television. His large face was red and shining with a film of sweat, but instead of using his usual handkerchief, he just wiped the sleeve of his hospital robe across his face, breathing heavily. Ted knew Carl wasn't expecting visitors. He never had visitors. He had no wife and never spoke of any family or friends.

"What are you doing here all alone? You usually have an entourage with you. Or are they out smoking more dope?" Carl asked.

"I don't know where Jonathan and Rick are. I'm just sitting here watching Lana Turner dupe some mark into bumping off her dud of a husband in trade for some pussy."

"You and Jonathan have become pretty good friends, I see," Carl said, crossing his legs at the ankles in a prim grandmother pose. "I suppose it makes sense; you both have been in the army. You can share war stories."

Ted shrugged his shoulders. "Jonathan was in the war, not me," he said, staring straight ahead at the television, hoping that Carl would get the hint and get lost.

"Want some advice?" Carl asked, looking around for prying ears.

"No," Ted said, not turning away from the television.

"I'd stay away from that Jonathan Pressman if I were you."

"You would, would you?"

"I see things you don't, Theodore. Nothing gets past me."

"I'll keep that in mind. And if you want to call me by my full name, it's Edward, not Theodore."

Carl had been in the hospital the longest of all of them in Room 215W. He was one of the few involuntary patients in the hospital, and, after almost four months, no one seemed to think he was safe enough to be let out yet. After spending all this time with Carl Gruber, Ted concluded that that was probably for the best. The only nice thing Ted could say about Carl was that he had never ratted out the rest of them to Dr. Shackelford about the marijuana… or anything else that went on in 215W. At least not that Ted knew. The truth was that no one knew what Carl was saying during his sessions with the doctor. Who knew what they were saying about anyone else in Shackelford's office? Maybe all of them, except Ted, were ratting on each other.

"I want you to know that I did *not* take a classroom of kids hostage like Rick said the other day," Carl said.

"Okay. I believe you, Carl."

"I'll tell you exactly what happened."

"You don't have to."

"I don't mind telling you."

"I don't want to know, Carl."

"I had been on medical leave for stress for a few weeks," Carl began. "I had wanted to go back to my class, but my family doctor wouldn't approve it. He said I should take the rest of the school year off and return to work next September. Then one day, I was sitting at home, doing nothing but watching television, just like you are now, and I thought about my class and how I was never able to say goodbye to them formally. I disappeared one day. I'd been their teacher for almost five months. Five months! So, you can imagine how scary and upsetting it would be for a child to have their teacher just... vanish into thin air!"

Fat air was more like it, Ted thought, watching Lana climb up a cliff in heels after shoving her slob of a husband and his car into the sea.

"So, I thought to myself, since I wouldn't be back until the next school year, that I would go back, just once, and have a little visit with my class. All I wanted to do was say goodbye to them, but more *importantly* to show all my boys and girls that I cared. Well, apparently, that's a doggone crime these days."

"I said I believed you, Carl. This here is an important part in the movie."

"The rest only happened because that stupid substitute teacher made a great big fuss about my visit," Carl said, spitting a bit as he spoke.

"Jesus Christ," Ted sighed.

"This substitute teacher gets on her high horse and tells me that I couldn't come into *my* classroom! Not even to speak to my kids. She told me to go home. Said I should call the principal first so that they could set something up. She might as well have just told me to shove off! Well, little Miss substitute whatever-her-name-was had forgotten that this was *my* classroom! So, I told her, as nicely as I could, mind you, to get out of my way and that I was coming in whether she liked it or not! But I never pushed or shoved her like they said I did. Never!"

Ted chewed harder on his gum and tried to concentrate on the television. Why exactly was Lana now running into the ocean? Probably just so the movie studio, MGM or Warner Brothers, could show a little skin. As much skin as the Hayes Code would let them, that is. Who would have thought the sight of Lana Turner in a thirty-year-old film could still give Ted a bit of a boner? Or maybe it was the sip of rye before coming into the lounge. Perhaps it was both. Skin and booze were two of Ted's favourite things.

"I had stopped at the grocery store on the way to my school and picked up a big bag of Macintosh apples for the kids. A huge bag!" Carl said, now sitting forward in the teal chair like he was ready to pounce all three hundred pounds at this spectral substitute teacher who had probably forgotten all about Carl and his fucking apples.

"Carl…" Ted said.

"I had been teaching them about nutrition and the four basic food groups before I went on my medical leave and told them at the end of the module that I would bring them all apples. Now, Ted, you tell me, what's so wrong with a teacher bringing their boys and girls apples? But from the way that bitch substitute teacher flipped her wig, and that's exactly what she did, Ted, she *flipped her wig*, you would have thought I was barging into the classroom with… oh, I don't know… a loaded pistol or something. It was just a bag of *fucking apples!*"

"Okay, okay. Settle down."

Carl's red face became redder as an orderly closely watched them from across the lounge. Ted wasn't worried about Carl getting violent with him. As far as Ted knew, the only person Carl had ever really hurt was the policeman whose knee he had taken a chunk out of in the school playground that day when they tried to drag him off school property.

"Then I told this know-it-all substitute cunt to leave me alone with the kids for a few minutes." Carl looked shocked at his own language and lowered his voice. "That's all I wanted, a few gosh-darn minutes. I tried to tell her my kids were worried and probably had a lot of questions about what had happened to me, and all I wanted to do was answer them. And then… well, you know the rest. Everyone knows the rest."

"They called the police, and they hauled you here."

"Right! They called the police, took me to jail first, and then hauled me here. But no one was being held hostage. No one! And I really get angry when people say that. If I were holding my boys and girls hostage, would I have gone outside to speak to the police when they came? I went out there completely reasonable, ready to have a civilized discussion. And then the police, who I always admired and defended when people, people like… *like you*, who call them pigs and say they were nothing but fascists, attacked me! Four of them! Right there in the middle of the schoolyard. One of them tried to drag me away by the arm, and the next thing I know, I'm on my back, and two of them are on me, one with his knee on my throat. Right here!" He grabbed himself around the throat so hard he left a pink mark over his Adam's apple as sweat dripped down the side of his face.

The orderly across the room had been joined by a second orderly. Both began to walk slowly toward Carl from behind.

"If you don't calm yourself down, they're going to come over here and calm you down," Ted said.

"Later, they said I bit one of the policemen. I never bit anyone! I'm a teacher, for God's sake! I've been teaching for twenty years! Did you know that? Twenty years! Teachers teach! They don't go around biting people! I didn't find out until later that the whole thing was plastered all over the newspaper and on the 6 o'clock news. You'd think I was Jake Ragno, for goodness' sake." He picked up the newspaper's front section from the coffee table and then threw it on the floor at Ted's feet.

Patients and visitors were now looking over at them, and the large orderly was standing just steps behind an oblivious Carl, whose face was now purple and sweat dripped down his neck to the folds under his robe. Snot ran out of Carl's right nostril, and he wiped it away with the sleeve of his robe. Finally, he sat back in his chair, looked up at the nicotine-stained ceiling, and took a few deep breaths.

"And do you know that not once did anyone ever ask me my side of it? How am I going to face those kids again once this is all over? How am I supposed to go back and teach school again? Or what if they won't let me teach again? Teaching is the only thing I know how to do."

Ted thought about his job at Wentworth Steel. What if they didn't let him go back after all that happened?

"Rick was just kidding around with you," Ted said. "He made some crack about my scar, too, remember? And I just laughed it off and forgot about it."

"Well, I didn't think it was very funny. I never took anyone hostage."

On the television, John Garfield was headed to the electric chair. With Carl's freak-out, Ted had missed what had happened to Lana Turner. He would have to wait until it again popped up on some late show. One thing is for sure, Lana didn't get away with murdering her husband. The Hayes Code always got them in the end back then, unlike movies today where you never know if the bad guys will get away with the terrible shit they do. Just like in real life. Look at *Chinatown*. Ted thought that *Chinatown* had the darkest ending ever. The child-molesting grandfather not only got away with murder, but they hand over his granddaughter (who was also his own goddamn daughter) to him on a silver platter at the end. It had been almost unbearable to watch. Gloria couldn't even sleep the night they had seen it together at the Century Theatre.

"Anyway, I just wanted you to know all that," Carl said.

The two orderlies were wandering away from them, likely content that Carl's episode was over for now, when Ted saw Jonathan enter the lounge and walk toward them.

"So, are you planning on keeping that beard once you get home, Comrade? Are you trying to look like Trotsky?" Jonathan asked, sitting down beside Ted on the vinyl couch.

"Where've you been?"

"Taking a walk outside," Jonathan pulled down the brim of his Montreal Expos cap, turned to Carl. "Having a good day?"

Carl, his face merely a tad pink now, nodded and, with a grunt, pulled himself out of the chair, giving Ted a 'remember what I said about this guy' look, and trudged toward the exit. Carl liked to be one of the first in the cafeteria when dinner was served.

"I'm digging my new beard," Ted said, rubbing his hand over his chin. "I never really tried growing one. Before the army I was too young to grow one, and by the time I could, I was with Gloria, and she doesn't like beards. She complains whenever I forget to shave, even for one day."

"Che had a beard, too," Jonathan said. He reached over, ran the back of his hand over the whiskers on Ted's cheek, and smirked. "So did Lenin and Marx, for that matter. I'm not sure about Engels. Did Engels have a beard?"

"A huge one," Ted said.

"Did Mrs. Che, Mrs., Marx, Mrs. Lenin, or Mrs. Engels complain about their husbands' beards, I wonder?"

"That I don't know," Ted said. "Probably not when they were going down on them. But every time Gloria visits, she asks when I'm going to shave it off."

"So, when will you?" Jonathan picked up the front page of the newspaper off the floor.

"Maybe never."

"With those round John Lennon glasses and beard, you're looking more and more like Trotsky. And with that gold shirt you're wearing, I'd call your look *communist chic*," Jonathan said.

Ted grinned. "I'm a socialist, not a communist, Jonathan. I could explain the difference if you want."

"Please don't," Jonathan said. "But speaking of communists—"

"I thought we were speaking about socialists," Ted said.

"Speaking of communists *and* socialists, I think one of my uncles was a Bolshevik in the old country. You two would have a lot in common."

"Once again, Jonathan, I am a socialist. I am neither a Bolshevik nor a communist."

"I think my Bolshevik uncle ultimately threw himself on his own bayonet," Jonathan said, smiling widely and showing his straight with teeth.

The room was getting cooler. Someone must have turned the air conditioning up. Across the room, a blonde woman with a ponytail sitting alone, smoking and doing a jigsaw puzzle, paused to button up her red cardigan.

"Oh shit," Ted said.

"What is it?" Jonathan said, turning around toward the door.

There at the door of the lounge, was Sonny Ferro looking around the room frowning. For a second, Ted's flight instinct kicked in as he looked around to see if he could somehow scurry out the emergency door that led to the garden and sneak back to Room 215W before

Sonny spotted him but gave up as Sonny began walking toward him.

"Sonny! It's good to see you."

"Hi, Ted," Sonny said seriously.

Sonny Ferro, President of Steelworkers Local 2010, was a tall, stocky balding Portuguese man with dark eyes and a beer belly that hung over the waist of his work pants. He wore a flat brown cap and kept his hands in the pockets of his open blue and white union jacket. Ted had the same union jacket because he was treasurer of Steelworkers Local 2010—or at least he had been treasurer before he'd come to the Hamilton Psychiatric Hospital. Odds were he wasn't treasurer anymore.

"We gotta talk, Ted," Sonny said.

"Sure, Sonny, I just…"

"Now."

"I… um… I wanted to talk to you too, Sonny."

"Alone," Sonny said in a tone honed by years as a union boss.

Ted stood, and the two men walked across the lounge to one of the empty tables in a deserted part of the lounge near a window that looked out toward West Fifth Street. To look as ill as possible, Ted walked slowly, shuffling his feet.

"Got a cigarette, Sonny?" Ted asked, sitting down at the table. His heart began to race again, and he felt light-headed.

This is going to be bad.

Sonny nodded, took a pack from his jacket pocket, and tossed it across the table toward Ted.

"Thanks, brother," Ted said. With his hand trembling, he pulled his lighter out of the pocket of his jeans and lit the cigarette like he was facing a firing squad.

This is it.

"I can't wait to get out of here and get back to work," Ted said. He gently touched the scar on his throat with his index finger and grimaced slightly. "But I'm still healing up, you know, Sonny."

"Uh huh," Sonny said, seemingly unmoved.

"But I'm hoping to get back to work in time for the Labour Day parade. You know, Sonny, I haven't missed marching in the Hamilton Labour Day parade with the Steelworkers since 1966. Do you remember that? That was the first year I ran for shop steward at Wentworth. Christ, I lost by a landslide! I was so green then, you remember? It took me two more tries before I finally learned the ropes and won. You know what I mean, Sonny?"

"Cut the shit, Ted!" Sonny said as he slowly leaned forward. "Where's the eight grand you stole from us?"

Two

Gloria hated wearing her work clothes downtown.

In her black slacks, a pink short-sleeved polyester blouse, and clunky black work shoes, she sat alone on a seat near the front of the King Street bus staring out the window and hoping she wouldn't run into anyone she knew. The kerchief she tied around her head during her shift at Munro Steel, along with her dinner, a chicken loaf sandwich, was in the black leather purse she had set beside her on the orange vinyl seat. The purse was covering the words *FUCK YOU* that someone had written on the seat in blue ballpoint pen, more boldly than they needed to in Gloria's opinion.

She looked down and checked the time on her silver-plated wristwatch. It was past eleven-thirty. She gently bit her bottom lip. Gloria was on the swing shift all week and had to be up at the hospital by noon, or she risked being late for her 3pm shift back in the east end of the city. She yawned and, trying to conceal it, covered her mouth with the back of her hand. It was already a long day, and she wouldn't get home until close to midnight.

The bus came to a stop outside Diamond Jim's nightclub. Diamond Jim's was in a block of downtown buildings on King Street that included pawnshops, arcades, and the sorts of bars that Hamilton's less affluent alcoholics convened outside of every morning, waiting for the doors to open so they could fill up on one-dollar draught beer.

Diamond Jim's was certainly past its prime when the likes of Vic Damone and Frankie Laine had sung there. Still, at night its enormous red sign sporting a man in a tuxedo and top hat holding a cane with a huge glowing diamond on the tip still shone brighter than any of the electric signs lighting up downtown Hamilton. In the middle of the day, with its faded and chipping red and gold paint and odd missing bulb, the Diamond Jim sign just looked absurd. Gloria sighed. It must have been at least a decade since she'd been inside.

And both Jim and I are looking a little worse for wear.

Gloria had once seen The Platters at Diamond Jim's. She tried to remember what year that had been. But the truth was, they hadn't been the actual Platters at all since most of the original members had left the group by the time they had rolled into Hamilton. There had been, Gloria recalled, only one authentic Platter left among four fakes. Still, they had sung "The Great Pretender", one of Gloria's favourite songs, almost as well as on their old records.

I looked pretty good that night, Gloria thought as the bus continued down King Street. That night she had worn her brown fox fur coat, the one she had bought at Modern Furs, after saving up every extra dime she possibly could for over a year. It wasn't the best fur, but that night, with her black hair up and in a pale pink dress that made her light brown skin look like she had just returned from a holiday in Miami Beach, she had looked darn good walking under that blazing sign into Diamond Jim's. That very well could have been, she thought with some sadness, the last time I looked good. *Really* good. Maybe it was the best I ever looked. Better than I'll ever look again. Her fox coat was long gone. It had been hocked along with Ted's Kodak camera in a last-ditch and utterly futile attempt to save their first house. She had tried to save up enough money to buy another fox coat but then... what had happened? Ah well, Gloria thought, no sense crying about an old coat now. And no one could ever take away from her that night with The Platters at Diamond Jim's.

The bus passed a variety store with a busted 7-Up sign where six teenage boys stood in a semi-circle smoking cigarettes and laughing. Gloria instinctively slipped her hand onto the strap of her purse. She never felt comfortable downtown, among the bands of teenagers outside record stores, the bums in Gore Park, and all the eerie old buildings from the turn of the century that ran along King Street. Those old buildings hovered too close to the sidewalk, suffocating her as they looked down with their soot-stained red and brown brick and their tiny windows on the top floors pushed open, letting out the heat and letting in the Hamilton smog from the steel mills.

The bus rattled past the Pagoda Chop Suey House and the Chicken Roost Restaurant and turned onto James Street before stopping at Hunter Street, where a stream of kids, in their late teens and early twenties, probably off to Iroquois College on the mountain, noisily filed in the door, filling up most of the empty seats in the back of the bus. Gloria admired the easy way the girls chatted these days. They were all hair and teeth and dressed so nicely in bright colours. Skirts, she noticed, had gotten longer again. Miniskirts had gone out of style because women my age had started wearing them, she thought. A few years back, Gloria's sister, Doris, had had a purple miniskirt that was, to Gloria's mind, far too young for her. Young girls like these probably looked at Doris and other older women in those clothes and said, 'count me out!' And that was the end of the miniskirt.

Across the aisle from Gloria sat a boy and girl holding hands. The boy, with a good-humoured face and shiny full lips wore a dark blue T-shirt, jeans, and a denim jacket. He has the same sandy-coloured hair as Ted, Gloria thought, but this boy's hair was feathered back over his ears the way the kids were wearing it these days. The girl beside him wore a red blazer, white blouse, and tight blue jeans with fancy stitching up the legs. Her hair, blown out at the sides, was too platinum-blonde not to be bleached, but Gloria still admired how it bounced with each pothole the bus hit. That was one thing Gloria had never tried: bleaching or colouring her black hair, even though a few strands of grey had begun popping up. The girl with the bouncy hair leaned close into the boy and rested her head on his shoulder. That girl looks so pretty, Gloria thought. They all did. But everyone looks like a beauty when they're nineteen, they just don't appreciate it. *I looked pretty at nineteen too, even though I had two kids by that time.*

The boy put his arm around the girl and kissed the top of her head. Together they sat that way with their eyes closed as the bus began its ascent up Hamilton Mountain. Gloria turned away and, resting her chin on her hand, looked out the window. She had lived in Hamilton all her life but was still rather unfamiliar with the mountain. East end folks like her and Ted stayed on their side of the city for the most part. Oh sure, there was the occasional trip downtown to Eaton's or Kresge's to shop or to visit a nightclub like Diamond Jim's but that was it. The last time she had been up on the mountain before Ted had gotten sick was when she had Josh in the Henderson Hospital maternity ward a decade earlier. Everything Gloria wanted was in the lower city.

Gloria looked at the weeds and wildflowers growing along the foot of the mountain. Every time she made this trip up to see Ted she thought about how, years ago, her mother would take an old wicker basket and hike along the base of the mountain in search of goldthread, a healing plant, her mother had called it. As a little girl, Gloria's mother had learned to use goldthread from her own mother on the Nett Lake Indian reserve in northern Minnesota where she'd been born and raised. Whenever Gloria or her siblings had stomach trouble, her mother would brew a strong tea from its leaves and long yellow roots and have them drink it as she rubbed their bellies and sang old Indian songs to them. The tea tasted terrible but always made Gloria feel better. As she grew older, Gloria would brush off her mother's old Indian remedies, embarrassed by them, just like the native songs and odd Indian words her mother would use. Now Gloria wondered if any of these plants growing along the mountain road might be goldthread. She had no idea what the plant looked like in the wild, and her mother was long gone.

If she could do it all again, she would have paid closer attention to those sorts of things. She would have learned one of her mother's Indian songs to sing to her children or would have written down some of those Indian words, now long forgotten, that her mother had used. Who would have thought that words could be so easily lost?

The bus turned and twisted on the road up the mountain as she watched the jagged limestone wall a few feet from the window. It wasn't even a real mountain at all. The Niagara Escarpment was just stone chiselled out by receding ice thousands of years ago, or that's what Gloria had been told in school. She briefly wondered what this area would look like a thousand years from now. Maybe it would be covered in ice again.

"I didn't do any studying," the girl with the bouncy platinum hair finally said.

"It won't be that hard," the boy beside her answered.

"No, stats are pretty easy," the girl replied. "At least it is for me." She sat up, flicked her blonde locks, and laid her head back on the boy's shoulder as the bus reached the top of the mountain and continued down West Fifth Street.

Once Gloria had wanted to be a nurse. Her mother had told her that she would be a good one, considering how well she looked after her younger siblings, but Gloria had only made it to grade ten. In those days, it cost money to go to high school. The textbooks cost money, and then there were the clothes. They cost money too. Unlike these Iroquois College girls who probably had a different expensive outfit for every day of the month, Gloria had only one nice plaid skirt and a white blouse. Every day she would wear a different coloured scarf or trade sweaters with Doris to make it look as if she had several outfits, and after school, she would wash out that same skirt and blouse as gently as she could. She thought she was fooling them until one day, as she sat in English class, a note flew over her shoulder onto her desk. She slowly opened the folded note and read: *Why do you always wear the same clothes?*

Gloria quit school that same day.

After that, she knew her future would be spent in one of the many factories around Hamilton. And that had seemed all right with her at the time. There wasn't much choice, really. Without an education, it was either a factory, clean houses like her mother did, or marrying someone who made enough money that a woman didn't have to work, which didn't happen too often to the girls in the east end.

"Lovely day, isn't it?" said an elderly lady as she sat down slowly in front of Gloria in the handicap seats.

"Yes, it is," Gloria said smiling as she reached up and pulled the cord, ringing the bell. The next stop was the Hamilton Psychiatric Hospital.

"So many young people on the bus at this time of day," the elderly woman said sounding annoyed. "This section of the bus must be reserved for the older ladies like us, eh?"

Gloria chuckled to herself. Older ladies like us? As the bus slowed and stopped in front of the hospital, Gloria smiled and picked up her purse off the orange seat as she stood up exposing the bold blue *FUCK YOU*.

"Yes," Gloria said smiling. "I suppose it is."

She stepped carefully off the bus with her purse held tightly in one hand and an overstuffed plastic Bi-Way shopping bag in the other. Three years earlier she had fallen getting off the Parkdale bus on her way to work and had broken her right index finger. For most people a broken finger isn't a big deal but for Gloria, since a big hunk of her pay is piecework, it was devastating. Even with Ted's paycheque the family was on powdered milk and Hamburger Helper for three months to get by.

"Good Lord! It's too bloody hot for May," Gloria said, walking briskly up the concrete pathway toward the hospital's doors.

She manoeuvred her purse from her wrist down to her elbow, wiped away the sweat from under her bangs with her free hand, and then swiped her palm across the hips of her slacks. It was time for her summer perm. Gloria and her siblings all had hair like their mother, black and straight. Indian hair, her mother called it. Gloria only treated herself to a perm twice a year, once at the beginning of summer and then at Christmastime. All Gloria needed was a bit of a wave; she did not like the crazy frizzy perms with tight curls women were getting now. Doris had thought that getting one of those perms would make her hair look fuller but instead, all those curls of thin dyed-red hair going every which way only made Doris look clownish. Luckily, Doris only tried that once and now had a nice wave and, though she still insisted on dying it, she had recently chosen a really attractive shade of amber brown that took years off her.

As she headed into the Hamilton Psychiatric Hospital, Gloria tried not to make eye contact with the two men in slippers and hospital robes smoking outside the entrance. The men never had their robes tied because belts were not allowed in the hospital unless it was those thin shoestring-type ties on the hospital robes. When she had taken Ted's terrycloth bathrobe up, they had made her put the belt back in her purse to take home. "We wouldn't want anyone to hurt themselves," a nurse had said. *Have you seen Ted's throat?* Gloria had thought. If they want to hurt themselves, they will.

Gloria slowed her pace to allow the automatic door time to open for her. It was almost noon, and she would only be able to stay at the hospital with Ted for an hour and a half at most. And the doctor had told her on her last visit that he wanted to speak to her today. Why does Dr. Shackelford need to speak to me *again*? she thought as she walked toward the reception desk. Just how much more light could she throw on this whole horrible thing? And his questions were becoming far more personal than she would expect or appreciate. Some of the things Dr. Shackelford had asked Gloria she had never even discussed with Dr. Heller, her family doctor during her annual pap smear. All Gloria knew was that she had been sleeping that night when Ted had burst into the bedroom holding his throat, bleeding, and making those loud horrible gurgling noises. It was the worst night of her life.

She passed a young woman in a white nurse's uniform at reception and quickly waved.

"Hi, Deanna," Gloria said without stopping.

Deanna, on the phone, smiled and waved back. After two months, Gloria no longer needed to go through the formalities of stopping at reception and telling Deanna who she had come to see. Deanna had even remembered Gloria from when she would visit during those three months Doris has been a patient here. And that was three years ago.

Gloria walked into the hospital lounge and saw Ted sitting exactly where she had left him on Monday, with his roommate Jonathan, on opposite sides of that couch watching television. One of the things she had brought with her in the Bi-Way bag was two clean pairs of pants and a few pairs of socks and underwear. Gloria tried to bring up enough pairs of freshly washed pants so Ted could change into a clean pair every other day, but he had been in those olive-green workpants for three days now and she was afraid she would have to beg him to change out of them before she left.

Gloria inhaled deeply, steeling herself against the place, held tight to her plastic shopping bag, and walked over to the two men. She hoped that Jonathan would have the courtesy to leave when she sat down. Sometimes he would just sit there during her entire visit with Ted. And Ted would never ask Jonathan to leave, which would irritate Gloria even more.

"Hi, Ted." Gloria tried to look as pleasant as she could while utterly exhausted.

Ted smiled. "Gloria, my love!" He stood, hugged her, and softly kissed her neck.

She still wasn't used to Ted's new beard and, although she did not really like it, as his beard touched her cheek, she imagined what the whiskers would feel like as they scratched across her lips, down her throat and over her breasts and body when Ted was finally home. She was a little surprised at how much the thought thrilled her.

Ted sat back down on the vinyl couch and crossed his legs. He wasn't wearing any socks again, only the pair of brown leather loafers he wore the night they brought him in, which needed a good shine. What are the odds he would wear his slippers for a couple of days and let me take those shoes to be shined at a shoe store downtown? she wondered. Probably not good odds, she concluded. Besides, what did shabby shoes matter in this place.

"I brought you two clean pairs of pants," Gloria said, sitting in the matching teal armchair beside the sofa. "A pair of corduroys and a pair of blue jeans. You've been in those workpants for days, Ted."

Why don't they make him shower every day? she thought. They should make all of them shower every day. Who doesn't feel better after a shower? There were, Gloria believed, few things in the world that aren't made at least a little better with some soap, hot water, and a good scrubbing.

"Yeah, I guess I could stand to change pants, eh?" Ted said, scratching the whiskers on his jaw.

Ted was wearing the button-up dark yellow shirt she had brought up on her last visit on Monday, the one she had bought him last Father's Day as a gift from Josh. That mustard-yellow colour always made those green eyes of his stand out. He still looked a bit dopey to her but seemed better. Maybe he had even gained a few pounds back. His hair, longer than he had ever grown it, looked good on him, alluring.

"Hello, Jonathan, how are you?" Gloria asked, turning to Jonathan, and giving a tired smile.

"In the pink," Jonathan said. He took off his baseball cap, ran his hand through his shaggy black hair, and put the cap back on, tilting it slightly to the left.

Gloria turned back to Ted, reached over from her chair, and gently placed her hand on his knee. "You should try to change your pants every other day, Ted," she said softly. "If you run out of clean ones, just wear a pair of hospital pyjamas until I can bring you up more, okay?" Ted looked about to speak but she cut him off. "I *know* you don't like wearing pyjamas all day but it's better than sitting around in dirty pants, isn't it?" She checked her frustration.

"I'll change my pants every other day. Scout's honour." Ted held up three fingers in a scout salute and looked up at her with his green eyes and, for a moment, all she wanted was to have him put his arms around her. The first time she had seen those eyes, at Munro Steel, she'd been immediately smitten. So had he.

Gloria handed Ted the plastic Bi-Way bag. "There's clean shirts in there too," she said. "I also brought you a box of Licorice Allsorts and a carton of cigarettes. Give me those work pants before I go. I'll take them home and wash them."

Ted took the bag from Gloria and laid it on the floor between him and Jonathan.

"Ah, thanks." Ted tapped his scuffed shoe against the tin. "Licorice Allsorts and cigarettes. I'll use it to bribe the doctors into only giving me a hundred volts in the head next time instead of one hundred and fifty."

Gloria frowned and looked down at her feet.

"Hey, I'm just playing around with you, Gloria. I'm going to eat the Allsorts watching the Tiger Cats game tonight… or maybe a

Maple Leafs game. There's got to be some game on TV tonight, eh. What day is this?"

"Wednesday," Jonathan said. "Football season hasn't started yet."

"See, Gloria, Jonathan knows football season hasn't started yet because they only gave him eighty volts yesterday. He probably bribed the orderlies with Hershey Bars."

"It was eighty-five volts. And I bribed the guy with silk stockings. It's a weird staff here, what can I tell you." Jonathan said.

If this was hospital shtick, Gloria didn't think it was funny. Who knows what kind of damage they were doing to Ted's head with all that electricity? Doris had never been the same after all her shock treatments. There were subtle differences in her personality that no one, except a sister, a close sister like Gloria, could detect.

"Maybe I'll save the licorice until Saturday and eat it during the *Wide World of Sports*. Evel Knievel must be jumping over something or other. He always is," Ted said.

"I heard he just crashed and broke every bone in one leg from his right knee to his big toe," Jonathan said.

"Talk about the agony of de-feet," Ted said.

The two men laughed loudly.

"I'll bring up more cigarettes Monday," Gloria said, trying to put an end to the foolish banter.

"There's the cigarette machine in the cafeteria if I run out before then," Ted said.

"Do you like licorice Allsorts, Jonathan?" Gloria wasn't really interested in the answer but was brought up well enough to know to include him in their conversation.

"Not near as much as Ted does. He gets a lot of caramel corn brought up to him too. He's got a real sweet tooth."

"Caramel corn?" Gloria turned to Ted. In fifteen years, she had never seen him put any caramel corn in his mouth.

"Ted usually shares it with his roommates. It's the Communist in him."

Ted smiled. "It's the Socialist in me."

Gloria crossed her arms and thought, not for the first time, how much Jonathan looked like the guy from *Deep Throat*. She had forgotten the actor's name, but she did remember that he was quite handsome and had a thick black moustache and a goofy grin, like Jonathan. Ted had dragged her to see that movie at the Tivoli Theatre a few years ago. It was the first (and only) dirty movie Gloria had ever seen and she had been somewhat disappointed that it wasn't nearly as exciting as everyone had promised. Doris had seen it too, telling Gloria that she had laughed through the whole thing, but Gloria didn't laugh. For the most part she mostly felt sorry for the girl in the film. Still, she was not about to say to Jonathan "Hey, you look like that guy from *Deep Throat*," no matter how much he did.

It didn't look like Jonathan was going to leave so Gloria sat back in her chair and hoped the doctor would call for her soon. "What's this? *Match Game*?"

"*Match Game 77*," Ted said, as if it made a difference.

"We're better at *Wheel of Fortune*," Jonathan said. "If they had a *Wheel of Fortune* Lunatic Week like they have a College Week... Ted and I would clean up."

"Would you like the rest on gift certificate or account?" Ted said.

The two men laughed loudly again and Gloria, having no idea what they were talking about, briefly considered smiling out of politeness but decided not to. She was too tired.

"There's Rick," Ted said.

Gloria turned and saw Rick, the young boy who shared a room with Ted and Jonathan, standing by the lounge door frowning. *That poor boy.* Gloria hoped he was getting the help he needed. He was about the same age as her oldest son, Kevin, and... well, seeing a boy that young in here just broke her heart.

Rick gestured toward them putting his thumb and index finger to his mouth a few times and tilting his head toward the garden window.

"I'm going to go out for a smoke with Rick," Jonathan said, slapping his thighs. "I'll see you folks later." He hopped up quickly, re-situated his baseball cap on his shaggy head, and walked with Rick out of the lounge.

Gloria was not so naive as not to know the sign for 'let's go for a toke' when she saw it. She had spent enough time around Ted's good-for-nothing Socialist Party and union friends to know it when she saw it. *God, I hope Ted isn't doing pot up here on top of everything else!*

Gloria got up from her chair and sat beside Ted on the couch. She took his hand. Yes, he looked tired. There were already the beginnings of laugh lines in the corners of his eyes. *Laugh lines!* Now that's a good one. And though he may have gained a pound or two, she wished they would feed him more here. Still, his eyes, even behind dirty eyeglasses, seemed greener than when they'd met. She didn't know eyes could change colour like that. Though it may just be the fluorescent light above them. Those eyes could still take her breath away.

"Well, you sure are looking better than you did the other day," Gloria said.

"I hope so." Ted gave her a half-smile, leaned over, and picked up his green cigarette pack off the coffee table in front of him. "That wasn't long after shock treatment."

"Yes."

"It's the medication that slows me down more than the shock, I think."

Ted had stopped wearing the bandage around his throat. Gloria was surprised that the scar didn't look as bad as she had expected, but it certainly was not something he could hide. How many times over her lifetime will she have to explain that scar to people? she thought. An accident? That was *almost* true.

"They aren't giving me anymore," Ted said, lighting a cigarette.

"They aren't giving you any more shock treatments?"

"Nope."

"Well, that's good news!"

"Yeah, good news."

"It made you so forgetful, Ted."

"That's how it works." He chuckled. "All that electricity causes short-term memory loss, so you don't remember why you're so goddamn depressed."

"Well, if the doctor says you don't need it anymore it must have worked."

"I guess it did."

"So, you aren't depressed anymore?"

"No, I'm not depressed."

"Good," Gloria said, sitting back in her chair. "That is the best news I've heard in a long time."

"I wouldn't say I'm exactly happy either."

"Ted, can we just be grateful you don't need more of that... that treatment?"

"You're right. We can be grateful for that." Ted said.

In early April, not long after Ted had been brought in, Gloria thought she saw someone she knew—well someone *else* she knew at the hospital. It was Carole, a girl Gloria had grown up with back on Normandy Road in the city's east end. Carole always was a tad odd, and it wasn't too difficult for Gloria to believe that Carole would have ended up in here. In grade three Carole had stopped talking. You would think, Gloria thought, that the teacher or somebody at the school would have made a very big deal about a little girl who suddenly became mute, but no. No one had seemed too concerned about it at the time. As Gloria remembered, the teacher just shrugged her shoulders, put Carole in the back of the classroom, and forgot about her. Today, if a kid suddenly stopped speaking, they would surely send them off for some kind of counselling. A few years later, right out of the blue, Carole started talking again and, once again, no one seemed to mention it. After that Carole became pretty normal, for the most part. She had married early, earlier than Gloria had, and the last Gloria had heard was that Carole had had a bunch of kids in quick succession, five in six years or something and moved to somewhere on the west mountain. Gloria hadn't thought about Carole for years, not until a few weeks previously when Gloria, who had been watching television with a practically comatose Ted in the lounge, had looked up and seen Carole across the room. She was older, of course. Her blonde hair was up in a ponytail, just like she had worn it in the 1950s, and she was wearing a blue hospital nightgown, house slippers and a red cardigan. She sat alone, smoking a cigarette nervously with an ashtray on her lap. When their eyes finally met there was, Gloria had thought, a moment of recognition on the woman's face but before Gloria could smile or wave, Carole quickly turned away.

From then on, the woman in the red cardigan would quickly disappear whenever Gloria walked into the lounge. However, Gloria had not seen Carole in a couple of weeks. She had probably been sent back to her brood in the west end of Hamilton with a few words of advice and a handful of prescriptions to get her through her day. Now Carole was likely back in her west mountain home just trying to live life as best she could, Gloria thought. *Just like the rest of us.*

"You know you don't have to come up here to see me so often," Ted said.

That was abrupt, Gloria thought. He certainly could have put it a bit more nicely even if it were true. "I know I don't have to, but I want to."

"It's just that I know you're tired. Coming all the way up here before work and all. That puts a lot on you. Too much. I feel guilty."

"I'm not so tired," Gloria said, though they both knew that wasn't true.

Why did she feel the need to keep coming up to the hospital so often? It was like something might break if she didn't; maybe it was their marriage or maybe it was something else but, whatever it was, Gloria was determined to continue coming up there three times a week until Ted came home. What wife wouldn't do that? And she liked being close to him, even if it was only a few times a week. It made her feel less afraid about everything. It pushed away at the doom.

"Doris brought me flowers and candy yesterday," Ted said, butting out his cigarette.

"She told me," Gloria said. "If I wasn't on the swing shift, I could have come up with her. That's the worst thing about the three-to-eleven shift, by the time you wake up everyone has gone to work and by the time you get home at night, everyone is asleep. I'd even take night shift over swing shift."

A young female patient walked past and stopped for a few minutes to watch the television before walking away.

"What kind of flowers did Doris bring?" Gloria asked.

Doris had not told Gloria she planned to bring up flowers, but she would never show up at a hospital without bringing something. They had learned that from their mother, who had placed manners above almost everything else, probably because they didn't have much of anything except their manners.

"Lilies."

"Lilies? Really?" An odd choice of flower, even for Doris. Lilies were more for Easter Sunday and laying on caskets than for hospitals.

"They're nice, but they stunk up the room."

"What kind of candy did Doris bring? Not more Licorice Allsorts?"

"No… a tin of caramel corn."

Ted reached over and stroked the back of Gloria's hand with his fingertips. The callouses on his fingers, a combination of steelwork and years of guitar playing, felt good as they scraped slightly against her skin. He took her hand and held it tightly.

"Have *your* sisters been up to see you this week?" Gloria asked.

"No, thank Christ."

"They mean well."

"Uh-huh."

Gloria frowned and looked around the lounge. "If that doctor of yours wants to speak to me today, he'd better come and get me soon. I don't want to be late for work. Should I go ask a nurse or look for him myself?"

"They know you're here," Ted said, still holding firm to her hand. "How's Josh doing? Is he getting excited for school to let out?"

"He's fine. But I'm not looking forward to him being underfoot the whole summer."

"He has Cub Scout camp at the end of July. That will get him out of your hair for three weeks."

"I know," Gloria said. "But…"

"But?"

"He doesn't want to go."

"He'll enjoy it once he's there. Troy didn't want to go to camp either, and he ended up having a great time. When we picked him up, he pouted all the way home. Remember that?"

"Josh isn't Troy."

Gloria folded her hands and placed them on her lower stomach below her belly button. She had gained at least ten extra pounds since this whole ordeal started, and as Ted had been getting skinner, she'd been getting fatter. It was as if Ted had magically passed the weight from himself to her. And while she has been working harder than ever these last two months, he has been up here with his feet up, watching game shows and old movies. It's like every day was summer camp for Ted.

"No, Josh isn't Troy, but he should still go to Cub Scout camp. The kid needs to spend some time with other boys, Gloria. He's too in his head, you know," Ted tapped the side of one of his temples with his finger.

"Well, let's not argue about it now," Gloria said.

It was true that Josh was nothing like her first two boys. Gloria didn't see what was so wrong with her youngest son. Ted worried too much. Josh was Ted's first son, but he was her third. Kids didn't need so much obsessing about in Gloria's book; they would grow up the way they wanted, and there wasn't much anyone could do about it. Ted still thought he could create Josh in his own image. Sorry, but it doesn't work that way. Besides, any kid worth their salt will ultimately tell their parents to drop dead and do precisely what they want to do. At least any kid with a spine will. And who wanted a spineless kid?

"Oh," Gloria said, suddenly remembering something. "I wanted to ask you about the dog. I know we said we would get that golden retriever puppy from Bill, but I don't think this is the best time to get a dog, do you? And since we never told Josh about the dog in the first place, it won't matter to him. Bill said he could find someone else to take the dog if it's a bad time for us. He said it wouldn't be hard finding homes for purebred golden retrievers even if they didn't have their papers."

"Bill who?" Ted let go of her hand and reached again for his cigarette pack.

"You know, Bill Hunter from Munro Steel."

"No, I don't know any Bill Hunter."

"Ted, you worked with Bill before you went to Wentworth Steel. He's a truck driver at Munro. We were going to buy a golden retriever from him when his dog had puppies."

Ted shook his head.

"Bill is Indian," Gloria said with some frustration. "He lives out on the Six Nations Reserve. He drove us home when you got too drunk to drive at the last company Christmas party."

"Oh, sure..." Ted finally said. "I remember Bill. He's a good guy, but he's got a crazy wife, doesn't he?"

"Isabelle is his wife's name, but I'm unsure if she's still in the picture."

"She was one crazy woman."

"But Ted, do you remember we told Bill we'd take a puppy from his dog's next litter? He said we could have one for thirty dollars."

"Yeah, yeah, I remember," Ted said.

Gloria wanted to reach over and clean his glasses but decided it was time for him to start doing that himself. She wasn't coming up here just to make sure he had his socks on, clean pants, and eyeglasses without gunk all over them.

"Well, what I'm saying is," Gloria said in a staccato tone. "I'm just not sure it's the best time for a dog. Troy said he'd help take care of it, but he just started that new job at the gas station, and he'll never be home, so I know he'll only do it for a week, and the puppy will just end up being another job for me."

"I think it would be good for the boys to have a dog." Ted's eyes wandered back to *Match Game 77* on the television.

"Sure, it would. I just don't think it's the right time."

"So, does Bill know I'm in here?"

"Bill? Yes, he knows you're here."

"I guess everyone at Munro knows now," Ted said softly

"No, not everyone knows."

"I wish..." Ted said, looking down at his scuffed shoes, "I really wish you hadn't told them, Gloria. It... it makes everything ten times worse knowing people are sitting around Munro talking about me."

Gloria moved closer to Ted and put her lips close to his ear, so close that his long hair tickled her face. "Everyone is caught up in their own problems, Ted. No one, and I mean *no one*, has the time to worry about anyone else's problems these days, yours and mine included."

"Get the puppy," Ted said, staring ahead at the television.

"Are you sure?"

"Get the puppy."

"Because, like I said, if it's a bad time to bring a dog into the house, Bill said—"

"Just get the fucking puppy!"

"All right, all right," Gloria said, lowering her voice and moving away. "You don't need to get upset. Doris already said she'd take me up to Bill's house on the reserve to pick the thing up."

"You have to go all the way up to Six Nations? Bill can't bring it to our house before you start work?"

"I'm not going to ask him to do that if we're buying the dog," Gloria said.

"Just make sure it's a male," Ted said.

"We can't pick it up until it's weaned in a few more weeks, so we still have time if you change your mind. I won't tell Josh until we bring the puppy home."

"So, why is Bill's crazy wife out of the picture?" Ted asked. "Did she run off with another guy?"

"I don't know anything about it. And I'm not interested to know. See, I told you people were far too caught up in their own problems to care much about other people's problems."

That was true. Gloria didn't know why Isabelle Hunter was out of the picture. She had only heard Isabelle left Bill from some girls gossiping in her department at the mill, so who knew if it was even true, though the girls were usually right about that sort of thing.

"I'm sorry I snapped at you, Gloria. Can I just plead insanity?"

He smiled and put his hand on her left thigh, moving it higher and higher until she laughed and pushed it down to her knee.

"Give me those glasses," Gloria said, smiling.

She reached over, took off his eyeglasses, and then rooted in her purse for a clean Kleenex to clean them. "They're filthy. Just like you."

"Just like me." Ted leaned over and kissed her on the neck.

And for a few minutes, as she cleaned her husband's glasses, Gloria could believe everything would turn out all right in the end. Soon, she thought, Ted would be home, and it would be just like it was before he got sick, and, by Christmas at the latest, they would have put this place and these horrible months behind them forever. All of them. Her, Ted, Kevin, Troy, Josh, and the new dog around the Christmas tree with the hospital long forgotten. In her mind's eye, she even pictured herself in a fresh fur fox coat like the one she had pawned, only more modern and stylish. Feeling better, Gloria began to hum "The Great Pretender" to herself as she cleaned each round lens of Ted's wire eyeglasses.

"Baby, I have to tell you something," Ted said quietly. "It's bad. I've..."

She looked up and into Ted's green eyes. Yes, she could see it. It was bad.

Oh, God, what now?

"Sonny from the union came by." Ted covered his face with his hands. "And we have a big problem."

Gloria sat alone outside Dr. Shackelford's office, nervously twisting her wedding band on her finger. The old wooden chair, one of three lined up in the hallway and no doubt a leftover from the old Hamilton Asylum days, was causing her lower back to ache, and she shifted uncomfortably from side to side. If, years ago, someone had told Gloria that someday her husband would be in the Hamilton Psychiatric Hospital... well, if she were candid with herself, Gloria would have to say she wouldn't have been all that surprised considering that crazy family he came from. All the signs had been there from the get-go, but Gloria had chosen to ignore all of them, even the bright neon one, evident from the first time Gloria had met Ted's family, that had flashed as bright as the Diamond Jim's sign, spelling out RUN in crimson red.

The heavy wooden door beside her suddenly opened and Dr. Shackelford, a short white-haired man, wearing a lab coat with a permanent coffee stain on one sleeve, stood in the doorway.

"Come in, Mrs. Moore. How are you today?"

"I'm fine, thank you," she answered as she rose from her chair. Her back was stiff from sitting in it. "But I can't stay more than forty-five minutes today. I'm on the afternoon shift."

Dr. Shackelford held open the door and gestured for her to come through. Gloria could smell smoke as she passed him and was perturbed that he had kept her waiting so that he could have a cigarette.

The office was large but shabby-looking for a relatively new hospital. There was a worn green rug and the same cream-yellow-coloured walls that lined the hallways of the hospital. An oak bookcase on one wall held shelves of old books intermingled with the odd family picture in gaudy gold frames and a few pieces of bric-a-brac. Behind him, on the wall, hung his diploma from The University of Western Ontario. The lime-green curtains were opened to show the traffic building on West Fifth Street.

Gloria sat down in one of two small chairs in front of a large oak desk and placed her purse on her lap. "Will Ted be coming home soon?" she asked.

"We hope so but not quite yet." Dr. Shackelford seated himself in a large leather chair behind the desk and moved a green glass ashtray to the side.

"How much longer will he have to be here?" she asked.

"I think we're looking at about eight weeks. Maybe more."

"Eight weeks?"

"Ted has been responding well to treatment. And there's a light at the end of the tunnel." He glanced down briefly at an open manila file lying on his desk's light green ink blotter.

"That is exactly what it has been like, Dr. Shackelford, being in a dark, scary tunnel."

The doctor closed the folder and placed his hands flat on top of it. "Not to say there still isn't more to do," he said.

"Will he be normal again?" Gloria asked. She wished she sounded more medical, using the correct terms but didn't know them.

"Normal?" The doctor said, leaning forward as if the word itself was too intriguing to ignore.

"The way he was before all this?" Gloria said.

To be honest, that wasn't what she wanted at all. If they could make Ted the way he was, say, ten years ago— but Gloria knew no one could do that.

"That's our hope," the doctor said. "What we wanted to know is—"

"Yes?"

"Ted is depressed, you know that, but there's also an underlying anxiety and rage that can be violent. He showed you that the night he was brought in. We have tackled the depression and now want to work on the anger."

Gloria nodded.

"Where do you think Ted's anger originates?"

"He's been here all this time, and you haven't asked him that yet?"

"What I'm looking for is your perspective, Mrs. Moore."

"I don't know," Gloria said, shaking her head slightly. "Some men get angry. My first husband was angrier than Ted ever was." She wondered if Dr. Shackelford was from Hamilton. Most men Gloria knew, her brothers, the men she worked with, all carried chips on their shoulders as if they believed they'd somehow gotten the bum end of the stick. Did this doctor think these men in the steel mills were a bunch of sissies? They did challenging, dirty and dangerous work, and if these men weren't hardened before they went into the blast furnaces and coke ovens, they sure as hell were when they came out.

"Has Ted ever been violent with you?"

"No, never," Gloria said, not entirely truthfully.

"And he drinks?"

"Yes, he drinks."

"Did this last episode start with excessive drinking?"

"He drank as much as he ever did when this mess started. Yes, he was drinking a lot, but I don't know if you'd say it was *excessive*. At least for him."

"Alcohol should be avoided when taking Thorazine."

"Well, you try and stop Ted from drinking. Do you seriously think I haven't tried all these years?"

"No one is blaming you or anyone else," the doctor said, in a voice so patronizing that it sounded to Gloria like he was indeed blaming her, at least partially. He reopened the file on his desk and picked up a pen lying on his blotter. "Could you tell me again how it all started?"

Gloria rechecked her watch. Thirty more minutes, and then she'd have to leave whether the doctor was done with her or not, besides she had told him all this the first time she met him when Ted was still strapped down to his bed. She wanted to ask him to finger through that file and just read his bloody notes, but instead she just sighed deeply.

"It started when Ted said he saw little black bugs crawling in the kitchen cabinets. I was horrified when he told me. I have never had any bugs in my house."

"Uh-huh," the doctor said. He turned over the top page in the file and began writing on its blank backside in a scratchy cursive.

"Anyway, after Ted told me he saw the bugs, I stood on a kitchen chair and checked all the cupboards. I pulled out all the dishes and boxes and cans but didn't find a thing. I said to Ted, 'Point to them! Show me where these bugs are, *specifically!*' Finally, he looked through the cupboards but couldn't find any."

"And did you think there were bugs?" the doctor asked without looking up.

"I did believe him at first. Ted had never seen things that weren't there before, so I cleaned out every cupboard in the kitchen, top to bottom, looking for these bloody bugs, but, of course, I didn't find one single bug, not even a dead one. By then, I thought the bugs were all in his head, and I told him that maybe it was just a reaction to the new medication they had put him on."

"The Thorazine," the doctor said.

"Yes, the Thorazine."

"What happened when you told him it was probably just the medication?"

"He didn't mention bugs again. I don't know if he stopped seeing them or not. You would have to ask him. I'd like to know myself. I still look for bugs every time I open a cupboard door."

As the doctor kept scribbling in his notebook, Gloria wondered which words of hers he was choosing to write down. What was he adding or leaving out from her story? He couldn't be writing down everything she said. Perhaps he had just written *wife dresses like a cleaning lady.*

"There are no bugs in my house, Dr. Shackelford," Gloria said.

"No," he said. "I'm sure it was a hallucination."

Dr. Shackelford turned to a new page. Gloria checked her watch and shook her head. If he hadn't kept her waiting for so long…

"Ted told me he's a twin," the doctor said.

"Well, that's what his mother says," Gloria said.

"What his mother says?" the doctor said, looking up. "Don't you believe it?"

"The story just seems so strange to me," Gloria replied.

"Strange?"

"Supposedly, his mother, Anna, was three or four months pregnant with Ted, and one day she was walking down Ottawa Street doing some shopping when she had a breakdown—that's the word she always uses when she tells the story, and trust me, she tells it a lot. *Breakdown.* As if she were an old Studebaker." Gloria rubbed her hands up and down the leather arms of her chair. "And she miscarried right there on the sidewalk."

"And you don't believe it?"

"Ted does. I don't know what to believe. That family is full of farfetched stories of long-lost money, stolen artwork, and famous relatives. My sister, Doris, calls them "Moore Stories." Fairy tales, if you ask me. According to them, they are related to Norwegian royalty too. Did Ted tell you that one?" Gloria said.

"And the twin?"

"Only Ted's mother knows exactly what happened that day. And time always seems to twist the truth toward how we want it. Ted's mother believes there was a twin, so what does the honest-to-God truth matter?"

"And after the miscarriage, Ted was born?" the doctor asked. He had stopped writing and was sitting back in his chair.

"That's how the story goes. After the *breakdown,* she kept

getting bigger and bigger, and then four months later, Ted was born. Anna loves telling that story. It's grotesque if you ask me. Maybe because I know how messy a miscarriage is."

Gloria looked out the small window at the traffic along West Fifth as a black and gold HSR city bus went toward the mountain brow headed down the escarpment.

"Now I think about Ted's mother every time I'm on Ottawa Street. I say to myself, that's where my mother-in-law *broke down*. Is that even possible, Dr. Shackelford? Can you lose one baby and still deliver its twin months later?"

"It's possible... but rare," he said.

"Well, I've never heard anything like it." She picked up her purse and held it close to her chest. "But if you say so. Maybe Ted's mother was telling the truth the whole time. I didn't think she was lying all this time; I just thought she was confused. She even named the twin she miscarried on the street. She named him Gabriel, like the angel. Did Ted tell you that his mother used to perform a séance for Gabriel every year on his birthday... or his miscarriage day. It's disturbing! She would gather the entire family around the kitchen table and try to get in touch with him. She still might do it, calling out for him all alone in her apartment, for all I know. Anna says Gabriel protects the family. If that's true, he's done a lousy job of it so far."

"I'm hoping to get Ted's mother up for a session with Ted. I think it could be beneficial," the doctor said.

"Don't count on getting Anna up here. She hasn't come up once to visit Ted since he's been here."

"We'll cross that bridge when we come to it."

"She always thought Ted was destined to be special since he was the twin who lived. I'm not sure if she still believes it now."

It was all mysticism, signs, and luck with Ted's mother. Not that Anna had had much luck herself in her life. Gloria avoided Anna's mystic talk of signs and hidden meanings; they frightened her. When Anna first came to visit Gloria at the maternity ward of the Henderson Hospital, she had been thrilled that Josh had the good luck of being born with a caul over his face, an especially charmed and fortunate sign, according to Anna. "Your boy," Anna had said, "is destined for something *very* special, just like Ted is." Gloria never felt particularly lucky about having Josh born with a caul. She had screamed when she first saw that disgusting thing looking like a rancid purple sausage casing covering Josh's face. She had thought he was deformed, dead, or both as they whisked him away. It took some time for the doctor and nurses to calm her down and explain that they would gently remove the caul with warm water and bring Josh back to her. If that's what passes for good luck, you can keep it.

"Do you think Ted believes he is destined for greatness?" the doctor asked.

"You'll have to ask him," Gloria said.

"I would like to know what you think."

"Maybe. Maybe he does."

"All right," the doctor said. "The nurse will ask Ted to join us in a few minutes."

"But why does Ted need to be great? What's wrong with being exactly who he is? A working man. A *good* working man. Ted works hard, and he's treasurer for his union at Wentworth Steel—well, he was treasurer before all this. So here I am, left alone trying to pay the bills, keep all this from Josh, keep working, and making three or four trips up here every week, and now... and now Ted just told me I have to find eight thousand dollars someplace. How can I do that? Our house is only worth eighteen thousand and we have a sixteen-thousand-dollar mortgage."

"Yes, Ted was worried about how you would react when he told you about the missing money; we discussed it earlier this week."

"And it all falls to me while Ted's wrapped up in this cozy cocoon, wearing the same pants for days with his feet up watching television. A little electricity in his head and he forgets it all, but I can't forget, can I? I'm not allowed to forget any of it—hospitals, the boys, work, and now this bloody eight thousand dollars!"

Dr. Shackelford leaned back in his leather chair and nodded with such dramatic empathy that Gloria wanted to scream. He was, after all, Ted's doctor, not hers, and he was only interested in treating Ted. Her problems and her boys' problems were of no interest outside of how they affected Ted.

"Let's put aside the eight thousand dollars for now," the doctor said.

"As if I could," Gloria said. "I'm just so afraid."

"Afraid?"

"Afraid of what will happen if we don't find the eight thousand dollars. Afraid of what will happen once Ted finally comes home. And what he might do next time."

"Do you mean what Ted might do next time with money, himself... or your son?"

The door opened, and Ted walked into the office.

"Come in, Ted. You're right on time," the doctor said.

Ted had showered and changed into the corduroy pants she had brought and a clean white shirt that made the scar on his throat look even more pronounced. His long hair was slicked back and looked darker wet. He was chewing gum, and his glasses were a little steamed up. He seemed happier to Gloria, even sexy.

He walked to the empty chair beside her. She would think he'd been drinking if she didn't know better. What was she thinking—if Ted wanted booze, he'd find a way to get it.

"Are you telling her I need more shock?" Ted smiled and fell back in the chair with a dull thump.

"No," the doctor said. "I told you we were done with that for now."

"For now, he says," Ted said, between chews.

"The ECT seems to have worked as well as we can expect. Your depression has eased. I told your wife that you are doing quite a bit better."

"Great. So, when can I go home with your seal of approval?"

"Soon, but it's time we talked about something else, Ted."

"What's that?" Ted asked. He looked over at Gloria and then reached for the pack of cigarettes in the right breast pocket of his shirt. "The eight thousand dollars?"

"No, we'll talk about that some other time."

"Then what?"

"I want to talk about something more difficult, Ted."

"More difficult than the eight thousand dollars? Good luck," Ted said, lighting his cigarette.

"I want to talk about the night you came to us."

"It was a dark and stormy night," Ted said, grinning.

"Ted, can you please just tell the doctor what he wants to know? I have to leave for work, and I can't afford to be docked. *We* can't afford to be docked," Gloria said.

"I already told you I don't remember anything about the night I came in. Or the first couple of weeks I was here, for that matter. Shock will do that to you."

"Yes, I know," the doctor said, "but I think it's time we all discuss something you said to me when you were admitted here. Something I found rather disconcerting."

"Okay," Ted said. "So, what did I say?"

"The night you were admitted," Dr. Shackelford said, leaning forward. "You told me that before you took that piece of broken beer bottle and cut your own throat..." he hesitated and took a deep breath.

Gloria's eyes darted between the doctor to Ted. She had stopped breathing.

"Well?" Ted said, growing agitated.

"You told me that before you cut your own throat, you were thinking about slashing your son Josh's throat."

Three

"If you're brown, hang around," Aunt Doris said, smiling as she sat at the kitchen table rooting through her purse.

Aunt Doris was always saying that. She said it about her brown Cadillac, a bottle of beer, the new beige shag rug in her living room, and even about a batch of chocolate pudding she once cooked. Today Aunt Doris was talking about pennies. She insisted they were the best of all coins due to their color. She called them Indian coins. And Aunt Doris was, like Josh's mother, an Indian. That meant, by extension, Josh was Indian, too, though a bit less so. The only blond in the group of dark-haired brothers and cousins, Josh often wished his skin were browner to prove that he was just as Indian as them.

"Give me a break, Aunt Doris," Josh said. "I'm ten and a half. Pennies suck, and everyone knows it."

Josh may have fallen for that crap when he was a kid, but now he knew that unless you had a bathtub full of pennies, they were pretty much worthless and bought you nothing but shitty penny candy or one lousy shoelace licorice. And what good was one shoelace licorice? It took at least three to be able to braid them. And he would need at least twenty "Indian coins" to buy one Three Musketeers bar.

"Well, they're prettiest of all the coins," Aunt Doris said. "I think so, anyway."

Josh rolled his eyes. The prettiest coins are the ones that are worth the most.

Aunt Doris handed Josh a pink two-dollar bill, a quarter, and all the pennies she had in her purse and then placed the purse back on the blue Formica kitchen table beside her cup of tea. She always gave him some loose change for going to the corner store to buy cigarettes for her, though Josh knew his mother would have made him go to the store for her whether his aunt paid him or not.

Josh took the money and put it in the pocket of his shorts.

"You don't happen to have eight thousand dollars' worth of pennies in there, do you?" Josh's mother asked, with a weary smile from across the kitchen table.

"Stop worrying, Gloria." Aunt Doris picked up a Peek Frean cream cookie off a saucer in the middle of the table. "Hannah is loaded. When that mother and sister of hers dropped dead, they left her a bundle. She'll help you out. After all, we're family. And family is important, isn't it, Josh?"

Josh shrugged. He had never really thought much about it.

"I wouldn't bet the house on it. Hannah never liked Ted very much," Josh's mother said.

"Who's this, Hannah?" Josh asked, grabbing a chocolate cream cookie from the saucer.

Josh had never heard that name before. He would have remembered if someone had come to his house with a dumb-ass name that rhymed with *banana*. And, besides, who couldn't like his father? Everyone liked his father. Josh didn't even know this Hannah and already disliked her.

"Hannah is our cousin," Aunt Doris said, after a few suspicious seconds of silence.

She looked over to Josh's mother like there was more to be said. Aunt Doris never skirted around Josh's questions the way his mother would. Still, it seemed strange that Josh had never met his mother's cousin before. He saw his cousins all the time. And he had a ton of them!

"We're going to visit Hannah this afternoon," his mother said, holding tight to her teacup. "And you get to come with us."

"Why do I have to go?" Josh asked. "I don't want to meet this Hannah."

"You're going because I asked you to. And make sure you don't say anything about... well, about, well, anything when you get there, you understand?"

That's when Josh knew there was something up with this cousin Hannah.

Aunt Doris pulled a crumpled light-pink Kleenex from her purse and patted her chest, running her hand below the neckline of her tight yellow T-shirt. She left the Kleenex in her cleavage like a sponge. "My God, it's hot. They said on the radio that it's the hottest May on record. And it hasn't rained—not a good rain— since April."

Aunt Doris wore a pair of faded cut-off denim shorts that Josh's mother had told her a few times were cut too short and bare feet. Aunt Doris looked more like Josh's mother than any other of his mother's siblings. Both had the same oval face and high cheekbones, but his aunt had dyed her hair light brown while Josh's mother had black hair. In Josh's ten years, he could remember his Aunt Doris having at least three different hair colours: red, light brown and, once, even blonde like his. Unlike Josh's mother, Aunt Doris liked to dress with pizzazz, in bright colours with lots of gold jewelry, and she wore makeup on her eyes and cheeks. Josh's mother never put makeup on, except maybe some lipstick on the rare nights when she dressed up fancy for a wedding or something. Still, even then, his mother's lipstick was practically the same colour as her natural lips, never bright red and shiny like the lipstick Aunt Doris wore.

"It's one of the hottest Mays I can remember," Josh's mother agreed. "But I think the summer of sixty-one when I was pregnant with Troy was hotter. Or maybe it just seemed hotter."

Today Josh's mother wore dark green slacks and a white and pink blouse. She had already changed out of the short pants she had been wearing earlier that morning when she did the laundry. Josh's mother would never go farther than their front yard in a pair of short pants.

"Look." Aunt Doris lifted her arm revealing a perspiration mark on the armpit of her yellow T-shirt. "I'm already soaked under the arms. Why don't you turn the air conditioner on?"

"It's too expensive to run all day," his mother said. "I only put it on at night for sleeping. And, besides, there's a bit of a breeze coming off the lake through the window. Can't you feel it?"

"No! All I can feel is heat and more heat!"

Josh thought, there's no breeze off the lake, wiping cookie crumbs off his face with the back of his hand. Josh liked when the air conditioning was running on full blast with all the windows and doors shut. It made their small house feel like a cave, hidden from the rest of the world.

"My air conditioning is on right now, and nobody's even home," Aunt Doris said proudly. "But it'll be nice and cool when I get home later."

"Oh, that's just burning money, Doris. And I can barely afford food right now."

"Ken likes it cool when he gets home from work. Not too cool, but just cool enough. He doesn't like it too cold."

"We can't have Ken uncomfortable when he walks in, can we?"

Josh's mother didn't even try to hide her dislike for Josh's Uncle Ken anymore, Josh thought walking out of the kitchen toward the back door. Not since his aunt had shown up at their back door one Sunday morning with her face purple and swollen after he had beaten her up. She stayed with them for a few weeks before moving to Josh's Aunt Lydia's for a couple of months. Then she went home. Aunt Doris had moved out and then moved back in with Uncle Ken at least three times that Josh could remember. The exact number of times her hair changed colour, he thought.

Josh sat down on a step by the back door and pulled his tattered blue sneakers over his bare feet. A few days earlier, he had gotten a shard of glass in his foot while walking to the corner store barefoot, and now he was a little wary of going without shoes. Still, most of the kids around his neighbourhood went barefoot in the summer months despite the occasional shard of glass or sharp stone.

"And don't be fooling around out there, please! We're leaving for Hannah's as soon as you come back!" Josh's mother yelled as the storm door slammed behind him.

"Get off my freaking back," Josh said under his breath.

He swung the back gate shut with a clang, skipped down the driveway, and suddenly stopped. It wasn't a good idea for a boy to skip on Alkeld Street. Girls could skip all they wanted, but boys had to walk. That was a rule. There were a lot of rules on Alkeld that were best not broken, so he tried to walk as boy-like as he knew how to down the street.

Train tracks bordered the east end neighbourhood where Josh lived on the south, colossal steel mills lining the bay on the north, and a sewage plant and the Red Hill Creek to the east. Smaller steel fabrication plants, warehouses, and factories were scattered on the streets around Josh's neighbourhood. At the end of Alkeld was the East End Scrap Metal company, where Josh and other neighbourhood kids would often play on the scrap in their yard when it closed for the day and on weekends, bouncing up and down on a rusted piece of metal slab, climbing piles of twisted aluminum, or rolling barrel-sized steel coils. It was the closest thing to a playground they had.

As Josh strolled down Alkeld Street, enjoying how the lump of change felt jingling in his pocket, he thought about what his mother had said about eight thousand dollars. She was out of her mind if she thought that would slip past him. Why did his mother need so much money? Was it because his father was in the hospital and couldn't work at Wentworth Steel? Maybe the whole family was headed to the poor house like his mother always said they would.

It was quiet on Alkeld Street today. Where were the other kids hiding? Josh wondered. Two other kids were at the top of the street near Woodward Avenue, but that was it. Saturday morning cartoons were over, so more kids should be out.

The corner store was only two blocks away, and as Josh walked, putting in the odd double-jump when he thought no one was looking, he sang "Don't Give Up on Us", quietly to himself, thinking that Hutch, with his blond hair, moustache, and brown leather jacket, was much better than Starsky. And Starsky, as far as Josh knew, never had a big song on the radio. Yes, Josh would have preferred darker skin like his mother and aunt, but he liked his Hutch-blonde hair. *I should find someone on the street to play Starsky and Hutch with.* They could pretend they were cops sharing an apartment in

California and catching perps and pervs (as Hutch would say) during the day in their cool red and white "Zebra Three" Gran Torino and then pretend to make dinner and watch television together on the couch at night. Josh would have to play Hutch, though. He was the one with blond hair, after all.

As Josh passed the smallest house on Alkeld Street, Shannon Perry came out of the front door and sat down on the top step of his rickety old wooden porch. He was wearing only a pair of red gym shorts that were a bit too small and held a lit cigarette between his fingers.

Shannon Perry was twelve years old and had lived in that small lime-green house on Alkeld since before Josh and his family moved into the neighbourhood. Shannon had no father, just his mother, Janet, who worked steady nights in a nearby boot factory and spent the rest of the time sleeping or walking around her house in a bathrobe and slippers. He had bushy mousy-brown hair, always wet-looking from grease and flipped up a bit at his shoulders, and the beginnings of a peach-fuzz moustache on his upper lip. He was the neighbourhood troublemaker. Once, even being brought home in a police car, causing considerable excitement on Alkeld Street. He was a tough kid, for sure, but Shannon wasn't a bully to younger kids like some on Alkeld, and he was never mean to Josh. Shannon was always nice to him. Josh didn't exactly know why Shannon liked him, but Josh was happy to take it. Josh was no idiot. He would rather have Shannon Perry as a friend than an enemy. Earlier that summer Shannon had split open Warren Dickenson's bottom lip after Warren had called Shannon's mother a whore. Josh didn't know whether Warren was right about Janet Perry being a whore, but Walter was crazy for saying it to Shannon's face. You didn't want to get on Shannon's bad side.

Josh's mother hated Shannon and forbade Josh to hang around with the boy, but Josh didn't care. He would talk to Shannon Perry anytime he wanted to. Josh treated people who were nice to him kindly and those who were dicks he'd try to ignore or, if he couldn't ignore them, then Josh would have to fight them. Not that he wanted to. He never *wanted* to fight, but that was how you settled things on

Alkeld Street. Sometimes Josh would win a school fight, but most of the time he'd get his ass kicked—but so did everyone else. That was just the way it worked.

"Hey, Shannon," Josh said with a wave as he passed.

Shannon nodded and took a long drag of his cigarette without saying anything. *How cool is he?* Really cool people don't even have to speak. You just know they're cool. Josh hoped to be that cool one day. Cool enough he didn't even have to speak. As Josh proceeded down Alkeld he tried to mimic the way that Shannon walked, slowly with indifference and a hint of danger. That's how boys walk.

Josh climbed the chipped cement stairs of Little Variety and opened the door. Behind the counter, Boris, the owner, sat up as the bell over the door jingled. He must have been napping, Josh thought, walking past a stack of afternoon newspapers by the counter with a big colour photo of Jake Ragno on the front page. He was in a suit and placing flowers on the graves of his wife and kids. That boy's grave is empty, Josh thought.

Josh breathed in deeply. One of his favourite things was the sweet scent of the corner store in the summertime. It seemed like everything in the store, fresh Wonder Bread, sugary cereals in boxes, Twinkies, and cupcakes in cellophane, and even the candy under the counter was getting overripe, swelling and sweating in their packaging and smelling sweeter and sweeter with every passing hot day. Boris' Little Variety never smelled this good in the winter.

"Hi ya, Boris," Josh said as the ice cream freezer, overfilled with different flavoured Good Humor ice cream, hummed loudly at the back of the store.

"Hello, kid. How's your papa?"

"He's fine. He's still in Montreal with my uncle."

Josh's mother had told him the best way to handle questions about his father was to lie since, she had said, it's none of their business. Josh had no moral qualms about this as he decided that it's not lying if they *make* you lie.

Boris nodded and sat back on his stool against the window. Boris never bothered to learn all the kids' names in the neighbourhood, choosing to call most just 'kid.' He was wearing what he wore all summer, a button-up short-sleeved white dress shirt, short black pants, and long black socks with sandals. Josh figured socks and sandals were how men dressed in Yugoslavia, where Boris was from. None of the other men on Alkeld Street ever dressed like that.

In the back of Boris' Little Variety, a doorway led to another room where Josh could see a flickering light. Sophie must be watching TV, he thought. Boris and his wife Sophie had kids, but they were older now and had moved away, so it was just the two of them living alone in the back of the store. Josh sometimes saw Sophie working behind the counter, but not very often.

Josh bought his aunt's Export-A cigarettes and had thirty-one cents left over in change. He bent down and, careful not to put his hands on the glass and irritate Boris, looked over the alluring candy behind the counter. There were bubble gum cigars, giant jawbreakers that turned colours as you sucked them, Hot Tamales, candy necklaces, Pixy Stix, rockets, Pop Rocks, candy cigarettes, marshmallow bananas, fireballs, Jujubes, caramels, bottle caps, Fun Dips, Mojo toffees, Red Vines, and Pez refills. It all looked so beautiful.

Josh bought a Three Musketeers chocolate bar and licorice strings, all purple because that was the only colour of licorice laces Boris had left.

Boris leaned back in his chair. "Bye, kid."

Josh waved goodbye and walked out, putting his Three Musketeers in his back pocket to get it a bit melty as the bell jingled again behind him. He had planned to braid the licorice when he got home but decided since they were going to this Hannah's, he might as well just eat them now and he shoved one purple string in his mouth as he walked down the stairs of the store. As he started back down, Alkeld he slowed down his pace. The sooner he got home, the sooner they left for his mother's cousin. He felt queasy. Josh didn't enjoy meeting new people; it made his stomach flip-flop. And there was something up about this Hannah that his mother and aunt weren't telling him. That made his gut quiver even more.

"Hey Shannon, you want a licorice string?" he yelled, approaching the Perry's house.

"Sure!" With a lit cigarette in his mouth, Shannon walked across his patchy lawn of weeds and took one of the long strands of purple licorice strings from Josh. "Thanks, man."

Shannon shoved one end of the licorice string in his mouthful of crooked teeth and chewed it without using his hands so the licorice would inch up to his mouth with each bite. Josh sometimes ate his spaghetti that way when his mother wasn't around. Josh noticed Shannon had the telltale yellow-brown bruises under each eye, remnants of a recent punch to the nose. For both boys and girls, such crescent-moon bruises were common on Alkeld Street. Josh wondered if Shannon had won or lost his fight.

"Those your cigarettes?" Shannon asked, pointing at the pack of Export-A in Josh's hand.

"No, they're for my aunt."

"That's the same brand I smoke." He extended his hand with the cigarette. "You want a drag, Josh?"

"Right here in the middle of the street? No way."

Even though Josh smoked now and then, like most kids his age on Alkeld, he would never do it right out in the open. Instead, he would hide away in the bushes near the railroad tracks, along the banks of the Red Hill Creek, or, most often, behind one of the many garages in the neighbourhood. These were safe places. Grown-ups never looked to see what was going on behind the garages and sheds on Alkeld Street; they were forgotten fragments of their parents' property, small strips of territory overgrown with weeds between the garages and wooden fences, reclaimed by kids for smoking, kissing, and other stuff you would never tell your parents.

"Go on," Shannon said. "No one's looking."

Josh knew from living on Alkeld Street that there was *always* someone looking. "Nah," he said. He put his hands behind his back so anyone watching would see the refusal plain as day. "Next time."

"Hey, is your mom home now?" The older boy took a final drag of the cigarette before flicking the butt across the sidewalk and onto the boulevard, where it smoldered in the dry grass.

"She's home. But we're going out to see her cousin now."

"That's the pits. Nothing worse than relatives, eh, man?" Shannon looked Josh over from head to foot. "How old are you now, Josh? Eleven?"

"Ten," Josh said, somewhat impressed that Shannon thought he was older. "And a half."

"That's cool. I'll be thirteen July twenty-second." Shannon lifted his right arm in the air showing the callow light-brown hair in the middle of his armpit. "See that? I'm starting to get hair under my arms. I'm practically a teenager already. Two months early! The school nurse even sent a note home to my mom telling her to buy me deodorant because I was starting to smell. Only grown-ups smell, you know." Shannon beamed proudly.

"You're getting a moustache too."

"Yeah," Shannon said. He rubbed the down on his upper lip with his forefinger. "It should look pretty good by the time school starts again. Like Burt Reynolds, probably."

Josh had a strange urge to reach over and gently touch the peach fuzz on Shannon's upper lip to see what it felt like but didn't. Though he didn't think Shannon would mind all that much, being so proud of it.

"If we have cake or something on my birthday, you could come over for some. My mother makes good cake. She's a dumb tit when it comes to everything else in the world, but she can make a pretty good cake," Shannon said.

"I would," Josh said. "But I'll be at Cub Scout camp then. It's for three weeks. I don't want to go."

"Three whole weeks?"

"Uh huh."

"Christ, that's shitty luck, man," Shannon said, shaking his head. "And you know all those Cub Scouts are fags, don't you? All that sleeping in the same tent and weird shit goes down, man. You know what I'm saying, or are you too young?"

"I know what you're saying. I'm not a baby."

"You keep your sleeping bag done up tight, man. That's all I'm sayin."

Shannon spit a light-purple gob far down the sidewalk. Josh wished he could spit at such a distance, but whenever he tried his spit mostly just landed on his chin. He had to practice spitting more.

69

"What grade are you going into in the fall, Shannon?" Josh asked.

"Six. That is if Mr. Tanner passes me next month, the fucking faggot."

Josh figured that Shannon must have failed two grades. Josh would be going into Mr. Tanner's grade-five class in September and would catch up with Shannon if he failed again. It did seem odd to Josh that Shannon failed so often because Shannon didn't seem stupid like most kids who failed grades in school. Shannon just seemed... not to care.

"You want another one?" Josh asked, holding up one of the last two pieces of purple licorice.

"Nah, you have it. I'm getting too old for licorice anyway. Hey, did you know I built a wicked fort down by the creek?"

"A fort?" Josh asked, intrigued.

"Yeah, it's fucking awesome! And it's hidden really good so no one can find it, but I'll show you sometime. We can smoke in peace without our mothers or these nosey bitches looking out their windows bugging us. Nothing faggy though, you know what I mean, Josh?"

"Sure. But I gotta go now."

Josh didn't want his mother yelling his name out the back door. Most mothers on Alkeld Street did that. The names of random kids being shrieked out by mothers on the street were almost as common as the sound of the CN train rattling by just past the trees.

"Hey, your dad still away?" Shannon asked, picking some lint out of his belly button.

"Yeah. He's in Montreal visiting my uncle."

Shannon looked at the ground and nodded. "Okay, take it easy, Josh," He turned around and walked back to his front porch.

"But if I don't go to camp, I'll come over for some birthday cake for sure," Josh shouted.

Josh still believed that he could somehow get out of this whole shitty camp thing. He was a smart guy, one of the smartest guys in his class. Sure, there were a couple of girls who were smarter, but they were girls. Girls were always better at tests and knowing answers. They always did their homework too. When it came to the boys, Josh was head and shoulders above all of them. No boy in his class got better marks than Josh.

He walked faster now, thinking about Shannon's secret fort down in the creek. Josh loved forts, they were almost like having your own house, but forts were only for those big enough to fight for them. Once he and Tonya, a girl in the neighbourhood, had made a nice fort in the trees along Red Hill Creek. It wasn't the best, but they had spent almost a week last summer building and decorating it. It even had wallpaper. Tonya had gotten her hands on one of those wallpaper sample books, and they had covered the plywood walls with the different pages using a stapler and some masking tape. Still, their fort was quickly discovered and taken over by bigger kids. He would be the bigger kid soon enough. Josh hoped by then he had better things to do than pick on younger kids by taking the fort they had worked a whole week on. He wondered if Shannon would want to play *Starsky and Hutch* down at the fort some time. But Shannon might want to be Hutch since he was growing a moustache too.

Fifteen minutes later, Josh, his mother, and his aunt all climbed into his aunt's steaming hot car. He was already ailing from the scorching June heat and suffocating humidity. Unlike his darker-skinned aunt and mother, who seemed to flourish in the summer, Josh drooped in the heat.

Aunt Doris drove east down Broadridge Avenue past Red Hill Junior High, where Josh would be going in a year, toward Eastgate Mall. As they went over Red Hill Creek, Josh wondered if they were passing over Shannon's fort.

"Can you imagine being buried there?" Josh's mother said as they passed Restland Cemetery on Nash Road.

"What's wrong with Restland? It's close to everyone you know. We can visit you every time we go to the mall," Aunt Doris said with a smile.

"I want to be buried in Ancaster, his mother said. "I went to a funeral out there once. I forget whose funeral it was, but it was clean and not a factory in sight. Who wants to spend eternity looking up at some boot factory and a closed-up roller rink? And it's less than a mile from the dump. You can see the incinerator."

"The roller rink won't be empty forever," Aunt Doris said.

"That's not the point," his mother said, smiling.

"You've lived your whole life in the east end of Hamilton, and now you want to pull up stakes and go to swanky Ancaster to be put in the ground? You never go to Ancaster. You don't know anyone in Ancaster. You don't know anything about Ancaster, Gloria," Aunt Doris said. She laughed heartily.

Josh's mother chuckled too. "Well, it's never too late to get to know a new place."

Aunt Doris turned onto Queenston Road. Queenston was one of Josh's favourite streets in Hamilton, it had the McDonald's with the golden arches, the A&W where they brought your food to your car on a tray and placed it on your window, and the Ponderosa, where his father would always order a steak, well-done and the smell of cooking beef filled the car as they passed. His aunt pulled into the driveway of one of the many high-rise apartments that towered along Queenston Road and parked her car at the very end of the parking lot, away from any other cars. Aunt Doris liked to have room around her car when she parked, happy to choose a spot far from the door if it meant she didn't have to squeeze her big brown Caddy between two cars.

"So, this Hannah is Indian too?" Josh asked.

"Yep," Aunt Doris answered. "Her mother and our mother were sisters. Their father, your great-grandfather, brought them all up here to Canada from Minnesota when they were little girls."

"Why?"

"Because their mother died," Aunt Doris said.

Josh could point out Minnesota on the map and knew that, relatively speaking, it wasn't that far from Hamilton. It was much closer than England, where his Grandpa Moore was from, or Norway, where his other grandmother was born. But everything looked close on maps and globes. Even Africa, where his father had once been a soldier, didn't look all that far away.

His aunt turned off the car, and they sat quietly for a minute while Josh waited with his hand on the door handle.

"Are we getting out, or what?" he asked.

"You have to tell him before we go in," Aunt Doris said.

His mother sighed and turned around. "Josh, I want to tell you one thing about Hannah."

"What? What about Hannah?"

"Hannah is very… large," his mother remarked.

"Is that all? Can we get out now?"

"She's very, *very* large," Aunt Doris said.

"I'm starting to think maybe you and Josh should go over to Eastgate Mall and let me go up alone," his mother said. "Lydia said it was even worse the last time she visited Hannah."

"Yeah, let's go to Eastgate, Aunt Doris."

"You'll need me there to help guilt her into it if she squawks. And she should see exactly who she's helping. Who can resist this one's face?" His aunt gestured with her thumb toward Josh.

"We'll only be up an hour. Tops! I'll tell her I have to pick up Ken at work, so we're not trapped there all afternoon."

"All right," his mother said, after a few seconds. "Just remember your manners, and don't say anything that will embarrass me or your Aunt Doris. And don't mention anything about how big she is or how…"

His aunt and mother looked at each other.

"Just don't say anything about anything," his mother said.

"I won't say anything," Josh said, stepping out of the car. "So just how fat is she, anyway?"

"Fat." Aunt Doris said, slamming her car door closed.

The front entrance of the apartment had on either side of the steps leading to the lobby, two large stone lions sitting and staring straight ahead at the Hudson's Bay department store across the street in the mall. They almost seemed to Josh to say, "I wouldn't go up there if I were you…"

Josh thought this must be a fancy apartment, walking up three wide marble steps to the front door. The lobby was decorated with red and gold paisley wallpaper and gold-flecked mirrors covered one wall. This was the sort of place he would live when he got older. Josh had no intention of ever living in a house with creaking stairs and a musty basement that leaked and flooded with spiders in the garage like all the old houses on Alkeld Street when he grew up. He was going to live in an apartment building like this with elegant stone lions, an elevator, and a balcony. He wondered if this apartment had an indoor pool; all the best apartments had pools.

His aunt walked to the intercom panel and looked for her cousin's name in the long list of names punched in shiny black plastic Rotex labels. "Here it is."

Josh looked at the black label on the panel: *& Mrs. Sinclair* 2232

"I think this used to say *Mr. and Mrs. Sinclair* but someone has cut off the *Mr.*," Aunt Doris said. She pushed the buttons on the panel and the intercom buzzed like a busy phone signal.

"Yeah?" a manly voice asked a moment later.

"Hannah?" Aunt Doris said, looking cautiously at Josh's mother. "Hannah, it's Doris and Gloria."

They didn't mention me, Josh thought, and the front door clicked open.

As they stood waiting for the elevator, Josh wondered just how fat this cousin would be. She must be awfully big if they wanted to warn him, like a yellow street sign.

Fat lady ahead.

Josh noticed the smell before they had even made it to Hannah's door at the end of the hall. It became a little stronger as they made their way down the worn red carpet that lined the dark hallway. By the time his Aunt Doris knocked on the door, it was undeniable. The door opened, and a horrible stench hit Josh like a cudgel between the eyes.

"Well, come on in," a colossal woman said crossly. She backed up down the hall to let the three of them in the door, since her size made it impossible for Aunt Doris or his mother to get by her.

Josh's face scrunched up in an agonized grimace as he crossed the threshold into the apartment. He had never smelled anything like this before. The smell was like a hamper full of dirty clothes intermingled with the tang of stale cigarette smoke, rotting food, dog shit, and something worse.

Manners or not, Josh made up his mind that this woman was not going to touch him like his dad's sister, Bonnie, who thought she could grab him, mess up his hair or jiggle his belly and tell him he was getting chubby. Luckily, Hannah did not try and touch him at all. Instead, she put her fat hand on her hip while her face contorted its hanging folds into a scowl, apparently, Josh thought, annoyed that his mother had brought him along. That was fine with Josh. He didn't want her liking him, and he wasn't going to like her.

"Come on." Hannah turned around and lead them down the hall. She walked with a limp, puffing hard with each step.

They walked past cardboard boxes stacked from the floor to the ceiling against the dining room walls and the living room corner. The patio doors were open slightly but, having boxes piled halfway up the glass, no breeze could blow away the stench that clung to the apartment.

"Oh, you got a new dining room table," Aunt Doris said as if none of them could smell at all.

"Two years ago. You'd know that if you came more often. The old dining room table is lying against the wall of my bedroom. I'm going to sell it sometime. But I don't have a front yard for a yard sale, so I'll have to put it in the newspaper. But all that takes money and I'm not made of money no matter what some people think."

Josh had never seen anyone so big right up close to him before. She had bulging eyes and a flame of bright orange hair that was grey closer to her head. She wore a huge dress with a pink flowered print that hugged her folds of fat so closely that she looked like she had been put together in four round sections like a snowman. Her feet were bare with small wiry black hairs on the big toes and deep spider web cracks encrusted with grime crept up her heels. She wore rings on almost every one of her large fingers, each with big square or football-shaped yellow, red, and green stones. Probably just glass, Josh thought.

"Go sit on the sofa and be quiet, please," Josh's mother whispered. "Do you want me to ask if she has a soda or something?"

"I don't want anything from her," Josh whispered back. "It smells."

He wanted to add 'like shit' but he didn't. First of all, his mother would probably slap him across the back of the head when they got back to the car, and second, the apartment didn't smell like shit. It smelled worse than shit. The stink seemed to ooze out of the walls like a living thing, moving between them and forcing its way into their bodies through their noses and mouths. He felt violated.

Her eyes pleaded with him. "I know it does, Josh, but please *please* don't be rude. For me? I honestly never thought it would be this... bad."

"All right," He wouldn't say another word, at least for now. They would surely talk about it when they get back to his aunt's car. Aunt Doris wasn't going to stay quiet about this.

Josh went to sit on the sofa, but the upholstery was grimy with dark stains, so he sat in the wooden rocking chair by the cardboard boxes stacked against the living room wall and pulled his knees up to his chest. He yanked the collar of his T-shirt over his mouth and nose and sat quietly, watching a man playing an accordion on the television in the corner. He would never live in this apartment building. Not ever!

Over the couch was a painted portrait of, Josh deduced, a younger, thinner, dark-haired, and much prettier Hannah, wearing a low-cut black dress with a strand of pearls. Josh had never met anyone who was in a painting before, and he compared the woman in paint to the woman who opened the door. *Is that what time does?* Through the cut-out in the kitchen wall, Josh watched his mother pick up the electric kettle that sat on Hannah's avocado-green countertop as Aunt Doris and cousin Hannah sat at the round wooden kitchen table smoking. *Why was his mother making the tea? His mother never asked guests to make tea when they came to their house. Where are* your *manners, Hannah?* Josh thought.

"So where is George living now, Hannah?" Aunt Doris asked.

"I don't give a damn where he's living or even if he is living."

Josh kept his eyes on the kitchen. There were boxes piled up on one side of the kitchen as well. *Why were there cardboard boxes all around the apartment?* A small bug that looked like a tiny black beetle crawled over his forearm and Josh flicked it off toward the television.

"A friend of mine from the bingo called me the other day and said she saw them together. Right out in public at the bingo. And that's *my* bingo too!" Hannah said, her large face getting redder and redder. "I've been going to that bingo for years! You know how that makes me look? Well, I haven't been able to go for a while since I hurt my knee, but I'm still known there. And I know everyone is laughing at me."

Aunt Doris made a tsk tsk sound as Josh's mother first put a cup of tea in front of Hannah and then served Aunt Doris and herself.

"And now I hear they're living together in an apartment near Gage Park. But you know what, I don't care; they can both go straight to hell," she said, swiping her hand in the air and knocking ashes from the cigarette between her sausage-like fingers into the middle of the table.

"Right!" Aunt Doris said. "Straight to hell. The both of them!"

"Say," Hannah said, smiling for the first time since they had arrived. "Do you girls remember when your mother used to have me babysit for you while she cleaned houses when you were little? Remember all those boys that used to come over to see me? Remember how they came over all the time? Finally, your mother said to me, 'Hannah, there are too many boys around here!'"

"I remember," Aunt Doris said, nodding. "You were one popular girl."

Josh didn't buy it.

"I just picked the wrong one to marry," Hannah said. "And I would never have married George if I hadn't been pregnant. And then what happens? I lose the damned thing a month after we marry."

Josh pulled his T-shirt higher on his face to just below his eyes. Ten minutes in here and he was ready to make a run for it like George had.

"And that's why I can't go to my regular bingo anymore."

"That's terrible," Aunt Doris said. "Isn't that terrible, Gloria?"

"Yes, it is," she said.

"I thought about going to that bingo under Baldock's Grocery on Barton, the one near Kenilworth, but people say their bingo smells as lousy as their meat. And I've heard it's not as on the up-and-up like my regular bingo, so I just don't go to any bingo anymore. All I do is play the one on the cable channel, but I think that one is rigged too."

"Everyone always said Baldock's meat was bad. I was never sure if that was true, but I was always afraid to buy meat there," Josh's mother said.

"I wouldn't touch Baldock's meat with a ten-foot pole," Aunt Doris said. "But I have gone to the bingo in their basement. I didn't think it was rigged though, Hannah. And it smells like all bingos, like stale smoke and coffee."

"Did you win?" Hannah asked.

"No, but I never win," Aunt Doris said. She laughed and slapped Hannah on the arm.

"And do you know what George suggested to me before he packed up and left? I should say before I *told* him to pack up and leave?"

"What?" said Aunt Doris.

"George said, and you two aren't going to believe this... George said that the three of us, him and me and that woman, should all live together here. In a one-bedroom apartment, if you catch my drift."

"Yeah, George was always an odd-duck, wasn't he, Gloria," Aunt Doris said.

"There was something always a little off about him," Josh's mother agreed.

"He's a bastard!" Hannah said.

While his mother and aunt continued to sip tea at Hannah's kitchen table and listen to her spew hatred toward George, Josh tried to listen to the polka music on the television. He had to take a leak but didn't want to use that woman's toilet.

"George just did it at the worst possible time," Hannah continued. "First Mom went in '71, then Gwen in '74, and then poor Naomi drops dead in '75. You two don't know what it's like to lose your mother and your two sisters so quickly and so close together. Now all my sisters are gone, and I only have three useless brothers left. It's just like that song "Ten Little Indians". We're all disappearing one by one. You two will soon learn that with your own family; before you know it there'll only be one little Indian left. And do you think that one will feel lucky about being the last? Fat chance."

Josh started to softly sing "Ten Little Indians" but stopped. Was that really what it was like? Losing people you love, one by one, until only one was left? So far, no one in his family had died. Or, if they had, they died like his mother's mother long before he was born. Now he wondered, which one of us will be the one little Indian left? Since he was the youngest in the family, naturally he assumed he would be the last, standing over everyone's grave. All forever being towered over by a boot factory across the street. He suddenly felt ill.

"So, Gloria," Hannah finally said. "Doris said on the phone you were having money problems… again. I'm not sure what you expect me to do about it?" She crossed her arms, only able to touch her fingertips together over her stomach.

Josh's mother folded her hands on the green plastic placemat in front of her and nodded.

"Yes. We need eight thousand dollars."

"Pfft, you can't be serious!"

"Lydia will lend me two thousand, but I need six thousand more. You know I wouldn't ask if it wasn't important but… we're in a bind." She lowered her voice. "A terrible bind, Hannah."

"Not for the first time either," Hannah said.

"No, you're right, it's not the first time," his mother said, looking down into her cup of tea.

"Since Mom died and left me a few bucks, I've had family members coming out of the woodwork, family members who never come to see me any other time, mind you, they traipse in here with their hand open as if to say, 'fork it over, Hannah.'"

"We're not coming out of the woodwork, Hannah," Aunt Doris said firmly.

"I can give you a forty-dollar payment out of every paycheque I get," Josh's mother said, looking up. "I figured out that's as much as I can afford. Then when Ted gets working again, we'll be able to double that and pay you off even sooner."

Cousin Hannah grunted, leaned over, and took one of Aunt Doris' cigarettes without asking.

"What's the problem? How did you get eight thousand dollars in debt?"

"Well," Gloria said, and then paused. She lowered her voice so low that Josh could only make out a few words. "Money... borrowed... union..."

"Borrowed or took?" Hannah asked.

"Took," Josh's mother said.

"Gambling?"

"Yes."

"That's Ted Moore for you!"

Josh's bladder was full, and he had to piss, but he wasn't going to ask this woman where the bathroom was. He stood and walked down the hallway, past the portrait of Hannah, and found a bathroom near the front door. The bathtub had no shower curtain and was full, to the ceiling, with more cardboard boxes, just like the living room and dining room. How did she shower? Josh lifted the toilet seat and, finding brown splash stains underneath, he pissed quickly, pushing it out of his bladder as hard as he could. Then, he grinned and aimed his penis toward the side of the vanity and, once it was soaked, then aimed down to the floor leaving a puddle of piss on her bathroom floor. *That will teach you for treating my mother like that.* Still, it didn't seem like enough.

He flushed, kicked the toilet seat and lid with its grubby stained mint-green shag toilet cover down with his foot. His head swam in a fetid pond while down his throat the fumes solidified into a grimy finger that swivelled the contents of his stomach. He walked out of the bathroom, stopped, and put his nose against the front door to get some fresh air in his lungs, then he walked back to the rocking chair and put his T-shirt back over his mouth and nose. The room seemed hotter and fouler.

"Sorry, Gloria, but I can't help you. You'll just have to find some other way to get out of this mess. I'm not about to hand over that kind of money to a drunk, a thief and gambler."

"You're not giving it to a drunk and a thief, Hannah. You'll be *lending* it to Gloria. You'll be doing it for that poor hungry boy out there watching television. And she will pay you back," Aunt Doris said.

"That hungry boy looks pretty well-fed to me," Hannah said. "And where did Ted end up after all this? In the booby hatch! And who knows how long he'll be there. Who knows if he'll ever bring in a paycheque again? A lot of people go in there and never come out!"

"Hannah," Aunt Doris said.

"All right!" Josh's mother said. "Let's just forget it. If you can't help me, Hannah, then you can't help me. I'll figure something else out."

"And who knows what's going to happen with George? What if he comes back? I'd have to tell him where a big hunk of our money went. I could see him turning right around and going back to that woman."

"Like I said," Josh's mother said politely. "It's fine, Hannah. I'll manage. Does anyone want another cup of tea?"

"I told you not to marry him, Gloria," Hannah said.

That was it. Josh yanked the T-shirt he had covering his face down and, lifting his head to the brown, nicotine-stained ceiling, began rocking faster. He focused on the image of Hannah's dirty toilet until his stomach began to turn and vomit pushed against the back of his throat. He breathed the rancid air deep into his lungs and continued to rock faster and faster until he began to gag. Finally, as the polka show was ending, he stood and walked toward the kitchen.

"Josh," his mother said, putting down her cup, "you don't look so good—"

Suddenly the contents of Josh's stomach were forced up and out a good foot from his mouth. A stomach-full of yellowing Lucky Charms and curdled milk from breakfast intermingled with pieces of purple licorice laces splashed against the green wall of the kitchen and on Hannah's lap and down her legs onto the parquet floor. *Bull's-eye!*

Hannah screamed.

Josh's mother jumped up from the table and grabbed some green paper towels from the kitchen counter.

"I'm so sorry, Hannah, he's been sick," his mother lied. "I probably shouldn't have brought him today."

"No, you shouldn't have!"

Aunt Doris took more paper towel and, dropping to her knees, began cleaning up the mess on Hannah's kitchen floor.

"Just go! I'll clean it up myself. Just get him out of here... before he pukes again! Jesus Christ! I just cleaned these goddamn floors!" Hannah yelled.

The three of them made a quick exit out of Hannah's apartment while Josh's mother kept apologizing. Josh was only sorry his belly wasn't fuller. Finally, out in the hall he breathed in deeply as they waited for the elevator.

"I'm so embarrassed," his mother said.

"She's the one who should be embarrassed," Aunt Doris said as they stepped in the elevator. "Getting to the point that your apartment smells so bad that it makes children sick to their stomach. She should be mortified! That was at least ten times worse than my last time there. And it wasn't two years ago like she said either. And what's with all those boxes of junk around? Can't she toss anything out?"

"Feeling better?" his mother asked, rubbing his shoulder.

Josh nodded. The taste of vomit was sour in his mouth, burning the inside of his nose.

"I think I know why George left," Aunt Doris said. "For fresh air."

The elevator doors opened, and they stepped into the red and gold lobby. It didn't look fancy to Josh anymore.

"I should go back up and help her clean it up, Doris. She has bad knees."

"Oh, screw her! If she doesn't understand the idea that you're supposed to help family out when they need it—she doesn't deserve our help. Christ, what a piece of work! I always said Hannah was one selfish broad, sitting up on the money her mother and sisters left her like a stuffed chicken sitting on her eggs."

Josh's mother had him sit on the marble steps. Beside them the stone lion looked down at them. He's saying *Told you so*, Josh thought.

"I shouldn't have taken him up there," his mother said, sitting down beside Josh. She gently rubbed his back. "He has a weak stomach. He always has. I just never in my wildest dreams thought that it had gotten that bad... it's like she gave up."

"Her mother would roll over in her grave!" Aunt Doris said, leaning against the lion's pedestal with her arms crossed. "Her mother was neat as a pin. And did you hear her say she had just washed her kitchen floor? I nearly fell over when she said that."

"She's really gone downhill fast. I feel sorry for her. Maybe we should have visited her more often, Doris. Especially after George left."

"Bull! I can actually smell her apartment on my shirt now." Aunt Doris pulled the bottom of her yellow T-shirt up to her nose and grimaced. "I only hope it will blow off us in the car with the windows open."

Josh's mother pulled a Kleenex out of her purse and gave it to Josh who blew snot and puke from his nose into it.

"And what was that crap she was saying about only marrying George because she was pregnant and then lost the baby?" Aunt Doris continued. "Hannah was never pregnant; she just said that so George would marry her, and we all know it. She's not fooling anyone, even all these years later. And, while we're at it, I don't remember any swarm of boys coming over to our house when she babysat us, either. In fact, I can't remember one boy coming over to see her. She lives in a fantasy world, if you ask me." She sat down close on the other side of Josh with a grunt and lit a cigarette.

"What are we going to do now?" his mother said.

"But if you had to throw up on her feet, Josh, you did it at the perfect time," Aunt Doris said.

"I'm hungry," Josh finally said. "Can we stop at A&W?"

Josh stood outside his house with a tennis ball in his hand trying to think of a good wall to bounce it against. Since it was Saturday, he decided to head to East End Scrap Metal at the end of Alkeld Street where the parking lot would be empty and he could bounce the tennis ball against their red brick wall and no one would be around, except for maybe some neighbourhood kids playing on the scrap metal that rusted in the back.

Josh walked toward the end of Alkeld, bouncing the ball and counting. He wanted to see how long it would take to bounce his ball six thousand times but stopped when it became boring after hitting just over fifty bounces. Josh had been worrying about those six thousand dollars since they visited that cousin Hannah. If his mother hadn't found six thousand dollars yet, maybe she could ask some of his father's sisters. He wasn't sure if his Aunt Sue and Aunt Peggy had six thousand dollars but what about Aunt Wilma in Georgia? Weren't all Americans rich?

For a few minutes Josh bounced his tennis ball against the East End Scrap Metal building, enjoying being alone in the shade when he suddenly saw three boys on bicycles come riding quickly up the driveway toward him. Tony Sheehan led with Gavin Mulligan and Danny Jacovitch coming up behind.

"Playing with all your friends?" Tony said as the three boys rode their bikes in circles around Josh.

Tony Sheehan was a thin tall boy with dark brown hair and a chip in his front tooth that he had gotten while belly-whopping on the small hill beside Laura Secord School last winter. Tony was two years older than Josh and had a younger sister, Eva Sheehan, who was in Josh's class. Eva wore skirts over her pants for some weird reason. Unlike his sister, Tony dressed pretty much normal.

Gavin and Danny were, like Tony, also two years older than Josh and in grade six. Gavin, shortest of the three, with black curly hair, dark eyes and braces, had the kind of bike that most kids in the neighbourhood coveted. It had a banana seat and a long sissy bar in the back that towered over Gavin's head. It was cool but Josh preferred his own Schwinn Sting-ray. Josh's bike was, in his opinion, probably one of the best on Alkeld Street, even with the deep scratch his father had made in the crossbar with the beer bottle.

"So, where's your dad, Josh Moore?" Tony Sheehan asked. He grinned showing his broken front tooth.

"He's in Montreal visiting my uncle." Josh tossed the tennis ball between his hands and looked Tony straight in the eye. "If it's any of your business."

"Wrong!" Tony yelled. He stopped in front of Josh and stood straddling his bike while Gavin and Danny circled them. "Want me to tell you where your dad is, Josh Moore?"

"Yeah, tell him where his father is!" Gavin said, stopping abruptly in front of Josh. He folded his arms and sat back on his banana seat with one foot on a pedal and the other on the ground.

Josh tried to ignore them. He walked around the boys, continuing to bounce his tennis ball as nonchalantly as he could as he walked past the rusted coils and sheets of metal back toward Alkeld Street. His heart raced in his chest. The three boys slowly rode behind Josh, laughing to themselves, until Tony shot quickly past him and then turned, stopping in Josh's path, his tires crunching the gravel and stone driveway.

"Your dad is locked up in the funny farm, Josh Moore," Tony said. "And everyone knows it!"

Gavin and Danny laughed like they had never heard anything so funny in their short stupid lives.

"You're crazy, Tony Sheehan," Josh said, walking as intrepidly as he could around Tony's bicycle. "I told you my dad is in Montreal."

"Wanna bet?" Tony yelled behind him.

"He's in the funny faaaaaaaaaarm!" Gavin said, riding quickly past Josh.

"Well, at least I have a father, Gavin Mulligan!" Josh yelled. turning back onto Alkeld.

Josh instantly regretted saying that. He wouldn't usually antagonize bigger kids when there were three of them, but he was angry, feeling the tears burning behind his eyes but refusing to cry in front of these three assholes.

Gavin stopped laughing but Tony and Danny began laughing even harder.

"The little prick has you there, Gav," Danny said.

Gavin hopped off his banana seat and dropped his bike with a thud on the sidewalk, then walking up quickly behind Josh, Gavin shoved him hard using both hands. Josh stumbled, but he didn't fall.

"What did you say to me, you little shit?" Gavin said.

Josh kept walking away, hoping they would just leave him alone or, if not, at least make it fair and leave it to just Gavin and him to fight. He'd lose, for sure, but Gavin wouldn't go home unbruised if a fight was going to happen. And it sure looked like it was about to happen.

"Leave him alone!" someone shouted.

Josh turned and saw Shannon Perry. He was holding a Fudgesicle in his right hand and looked more bored at what was going on than anything else, as if he knew everyone was going to do exactly what he said and he wasn't going to have to break a sweat.

Gavin immediately turned and hopped back on the banana seat of his bicycle and drove away followed by a laughing Tony and Danny.

"Your father is in the nuthouse, Josh Moore!" Gavin shouted, as he rode away down Alkeld Street.

"And your mother sucks cocks in back alleys for beer, Gavin, you fucking queer!" Shannon yelled after them. Then he stuck what was left of the Fudgesicle back in his mouth.

That was it. The battle was over.

"I can fight my own battles, you know," Josh said, finally feeling tears roll down his cheeks. He tried to wipe them away before Shannon saw them.

"I know you can," Shannon said, tossing the Fudgesicle stick on the grass. "I saw you fight that Willy Lloyd kid last winter. You didn't win but you got a few good licks in. I just don't like kids picking on younger kids. It's a shitty thing to do."

Shannon picked a short cigarette butt out of the front pocket of his jeans and lit it with a match from a penny matchbook.

"You got snot hanging from your nose," Shannon said, taking a drag from his cigarette, inhaling like a grown-up.

"It's true, you know," Josh said. He wiped the snot from his face and cleaned his fingers on the leg of his shorts.

"What's true?"

Josh looked down at the asphalt. "My dad *is* in the nuthouse." He could feel more tears well up in his eyes.

"Yeah, I know he is. Me and my mom were watching the night they took him away," Shannon said.

"He cut his throat in our garage. On purpose. After they took him away in the ambulance, they took him to a regular hospital to stitch up his throat first and then took him to the mental hospital on the mountain. My mom made up the story about Montreal for me to tell people. Not sure why. Everyone knows the truth."

"Do you know why your dad cut his throat?"

Shannon passed the cigarette to Josh who, taking it, sucked the smoke into his mouth and blew it out without inhaling. Josh didn't care if someone on Alkeld Street saw him and snitched to his mother. Fuck em! Snoops around here knew everything anyway, he thought.

"No, I don't know why he cut himself." He took one more drag off the cigarette and handed it back to Shannon. "I've tried to listen to my mom on the phone through my bedroom door at night when she thinks I'm sleeping but haven't heard her tell anyone why he did it. Maybe no one knows. Alls I know is he did it."

"That's wild," Shannon said, shaking his head. "Could it have been an accident? I once cut my knee on a piece of glass."

Shannon lifted his cut-offs to show his scar. He was beginning to get hair on his shins and lower legs that got darker and fuller toward his ankle. His scar looked like a lightning bolt.

"Glass leaves an awesome kind of scar," Shannon said. "Like nothing else. Wait till you see your old man's throat. I bet it'll look really cool."

"I don't think it was an accident."

"No, it probably wasn't if they put him in the nuthouse."

"If I ever find out I'll let you know, though,"

"Okay," Shannon said. "If Gavin or that bunch of fags bugs you again, let me know, man." He tossed his cigarette onto the middle of Alkeld Street, hocked up some light-green phlegm, and spit on the sidewalk. "I know you can fight your own battles and all, but they're older and bigger, and I just thought you might need some help."

"Thanks," Josh said. He hoped that just being afraid of Shannon would keep Gavin and the rest of them away from him for a while.

"Want to come over to my place and listen to records? I have a new KISS album. I stole it from Sam the Record Man. I just walked right out with it, and they didn't stop me."

"Nah," Josh said.

He didn't feel like listening to records right then. And he didn't like KISS that much either.

"Or, if you want, you could come and see my fort. There's a shortcut behind East End Scrap down to the tracks."

"Ah..."

"It's a cool fort. Probably the coolest fort ever made down there. I keep some stuff hidden in it too. Some pretty cool stuff," Shannon said.

"Like what?" Josh asked.

Josh had a secret box under his captain's bed that no one knew about that held some of his favourite things. It had the Queen's Silver Jubilee coin they handed out to everyone at school, half a robin's eggshell, a paperback book about the Evelyn Dick murders with gory photos of her husband's chopped-up body, and an AMWAY catalogue with a set of glasses that had pictures of men and women on them whose clothes would slowly disappear when the glasses got cold. Josh could almost make out the naked bodies on the last glass. Almost!

"You know, nudie mags, *Playboy* and *Hustler* and other stuff. You can smoke all you want down there too. I always let my friends smoke as much as they want in my fort. And I have two cigarettes left that we could share."

Josh wondered what friends Shannon was talking about since he didn't seem to have any. And what about these nudie mags?

"Okay," Josh said, shoving his tennis ball down the front pocket of his cut-offs.

The two boys walked, with Shannon leading, through the brush at the end of Alkeld Street behind East End Scrap Metal toward the path to the railroad tracks. Josh knew of a lot of paths that lead to the railroad tracks but had never taken this one. It wasn't well-worn like some others, and Josh wondered if Shannon had made the path himself. Bushes with long thorns scratched Josh's bare legs as they came upon the clearing opening to the CN railroad tracks some fifty yards before it crossed Red Hill Creek. Though his mother forbade Josh from going down to the creek, Josh had been going there for years, to smoke or skip rocks in the creek or to just explore, always remembering to kick off the red dirt from his sneakers before going home. And she never knew the difference. She fell for anything.

They walked along the train tracks until they reached the old stone bridge over Red Hill Creek, ignoring the black and white *Danger, Trespassing on Railway Property Is Illegal. Offenders Will Be Prosecuted* sign on a metal post along the tracks.

Shannon made his way down the red clay hill of the creek as Josh grabbed a tree branch for support and carefully followed Shannon down to the creek's bank. In the murky brown-green water, Josh saw a large gold carp with ugly lips sucking on some creek scum.

"Watch this," Shannon said. He picked up a large rock and hurled it at the fish. The water splashed up with a loud plunk.

"Did you get him?" Josh asked. "Those giant goldfish give me the creeps."

"Nah, the fucker just swam away," Shannon said. "You know where they come from, don't you? It's from people who flush little goldfish down the toilet. Then the fish eat all that shit from the sewage plant and grow into those monsters."

Shannon turned and walked into the darkness under the railroad bridge spanning the creek. Josh hesitated. He had never ventured under the arches of the old stone bridge before. Looking under the bridge, he could see only an old sleeping bag, broken beer bottles, and where someone had written FUCK CUNT in red spray paint on the tunnel wall. He could see the other side, just thirty feet away, but about ten feet of complete darkness was in the middle.

"Come on, Josh. You're only in the dark for a second. Don't be a baby after you came all this way."

Josh walked slowly at first and then, summoning his courage, ran quickly toward the light on the other side, accidently stepping into the edge of the muddy creek at one point. Now he had one wet foot he would have to explain to his mother. He would come up with a lie later.

"Most forts are on the other side of the bridge," Shannon said. "That's 'cause it's easier to get to. But if you want to get to mine you got to either walk under the railroad bridge in the dark, which most people are too chicken shit to do, or climb down through those thorn bushes on the bank up there and that's almost impossible without getting stabbed to death. Well, here it is, man."

"Did you make this or find it?" Josh asked.

He surveyed the fort from the outside. It was right against the hill where a tree grew diagonally from the red mud of the embankment. Shannon had hidden it behind a bunch of thorn bushes. Josh would have walked right past it if he were hiking along Red Hill Creek. He was impressed.

"I made it myself, of course," Shannon said with a grin. "I walked along the creek, from the mountain to the sewage plant, until I found the perfect place that was really hidden good. You like my fort, Josh?" Shannon carefully moved some of the thorn bush branches near the tree's root hiding the entrance and motioned for Josh to go in.

Josh got down on his knees and crawled into the fort. It was surprisingly large, twice the size of the one he had made with Tonya, and smelled of mushrooms, damp clay, and rotting leaves. Inside, two sheets of plywood were used as a lean-to against the tree root and covered with maple branches. The floor had a dirty grey rug that was damp even though it had not rained in a while. It could easily fit four or five people.

"It's totally wicked, Shannon!"

"And it's totally private!" Shannon said, crawling in behind Josh. "I brought a girl here once."

"What girl?" Josh asked. He didn't know any girl in the neighbourhood that would have made the dirty trip in the dark under the bridge.

"You don't know her. She's older."

Josh wasn't sure if Shannon was lying or not. He had a feeling in his stomach when he thought someone was lying, but he usually didn't make a big deal out of it when someone lied. All they wanted to do was make themselves sound like a bigger big shot than they were. Josh lied from time to time, himself.

"She let me finger her. Both her pussy and ass."

"Oh yeah?" Josh said.

Maybe his mother was right about Shannon being too old for Josh to play with. Or maybe he *was* a pervert like people on Alkeld Street said. Not that it bothered Josh all that much if Shannon was a pervert. As long as he keeps his fingers out of my ass I don't care, Josh thought.

"Does it stay dry in here in the rain?" Josh asked.

"Pretty dry since the tree grows at an angle and keeps it covered, but I've only been here when it's been raining a little bit. I think if I put more branches on the top it will stay even drier, but if I use too many branches, people will come over to see why the fuck there's a pile of branches against a tree."

"It would be cool in the rain," Josh said.

"I don't come down if it's raining hard because the creek can get really high really fast when all that rainwater comes down the mountain to the lake and even though *I think* I've made the fort far enough from the creek… it could be dangerous. And you can't go under the bridge when it's raining because the creek rises so high it floods the path underneath. But it hasn't rained much this spring, so I've been lucky."

"My dad brought me here last spring to see the creek rise. It almost hit the railroad tracks."

Shannon lit a cigarette and pulled a magazine with brown water stains from under a pile of dry leaves. "Here, have a look at this *Hustler*," he said.

Josh leafed through the crunchy pages of the magazine. It had *both* naked women and men in it. One had a man with a hairy chest and moustache dressed as a policeman with four women with huge breasts. Over eight pages, their clothing quickly disappeared, and they were in every sort of position, on their back or their knees, their tongues always a few inches from the other person's body. By the last photo the man with the moustache was wearing only a gun belt and black boots. He was sitting in a black leather chair, his legs open, and his fat wiener hanging out, while the four women were standing around him smiling at his big penis and holding their big boobs in their palms. Josh had no idea why they would be holding up their boobs, as if for inspection.

Josh thought that if that was my magazine, I would put it in the box under my bed. It was ten times better than the AMWAY catalogue and those water glasses of men with the disappearing clothes that didn't show anything. Josh wondered if Shannon would notice if he snuck down here sometime and took it—just the last page.

"Hey, Josh," Shannon said, almost reading Josh's mind, "don't ever come down here without me, okay? This is *my* fort."

"I won't, Shannon, I promise."

"And don't show it to anyone else either, all right? If you do, I'll get pissed off and you and me, we couldn't be friends anymore. You can come down to the bridge to see if I'm here, we'll make some kind of signal, but if I'm not, don't come in. I'll know if you did. Just keep it a secret."

Josh promised.

Shannon didn't have to worry. Josh was pretty good at keeping his mouth shut. He liked having secrets with people. He had a few with his mom and some with his dad. He had kept every single one of them. He could easily keep Shannon's fort secret.

Shannon pushed away another branch and there, wedged between the tree's roots, was a rusted Chock-Full-Of-Nuts coffee can. He opened the can and pulled out another folded-up page from another nudie mag that was just a picture of a woman with her legs wide open and under that, stuffed into the coffee can, was some fabric.

"Look at that," Shannon said, handing Josh the folded page. "That's some big cunt, eh?"

"Yeah," Josh said, though he didn't know a large one from a small one. "What else is there in the coffee can?"

Shannon put his hand in the coffee can and pulled out three pairs of women's underwear. He unfolded and held them up one at a time: two white and one pink. One was much larger than the other two. What are they for, Josh wondered? They were discoloured and dirty from the rusty can.

"Panties! All the girls who come in here have to leave their panties behind. That's the rule," Shannon said.

Josh nodded, wondering if Shannon was going to ask him for his underwear. *Would I give Shannon my underwear if he asked? Maybe.*

"You have older brothers right, Josh?" Shannon said.

"Two."

"They have any magazines like this around?"

"I don't know. I've never seen any around."

"You should look in their bedroom. Under their bed and in their drawers," Shannon said, passing his cigarette to Josh. "I'd pay you for them. And you can be a member of my club and use the fort whenever you want, as long as I'm here too and only if you ask me first. Then you can bring some people here too, if I say it's all right and I like them. You know, as long as they aren't fags, you know what I mean, Josh?"

"Only one of my brothers still lives at home. I'll look in his bedroom," Josh said, not meaning it. If Troy caught him rifling through his drawers, he'd beat the shit out of him.

"Well, if you can't get a nudie magazine... could you get me a picture of your mother? There must be a bunch of photos of her around your house. Grab one for me she won't miss."

"I could ask her."

"No, don't ask her! Just take one."

Josh took a drag off the cigarette, and the smoke burned the inside of his mouth, but he was getting used to that by now. Soon he would teach himself how to inhale like Shannon and the grown-ups. He blew the smoke across the fort and let the cigarette dangle off his lips like Shannon had.

"But there's another rule for my fort. Any girl you bring here has to show me her tits to get in," Shannon said.

That seems fair, Josh thought, but none of the girls Josh knew had tits yet.

"Hey, you know Tony's Sheehan's sister?"

"Eva?"

"No, the older one, Deena. She's sixteen. She wanted to see my fort, so I brought her down here once and I told her she had to show me her tits first. So, she did. She had great big tits, too. She said she'll go skinny dipping with me when the creek gets deeper. She'll probably let you watch us. Or you could hide in some bushes and watch if she doesn't."

"Yeah, I could hide on the other side of the creek where no one ever goes," Josh said, trying to think of the perfect place to hide. He wondered what Deena and Shannon would look like naked in the creek and if Shannon had started growing hair around his wiener too.

"Hey, Shannon!" Josh suddenly said. "You don't think that Ragno kid they're looking for might be somewhere in Red Hill Creek, do you?"

"He could be. I thought I found him once. I saw a garbage bag lying along the creek just down from here and it reeked. So, I ripped it open with a stick and I thought I saw an arm, but it was only a dead cat full of maggots. It was there for a while and then one day it was gone. Something else must have eaten it."

Josh was starting to get uncomfortable. The damp rug was making his ass damp, and branches from the tree's lower boughs were poking into his back.

"Are you still going to that Cub Scout camp, or did you find a way to get out of it yet?"

"No, I don't think I could get out of it unless I got sick or something," Josh answered, pushing a branch out of his back and bending it downward, toward the tree's root.

"Yeah, it will be full of faggots, I bet. Will there be girls at the camp too or only boys?" Shannon asked, flipping through the pages of the magazine. Stopping every so often to, Josh thought, admire some lady's pussy or tits.

"Only boys."

"Really faggy," Shannon said, still not looking up from his magazine.

"I'm still trying to figure out a way to get out of it."

"Too bad it wasn't a camp with both guys and girls. Now that would be awesome! Imagine all those girls showering together and going swimming… in little bikinis. Fuck, man!" Shannon rubbed his crotch. "Ha! But you're just turning eleven, you'll learn about that stuff when you get older, Josh. Give it another year or so!"

Showers? Josh thought. He didn't even consider how they would shower those weeks at Cub Scout camp. Would they all have to shower together? He was terrified and thrilled at the same time.

"I should probably go now, Shannon."

"Okay. But before you leave, we must tell each other a secret. And promise not to tell anyone else ever. Then we'll be fort buddies for life."

Josh thought. He knew not to mention how much he wanted that picture in the magazine of the hairy cop with the moustache with his dong out. Not after all that talk about faggy stuff Shannon said earlier.

"Okay, you go first," Josh said.

"All right," Shannon said. He looked up and pursed his lips for a few moments while searching, Josh thought, for a secret suitable for fort buddies. "Hmm. Nah, I better not tell you that until you're older," he said, smiling. "Okay, I have a secret I can tell you."

"What is it?" Josh sat on his knees even after he started sinking into the damp ground. When he walked home, he would have two brown wet marks on his bare knees.

"I heard my mother tell my social worker that my father was her uncle," Shannon said. "You ever heard of someone having a baby with their uncle?"

Josh hadn't. He certainly could not imagine ever getting married to any of his aunts. It just seemed… wrong. So wrong it seemed they shouldn't even be talking about it—even as fort buddies.

"Then my mom told the social worker that my father, her uncle Roy, died when I was a baby. She said he was sniffing glue from a bag. Later they found him with the bag over his head, suffocated, in Vancouver somewhere."

"Wow," Josh said.

"And you can never tell anyone, Josh. Not ever."

Josh shook his head. Still, he had no idea how anything like that could happen and he would have to think about it more later. He might ask his Aunt Doris if she had ever heard of anything so crazy as some girl marrying her uncle. He wouldn't tell his aunt who he was talking about though, because he had made a promise.

"Now you tell me a secret, Josh."

"Um… okay. I made myself throw up on my mother's fat smelly cousin on purpose."

"Why?"

"She was saying rotten things about my father so first I pissed on her bathroom floor then I made myself sick by breathing the smelly air in her apartment and rocking back and forth in a chair until I was ready to puke, then I walked up to her and… bleech!" Josh smiled. He was still proud of himself for hitting Hannah perfectly with his puke.

"Sheesh, that's a lousy secret," Shannon said, looking disappointed. "Half the people around here have a stinky fat relative and I'm sure some have puked on them on purpose too."

Shannon was waiting for a better secret. Josh looked up at the tree trunk beside the red clay of the hill. *Should I tell Shannon?*

"Okay, Shannon, this is my biggest secret…"

"Yeah?"

"I was in the garage the night my dad cut his throat open. I watched him do it."

"You saw your dad cut himself?" Shannon looked shocked and Josh knew he had given a good enough secret to be a fort buddy.

"Yeah. He smashed a beer bottle on my bike, took a piece of the broken glass, and made one quick cut. After he started bleeding, he just walked past me into the house with his hand over his throat dripping blood."

"Holy shit!"

"Then when my mom started screaming, I ran into my bedroom and stayed there until the ambulance came. My mom doesn't know I saw the whole thing."

"Did your dad know you were there?"

"Not at first. I was lying in bed when I heard the backdoor slam, so I got up and followed him to the garage. The garage door was open, and I stood just inside the garage because it was raining, and I was barefoot. I watched him for a while, pacing around the garage, drinking a beer, and mumbling to himself. I was going to ask him if he was okay, but then he saw me and looked at me like… like he was scared of me."

"So, what did you do?"

"I just stood there watching him. Then he walked slowly backwards to the back of the garage where my bike was parked, smashed his beer bottle over the crossbar, and did it." Josh made a sweeping gesture across his own throat with his finger.

"Weird!" Shannon said. "But it's a great secret so you are officially a fort buddy, Josh. Do you want me to walk you back or can you go home yourself?"

"I can go myself," Josh said.

"Okay," Shannon said. "I want to look at my magazines again, anyway. But I'll watch to make sure you get back under the bridge and up the hill. Sometimes it's hard to get up, even for big kids. And remember to let me know if Gavin or those other faggots bug you again."

Josh climbed up the bank of the creek, sliding a bit only once, while Shannon watched, then he waved goodbye, and Shannon walked back under the bridge to his fort. Walking home along the train tracks, Josh thought that, as forts go, Shannon's was pretty good. Josh liked being a fort buddy.

This was going to be a good summer.

June 1977

Four

Ted sat alone on his hospital bed with his back toward the door, staring out the window and enjoying some time alone. Gloria would not be up today; she never came up on Sundays. June had arrived at the Hamilton Psychiatric Hospital and the small garden, nursed better than most patients with trimming, weeding, planting, raking and twice-daily watering by groundskeepers, was a lush oasis in the otherwise brown aridity of the sprawling hospital grounds.

Ted had thought they would finally see some rain this month, but no, any clouds that did appear seemed hell-bent on holding tight to their precipitation, taking it with them as they traveled east. Ted hoped that his lawn was being watered properly. During one of her visits, he had told Gloria to make sure Troy put the sprinkler on both the front and back yards every evening when the sun sunk behind the trees. Still, when he finally returned home, he wouldn't be surprised to find a mass of brown ugly brown blades dotted with dandelions and prickly Canada thistles.

Resting on Ted's lap was a canister of caramel corn that his sister-in-law, Doris, had brought up yesterday afternoon. Ted didn't like caramel corn. He never had. Even when he was a kid, he never bought a box of Cracker Jack on those rare occasions he was given a nickel or two from his mother or Abe. And now that stuff just got stuck in his dentures.

Ted pulled off the canister's red plastic lid and waited a few seconds, listening for footsteps in the hallway. Hearing nothing but nurse's chatter down the corridor, he shoved his hand into the middle of the caramel corn and pulled out a small bottle of Canadian Club rye whiskey hidden inside. The amber liquid glistened in the sunlight that flooded in from the window and refracted a golden shadow over the front of Ted's white T-shirt as he gently rocked the bottle in his hand. A feeling of excitement ran like an electric charge through his body.

It was easy to convince Doris to smuggle the odd bottle of booze into the hospital for him. Doris was always up for a caper, and Ted thought she enjoyed the thrill of sneaking a forbidden bottle of whiskey past hospital staff weekly. Using the caramel corn as camouflage had been Doris' idea. Doris understood because she had once been a patient here and also liked to drink, just like Ted. And Doris knew how to keep a secret.

"What if they catch you?" she had said.

"What do you think they'd do? Call the goddamn police on me? Come on, this is the seventies, Doris. Crazy people aren't treated like criminals anymore. We're celebrated! If they found out I was drinking a bit in here, they would just increase my Valium or something."

Doris didn't know that Ted also had a buddy from the Socialist Party bring up the odd bottle, and when he needed it, he could pay one of the night orderlies a hefty price for a pint. Yes, he had his bases covered.

Ted unscrewed the bottle cap and, putting his nose over the rim, deeply inhaled the woody alcohol scent. His cock stirred in his brown corduroys. Although Ted was usually more careful, rolling the bottle in a newspaper and taking it into the john to drink in peace, he took a quick swig, enjoying the pain as it clawed its way down his throat and warmed his guts.

As his throat burned, Ted thought of the Old Man dying of esophageal cancer at St. Joseph Hospital and took another swig, scorching his throat even more but then, soothingly numbing it. *I guess the apple doesn't fall far from the fucking tree.* Ted took one more mouthful and then, hearing footsteps in the hall, screwed the black plastic cap back on the bottle as tight as he could and slipped it under the pillow. He would hide it in the pocket of his union jacket later.

"Eight thousand dollars," Ted said quietly to himself, shaking his head.

Only six thousand now that Gloria hit up her sister, Lydia, for two grand. Too bad Doris couldn't help them out with this as easily as she did with the bottle of rye. If it wasn't for Ken, that asshole husband of hers, Doris would give Gloria that six thousand bucks today. Now there was no one left to ask. Even big old Hannah had refused to help them out.

Ted put his head in his hands. This wasn't the first time he'd fucked up. He lost paycheques and rent money betting on the goddamn horses before. Once they had even been evicted from a house they were renting because of a long losing streak. He had endured the tears of his wife and the occasional busted plate against the kitchen wall and, one time, had all his clothes tossed out on the front lawn. Each time Ted had promised Gloria he would never do it again. And each time he did.

You could set a clock by my fuckups. And hadn't Ted been so proud when he finally ran and won a place on the local union executive. He had run twice before, and lost, but last year he had finally won, not by a landslide, but by a good margin. And he had even beat out Kurt Marshall, a Mason. That is no easy thing beating a Mason since they all stuck together like rebar in concrete. Still, Sonny had pulled some strings, made some deals, and when the votes were counted, Ted had won the spot of Treasurer of Steelworkers Local 2010.

But then, like clockwork, another fuckup.

First, he was just in for a few hundred to a few street bookies. They let it ride for a while, and then a 'sure thing' didn't pan out, and suddenly, he was in the hole to them for over a grand, more than he had ever owed before. Ted then went to the loan sharks and began betting more and more to cover the grand he owed. What the hell was he thinking! Less than three months later, he was in for five thousand dollars with one loan shark. It was leg-busting time and Ted turned to the union's money to pay off the loan sharks, promising himself he could pay it back quickly with a few long shots if he got the right tips at the track. After that, he bypassed the sharks and just used the union cash. It was like he was watching himself fuck up his life in slow motion and not able to do anything about it except fuck it up more each day. Then Dr. Heller put him on pills for depression and anxiety, and then… here he was with a five-inch scar across his throat. And it had all started with a few hundred bucks. *God, what the fuck is wrong with me!*

He slipped his hand under the pillow and caressed the cool bottle of rye with his fingertips. Looking back, Ted had always hoped to be a better man than his Old Man or his stepfather, Abe. And even at that moment, in the nuthouse with a bottle of rye hidden under his pillow and a jagged scar across his throat, Ted still knew he was a better man than either of them, not that that was saying much. Perhaps, Ted thought, rubbing his fingers up and down the bottle, *I should have placed the bar a bit higher. I could have done better—even for an east-ender.*

Ted was born and raised in the east end of Hamilton and was proud of his east end roots. He grew up on Waterloo Street, just around the corner from where he now lived on Alkeld Street. He often thought that though he may have taken the long way, through Africa, he still ended up right back where he started. The east end wasn't the worst part of Hamilton, but it was close. East-enders could always say (and often did) "at least we aren't the north end." Ted's father, Walter Moore, whom Ted and all his siblings now referred to simply as the Old Man, at least until he got sick, was a tall and burly blonde-haired jolly Englishman who had left his family home in the southwest of England the very first chance he had to come to Canada. Although a young man with all of Canada at his feet, for some reason Walter Moore chose to stop in Hamilton, where he drove 'the Beltline' trolley up and down King Street for the Hamilton Street Railway for the next forty years, except for two years during World War Two when he had been in the army.

The Old Man probably never should have married or had kids. He was most happy back then, spending the money he made on the HSR Beltline drinking with tramps and getting into bar fights in dumps like the Windsor Hotel. His years in Europe during the war were the only time Ted's mother, Anna, saw any of the Old Man's income with any reliability, as the army would automatically send a large portion of a soldier's pay back to the wife on the home front. No, Ted's mother was never the kind of soldier's wife keeping a candle in the window or standing on the front porch in a shawl waiting for her husband's return; she was just happy to finally feed her kids with some regularity. Many years later, Anna would confide in Ted how much easier their lives would have been if the Old Man had died in the war.

When the Old Man returned home to Waterloo Street from the war early, claiming a bad back, the money once again dried up, and Ted's mother returned to begging for food money even as the Moore babies continued to come with increased frequency. For the remainder of the war, the Old Man would disappear for weeks at a time, shacking up with some woman or other, most likely some woman whose husband was fighting in Europe. The years following the war were miserable for everyone as the Old Man's drinking worsened, even less money came into the house on Waterloo Street, and fighting escalated between Ted's parents. Once Ted's mother, out of desperation, had even taken four-year-old Ted to the HSR trolley garage on Wentworth Street so Ted could toddle up to the Old Man after his shift and beg the Old Man for food money in hopes of shaming him in front of his fellow trolley and bus drivers (for the record, the Old Man gave him a dollar in quarters from his HSR coin dispenser belt). And then one April, when Ted was seven years old, the Old Man packed up his army duffle bag and left for good, leaving behind Ted's mother and eight kids. Ted never stepped foot on the Beltline trolley again. Some twelve years later, when Ted himself was discharged from the army, he would again see Walter Moore.

It wasn't long after his father left the east end for parts unknown (Ted would later find out he had only moved downtown to the north end of John Street) that his mother moved the shorter, less attractive, less jolly, red-haired Abe Murphy into their house on

Waterloo Street. And although Ted's older sisters will still swear on their *Living Bible* that Abe didn't move in for months and months after the Old Man left, Ted and his older brothers Jack and Noah agree that Abe had moved in practically the same day Walter Moore moved out. Ted had come to believe the truth was probably someplace in the middle. There was no doubt that Ted's mother had seen Abe Murphy for some time before the Old Man left, but Ted would never ask her for the details.

Today no one in the family, except Ted's youngest half-siblings Bonnie and Andy, Abe's biological children, still saw Abe regularly. Ted would drop in to see Abe and his new wife, Gert, occasionally but never told Gloria when he did. Gloria steadfastly refused to see Abe or allow him in their home. But in Abe's defence (and if anyone needed a defence it was Abe) Ted could not deny the fact that the guy took on the feeding, clothing, and sheltering of eight kids, none of them his own, when he didn't have to. Abe brought his paycheque home every Friday at 5:30 pm like clockwork and handed it over to Ted's mother with a smile. Abe was, Ted still believed, a fine stepfather in many ways. His job at the Firestone tire plant made them better off than most families in the east end, certainly better off than they had been living. As soon as Abe moved in, he undertook to fix up the long-neglected house on Waterloo Street, making it over in his image: painting the exterior shamrock green, hanging lily of the valley wallpaper in the living room, and putting up a swing set in the yard for Ted, Dale, and Tessa. But first, and most importantly to Ted's mother, Abe installed an indoor bathroom, finally tearing down their old double-seat outhouse, the last remaining shithouse on Waterloo Street. By the time the new bathroom was completed, Ted's mother had taken Abe's last name and was known as Anna Murphy, even though she and Abe would never marry.

That was the first fault line that ran through Ted's family—names. Even in those early days after the Old Man left, the rebellious Moores lined up on one side, and the smaller (and in many ways, more brutal) Murphys lined up on the other. That left Ted and the younger Moore siblings, Dale and Tessa, who had been only two and one when the Old Man left, stuck in the middle. The family had not yet begun the epic battle that would ultimately tear them apart and end in at least one casualty, but the warring factions were in place from the beginning, just biding their time for something to set it off. And when it came—

Ted lit a cigarette, laid back and stared at the yellowing hospital ceiling. Maybe little Ruth, dead at only six months, was the smart one getting out when she did. Dead from the effects of syphilis brought home by the Old Man and infecting Ted's mother when she was pregnant. Maybe all this started with the syphilis, Ted thought. Could that be why his family, Moores, and Murphys, were so fucked up? Perhaps they were all affected by some lingering affliction that infected their DNA and made every single one of them go off the rails somehow. *And all of Ted's brothers and sisters had, whether they wanted to admit it or not, gone off the rails somehow.*

"Your sisters are here to see you, Mr. Moore," Nurse Debbie said, leaning into the room. She then turned and tip-tapped in her white nurse's shoes back down the hall.

"Shit!"

Ted quickly hopped out of bed, grabbed the bottle under the pillow, and took a swig. Then another. Then he shoved the whiskey into the inside pocket of his union jacket hanging in one of the four lockers by the door. Good thing it smells like alcohol all through this joint, he thought. Then, thinking twice, he walked back toward his bed, grabbed a piece of Doublemint gum out of his bedside table, shoved it in his mouth, and pushed his round metal glasses farther up his fleshy nose.

Sisters! That's all I fucking need right now.

Ted walked past the silver ashtrays along the corridor and stepped into the lounge with a small but unmistakable swagger. He hoped that others noticed it. Across the lounge, at one of the tables near the window, his older sisters Peggy and Sue sat looking grim. Grimmer than usual. Judging from their appearance, they had come straight from Sunday service. Peggy was wearing a matronly plaid skirt past the knees, lavender blouse, and a necklace of blue oval agate beads, almost the perfect size for skipping rocks, while Sue was wearing a purple pantsuit, a cream-coloured blouse, and an enormous gold cross on a thick gold chain that rested on her chest.

Both of his sisters had their hair dyed the colour of bourbon whiskey, though perhaps Sue's appeared to have a bit more water added to the bourbon, and both hairdos were styled in the same bouffant manner, just touching their shoulders with waves cemented firmly in place with hairspray.

"Hi guys," Ted said, walking up beside them, startling Peggy, who jumped a bit when he appeared. He sat down in an empty chair and grinned. Seeing Jonathan's Expos ballcap behind a newspaper two tables over made Ted feel less alone, less ganged up on. It felt like someone had his back.

"I think they should have free coffee here," Sue said. "You should mention that to whoever's in charge here, Ted."

"I will." Ted wished he had taken one more swig from the bottle before coming down.

Sue, the older of the two sisters, was wearing dark plum lipstick, green eyeshadow, mascara, and the same pancake makeup she had worn since she was a teenager that made her face appear a shade lighter than it was. Peggy, on the other hand, wore only light pink lipstick. Both of his sisters wore so much perfume; individually, he might have ignored the smell, but blended, his nose ached.

"You look so much better," Peggy said.

"I just mean if people… your family and friends, take the time to come *all the way* up the mountain to visit people on a Sunday then the least these people could do is have some complimentary coffee, don't you think? Am I wrong?" Sue asked.

"Complimentary coffee? You mean coffee that says things like, 'Hey, you look great! Have you lost weight?'" Ted said.

Two tables over Jonathan chuckled from behind *The Hamilton Spectator* as Peggy and Sue both looked at Ted quizzically and then looked at one another. No doubt they're thinking I've just come from shock, Ted thought.

"Ted, you should cover that thing on your throat with a bandage when you have company. At least until it heals a bit more. It looks awful," Sue said.

"You don't think it makes me look like I'm in a gangster movie or something?" Ted asked.

"We don't have a lot of time," Sue said. "I have to get a roast in the oven."

"We're having bats in the belfry pie for lunch."

"Ted..." Sue said disapprovingly.

"And when they say we're out to lunch here... they mean we're *really* out to lunch," Ted said. "And for dessert..."

"Fruitcake with nuts!" Peggy said. She bust into a loud guffaw. Then, as if suddenly recalling her lower-middle-class respectability, embarrassedly covered her mouth with a hand and cleared her throat.

"That's right! Fruitcake with nuts for dessert," Ted said, laughing.

Sue sighed. "If you two are done with this Gong Show. We just came from seeing Dad."

This was the first time Ted had heard Sue call Walter Moore anything other than the Old Man in decades. Maybe the closer we are to death, the more likely old terms of endearments like *Dad* get hauled out from the back closets where we tossed them years ago, Ted thought. Maybe at the end we're all called things like *sweetheart, dear, daddy, mommy, honeybunch*...

"Oh, Ted." Peggy clutched her agate beads. "It's heartbreaking, you know that? Him lying there on his deathbed in that Catholic hospital... surrounded by all those crucifixes while you're here in this awful place! And neither of you can see the other."

"I've spoken to him on the phone a couple of times."

"You didn't go into too much detail about this place, I hope," Sue said.

"I told him I'm in the nuthouse."

"It just breaks my heart," Peggy said, letting go of her beads. She lit an unfiltered cigarette and offered one to Ted.

"Thanks," he said, putting the cigarette between his lips.

"Do you remember how I'd sneak you cigarettes when you were a kid?" Peggy asked.

Ted nodded and scratched his beard. "That's how I learned to smoke; watching my big sisters."

Peggy smiled, reached over, and moved a lock of Ted's hair out of his face and behind one ear and a wave of nostalgia so strong and unexpected came over Ted that he almost teared up. "I'm liking the new beard. I don't care what anyone says, I think it makes you look like a cute Jesus," she said.

"That's exactly what I'm going for."

"I find it sad that you two can't even go five minutes without a cigarette. You're both going to end up with esophageal cancer, just like Dad," Sue said.

"I can't quit smoking now with Dad dying and Ted locked up here."

"I'm not locked up in here, Peg. It's a hospital not a jail."

"Could you see me trying to quit smoking now with all this stress? I'd be joining you here in less than a week, Ted."

He smiled. "That could be fun. Maybe we could get a family discount."

"I'm just saying," Sue said tersely. "If I can quit smoking then you two can quit too. All it takes is a bit of willpower and a lot of prayer. And if you ask me…" She looked around the lounge frowning. "This place needs a lot of prayers."

"I told you before, if you come here and start praying again, I'm going back to my room," Ted said.

"We prayed in the car before we came in," Peggy said.

"I'm surprised they didn't throw you both in straightjackets and admit you."

"What did you and Dad talk about on the phone?" Peggy asked.

"He told me that he remembered coming up here to visit Mom when they brought her here after Ruth died; back when it was the old Hamilton Asylum. He said they tied people to their beds in those days. Then he asked if they tied me to the bed. I told him no, today it's civilized; they just chain us to radiators when they get tired of beating us with broom handles."

"How old would little Ruth be now?" Peggy asked.

"I guess you didn't mention to the Old Man that it was his fault Mom was here in the first place?" Sue said.

So much for calling him *Dad*, Ted thought, flicking an ash in the ashtray on the table.

"My God, can't we all just let that go?" Peggy looked around and then lowered her voice. "It's a really ugly episode that I would like to forget. It seems no one in this family can ever let anything go. We just keep dredging up the same awful things over and over again."

"Don't look at me, I didn't bring it up," he said. "And Ruth would be forty-eight, Peg."

"I was thinking that maybe you could ask your doctor if he would let you out for an afternoon, even just an hour or two, to go and see your father on his deathbed? I could ask your doctor if you want me to," Sue said.

"It might be your last chance, Teddy," Peggy said.

"I'll ask," he said. "In a week or so."

"A week might be too late if you want to make amends and all that," Sue said.

"I have nothing to amend for."

"Now don't get huffy. Maybe he wants to make amends to you. Did you ever think of that? And besides, what does all that matter now?" Sue said.

"It matters," he said.

"I'm afraid it won't be long now," Peggy said. "The doctors say he only has a few weeks left. The cancer has spread and weakened his heart. His heart is like tissue paper, they said. Can you imagine?" She lowered her voice to a whisper. "Like tissue paper."

"Last night I tried to talk to him seriously again about accepting Jesus. But all he wanted to do was watch that stupid television," Sue said.

"He told Sue to put a sock in it."

Ted laughed. Now *that* was the Old Man.

"Ted," Peggy said gently, "I'm sorry we couldn't help you with the money you need. But, like I told Gloria, we have nothing saved. And the car just broke down and—"

"Did Gloria get the money together?" Sue asked. "Can you get a second mortgage on the house, maybe?"

"We already have a second mortgage."

"You're terrible with money, Ted!" Sue said. "You always have been since day one. I remember when I'd give you some money when you were a kid, it was always gone in a heartbeat. I'd say make this money last all week but no. Not you."

"You know what I was thinking about yesterday, Ted," Peggy said. "How you used to play 'Goodnight Irene' on the guitar. And how Tessa would sing along."

Sue bit her lip and looked away.

"I forgot that," Ted said, smiling. "That was before I went in the army."

"Tessa had a beautiful voice," Peggy continued. "I wish I had owned a tape recorder back then and had taped you two. Not that I could ever listen to it today without crying. But I would listen. I'd love to hear Tessa sing again."

"I'm in charge of calling Wilma and letting her know when it's time," Sue said. "And the moment she hears from me she'll hop on a plane and fly up from Georgia. But I'm so afraid I'll call her too late, and Dad will be lost forever."

"Who put you in charge?" Ted asked.

"Wilma did," Sue replied, straightening her collar.

"Of course, she did," Ted said caustically.

The lounge was slowly emptying of patients as, one by one, men and women in robes, gowns, and pyjamas made their way to the cafeteria for lunch.

"I was hoping Dad would accept Christ before Wilma got here," Sue said. "I had my Wednesday night ladies Bible study group praying about it just last week…"

Ted's sisters had not always been like this.

At one time Sue and Peggy were so severely cool and hip that Ted was in awe of them. In the 1950s, when they were teenagers, Peggy and Sue were tough east end girls, able to hold their own with anyone, including many of the boys in the neighbourhood. Back then the two of them had been in a girl gang, the Barton Girls. The Barton Girls would hang out at the Golden Pheasant on Kenilworth Street, drinking bottle after bottle of Pepsi, smoking cigarettes, and dancing together to rock and roll songs playing on the jukebox. At the same time, their boyfriends sat on the other side of the restaurant talking about cars and other girls. Not so dangerous or notorious as some

Hamilton girl gangs of the north end that took to wearing leather and denim like their male counterparts, the Barton Girls chose short suede or nylon jackets, Capri pants, colourful scarfs, and tight cashmere sweaters that hugged their cone-shaped bullet bras.

The Barton Girls had no real fights or rumbles that Ted could recall, other than with other girls who made a play for one of their boyfriends. Even the word 'gang' was a stretch. Still, Sue and Peggy, who must have been high in the Barton Girls hierarchy, would sometimes take Ted and his younger brother Dale to the Golden Pheasant to buy them Pepsi and french fries and slip them cigarettes when he and Dale were only about nine and eleven years old. Then the other Barton Girls would pat Ted's head and, getting close to him with their torpedo-bra tits, kiss his cheek and tell him how cute he was, even in his big horn-rimmed Buddy Holly glasses.

Ted didn't think his mother or Abe ever knew that Sue and Peggy were Barton Girls, but Abe eventually clued in that something was happening with the girls when they started wearing a ton of makeup and coming home late in strange cars smelling of cigarette smoke. Though Ted's mother appeared content to take her teenage daughters' antics in stride, Abe, it seemed, saw any independent streak in his stepdaughters, especially consorting with neighbourhood boys, as an affront to his authority. He fought back, once shoving Peggy's face under the tap in the kitchen sink, scrubbing her face until her mouth bled with a Brillo pad because he thought her lipstick was too red. Soon after he forced an eighteen-year-old Sue over his knee, pulled up her skirt and spanked her in front of Ted and all his siblings for coming home late. That spanking would be the last straw for Sue who moved out, to a basement apartment close to the Golden Pheasant with another Barton Girl, the very next week. Within a month or two Peggy would join Sue in the same apartment, ending Ted's days of Pepsi, french fries, and amorous touches from big-breasted Barton Girls at the Golden Pheasant.

When Sue and Peggy moved away from Waterloo Street, Wilma married an American salesman and was a young newlywed living in Georgia with her own problems. Back then Ted's older sisters muddled through their problems as best as they could. Jesus would not be their solution for a few more years. Around the time President Kennedy was shot, Wilma became a born-again Christian after a bizarre medical incident. Like Paul on the road to Damascus, Wilma was suddenly afflicted, unable to raise her hands above her shoulders, right in the middle of the A&P, as she told it, while reaching for a box of Pablum on the top shelf. The Atlanta doctor her husband had taken her to had called it hysterical paralysis caused by postpartum anxiety after her second son was born. He had seen it before and assured Wilma that it would eventually pass, but a day or two later Wilma had been convinced to pray with a Southern Baptist neighbour who asked Jesus to heal Wilma from the assorted demons in her arms. The next Sunday, Wilma's arms miraculously raised to the heavens and, discounting everything the doctor had told her, Wilma refused to believe that her healing was anything short of the Holy Spirit's intervention. She was, 'born again'. Over the next decade, Wilma had led Sue and Peggy to Jesus, both at the worst times in their lives. First, she broke down Sue when her oldest daughter, Mariah, died in a car accident and then, a few years later, Wilma returned when Peggy discovered her husband was messing around with another woman. It was Wilma's M.O. to drag people, kicking and screaming, if need be, to Jesus whenever they were in crisis. And when the time was ripe, she would fly up from Georgia, black leather bible in hand, and try to save the Old Man's soul before he kicked.

"Wilma wants to have a long talk with you too, Ted," Sue said. "Wilma says that you being a communist is the real reason you're here in the hospital and I agree with her. We've concluded that it's all because of your dark godless view of the world."

Of course, Wilma would set her eyes on me next, Ted thought. I must look like some low-hanging fruit to her, right now.

"I'm not a communist, Sue. I'm a socialist." He grinned, knowing Jonathan was probably chuckling behind his newspaper.

"Wilma says communism is one of the worst sins there is," Sue continued. "They burn bibles in Russia."

"They burn Marx in Georgia," Ted replied.

"I think you should be looking at your time here as a wakeup call," Sue said. "Wilma told me when Mariah died, 'When God wants to get your attention, first He'll begin with a tap on your shoulder… then a thump… and then eventually He'll have to resort to a two-by-four across the back of your head."

"Are you telling me that your God took Mariah as a wakeup call for you?" Ted asked. "Are you seriously saying your daughter was hit and killed by a drunk driver as part of some big plan to get you to come to Jesus? That's the way it works, Sue? If it is, I don't want any part of your God." He could feel his face and ears warm.

"I'm only saying we don't know God's plan. And you being in here, and all the electricity they gave you, that just might be His way of, you know, telling you it's time to follow Him. Think of this as your thump, Ted. You don't want to wait for God's two-by-four and lose someone you love—like Gloria or Josh the way I lost Mariah."

All Ted wanted was to get back to that bottle of whiskey. "I'm two seconds from getting up and leaving."

"That's enough, you two," Peggy said, sharpening her voice. "Let's all just calm down and talk about something else."

"All right, all right", Sue said. "But I know God has a plan for this one." She poked Ted in the side making him jump with a start. "No, I'm not worried about you. It may take until the end of your life, like Dad, before you finally accept Him, but I know you will. It wouldn't be heaven without my little brother."

Peggy smiled. "Ah, that's more like it."

"And then you'll be really angry you wasted all those years. I'm angry at myself for wasting so much of my life. We're going to get you. But it will be on God's time, I suppose."

"Don't hold your breath."

"Wilma planted the seed in this family a long time ago and it will worm its way through all of you, one way or another," Sue said.

"Like syphilis did?"

"Ted!" Peggy said, grabbing at her blue beads again.

"Sorry. I shouldn't have said that."

The three of them sat quietly for a minute as Jonathan, perhaps having had enough of Ted's sisters, folded up his newspaper and walked toward the lounge door where he met up with a woman in a ponytail wearing a red cardigan. The two chatted briefly and then they exited together. Ted didn't know the woman's name but had seen Jonathan speaking with her before.

"Any idea when you can go home?" Peggy asked.

Ted shrugged.

"Well, I'll be sure to tell Dad to hang on and wait for you," Sue said.

"Dad told us that Gloria went to St. Joseph's yesterday to see him. She brought him a little cactus," Peggy said.

"Yeah, Gloria always liked the Old Man. She calls him the father she never had. I told her he's the father I never had too," Ted replied.

"You know, for someone so willing to let bygones be bygones with Abe, you do have a chip on your shoulder about Dad," Sue said.

"Maybe it's because I expected more from my own father than I did from Abe."

"Or maybe it's because Abe didn't hurt you as much as he hurt us," Sue said.

Ted didn't like that. Mostly because he had thought about that himself over the years and, if Sue was right, it would make him an even bigger asshole than he wanted to admit.

"Any chance the Old Man will rally? Maybe make it home one more time? He's fooled them before. We all thought he would kick at New Year's, but he fooled us," Ted said.

"No," Sue said. "This is it."

"Well, I guess there's always a chance. We've always got prayer, right?" Peggy said.

"Sure, we've always got that," Ted said. "Can we please talk about something else?" He would welcome a little paper cup of *pills du jour* right now.

Peggy smirked. "Did you know Bonnie wants to be a gospel singer now?"

Now this was a surprise to Ted. Wilma could sing a bit and Peggy and Sue had nice enough voices, though nothing you would put on a record, hell even Ted could carry a tune when he was playing his guitar but his half-sister Bonnie Murphy? Christ!

"It's true," Sue said, laughing. "Bonnie has already asked around Zion Baptist if she could do a few numbers. That's what she calls them, 'numbers' like she's Billie Holiday or something. Our Pastor at Zion told her 'Maybe some other time' after I told him what she sounded like."

"And now she's been going around the other Baptist, Gospel, and Evangelical churches around Hamilton to 'test out the water' she says," Peggy said.

"I'm guessing the waters will be lukewarm at best," Ted said.

"One guess where she's getting the money for all that sound equipment," Sue said with a bit of a Barton Girls attitude. She reached over and took Peggy's cigarette out of her hand, took a deep drag and handed it back. "Microphones, speakers, and tape players aren't cheap."

Peggy leaned in close. "Luckily the rapture didn't happen just then while you had my cigarette in your mouth."

"Shut up, it's not like I'm having it all. Anyway, I think what Bonnie is doing is disgusting. I know Abe is horrible, but for Bonnie to fleece him like she does… she treats him like her own private bank. Just in the last year, she squeezed Abe for her second wedding and that pink motorcycle she never rides"

"She named it Tootsie," Peggy said, rolling her eyes. "I have to take Tootsie out for a spin, she says. Then one day the motorcycle disappears. She said it was stolen."

"She probably sold it," Sue said. "And after the motorcycle disappeared, she hit Abe up for the down payment for her and Ray's house. And now this gospel music nonsense. Why did she need such a big ugly house in the north end anyway? I suppose she'll keep taking his money as long as Abe keeps giving it to her. That's the Murphys for you. Mind you, no Moore has ever asked Abe for a goddamn thing! Not even poor Tessa."

Ted didn't point out that Sue had cussed. He liked to see a bit of the old Sue come out again.

"It's not like it's Abe's money anyway," Peggy said. "All he has is his pension from Firestone and his Canadian Pension. That doesn't add up to much."

"It's all coming from that wife of his," Sue said. "She buried two husbands and was rolling in dough when Abe married her. I hope she buries Abe soon, too."

"Men like Abe never seem to die," Peggy said.

Sue nodded. "Or when they finally do, they die comfortably in their own beds. It makes me sick."

Abe! Suddenly Ted felt invigorated. Just how much money did Abe and that hag of a wife of his have? Could he be persuaded to part with six thousand? Ted had never asked Abe for a penny since he left Waterloo Street for the army.

"Just wait until Wilma gets here from Georgia. She won't take no for an answer. She'll lead Dad to Jesus. Mark my words," Sue said.

"Sure, Wilma can tell the Old Man that his cancer is just another two-by-four to the head," Ted said.

"Just you wait," Sue repeated. "No one can refuse Wilma…"

But Ted had stopped listening. Would it be possible to convince Gloria to borrow that much money from Abe, a man she despised. Could she be persuaded? It would be to her benefit, after all. If it came down to either taking the six thousand dollars from Abe Murphy or losing their house on Alkeld Street what would Gloria do?

After his sisters left, Ted sat outside on a wooden bench in the shade of a large oak tree in the hospital garden on the gravel path between the hospital and the old Manor House trying to imagine what the area had looked like when his mother was a patient there in the 1930s. Would they have even let her out into the garden back then? The heat amplified every tiny sound around the grounds of the hospital and beyond, and Ted could clearly make out the cars rumbling on the other side of the building down West Fifth Street; crickets, katydids, and cicadas singing a strangely harmonious duet and, farther away, children shouting and, even farther, the splash of a backyard pool.

Ted had half-filled a Pepsi can with whiskey and was enjoying the numbness that had now reached his brain like a more pleasurable and familiar form of shock therapy, erasing unwelcome memories, and slowly placing him in a beautiful state of stupefaction. *Finally, relief.*

"Your sisters are grotesque," Jonathan said, sitting beside Ted on the bench.

"Yeah, they can be. But aren't all big sisters pushy like that?" Ted said. He had not seen Jonathan since they were in the lounge that morning and was glad to see him. Even in the nuthouse, it was good to have friends.

"I wouldn't know. I'm an only child." Jonathan pulled the visor of his Expos baseball cap down over his eyes to block a rogue beam of sunlight poking through the oak tree's leaves. "I did have an imaginary sister named Aleksandra spelled with a k. She taught herself the balalaika and read all of Hegel one summer just for fun, but that was it as far as siblings went for me. But yours are something else, especially the one with the big gold cross. I didn't know people like her existed outside of movies and Sinclair Lewis novels."

"Well, unlike Aleksandra with a k, my sisters have been through a lot of shit."

"First of all, Ted, you have no idea what Aleksandra has gone through. And second, who hasn't gone through a lot of shit."

Jonathan reached over and took the Pepsi can from Ted's hand. He sniffed it, grinned, and took a few large gulps as his huge Adam's apple bounced up and down like a tennis ball Bjorn Borg was preparing to serve.

Jonathan Pressman was not an east-ender. He grew up in the heart of downtown Hamilton. Jonathan's father owned Pressman's Tailors, a men's clothing shop on the north end of James Street. Ted knew Pressman Tailors. Everyone in Hamilton knew Pressman Tailors. The Pressmans, Jonathan had told Ted, had come to Hamilton from The Pale of Settlement in Russia in the early 1900s. Jonathan's grandfather had opened the suit shop soon after he arrived and Pressman's, as everyone in the city now simply called it, had been a Hamilton institution ever since. In the 1930s and 1940s Pressman's became a favourite tailor of Hamilton mobsters looking for double-breasted pinstripe suits and no mafioso worth his salt would be caught dead in Hamilton in those days without a Pressman's label in his suit jacket. The store still had a reputation as one of the best men's suit shops in Hamilton and had supported

Jonathan's grandfather, father, and their families for almost eighty years. Jonathan's mother had come to Canada with her family as a girl from the Ukraine after the First World War. She was the daughter of a watchmaker who had also opened a storefront on the north end of James Street just a few doors down from Pressman Tailors. At some point Jonathan's mother and father were introduced by their parents and, if not expected to marry, then strongly encouraged.

"I'm what you get when you cross a clothier and a horologist," Jonathan had once said to Ted.

Jonathan had gone much farther in school than Ted had ever dreamed, all the way to university. He had studied to be a pharmacist but left university a year before he was to graduate. Still, Jonathan's impressive knowledge of pharmaceuticals gave him some expertise when it came to the drugs the nurses would bring him in their little paper cups, much, it seemed, to the doctor's irritation. Jonathan had even outright refused to take one pill he was handed and demanded to have a consultation. After a chat with Dr. Shackelford that pill, whatever it was, disappeared from Jonathan's little paper cup. Like Ted, Jonathan was an army man too but, unlike Ted, Jonathan had been to war, a real war. Looking for adventure, one day Jonathan had walked out of university, hitchhiked down to Buffalo, and enlisted in the US army.

"What can I say?" he had told Ted. "Vietnam sounded like fun. So, while all those American draft dodgers were rushing up to Canada to avoid the draft, I went south and was tossed right into the middle of Vietnam. That's when they should have given me a couple of hundred volts to my head, eh? That's when I was really crazy."

Though curious, Ted didn't ask Jonathan too many questions about Vietnam. After all, Ted never liked talking about the Congo. He never told anyone about the horrible things he had seen there or his nightmares of being hacked up by Congolese militia with machetes. Nevertheless, whatever shit Ted had been through in the Congo, he knew Jonathan had been through worse in Vietnam. Much worse. And Ted admired the big-balled courage it took for young Jonathan Pressman to volunteer to fight in Vietnam. Nobody was ever impressed that Ted had been a UN Peacekeeper in the Congo. Today people mostly laughed when he brought it up. The whole fucking Congo Crisis was long forgotten or, if anyone thought of it at all, was now considered a 'non-war'. The day Ted returned from Africa in early 1964 all Abe did was chuckle and say "Big hero! What did you do? Fight some Pygmies?"

"But," Jonathan now said, handing the Pepsi can of rye back to Ted, "whether your sisters are bible-beating grotesques or not, I can tell they care about you. A lot of people here never have anyone visit them. Carl, for instance."

"I know my sisters love me," Ted said. He took a long drink from the can and smiled. "And one thing I've learned over the years, Jonathan, my friend, is that there aren't that many people around who really care about me. I'm just glad I have them, even if they are *grotesque* sometimes."

"Yeah, you're probably right, Teddy," Jonathan said, leaning back on the bench. He stretched out his legs onto the path and wiped sweat or whisky from his thick black moustache. "I can be pretty grotesque myself sometimes."

"You sure as hell can," Ted said with a wry smile.

Jonathan had recently begun calling him 'Teddy' out of the blue. Even though his mother and siblings occasionally called him that, Ted didn't mind. It was kind of nice to hear it from time to time.

"At least they didn't pray this time," Jonathan said.

"They prayed in the car before they came in."

Ted raised his Pepsi can toward the sky as if toasting God and took another swig. The scalding in his throat felt good and familiar. Back in basic training he and two of his buddies would drink rubbing alcohol from time to time to get a small buzz if there was nothing else around. It was no big deal at the time, and they weren't the only ones in the army doing it. One of Ted's friends taught him exactly how much rubbing alcohol they could drink before it would make them get sick or go blind. Later, when Ted was in Elizabethville waiting out his last two months in the Congo, he would resort to drinking rubbing alcohol alone and, once, Aqua Velva aftershave. Again, it was no big deal.

"You drink too much, Teddy," Jonathan suddenly said. He stared straight ahead at the Manor House across the garden without looking at Ted.

"Ha! Tell me something I don't know, Jonathan."

"Say, Teddy…"

"Yeah?"

"Why do you drink so much?"

Ted laughed loudly. No one had ever asked him that question before, even though he had been waiting for someone to ask it for years. Sure, lots of people (doctors, friends, family, coworkers) had told him to stop drinking, or have told him that he should learn to handle his liquor, but no one had ever asked Ted point-blank *why* he drank so much.

"Habit, I guess."

"Ah, okay."

Jonathan sounded disappointed by the answer and, perhaps, Ted had to agree, it was a tad too easy a response, at least too easy a response for Jonathan.

"Booze gives me everything I want."

"Everything? Maybe I should take up drinking."

"Take up the guitar instead, Jonny. It's cheaper than rye and always made me happy. You know… sometimes when I'm talking with Dr. Shackelford about shit, I wish I could find a guitar and just play it. I can't… sometimes I can't find the right words, but I know I could play what I'm feeling on my guitar."

"You mean play a sad song?"

"No," Ted said, shaking his head. "Not a song. Just notes and sounds… open minor chords… a melody made up on the spot that will never be played again. Christ! That sounds so stupid when I say it out loud! Never mind."

"It doesn't sound stupid at all. I think it could be more honest than words. I want to hear you play your feelings sometime, Teddy. Maybe you should have your sister-in-law bring you up your guitar instead of all these bottles of booze, eh?"

"I can play "L'Internationale" on the guitar too," Ted said, grinning.

"Every communist can, I hear."

"Like I said, Jonny, I'm a socialist. Not a communist."

From across the garden Ted could see Carl walking slowly, huffing and puffing, toward them.

"Teacher's coming," Jonathan said.

"Fuck," Ted said. He quickly lifted the Pepsi can and drank the last mouthful of rye.

"Hello, gentlemen," Carl said, stopping in front of them. "Have either of you seen our young friend Rick about?" He licked some orange cheese puff dust from corners of his mouth.

"Nope," Ted said.

"Maybe he's somewhere smoking reefer," Jonathan said.

Carl stood, waiting for someone to tell him to sit down but Ted decided to let him stand there for a while. He needed to either learn to ask to join them or be a man and just sit down without permission. For a teacher he sure had some weird traits. One would expect a teacher to be more forceful. Unless Carl could only be forceful with little kids. Some weak men got into teaching because they got a charge off bullying children. How would Carl's students describe their Mr. Gruber? Ted wondered.

Finally, Carl took a seat on the bench between Ted and Jonathan, requiring Jonathan to slide down closer to the edge to give Carl space. Carl wheezed and wiped his forehead with his polka-dot handkerchief, already dark with a day's worth of sweat and dirt.

"I was just reading in the newspaper about those Ragno children," Carl said. He stuffed his hanky back in his robe pocket with his orange fingers. "Did you two know that Jake Ragno doesn't live too far from here? Anyway, the paper said that Ragno tried to convince the police that the big hunk of carpet he tore out of his house the week of the murders was because his cat threw up on it. He swore he took the carpet to the dump up here on the mountain, but the police eventually found it, with the wife's blood all over it, incidentally, at the Nash Road dump down in the east end. The people at the dump fingered him. Say they remember him. For a murderer he's not very clever."

"Yeah, for a murderer he's pretty stupid," Ted said.

"I always expect murderers to be criminal masterminds like Professor Moriarty. But it usually turns out that they're idiots," Jonathan said.

"I keep thinking how hard it must be on those kids' teachers."

"Their teachers?" Ted said almost choking on his cigarette.

"I can honestly say that I have never thought about how the murder of two little kids would affect their damned teachers, Carl. I always thought more about, you know, grandparents, uncles, aunts, and their friends," Jonathan said.

"Teachers can get very attached to their students," Carl said in a way that made Ted want to push him off the bench.

"Apparently," Jonathan said.

"Once I had a girl in my class," Carl began. "Kimberly Tate was her name. She was the prettiest little thing; small for her age, always wore little blue dresses and black shiny shoes with buckles. Remember those? Girls used to wear them all the time to school when I started teaching. Every morning I would hear those little black shoes clickity-clack down the hallway as the little girls walked to class. They don't wear them now. It's all just sneakers now. I remember when sneakers were just for gym class."

"Carl, what the hell are you talking about?" Ted said impatiently.

"Well," Carl continued, "one day, I think it was a Sunday in June, a day just like today, actually, the principal of the school calls me up at home and I knew right away that something was wrong because a principal has never called me up at home before. So, he told me that little Kimberly Tate had drowned in her family's swimming pool that weekend right in the middle of a big birthday pool party for her older sister, whose name I can't remember. Anyway, the pool was full of kids, so no one noticed little Kimberly lying at the bottom until it was too late. Can you imagine being that mother having to live with that? The mother was right there and wasn't paying attention! You have to watch kids around pools. And cars! You have to watch kids around cars too. A few years before Kimberly drowned there was a boy, I forget his name too, he wasn't in my class, but he went to our school and one day he was riding his Big Wheel on the sidewalk and what do you think happened? He got run over by his own father who was backing up their car. Crushed him and his Big Wheel to a pulp. And this father had to go on living with himself too. Like I said, you have to watch kids. I have no idea how a parent can go on after doing something like that, can you? I wish I could remember that little boy's name."

"I always back into my driveway," Ted said. "That way I see everything when I back into it and everything when I pull out of it."

"Yeah? Me too. And for the exact same reason," Jonathan said.

"Everyone should," Ted said.

"Women don't like backing into driveways or parking spots though, ever notice that?" Jonathan said.

"Gloria's sister, Lydia, is a lesbian and she can back up a car with a camper on it like a pro."

"I'm trying to make a point here!" Carl said. "For a teacher, like me, it's very difficult to lose one of your students. And the teachers of those two Ragno children will never get over it. Just like I'll never get over Kimberly Tate or that other boy. Especially Kimberly since she was actually in my class. That's why I'm so protective of my kids. That's why I wanted to check out that substitute teacher that day I went back to my school with the apples, understand?"

Now this guy really should be making baskets, Ted thought. Hopefully they don't let him loose on some unsuspecting classroom of kids anytime soon.

"I saw your sisters visited you again today, Ted," Carl said.

"They're bible-beating grotesques," Jonathan said.

"You're disgusting," Carl said.

"Yes, Carl, that was my older sisters, Sue and Peggy. They like to come up on Sundays sometimes."

"That's nice, I don't have any sisters. I don't have any brothers either. I don't miss not having siblings. One can't miss what one never had," Carl said.

"One cannot!" Jonathan said.

"You should have just made one up like Jonathan. Aleksandra with a k played the tuba and danced the can-can at the *Folies Bergère*."

"I'm actually glad, right at this moment, that I don't have any family to speak of," Carl continued. "I'm sure they'd all be persecuted just like me if I did. It's the whole city, you know. The police force, city council, the mayor. They're all rotten to the core. All out to get me. All want me to rot in this place."

"Ted's sisters had just come from church. If you were wondering why they were dressed like Anita Bryant," Jonathan said

"Minus the orange juice," Ted said.

"Is a day without your sisters like a day without sunshine? Like they say in the commercial?" Jonathan asked with a playful smile curled up one side of his lip.

"I thought your sisters were dressed very nicely," Carl said. "I think it's nice to have some colour around here. I can't wait to dress up again. Get into one of my suits, a nice, starched shirt, and my favourite sky-blue tie. I almost forgot what that's like. It's amazing how much you miss nice clothes when you're in a place like this. I bet I'd feel like a new person if I could only get in a nice suit."

Ted put another cigarette in his mouth and offered one to Jonathan who shook his head. "The operative word here is nice," Jonathan said.

"But meanwhile," Carl went on. "I'm stuck here in hospital pyjamas while Ragno is walking around on bail. He's out, free as you please, until his trial in November. Does that make sense to you? Me neither! But it's all part of the plot! And do you know where Jake Ragno worked, Ted?"

"He worked for the city," Ted said.

"Exactly right! He worked for the city! The big corrupt City of Hamilton! And I'll tell you something else, gentlemen… They watch you two. They watch you all the time. They're watching you right now."

"So, if they're watching me and Ted right now then I guess they're watching you too, Carl," Jonathan said.

"They're only watching me now because they're watching you. They haven't watched me for a while now… weeks! But you two they watch very *very* closely."

"How do you know they're watching us, Carl," Ted asked.

"I'm a teacher. I watch kids all day. I have eyes in the back of my head, Ted Moore." Carl tapped the bald spot on the back of his head and nodded. "You must have eyes in the back of your head when teaching kids. Kids always try to get something past me, but they never do. I'm too good."

"Didn't Rick get past you, Carl? You came over here looking for him," Jonathan said.

"I've been watching everything around here. I see them following you two when you go to the lounge to watch television or outside for a cigarette; sometimes it's the nurses following you and sometimes it's the orderlies and then they go right in and tell Dr. Shackelford all about where you've been and what you've been up to."

"I think you're a little paranoid, Carl." Ted said. "They keep an eye out but we're not in prison for Christ's sake. Besides, Jonathan and I could voluntarily discharge ourselves today if we wanted. Say, why don't we do that, Jonathan? Let's blow this joint. Where should we go?"

"First we'll hit my folk's suit shop for some new threads." Jonathan said. "*Nice* threads, you know, three-piece suits. Then we'll go for a steak and a beer someplace, Cesar's Restaurant, I think. After that we'll go out and tie one on. Where should we go drinking, Teddy?"

"The Windsor," Ted said, smiling.

"Ah, so you want to go slumming," Jonathan chuckled.

"So, what you're both intimating is that since you are both voluntary patients now, you can discharge yourself and I can't?" snapped Carl.

"The only one I'd intimate with is Nurse Debbie," Jonathan said. "And you have some orange shit in the corners of your mouth, Carl."

"I'd discharge with Nurse Debbie too," Ted said.

"You're both disgusting! And if I was a betting man, which I am not, I'd say you two have either been drinking or you're high on dope."

"Nothing gets past Carl," Jonathan said.

"Hey, there's Rick," Ted said, pointing across the garden. "Looks like he's visiting with his mom."

On the other side of the garden, Rick sat at one of the old wrought-iron patio tables with his arms folded across his chest looking away from his mother as she sat on the other side of the table looking defeated.

"You mean it looks like Rick is ignoring his mom," Jonathan said.

"I should probably go over there and give his mother my regards," Carl said, licking the corners of his mouth. "I've spoken to Rick's mother a few times in the lounge. I'd like her to know that Rick is coming around quite nicely. Being a teacher, I have to observe kids all day and I can tell this lad is coming around." Carl rubbed his dirty handkerchief over his face and mumbled something about the heat before standing up with a loud grunt.

"Jesus Christ!" Ted said. "That poor woman doesn't want a parent-teacher interview right now, Carl. She wants to spend some time alone with her son."

Ignoring Ted, Carl walked across the garden toward where Rick sat barefoot, wearing pyjama bottoms, a T-shirt, and a robe. Rick looked up, grimaced, and said something to Carl that looked like a quick rebuff. Ted felt a pang of sympathy as he watched a crestfallen Carl turn and slowly shuffle toward the door leading back into the hospital's side entrance.

"Well, Carl can't say we didn't try to warn him," Jonathan said.

The June sun was falling over the trees in the west. There was the smell of barbecue in the air, charcoal and smoke. Ted's barbecue, a bright orange kettle grill with a dome lid, would still be gathering dust in his garage right now near his workbench, the lawnmower, and Josh's bicycle—. He shook his empty Pepsi can, wishing it was full again.

"Hey, Jonathan, you want to know the secret to why I drink?"

"Only if you want to tell me, Teddy."

"I drink because I can't stand myself."

A week later, Ted sat in the hospital lounge reading a copy of *Socialist Worker*. Gloria had brought him up another clean pair of pants and he was feeling optimistic as he bit into a Snickers bar from the hospital vending machine. The following week Spain was having their first democratic election since Franco died and the Socialist Party of Spain had great hopes of forming the government, as did Spain's Communist Party. Fascism was dead in Europe and would never return. It seemed like the whole world was on the left or moving in that direction. Canada was, Ted thought, also heading that way and the US (though a Johnny Come Lately) would wake up eventually. As he took a sip from his Styrofoam coffee cup, a nurse with short brown hair came up behind him and touched his shoulder.

"Dr. Shackelford wants to see you now, Mr. Moore," she said.

"Sure," Ted said, smiling. The nurse had just begun working at the hospital that week and had not yet been given a nametag. Ted watched her as she walked away, appreciating how the seam of her white skirt went over her round ass and up her back to the nape of her long neck to her Dorothy Hamill short bouncy hair. She looked to be even younger than Nurse Debbie. Twenty or twenty-one.

Leaving his coffee and *Socialist Worker* behind on the coffee table, Ted left the lounge and walked down the long corridor to Dr. Shackelford's office. Ted never knew when his appointments with the doctor were going to be, they were not at any set time. When Dr. Shackelford wanted to speak with him, some nurse would just come and find him in the lounge, garden, or his room.

For the first five minutes Ted listened, uninterested, to Dr. Shackelford talk about how good the fishing was at his cottage on Lake Huron. The drought had stressed the fish out as their habitat and food source shrank and they would strike any line thrown in the water.

"I want to talk about Thorazine," Dr. Shackelford finally said.

Ted hadn't really been listening to the fishing story and wasn't sure if the doctor was asking a question or answering one.

"What about Thorazine?" Ted said.

"You said you were mixing Thorazine with alcohol for a few months before you were admitted here. Thorazine by itself can cause dizziness, coordination problems, and impedes judgement. Mixing alcohol with Thorazine can make all these side-effects worse. What side-effects were you having?"

"Nothing to do with my drinking," Ted said, lighting a cigarette. "I was having some sexual problems. Trouble with, you know, cumming. I could fuck forever it seemed, but I could just never cum.

You'd think a woman would love that, being able to go so long, but no, turns out they don't. Who would have thought it, eh?"

The doctor remained quiet.

"And then I'd lose interest in fucking after so long and finally have to say, 'sorry, ain't gonna happen'. Then after all that screwing, I'd go to bed even more frustrated than when I began so I started to avoid screwing altogether."

"Hindered ability to achieve orgasm is one of the side effects," the doctor said nonchalantly, as if it was no big deal and that anyone should be able to live their life contentedly without ever having an orgasm again. "Any other side effects, Ted?"

"No, but that not being able to come was a pretty big one."

"Yes, you're right. It is."

"And it never really helped much with the depression I went to see Doctor Heller about in the first place. But one thing Thorazine did help with was the panic attacks I've been having since the army. But... alcohol helped with the panic attacks too and given the choice I'd take the booze."

"We've put you on something else. It's called Haldol. It should fix the sexual problems, but I still don't recommend drinking while you're on it. But if you do... try and limit your alcohol intake."

"Great."

"Do you think you have a problem with alcohol, Ted?"

"Probably," Ted said without hesitating. "All evidence seems to point to a problem with alcohol, doesn't it? If this were a courtroom you could probably bring in a bunch of witnesses: my wife, my mother, my kids, and they'll all tell you, 'Sure, that bastard has a problem with booze'. But of all my problems, and I got a fucking shitload of them, the alcohol one is the most bearable. Most bearable for *me*, anyway."

"You feel like you are in a courtroom?"

"Sometimes it seems like one. Like any minute you'll jump up and yell 'A-ha! Gotcha!' like Perry Mason."

"Do you think you may be an alcoholic, Ted?"

"Maybe. Who cares? Call it what you want. For years I've been going to doctors with overwhelming anxiety and crippling depression and these doctors have called me a lot of things. Let's see..." He began to count off on the fingers on one hand. "I've been called a heavy drinker, a binge drinker, a habitual drinker, a chronic drinker, and an alcoholic. I don't care what you people call it this time. Maybe I was all of them at different times. Who the fuck knows what I am today?"

"What do you think you are today?"

"Well, I'm probably someone who shouldn't drink. We've learned I'm definitely someone who shouldn't drink if I'm taking Thorazine. But I'll tell you this, I'll never stop drinking. It's one of the few things I have that makes it all bearable. So, you guys just figure out what shit in little white paper cups I can take that won't make me go crazy if I happen to have a drink along with it and send me on my merry way. That's all you have to do."

"We want to give you other tools to help you make life bearable, Ted."

"Yeah, well it's been weeks and weeks and I'm still waiting for them."

"Did you know Thorazine and alcohol could cause psychotic episodes?"

"Like the one I had in the garage? You're telling me a few months too late."

"Well, I'm not convinced what happened in the garage was an actual psychotic episode. It could have been several things."

"Slicing my own throat open wasn't a psychotic episode? Well, that's news to me."

"I said it *might* not be," Dr. Shackelford said.

"If I had known that alcohol and Thorazine could cause a psychotic episode I wouldn't have taken the Thorazine. And if you and your kind had just let me alone with my depression, I'd be home right now, still depressed but comfortable and soused in my La-Z-Boy chair watching baseball—but without this fucking scar across my throat."

"Can we discuss the night you came in again?" Dr. Shackelford asked.

"Nothing would be more fucking fun," Ted said. "Well, it's like this, I took a jagged piece of broken beer bottle and sliced my throat open, like you would, say, gut a fish. I don't consider it my best hour but that's what happened and that's that."

"And?"

"And sometimes I wonder why more people don't slice their throats open."

"What stopped you? What made you stop and seek help?"

"It hurt too much so I stopped. A perfectly rational response to pain."

"What were you thinking when it happened?"

"That I'd had better days."

"Tell me about it again, from the beginning."

Ted sighed and leaned back in his chair. "The socialists might win the Spanish election next week."

"Good for Spain," the doctor said. "And here in Canada, tell me again what happened in the garage that night."

"For the millionth time, I was in the garage changing a bulb in the headlight of my Chevy. When I finished, I saw that the new bulb I put in was burnt out as well. And that burnt out headlight bulb was like the straw that broke the fucking camel's back. I was drinking an API beer and smashed it against the crossbar of Josh's bicycle. Then I took a broken shard and cut open my throat. Left to right."

"Where was Josh at that time?"

"I don't know. In bed."

"You told me when you first came here that he was in the garage too."

"My wife said Josh was in his room until the ambulance came and I believe her. I don't know what I said the night I was brought here but Josh wasn't in the garage."

"Josh did not see you cut yourself?"

"I wouldn't have done it if Josh was there. Never!"

"Then why, Ted, do you think you told me when they brought you here to the hospital that Josh was in the garage watching you that night? Why did you tell me that when you saw Josh standing there in the garage that you became terrified you were about to lose control? And that you had to make a choice?"

"I don't know! Maybe because I was insane? They were dragging me kicking and screaming into the Hamilton Lunatic Asylum. Maybe I just *thought* I saw Josh in the garage, like those fucking bugs in the cupboard, but it doesn't matter because *Josh was not there.* Unless you know something I don't."

The doctor sat quietly staring at Ted.

It was easier when he was having shock. For those weeks Ted didn't remember anything of that night in the garage but when they stopped the shock treatment, those beautiful little holes in his mind began to refill with most horrific memories. Yes, Ted did remember everything that happened in the garage the night: he remembered that goddamn burnt-out headlight, he remembered how a cool spring rain had just begun, he remembered a winter's coat of dust on his barbeque, he remembered smashing the beer bottle against the bicycle, and how the sharp amber piece of glass felt in his hand—and Ted remembered Josh's face when he made the first slice into his throat. *Fuck it!*

"Alright, alright," Ted finally said. "Yes, Perry Mason! You got me! Josh was there in the fucking garage when I cut myself! Are you happy, now? He was standing at the garage door in his pyjamas watching me. And..."

"And?"

"And the reason I did it... the reason I cut my own throat that night was because I was trying to save Josh... from me."

"Good," the doctor said. "Now we're getting someplace."

That night Ted slept soundly and dreamed of lilies. They were white, had creeping anthers covered with shimmering orange pollen and, like the ones Doris brought, had the same rotten, deathly scent with a hint of the manure in which they were grown. In his dream Ted was wearing his army fatigues and carried the lilies, in a bouquet, down the empty halls of the west wing, trying to find a silver ashtray large enough to dump them. With each step along the corridor the stench of rotting lilies became stronger.

Ted awoke with a hard-on. Looks like the new medication is working, he thought. Then he noticed the same sickening stench from his dream wafting in the room. *What the fuck is that smell?* Ted reached over to the small bedside table and grabbed his eyeglasses. The sun was just rising. He looked over and saw Jonathan sleeping soundly in his bed. Across the room, Rick had kicked his blanket off and was sleeping in the fetal position with his hands clasped under his chin. Carl's bed was empty. Ted slid out of bed and walked barefoot across the room. Near the door leading to the hallway, he saw something white on the floor between Carl's hospital bed and the wall.

For a moment, Ted thought Carl had fallen out of bed. Then Ted saw Carl sitting on the floor, propped up straight beside his bed. He was naked with his bulging white belly covering his genitals. His hands, with his fingers still orange from his last bag of cheese puffs, were folded in his teachers pose over this stomach and his open eyes stared forward at the door. His hospital robe was twisted with one end wrapped around his neck and tied in a knot around the metal bedpost. Carl's face was reddish purple and blood from his nose had begun to crust on his chin and between his fat spread legs was a mound of orange-brown shit.

"For fuck's sake, Carl."

Five

"They gave up looking for that Ragno boy's body," Doris said.

She shook her head slowly, holding her cigarette firmly between her lips as she drove down Highway 6 south out of Hamilton.

"I saw that on the news," Gloria said somberly.

The thought of that poor little boy lying at the bottom of Lake Ontario for all eternity made Gloria want to cry. She wished she could just turn off the Ragno story for a while, but it seemed to be the only thing people in Hamilton were talking about now. It was the biggest murder story the city had seen since Evelyn Dick dismembered her husband and tossed his torso down the mountain back in the 1940s.

"They should chuck Jake Ragno in jail and throw away the key," Doris said. "Or wrap him in garbage bags and toss him in the lake like he did to his wife and kids."

Doris gripped her fingers around her faded tan leather steering wheel. She was wearing the 'Perfectly Puce' nail polish she had bought at Woolco last winter. At the time Gloria had thought puce would look good on Doris, or at least better than that candy apple red nail polish she usually wore, but now, seeing her sister's puce nails in the sunlight shining through the windshield, Gloria was having second thoughts. However, she wasn't about to tell her sister she didn't like her nail polish, not when Doris was driving Gloria twenty miles out of Hamilton to the Six Nations Indian Reserve. Gloria looked down at her nails, bitten down almost to the quick. She had no business telling anyone else about their nails. The puce wasn't so bad.

Gloria looked at the weeds and long grass along the highway waving gently in a slight hot breeze along with wildflowers. White Queen's Anne lace and purple crown vetch were the only ones she knew.

"Would you know goldthread if you saw it, Doris?"

"Goldthread! No, I don't think I'd recognize it if I were walking through a crop of it. It was just an ugly green weed with, I think, little white flowers. I'd sure as hell know it to taste it though! Jesus! That was revolting stuff, wasn't it?"

"It was," Gloria agreed. "It tasted like mud and dirty feet."

"That's it exactly! It tasted like someone went walking through the muck and then stuck their stinking feet in water and served it in a teacup."

Gloria chortled and nodded.

"And I think Mum made me drink it more than anyone else in the family because of those bad menstrual cramps I used to get when I was young. Once a month, like clockwork, she would make a batch of that godawful goldthread tea and make me drink it," Doris said.

Poor Doris! Yes, it always seemed as if Doris got everything worse than anyone else: worst case of measles, worst periods, worst childbirth and, even with Ted in the mental institution, Doris had the worst husband.

"Did you ever go with Mum to gather goldthread along the foot of mountain?" asked Gloria.

"No, I never did, but I do remember her coming home with her shoes all muddy and that old wicker basket of hers full of the goddamn stuff. Just an ugly weed with those long yellow roots that looked like tentacles. It looked so creepy. And there was always a bunch of it drying on the windowsill."

Gloria tried to picture how her mother looked all those times she had brought Doris a cup of yellow goldthread tea: Doris lying on the living room couch with a hot water bottle on her lower stomach and her mother's sympathetic smile on her tired face as she lovingly handed a teacup and saucer with little snowdrops on it to her. Suddenly Gloria felt somewhat envious, and was a little ashamed of being envious, of all the times her mother had made Doris goldthread tea, rubbed her stomach, and softly sang her Indian songs.

"As bad as goldthread was though, the tea really did work for my cramps. But today I'll take Midol over goldthread tea, thank you very much. Midol doesn't make me gag when I take it. So, what made you think about goldthread tea? Having stomach problems?"

"No, I've been thinking about it as I take the bus up the mountain to see Ted."

"Did you know Mum was still drinking goldthread tea right up until the day they took her to the hospital?" Doris said, lighting another cigarette. "She never thought the stomach-ache she had for months and months could have been cancer until it was too late. And when I think of her out there at the foot of the mountain, right at the end in such pain with her belly full of cancer, still wearing those old muddy shoes and carrying that wicker basket under her arm looking for that goddamn weed it just breaks my heart."

"I didn't know," Gloria said, looking away.

Gloria's mother had fallen ill the year after Gloria had gotten married to her first husband. Gloria had moved to Niagara Falls and then Kevin came along quickly and, because Gloria was dealing with problems of her own, she didn't see much of her mother after her wedding day. *If I had been living in Hamilton when she first started having such stomach pain*, Gloria now thought, *I would have made her go to the doctor. Then maybe she'd still be here—*

"She never made the boys drink that stuff when they were sick. It was always the girls," Doris said.

"The boys just refused."

"She let the boys get away with everything."

"I think she was more worried about us," Gloria said. "She knew what we had in front of us. Maybe she wanted to protect us for the short time she had us. I don't know."

"So, do you have any idea what you are going to do about the six thousand dollars, Gloria?"

"I'm not losing another house. I can't."

"I wish I could do more."

"I know you would if you could, Doris."

That was true. It was also probably true that Doris' husband Ken did have the money socked away but he kept it far away from Doris and he certainly would never lend it to anyone, least of all Gloria. Not since she and Ted had taken Doris in the last time she left Ken.

"I feel guilty for taking the money Lydia and Tara were saving for a down payment on a house. I think most of the money came from Tara," Gloria said.

"Having to come up with six thousand is a lot better than having to come up with eight thousand. And Lydia *wants* to help you and the boys," Doris said.

"Lydia didn't have to do that for us. Ted wasn't as understanding as he could have been when he found out that she was gay."

"Christ, that was years ago."

"Still, she didn't have to help us."

"Lydia isn't one to hold grudges," Doris said.

Gloria was still ashamed of how Ted had acted even if it was years ago. He had heard from one of his gutter friends that her sister, Lydia, was having an affair with an older woman she worked with. Ted came home that night and blurted out to Gloria that Lydia was a 'dyke'. And *everyone* knew it. Gloria had called him a liar, thinking it was just Ted's way of getting back at her for telling him her suspicions about Abe, so Gloria had called Lydia that night and asked her point blank. In retrospect, she should have kept her big mouth shut and let Lydia tell her when she was ready. Later, there was a huge fight between Lydia and Ted: yelling, denials, crying, and ugly words. And what did it accomplish? Lydia didn't speak to Ted for years. Even now there lingered a coolness between them that would likely always remain. However, Lydia was there for Gloria and her boys, putting her dreams of a home of her own with Tara on hold to help them out. Gloria would always be thankful for that. But she still needed six thousand dollars more.

Gloria had not slept a full night since Ted told her about the eight thousand dollars he had pilfered from the union treasury. The day Ted told her, Gloria had gone to work her afternoon shift at Munro and, though she had held herself together for a few hours, on her lunch hour she went to the lunchroom and sobbed, shaking in the stall. They were going to lose everything. After work that night she looked through the want ads to see if there were any part-time jobs. She could clean. She had cleaned houses with her mother when she was a girl and that would bring in some money but not enough. And even if they sold the house, they would only make a couple of thousand on it (if they were lucky) and then there were realtor fees and taxes that would probably gobble that up. And if the union decided to go to the police, Ted might end up in jail. She could never afford the mortgage alone. Gloria was weak from worry.

"Ted looks better every time I see him," Doris said. "I didn't take flowers with me this week. I thought the other guys in his room might give him the business, getting more flowers from his sister-in-law, so I just took him another tin of caramel corn. I remember when I was a patient there, some of the girls in my room were real bitches."

"It's good of you to drive up there when I'm working day shift. Ted appreciates it too, I know."

"Oh, I don't mind. After all, you and Ted came up and visited me all the time when I was up there."

Gloria decided just to let Doris think Ted had visited during her time at the psychiatric hospital. Ted didn't visit once. But Doris was pretty out of it when she was up there, even worse than Ted was. So, what did it matter now if Doris thought Ted had visited her. Nevertheless, Ted had driven Gloria up there every week. But he had sat in his car and never gone in.

"Well," Doris continued, "I don't mind visiting Ted as long as those sisters of his aren't there. Once I drove all the way up there and saw them, I turned right around and left."

"I try to work my visits around them too, but they mean well, and they've both been through a lot. And they love Ted. That's what I tell myself."

"Yeah, I know. Hey, what's the deal with that roommate of Ted's, that Jonathan guy?"

"What about him?"

"He's one handsome man! That Jonathan reminds me of someone, but I just can't put my finger on it."

"Yes," Gloria said, smiling. "He does."

"Six Nations is just up here on the right," Doris said, tossing her cigarette out of the window.

Being on the Six Nations Indian Reserve made Gloria feel less Indian than ever, overwhelmed with the feeling that she didn't belong there. And it wasn't because she herself was only half Indian, she and her whole family had lost something significant between the reservation in Minnesota that her mother had left as a child and their lives now.

And I don't even know what we lost.

The houses on the reserve were much like houses in the east end of Hamilton. They were small, nothing fancy, but these houses were spaced out more than those in Gloria's neighbourhood, and there were more trees and, of course, no smokestacks spewing out clouds of smoke on the horizon. Gloria was a tad surprised there were paved roads, expecting dirt roads throughout the reserve. That's silly, she thought. Why wouldn't their roads be paved? They aren't way up on some northern reserve; they had just passed a Dairy Queen and a Chevrolet Dealership a few miles back down the highway.

Around the houses, tanned dark-haired children played in the open spaces and yards. They reminded Gloria of her brothers and sisters when they were children. The difference was that all these children were growing up together while Gloria and her family were the only brown-skinned children in their east end Hamilton neighbourhood which was, incidentally, never very neighbourly to them. Growing up, the other kids (and even their parents) had called Gloria and her brothers and sisters filthy names like 'wild Indians' and worse. As long as she lived, Gloria would never forget that. Maybe it would have been better if they had all grown up here.

"You said you've been up here on the reserve before, Doris?" Gloria said, looking down at the directions that Bill had drawn to his house she had placed on her lap.

"Only once. It was for a dance a few years ago. It was amazing how everyone I met here treated me like long-lost family. They could tell I was Indian right away."

"We aren't Indians the way they're Indians," Gloria said.

"We're just as much Indian as anyone else here. Well... we're half Indian and that's almost the same thing. We just never had anyone teach us how to be Indian."

"Mum tried. We just weren't paying attention."

"Yeah. I know," Doris replied.

"Turn here onto Moccasin Trail," Gloria said, fingering her hand-written map. "It's number ninety-one."

"These are some big lots. Now, do they actually own the land or just the house that's on it?" asked Doris.

"I don't know how Indian reserves work. And don't ask Bill when you meet him either."

Doris smiled. "Contrary to popular belief, Gloria, I do have some class."

Doris drove around a bend and then stopped her car in front of number ninety-one. The house was a bungalow, about the same size as Gloria's house in the east end. It was wood and painted an eggshell white and in the front window an air conditioner hummed softly and dripped beads of water into a small puddle on the cement walkway in a shady spot in front of the house. It had a red Ford pickup truck parked in the gravel driveway and a huge front yard with patchy sun-scorched brown grass as a plastic oscillating lawn sprinkler sat frying in the sun, unattached to a water hose.

"I just hope he has a beer," Doris said, walking toward the house. "I'd kill for a beer right now."

A young girl, about eleven or twelve years old, stood watching them through the screen door. She was slender with long dark hair and wore a red one-piece bathing suit. Her hair was damp and matted on her head. *Must be one of his daughters*, Gloria thought. *She looks a lot like me when I was little.* Suddenly, an excited golden retriever appeared beside the girl, stuck its nose through a hole in the screen door, and sniffed at the breeze.

"I hope he doesn't bite!" Doris yelled to the girl.

"It's she not a he. Her name is Kanien," the girl replied.

"That doesn't really answer my question," Doris said softly.

Gloria and Doris reached the front steps and a man suddenly appeared and opened the screen door.

"Hey there!" Bill said, beaming as Kanien ran out of the open door and down the wooden stairs to where Gloria and Doris stood.

"That's Bill?" Doris whispered to Gloria. "Now that's one handsome man too."

"Come on in!"

Bill wore a wet pair of cut-off denim shorts and a short-sleeved baby blue velour V-neck shirt that had pulled up slightly over his biceps, showing a thick vein on each muscle. He was barefoot, and his legs were deep-reddish brown, much like Gloria's looked after a day in the sun. He was fixing the collar of his shirt, giving Gloria the impression that he had just thrown it on to greet them. His shining long black hair, still wet, was slicked back and hung down his back just past his shoulders.

The sisters walked up the creaky front steps into the cool house. The small living room was tidy and had a couch and a chair with a large television against one wall. The curtains were closed, and the room was dark except for a small lamp's glow on top of the television. A blue bedspread hung between the living room and what Gloria assumed was the kitchen in the back of the house. Gloria sometimes did that in her house on Alkeld Street to keep the cool air from the air conditioning in the living room. Who could afford an air conditioner in every room?

"This is my daughter, Alice," Bill said.

"Hi," the girl in the bathing suit said. Then she turned, ran behind the curtain, and the back door slammed.

"We have a pool in the backyard."

"Oh, lucky you! I've been trying to talk my husband into putting in a pool for years," Doris said.

"This is my sister, Doris," Gloria said, ashamed she had forgotten all about her for a moment.

"Hi, Doris," Bill said, still smiling.

"I was just thinking how much your daughter Alice looks like I did when I was a little girl. I know it's hard to believe now, but I was skinny when I was her age," Gloria said.

"That's because we didn't always have food," Doris said.

"There were a lot of times when I was a kid when we didn't have much to eat either. Always got by though, eh?"

"We certainly did," Doris said.

"The puppies are in the basement," Bill said. "But sit down, cool down and relax for a minute. We can go down in a little while, and you can have a look. Maybe I'll bring them out in the backyard for a run later or take them into the pool with their mama."

"Can puppies swim?" Doris asked, sitting down in the chair closest to the air conditioner while Gloria took a seat on the couch.

"Retrievers take to water quickly; that's what they were bred for, eh? Hunters used them to get ducks they shot down. That's how they got the name retriever."

"Well, who knew?" Doris said.

"Hey, you ladies want something to drink? It's a pretty hot day for a drive."

"Got a beer?" Doris asked. "I'd sell my soul for a beer."

"Beer, I got! How about you, Gloria? You want a beer too? I don't have any soda, but I have a jug of green Kool-Air for the kids."

"I'll have a glass of Kool-Aid," Gloria answered.

"I think I swallowed a ton of dust while driving up here, and green Kool-Aid ain't gonna cut it. Beer for me," Doris said.

Bill walked behind the blue bedspread and Gloria could hear the clink of bottles being opened in the kitchen as Doris scanned the room.

"I like that bear painting on the wall," Doris said. "And those wood carvings of ducks over there on the table, they must be authentic Indian art. I wanted to get something like that once, but Ken doesn't like Indian things. He calls them 'wa-hoo art'. Sometimes I wonder why he ever married an Indian girl at all."

Bill emerged from behind the blue bedspread holding two beers between the fingers of one hand and one glass of green drink with condensation already forming on the glass in the other.

"I was just telling Gloria I like your Indian art," Doris said, taking a bottle of beer from Bill. She took a few big gulps and sighed deeply.

"Thanks," Bill said. "So, you two ladies are Indian too, I see." He handed Gloria the glass of Kool-Aid and sat beside her on the floor with his back against the couch.

"Half," Doris said. She put the cold beer to her forehead and sighed loudly again.

"Our mother was born on a reserve in Minnesota. I forget the name of it," Gloria said

"It's on Nett Lake. She was a full-blooded Chippewa!"

"Ah, that's cool," Bill said, nodding. "You're Ojibwa."

"I'm a what?" Doris said.

Bill chuckled "Ojibwa is another name for Chippewa. I'm Mohawk. Mohawks are part of the Iroquois Confederacy."

"Are Chippewas part of that too, Bill?" Gloria asked.

"No, they weren't. But your people and my people *do* have a history."

"Ooooh, doesn't that sound exciting, Gloria?" Doris said with a big grin. "We have a history together. Is it a good history?"

"A bloody history," Bill said.

"Oh, dear," Doris said.

"We don't know much about being Indian," Gloria said. "Or anything about our Indian heritage, really. And now that our mother and aunts are long gone, we can't ask them."

Bill put his beer on a coaster on the coffee table. "Luckily you have lots of time to learn… if you wanted to."

Gloria finally took a sip of her green-lime drink. It was good but sweet. She always kept a jug of Kool-Aid in her fridge during the summer too, but it was always red. It didn't matter if it was strawberry, raspberry, punch, or cherry. If it was red, Josh was happy.

"Have either of you been out here on Six Nations before?" Bill asked.

He looked at Gloria with dark almond-shaped eyes. And such a smile! She even liked the way his incisors protruding slightly on both sides. Gloria looked down at his arm, resting on the cushion of the couch, so close to her hand. His skin was *maybe* a shade darker than hers, but not much. She never noticed how much alike their skin tone was at work, probably because Bill was usually in blue overalls during his shifts at Munro.

"No, never," Gloria said

"I have," Doris said. "I came out here for a dance once. I love it up here. It makes me feel more Indian. Did you say you have a pool?"

"Sure do! I threw it up last year during the summer shutdown at Munro. The wife never liked it, she said it took up too much of the backyard, but the kids love it and it's been so hot this year they're in it all the time, from morning to night practically. I'm just glad they're not in the house watching that damned TV. Want to go out back and have a look?"

"Yes!" Doris said, hopping up from the chair.

"Okay, follow me." Bill stood, walked across the room, and held aside the bedspread that separated the kitchen and living room for Doris and Gloria to pass into the sweltering, sun-drenched kitchen.

Gloria was impressed at how tidy the small kitchen was for a man without a wife living with a bunch of kids. Not only were his floors spotless, except for some wet footprints on the linoleum, the countertops, cupboards and even the chrome drip pans under the burners on the stove were shining. His wife may have run off, but he definitely has a woman around here, Gloria thought. Maybe she doesn't live here but some woman comes by and whoever this woman was liked Bill a whole lot. No woman would clean the black crust from under burners unless she thought she would be living there at some point in time.

"Are these all your kids, Bill?" Doris asked, stepping out of the back door onto the porch.

"Christ no! Not all of them. Some are neighbour kids. Since I put in the pool, ours has become the house on the street every kid comes to now."

Bill closed the kitchen door and the three of them sat down in kitchen chairs that had been brought out onto the wooden back porch. Though it was hot, there was a nice breeze from the west and the porch was shaded.

"I should have told you to bring your bathing suits with you. I could look around for suits for you ladies if you want; people are always leaving their bathing suits behind here," he said.

The pool did look inviting to Gloria. It was round with a white metal deck and fencing around it. White aluminum steps lead up to the deck where six deck chairs were lined up around two white plastic tables. Gloria tried to picture how much of her lawn would be left if Bill's pool suddenly appeared in her own backyard. Not enough, she decided.

"Can I go in like this in my shorts and T-shirt?" Doris asked.

"You, sure can."

"Doris, you can't go in," Gloria said. "You'd be uncomfortable driving home in wet clothes."

The truth was that Gloria couldn't let Doris go swimming in her clothes because Ken would have a conniption if Doris came home in wet clothes. And when Ken was upset Doris could very well end up with a black eye or split lip.

Doris pouted. "I wasn't going to go *all* the way in. I just want to put my feet in the water to cool them."

"Go ahead, Doris. Enjoy!" Bill said.

Doris kicked off her sandals onto the porch, climbed down the wooden porch steps to the lawn, and walked up the white aluminum stairs leading to the deck with her beer bottle in her hand. She sat on the side of the pool and, putting down her beer bottle on one of the white plastic tables, dipped her legs into the water up to her knees.

"It's so refreshing!" Doris yelled to them. "I don't even need to go all the way in."

She moved her feet slowly back and forth in the water while the children in the pool seemed to do their best to ignore this stranger with puce toenails on the side of the pool.

"What do you think of Six Nations so far, Gloria?" he asked.

"I really like it. All the time that I was growing up I had no idea that there was a reserve so close to where we lived in the east end. I thought, except for our aunts and a few cousins, other Indians were thousands of miles away."

"That must have been hard."

Up on the pool deck, Doris had talked the children into playing a game and was now tossing a penny into the pool to see who could be the first one to retrieve it and, after five minutes and about twenty tosses of the penny, Doris had charmed all the kids in the pool.

"Doris always wins over kids quickly."

"Indian pennies are the best!" Doris yelled out, tossing the penny into the middle of the pool again.

A thin boy, about six years old wearing a blue and red bathing suit, ran down the steps of the pool, across the grass, and up to the porch carrying an empty beer bottle.

"The funny fat lady in the pool asked if she could have another beer," the little boy said.

"We don't call people fat, Corey," Bill said.

"Sorry. Can I get the lady another beer?"

"Yeah. And get me another too!"

"I'm sorry, Bill. I should have brought a six-pack of beer with us for Doris. We didn't know we'd be stopping so long," Gloria said.

"I'd hate to think I'd ever begrudge a lady a beer or two," Bill said as the boy came barrelling out of the door with a bottle of beer in each hand and the bottle opener in his mouth. The boy handed them to Bill to open.

"The lady is tossing a penny in the pool for us to find. I got it first three times already," Corey said. He then took an open beer back and ran down the porch stairs and back to the pool.

"That's my youngest. And my only boy."

"He's adorable," Gloria said.

"Thank you, Bill!" Doris yelled from the pool deck. "You're a doll!"

"I like your sister. She's a kick."

"Everyone likes Doris."

Gloria enjoyed the scent of chlorine from the pool mixed with the nearby pine trees while she sat in the shade drinking her Kool-Aid. For a second, she forgot all about Ted and the six thousand dollars as she watched Doris, never tiring of throwing the penny into the middle of Bill's pool.

"So!" Bill finally said, finishing his second beer. "Are you ready to meet your new dog now?"

Gloria nodded. She followed Bill back into the hot kitchen and then down the creaky wooden stairs that lead into the basement. The basement was almost as cool as the living room but was damp with the earthy scent. The basement was brick cinderblock, painted light green with some wood paneling on one wall. There was a couch and an old dark green recliner in front of a small black and white television where two more children, little girls, younger than Alice, watched the *Friendly Giant*. At the back of the basement were a white washer and dryer, shining like they had just been polished. The woman who cleans the kitchen does his laundry too, Gloria thought

"It's too nice to be in the house. Get out and go swimming or play or something." Bill barked at the girls.

"Will you come swimming with us?" one girl asked.

"In a little while. Now get outside." Without arguing, the two girls climbed the stairs and went outside to join the others. "Those two, Darlene and Erica, are also mine,"

"When it's hot, Darlene, Erica and Alice like to sleep down here in the rec-room. Corey usually camps out in the living room with me when it gets really hot or sleeps on the back porch. One morning I found him asleep on the pool deck. He said sleeping on the metal deck was the coolest place he could find. I told him if I saw him sleeping by the pool in the dark again, I'd tan his ass. The back porch is fine for sleeping but I didn't want him rolling over in his sleep into the pool and drowning before he wakes up."

Bill walked past the washer and dryer through a pair of saloon doors at the back of the rec room to another smaller room.

"The pups are in here," he said. He walked along the furnace where he had built a wooden pen on the concrete floor covered with newspaper. Inside, four golden retriever puppies laid in a heap sleeping in one corner. Hearing Bill walk in, they immediately woke up with a jolt, jumped up on the side of the pen and began to howl like babies ready for a meal. Other than a small piece of dog poop covering half the face of Jake Ragno from a recent front page of *The Hamilton Spectator*, the pen and dogs were spotless.

"I have to have Alice change the paper in the pen. She does it a few times a day. But they're all ready to be housebroken. You can start as soon as you get him home."

"Are you sure they're ready to leave their mother?" Gloria said. "They still look pretty small."

"They're nine weeks today. Puppies can start being adopted at eight. I've already sold three."

"Oh."

"Now I only have two boys and two girls left. So... let's find you the males and you can pick," Bill picked up the puppies one by one and looked under them. "Their nuts just dropped, and it looks like both the males have two balls so you shouldn't have any problems if you want to breed them. Everything that should be there... is there. But if you want to get him fixed that's up to you, but I don't like fixed males. They seem to get fat and dopey after they've been neutered for some reason. But, like I told you at Munro, if you do want to breed them, I don't have any kind of papers."

"That's fine," Gloria said. She had no intention of ever breeding dogs.

"But just look at them." He held one of the puppies up by the scruff of the neck toward her. "You can tell they're full-blooded retrievers, eh?"

"I guess so," she said, not really knowing what a full-blooded retriever should look like.

Bill took the two male puppies out of the pen and put them down on the carpet by Gloria's feet and the larger of the two immediately jumped up onto Gloria's leg while the smaller one just sat down, sleepily, with his tongue sticking out. Gloria crouched down and began petting the larger puppy's head. The puppy became even more excited, jumping up and down, scratching her slightly through her slacks with his sharp claws, until Bill gently pushed the dog aside with his foot.

"Down ya get," he said.

Gloria then turned to the smaller more docile puppy. She didn't want a dog that was too rambunctious or yappy. Inside the pen the two females stood on their hind legs watching her, their front paws resting on the top of the pen, as they barked in a high-pitched yelp. Probably wondering where their caresses were.

I know how you feel, girls, Gloria thought.

Bill got down on one knee beside Gloria and stroked the smaller puppy behind the ears as the larger puppy jumped up and licked his face. "I got a soft spot for this little guy," he said as the smaller puppy began to doze off again. "He was the smallest of the litter."

"Thirty dollars you said, Bill?" Gloria stood up and tried not to grunt.

"Yeah, thirty. Like I said, they'd cost a lot more if they had their papers, eh?"

"I think I'll take the smaller one."

Bill put the larger puppy back in the pen and then picked up the smaller one by the scruff of the neck. "I think this little guy will make a great pet," he said, cradling the puppy like a baby. "And I'll tell you what, I'll give him to you for twenty-five since he was the runt."

"So how long do these types of dogs live?" Gloria asked.

"Tired of him already?" Bill said, chuckling.

"No… I was just wondering."

"Twelve years or so."

Josh would be almost twenty-three by then, Gloria thought. By that time, hopefully, he'll be out of this city with an education, a family, and a dog of his own.

"I'll put him back until you're ready to go." Bill placed the puppy back into the pen for his last hour or so with his brother and sisters.

Gloria nodded.

"I should prepare you for a few tears, though," Bill said. "Alice, especially, has a thing for this guy. She named him Tiny. Begged me not to sell him, but one dog around here is enough for me."

Great, now I'll be the big mean lady who steals puppies from little girls too.

"Is Ted coming home soon?" Bill asked, as they made their way up the basement stairs back into the hot kitchen.

"We're hoping he's home before Labour Day."

"That's not so far off, eh? Did I tell you I volunteered with the union to work on Munro's Labour Day float? I'll be driving the truck. This will be my first time going to the Hamilton Labour Day Parade."

"But you've worked at Munro for years!"

"I know," Bill said, stepping back onto the back porch. "I like to stay home on my day's off and spend time with the kids. But when the union asked me to drive the truck this year, I said, 'what the fuck?' Maybe the kids would like to see the parade for once."

"Your kids can march along with us, if they want," Gloria said, sitting back down on the kitchen chair and picking up her glass of green Kool-Aid. "Ted has had Josh marching with either his union or ours since he was old enough to walk. He always loved it. I signed Josh up to march with us again this year. I'm sure Ted will also be marching with Wentworth Steel if he's home. Ted keeps telling me he hasn't missed marching in a Labour Day parade since he came home from the army in the early sixties."

Gloria looked out toward the pool and gasped. "Doris! What did you do?"

Doris must have jumped in the pool while Gloria was downstairs with Bill and was now holding onto the side of the pool, happily drinking her beer.

"I fell in," Doris said as one of the kids brought her the penny to throw again.

"Luckily you emptied your pockets and put your cigarettes and keys on the deck before you *fell in*. Now you're going to have to drive home soaking wet," Gloria said.

"I was hot!"

"And now you'll have to explain it to Ken," Gloria said, looking sideways at Bill. "Ken is always so... touchy."

"Oh, who cares! If you're brown, hang around!" Doris shouted. She tossed the penny in the middle of the pool again. "Come and sit up here on the deck, Gloria!"

"Yeah, let's go sit on the deck," Bill said, getting up.

Gloria followed Bill down the back steps and across the few feet of lawn to the pool. She gingerly climbed up the wet and slippery aluminum stairs to the pool deck and sat in one of the lawn chairs near Doris.

"Watch out below!" Bill yelled, stripping off his velour shirt. He tossed it aside, showing the sunburn and slight peeling on his shoulders, then ran across the metal deck and cannonballed into the middle of the pool with a huge splash that made all the kids (and Doris) scream.

Coming up from the water, Bill's long black hair now reached halfway down his back. He grabbed his oldest daughter, Alice, and threw her in the air into the middle of the pool and for the next few minutes, tossed each of the kids the same way. Gloria watched his biceps flex, large and gleaming in the sun, each time he picked up a child.

"How about you, Doris?" Bill asked. "How about I toss you next?"

"Oh!" she said, laughing. "You couldn't lift me!"

"Okay, kids, that's it for now. The old man is exhausted."

He jumped out of the pool and water beaded and rolled off his caramel skin as his cut-off denim shorts dripped and clung tight to his buttocks. There was no hair on his chest except for a few stray strands around his dark brown nipples. He sat in the empty chair beside Gloria.

"Did you pick a dog?" Doris asked.

"She sure did," Bill said, grinning. "She bought the runt."

"I didn't want one that was too rambunctious," Gloria said.

"Good!" Doris said. "I'm glad you finally got a dog. You won't worry so much when you're alone at night with a dog in the house."

"Yoo-hoo!" a woman's voice yelled from across the backyard.

Gloria shaded her eyes with her hand and saw a woman walking toward the pool with a little girl walking beside her. The woman was slender with red hair. She wore a red and white striped bikini and had a beach towel around her neck. Her fair skin was freckled and a bit sunburned. She carried a pack of wieners and a bag of Wonder Bread hot dog buns in one hand and a bottle of Johnson's baby oil in the other. She's not even thirty, Gloria thought.

"Hello!" the woman shouted. "Is this a private party or can anyone join?"

There was a chorus of "Aunt Michelle!" from the children in the pool.

"Hey, Michelle," Bill said, standing up. "I was just about to put the barbecue on for lunch. You ladies are staying for lunch, I hope."

"I'd love a hotdog," Doris said. "And another beer if you have it."

"Only if you have enough, Bill!" Gloria said.

"We got plenty!" Bill said.

The little girl climbed up the stairs to the pool deck followed by the woman who smiled at Gloria and extended her hand.

"Hello there, I'm Michelle. I'm the neighbour."

She shook Gloria's hand a little too tightly and smiled broadly. There was a small gap between her front teeth that seemed to make her prettier for some reason, *Neighbour?* Gloria thought. *Why is a woman who was as white as Ted living on an Indian reserve?*

Suddenly Gloria was ashamed of herself for thinking such a thing. Wasn't that exactly what others had said about her and her family? Hadn't she been told her whole life that she was neither white enough nor Indian enough to be either?

Shame on me.

"Hi, I'm Gloria. And this is my sister, Doris."

"So nice to meet you two! How do you know Bill?"

"Gloria works with me at Munro. She's come to get herself a puppy."

"Oh, puppies!" Michelle said. "Aren't they just the sweetest things on the earth? I wish I was able to take one but I'm allergic, wouldn't you know it?"

Michelle bent down and picked up the empty beer bottles from the white plastic table showing her cleavage in her small bikini. "I hate glass beer bottles around the pool. They're accidents just waiting to happen. I'll take these inside."

"If I had known this was going to be a party," Doris said to Gloria under her breath, "I would have brought my potato salad."

After lunch Doris and Bill had persuaded Gloria to at least sit on the pool deck with her feet in the pool. Maybe a pool for the backyard on Alkeld Street wasn't such a bad idea. This was heavenly, she thought. And then, like a bolt of lightning in a clear-blue sky, the memory of six thousand dollars suddenly returned her to reality. There was no pool in her future. Not anytime soon, anyway,

"Is Michelle Indian too, Bill?" Doris asked, mortifying Gloria, once Michelle had gone into the house to do the lunch dishes.

"No," Bill said. "Her husband is Indian. He left her a while back and took off up north. She stayed on the reserve with her three kids. They're Indian."

"Just like us," Doris said.

"Just like you," Bill replied.

"Well, Doris… we should probably get that dog home," Gloria said, pulling her legs out of the water.

"We probably should," Doris agreed.

"Already?" Bill asked.

"It's after three," Gloria said.

"Oh, okay, I'll get the dog and meet you out front," Bill said. "Anyone who wants to say goodbye to the puppy meet me on the front porch in two minutes!" He yelled toward the pool. Then he quickly dried himself off, put his velour shirt back on, and walked back into the house.

"Me!" Alice shouted, jumping out of the pool.

"Me!" Darlene and Erica yelled in unison.

"Me too!" Corey yelled, following behind the girls.

"Should we go in and say goodbye to Michelle?" Gloria asked.

"Nah," Doris said, drying her hair as best she could with a beach towel.

Gloria and Doris put on their sandals, grabbed their purses from the back porch, and walked around the side of the house to the front yard where all the kids were waiting on the porch to say goodbye to the puppy.

Bill came out of the front door cradling the puppy in one arm followed by Kanien. He placed the puppy gently on the front porch.

"Let his mother say goodbye first," he said.

The puppy sat for a second, cocked its head, and scampered toward his mother. Kanien sniffed the puppy and nuzzled under its belly as the puppy rolled onto its back. Kanien licked the smooth skin of the puppy's underbelly and then licked the puppy's face.

She knows she's losing her baby, Gloria thought, suddenly choking up. Finally, Kanien poked the puppy once more with her nose and walked down the steps and laid down in the shade below the porch stairs.

"Alight, kids! I don't want any of that bullshit crying like last time, understand?" Bill said.

Bill handed the dog to Alice and walked down the stairs to Doris's car where Gloria and Doris were standing. "Michelle says goodbye. She's doing laundry now."

Doris gave Gloria a side look that Gloria understood.

"Oh, I forgot, one sec," Bill said. He ran back up the front porch stairs past the kids into his house, the screen door slamming behind him.

"She's doing his *laundry*," Doris said, under her breath.

"Shhh," Gloria said.

Bill came out the front door again carrying a small cardboard box, the sports section of the newspaper, and a brown paper bag.

"Put this paper in the cardboard box and put the box on the floor of the car by your feet, Gloria," he said. "He might piss or get car sick, eh."

"Let's hope he doesn't," Doris said.

"And this is some Puppy Chow." He handed Gloria the brown paper bag. "That should do you until you can get to the store. I mix the Puppy Chow with powdered milk and add water. Do you have powdered milk?"

Is he kidding? Gloria wondered.

"Yes, I have powdered milk," she said. "And you said Troy can start house training him right away?"

"Yep, he's already paper-trained. Tell your son to keep moving the newspaper closer to the backdoor, say over a week, and then put the paper outside the door on the grass. Then if he starts to piss or shit in the house, grab him by the scruff of the neck and toss him outside. Then treat him like he's the best dog in the world. He'll do anything in the world for you if he knows that's what you want. It really shouldn't take more than a week or two. Golden Retrievers are smart Trust me, it's easier than training a kid."

"Well, you trained three kids, Gloria, so this should be a breeze," Doris said.

"You can get him his first shots at the vet anytime now. There's an animal hospital on Queenston Road that's pretty good."

"I'll tell Troy. He's going to look after all that."

"Got a name for him yet?"

"Ted said the last time I went up to the hospital that he wants to name him Reefer," Gloria said, rolling her eyes.

"I think it's a great name," Bill said.

"So do I!" said Doris.

"I like your purple nails, by the way, Doris," Bill said, pointing to Doris's hands.

"Thank you! It's called Practically Plum," Doris said, holding out both her hands.

"It's puce, Doris. It should be called Absolutely Puce." Gloria said.

"Bring Josh by for a swim sometime. It would be good for him to see the reserve and get a bit of his Indian culture too," Bill said.

"Josh gets kind of nervous around kids he doesn't know. You should see the trouble I'm having trying to get him to camp."

"Then tell him to bring a friend with him."

"Okay, we'll see," Gloria said.

"Thanks again for the swim and beers," Doris said.

"Oh shoot!" Gloria said. "I almost forgot to give you the money for the dog. Twenty-five, you said?"

"I almost forgot too," said Bill.

Gloria rooted around her purse, around the fruit Lifesavers and plastic hair bonnet, looking for her pocketbook. She handed Bill a twenty and a five. He took the bills and then reached out and touched her arm above the elbow. It was just a friendly gesture, but there was, Gloria thought, something else. A chill started on her shoulder and went down the length of the arm. She glanced at his arm beside hers. It was almost the same hue. It didn't matter that they were, like he said, from different tribes with a bloody history. Chippewa and Iroquois. Goosebumps formed on her arm. Noticeable. He stared at her arm and then looked up at her. Her face grew warm.

"Okay, kids! That's enough with the goddamn goodbyes. Bring that dog down here now!" Bill yelled.

"I want to take Tiny down to her!" Alice yelled, pushing Corey aside.

Corey sobbed quietly and leaned on the railing near the stairs between Darlene and Erica. Alice stood up and, holding the puppy in her arms, began to slowly walk down the front porch steps. Then, as the girl stepped down on the second step, her left bare foot slipped out from under her on some pool water that had been tracked from the backyard and she tumbled sideways off the side of the wooden porch stairs onto the front yard.

She hit the ground hard landing on the puppy.

There was a thud and a horrible cracking noise that made Gloria jolt in shock as Doris covered her eyes with her hands. Alice, eyes wide in terror, slowly got up off the ground as the puppy lay motionless on the brown grass by the stairs, his mouth open and his pink tongue hanging out. Bill ran to the puppy and, picking it up gently with both hands, stroked his head between the ears as Kanien stood beside him.

"Come on, boy," Bill said. "Come on, little guy."

"He's dead! He's dead!" Alice screamed.

"You killed him!" Corey yelled.

Corey took a step back, covered his face with his hands, and sobbed while Alice ran up the stairs and into the living room, still screaming.

"Fuck! That's a waste," Bill said, laying the puppy on the ground.

"My, God! What happened?" Michelle yelled from inside the house.

"Michelle, get all the kids into the house!" Bill yelled.

Kanien laid down beside her puppy and continued to lick its face until Bill finally grabbed her by the collar and pulled her into the house too. Still, even behind the screen door, she stood watching her puppy. Her wet nose poked out though the hole in the front screen door.

Fifteen minutes later Doris and Gloria were headed back to Hamilton. None of the children, nor Kanien, were invited to say goodbye to the second puppy, the larger more rambunctious one, that, after calming her down, Bill had talked Gloria into taking home with her. The first puppy, Bill assured her, would be buried in a really nice spot on the reserve. And, Bill said, Gloria could still have the larger puppy for the runt-price of twenty-five dollars.

"My God! That was one of the worst things I've ever seen," Doris said. "I'm going to have nightmares for weeks. That poor puppy. That sound."

"If you keep talking about it, Doris, I'm going to start crying again.

"Okay. Let's change the subject. That Bill is a dreamboat," Doris said as she turned onto Highway 6 and headed back toward Hamilton.

"He is," Gloria agreed.

"He couldn't take his eyes off you, Gloria. I watched him watch you with those dark brown eyes all afternoon."

Gloria felt her face get warm again and she turned toward the window, letting the hot June air blow into her face.

"Oh, you dirty dog!" Doris said.

The puppy had pooped on the newspaper at Gloria's feet and then sat down in it. Now she would have to give him a bath when she got home.

"He's getting back at you because he knows he was your second choice," said Doris, laughing.

Nothing new there, Gloria thought. *It seems like most of my life all I ever got was my second choice.*

Later that month, Gloria sat at her machine, working another hot afternoon shift at Munro. The electric fan on the ceiling above her had broken during the day shift and Gloria had to rely on a small portable oscillating fan on a pedestal that the supervisor had placed between Gloria and her friend Miriam Svoboda's machines. All it really did was blow around the hot air, rotating its head from left to right like it was watching an excruciatingly slow game of tennis. Exhausted and flushed, Gloria kept a small hand towel tossed over her shoulder, reaching for it every few minutes when perspiration began to drip off her nose onto the olive-green machine.

Gloria's machine, the same one she had been sitting behind for almost two decades, had been re-painted every few years. Over the years they had painted it light green, dark green, olive green and every shade of green in between but within a few months it was always black again, covered with the grease that lubricated the internal parts. The machine had to be oiled at least once a day and since they never stopped the machine when it was being greased, often the hot oil would splash onto Gloria's arms and into her face if the machinist used too much.

Gloria's hands, swift at pulling down the mouth of the machine, flipping a switch by her thumb to cut the steel from the large coils that fed the machine then snatching the steel rods out and tossing them in the steel bin beside her, still moved with caution. Over the years there had been girls, momentarily distracted, that had lost fingers in the machines at Munro. Even the supervisor's daughter, only there at Munro as temporary help while on summer holidays from Iroquois College, had lost a finger in Gloria's machine. But now, after all these years, Gloria's machine had become more like an extension of her own body. It was as if Gloria's own hands were gripping the steel coil and slicing into it.

The house would be quiet when I get home, she thought. Except for the puppy that was always at her feet. Troy was either working at the gas station or off with his friends to one of the loud east end bars like the Derby or the Jockey Club. God knows what he was up to. He had told her not to expect him home tonight. And Josh was at Doris and Ken's for the night. Doris was taking Josh and his cousins to see *Smokey and the Bandit* at the Starlight Drive-In.

At 7:00pm Gloria sat in the lunchroom with a chicken loaf sandwich and a cup of lukewarm tea from the coffee vending machine. Nearly everyone else, including Miriam and Bill, had opted to eat outside beside the parking lot on the picnic tables tonight, but Gloria wasn't in the mood for factory merriment of jokes, talking about the weekend or the (mostly) innocent flirting between the women and men in the plant. She lifted the sandwich to her mouth and noticed her hands shaking ever so slightly. She had never been to a doctor but knew the cause; Gloria had seen the same thing happen to the older women at Munro. All the years she had spent with her hands gripped to that big rattling machine of hers was causing nerve damage to her hands. Now the tips of her fingers were also starting to go numb, and she was dropping the odd plate and glass at home.

This was Gloria's eighteenth summer at Munro, and she still had almost thirty years to go before she could retire. She inspected her right hand as it trembled the chicken loaf sandwich. God knows in what shape her hands would be like then. She already had the hands of an old lady.

Oh well, she thought as she bit into the sandwich, there was nothing to do about it now. She wrapped up half of her sandwich, tossed it into the brown paper lunch bag, and brushed the crumbs off the lunchroom table. Whether it was the heat or her visit with Ted that morning where he told her about his grand plan on getting the six thousand dollars, she couldn't eat.

All the scratched yellow Plexiglas windows in the lunchroom were open, but it was still stifling with heat, factory dust, and cigarette smoke hanging in the air. One of the things they were fighting for with their new contract with Munro was heat breaks. Most other factories in the city had already won them long ago. In the late sixties Ted and the rest of his shift had a wildcat strike at Wentworth Steel over heat breaks. It was messy, and some people were fired, but, still, they won their heat breaks.

Gloria hoped there wouldn't be a strike at Munro next month. It would be a terrible time for a strike, even if Gloria did agree to borrow that money from Abe. A pretty big *if* it was too.

The rest of Gloria's shift went by slowly, that was usual for a Friday afternoon. The girls were collectively obtaining a better mood as the last hours passed and plans were made of where to go for a few quick drinks before the bars had their last call. Bill passed a few times, smiling at her and Miriam each time he did. He must have been under a truck or fixing one of the machines in the plant, Gloria thought, because the back of his overalls had become dirtier and dirtier, caked with more grease and grime, each time he passed.

Gloria wondered how Michelle would get that grease out his work clothes. If I were washing Bill's work clothes, Gloria thought, I'd use Dawn dish soap on the grease first and scrub them by hand in the laundry tub to break down all that grease and then rinse them and put in the washer with Tide. That usually did the trick with Ted's work clothes.

"A lot of the girls are going to the Come by Chance for a drink after work. They never ask us to go," Miriam said, stopping at Gloria's machine after returning from the ladies' room.

"We're too old for them," Gloria said. She stopped working and placed her hands at her side.

"I can remember the days we used to rush out of here for a drink on Fridays after afternoon shifts. We'd go to the Jockey Club, remember?"

"These girls were babies then," Gloria said. "And we never asked any of the older women who were around then to join us either."

"You used to bring a dress and that fur coat of yours to work to change into, you remember that?"

"We thought we were really something, didn't we?" Gloria said.

Miriam dabbed the sweat from her forehead with some paper towel she had taken from the ladies' room.

"So," Miriam said. "Are you really going to ask him for the money?"

"I don't know," answered Gloria. "Unless something happens. I'm still hoping my cousin will have a change of heart at the last moment, so I won't have to go through with it."

Miriam nodded slowly. "Well, you have to do what you have to do."

Miriam disapproved. Gloria knew it. Miriam was one of her best friends, maybe her best friend after Doris, but what did Miriam Svoboda, unmarried and childless, know about what Gloria was going through? Tonight, like every night, Miriam would take the Parkdale bus down Woodward to her one-room apartment across from Edmund Park and tomorrow would get up early to spend the day with her elderly mother at Glen Echo Nursing Home and then go home and watch television. That was Miriam's life. That was all Miriam's life was going to be. If she disapproved, she was more than welcome to give Gloria the six thousand dollars and then Gloria wouldn't have to go see Abe at all.

At 11pm Gloria punched out and walked out to the Munro parking lot with her purse slung over her shoulder as Miriam, afraid of missing her bus, waved goodbye and walked quickly away to the bus stop. The younger girls, seven or eight of them, who had changed into their tight jeans and T-shirts all piled into two small cars on their way to the Come by Chance for last call. Gloria tried to imagine herself in those jeans and a tight T-shirt that showed off her chest and chuckled.

"Gloria, old girl, that ship has sailed," she said to herself.

Under a sputtering security light in the parking lot, Gloria saw Bill standing by the back of his red pickup truck with a cigarette in his mouth. He put his work boots, lunchbox, and overalls in the back of his truck and shut it hard with a clank.

"Hot day, eh," he said.

His black hair was wet from just showering in the men's locker room and combed back, hanging down his back like it was in the pool. He had changed into a white T-shirt, cut-off denim shorts, and a pair of brown leather sandals. The men, who always got dirtier, usually showered and changed before going home but, even though there was a shower in the ladies' locker room, the women at Munro never did. Those girls headed to the Come by Chance only did a quick wash of their face, necks, and underarms in the locker room, changed into a clean pair of underwear they keep in their purse, and then dabbed on some perfume. An east end ladies' wash.

"Days like this are why we really need heat breaks," Gloria said, stopping at the back of the pickup. "And they never did fix my ceiling fan. They said they'd have someone in tomorrow to look at it so, hopefully, it'll be working by our dayshift on Monday."

"When I get home I'm jumping right in the pool," Bill said.

"That would be nice."

"I'm not even putting on swim trunks. I'm just hopping in with my underwear." He flicked the ashes of his cigarette to his side and grinned.

Gloria blushed slightly as she pictured, quite unintentionally, how Bill would look getting out of his pool, standing on that metal deck with the moonlight on his back and wet white underwear hugging his brown skin.

"So, how's the puppy?" Bill asked, unlocking the driver's door of the truck. "What did you say you named him? Doobie?"

"Reefer. Ted's idea, of course."

"I knew it was either Reefer or Doobie."

"He's doing fine. Josh is over the moon having a dog. And the puppy is practically trained already."

"He must be eating a lot too."

"Oh, God, yes. He's like a bottomless pit. I said to Ted the last time I saw him that the puppy must be hollow inside."

"Ha, I know! Someday I'd like to come over to your place and see how he's doing. I feel attached to him. Maybe because we lost the little one."

"Of course, anytime you want. Do you think he still knows who you are?"

"Oh, retrievers are like elephants, they never forget. I'll be his daddy forever. Hey, I got an idea, why don't I drive you home and see the little guy right now. Climb in."

He took a final drag of his cigarette and threw it on the gravel beside of the truck.

Gloria looked around the parking lot. Most of the afternoon shift had already left for their weekend and only a few cars were left, mostly supervisors closing up shop.

"Alright, thanks" she said.

She walked to the passenger side of the pickup, opened the door, and climbed in, putting her purse on her lap. The pickup smelled like pine car air freshener and the pink hand soap that they used in the restrooms at Munro; the hand soap that came in big plastic jugs and looked like Thrill dishwashing soap but smelled like turpentine and overripe cherries.

"Troy should be home," Gloria lied. "Or will be home soon. And he can tell you how he housebroke the puppy so quickly. He's working an afternoon shift as well."

Bill drove down Woodward Avenue toward Alkeld Street, passing Laura Secord School.

"Schools look lonely in the summer, eh?" Bill said. "Like they've gone to sleep or something. Like they're just waiting for the kids to come back so they can wake up again."

"I think they have Alcoholics Anonymous meetings there a couple of times a week," Gloria said. "So, it can't get all that lonely."

"Do I turn left or right at the stop sign?"

"Left."

"I didn't even know there were houses down that way. And I've worked at Munro for years."

"People say that all the time. But here we are, just the same. It's the blue house with the black shutters." Gloria pointed at her house.

"That's a nice little house," Bill said, parking his pickup on the street in front of Gloria's house.

Gloria had heard people describe her house as 'nice' and 'little' many times. Well, it's better than being called ugly or creepy, she thought, stepping down from the passenger side.

"You got any beer?" Bill asked as he slammed the driver's side door

"Beer?"

"Yeah, brown boozy liquid with bubbles," Bill said, laughing.

She tried to remember the contents of her refrigerator. Doris had visited yesterday and drank a few, but there were, she believed, three or four bottles left. Since Ted had been gone, she really hadn't needed to buy any beer, except occasionally for Doris and Lydia. She didn't drink the stuff.

"I have a few in the cooler in the back of my truck if you're out. Me and the guys had a couple of them at lunch, but I have some left."

"I'm pretty sure I have a few bottles in the fridge," Gloria said.

They walked up the front stairs and Gloria could hear the high-pitched bark of Reefer as she put her key in the door.

"Shush, you!" Gloria said, unlocking the door.

Any doubt that Reefer would forget Bill after two weeks was gone when Bill walked up to the door. Gloria had never seen the dog that excited to see any of them. Reefer squeezed through the door before she had even opened it all the way and jumped up on Bill's bare legs wagging his tail and yelping. Then Reefer ran down the porch stairs to the front lawn, squatted, and peed.

"He's still pees like a girl," Gloria said.

"They don't start to lift their leg until they're near a year. It's a territorial thing. He's just a puppy. He's not territorial yet."

Reefer came running back up the front stairs and again began yelping and jumping at Bill's feet.

"Stop that!" Gloria said, trying to grab the puppy by the collar, but Bill scooped him up with one hand, cradled it in his arms, and carried him in the front door as the dog excitedly licked Bill's face.

"Ah, yeah. You remember me, don't you, boy?" Bill said.

Gloria turned on her living room lamp illuminating the small room and opened the front picture window curtains wide. Now all the busybodies on the street could see exactly what was going on in her living room— nothing.

Before she could tell Bill he could leave his sandals on, he had kicked them off by the front door. "Sit down and I'll get you your beer," she said.

She walked into the kitchen, opened an amber bottle of IPA beer, poured herself a glass of pink lemonade from a tan Tupperware pitcher, and then placed both drinks on the yellow countertop. She tore a piece of pink paper towel off the roll under the cupboard and patted her face. Her heart beat quickly. She closed her eyes for a moment and tried to collect herself. She picked up the drinks and walked back to the living room where Bill now sat in Ted's chair. At his feet, Reefer laid on his belly, dozing off.

"I think I owe you a few of these after all the beer Doris drank at your place that day," Gloria said, handing Bill the cold amber bottle.

Bill stretched out his arm and Gloria noticed that he had light brown down covering his arm that shone golden in the lamplight. She turned on the television to the late local news and sat down on the sofa, holding her pink lemonade in her lap with both hands.

"I like your sister," Bill said, after two big gulps of beer. "And I dig that she's interested in her Native heritage. She asked me a lot of questions while we were in the pool. She even said she wanted to go to a powwow with me and the kids."

"A powwow?" Gloria said.

"You know what I think?"

"What?"

"I think your ancestors are calling to you and Doris."

"Ancestors?" Gloria said incredulously. She smiled and shook her head. "You aren't one of those people who believe in spirits and ghosts like my mother-in-law, are you?"

"Well, I'm not sure what I believe, but it's kind of a nice way of putting it, eh? When someone, like you and Doris, who lost or got separated from their culture suddenly wants to learn more about their heritage and their history? It's like your ancestors calling you."

"We don't know anything about our heritage. Other than what

we saw growing up on television. It's so strange that being just one generation removed from my mother's reserve in Minnesota, we've lost every connection to it and our culture. I'd like to see a powwow too someday. Maybe I'll finally find someplace where I feel I belong."

Bill looked at her intently with his dark brown eyes.

"My younger sister Lydia went to a real powwow once. That's when she was dating a full-blooded Indian girl and... I mean—" Gloria stopped.

Even the puppy looked up at her, seemingly surprised by the sudden silence in the room.

"My sister, Lydia, is a lesbian," she said. "She's homosexual and we all love her and accept it. End of story."

Gloria had heard people say the worst things about Lydia for years and mostly expected the worse from people when she mentioned that she had a gay sister. Even from people she liked. Now she steeled herself against whatever Bill was going to say.

"You know," Bill said, "my mother once told me about an ancestor of mine who, even though she was a woman, had dressed in men's clothes and fought alongside other Mohawks with the English during the War of 1812. And they say that she was fucking fearless, more dangerous than most of our warrior men."

"Really? Is that true?"

"It's what my mother told me."

"What a wonderful story!" Gloria said. She would have to remember to tell Lydia about that, a woman warrior as fierce as any man. Lydia would get a kick out of it.

"I don't know if this ancestor was gay or lesbian or just liked to dress like a man," Bill said. "But I've heard some of our elders say that homosexuals once held esteemed positions in our culture. They were thought to have the souls of both men and women and, before the white man came, homosexuals were said to be our healers and storytellers. They were keepers of our knowledge and traditions. But then the white men came with their own churches and their own healers, and their own stories and they told us what we were doing, and what we believed, was wrong."

He gently rubbed Reefer's underbelly with his toes.

"My youngest brother, Chuck, is gay too," Bill said.

"You have a gay brother?"

"Yep, he lives in Toronto now with another guy in what he calls an 'urban reserve' with a bunch of friends. I call it a hippy commune in the city. But Chuck seems happy. We love him too."

Gloria smiled. "Do you want another beer, Bill? I still owe you a few."

"No, I should get going. If I have another, I'll fall asleep on the highway between here and Six Nations. And Alice will be up waiting for me. She likes to make me a sandwich or something when I get home from afternoon shift since Isabelle left. We had a couple of bad weeks after the puppy died, but she's better now."

"How long has Isabelle been gone?" Gloria asked.

"Over a year now. People say I should have known what was going on but... maybe I'm just an idiot."

"Do you miss her much?"

"I don't miss her much anymore, but I get lonely. Michelle helps some with that, eh?"

"I'm sure she does."

"And how long has Ted been away now?"

"Three months."

"Do you miss him much?"

"Yes. I don't think grown people are supposed to spend so much time by themselves. And I really hate sleeping alone."

Bill grinned widely, showing his protruding incisors.

"That's not what I mean," Gloria said shyly.

"I know exactly what you mean," Bill said. He put down his empty beer bottle on the coffee table and stood up. "Well, I better take off."

"Alight. I guess I'll see you Monday morning," Gloria said getting up. "Day shift again. I just hope they fix my fan by then."

Bill bent down by the door to slide the straps of his leather sandals over his heels. He had to keep pushing Reefer away as he jumped furiously up and down at his knees.

"Playtime is over, boy!" he said, softly shoving Reefer away again.

Suddenly, Bill stood up and quickly closed the front door with one hand. And there, with the two of them briefly hidden from any prying eyes of Alkeld Street, Bill leaned over and kissed Gloria gently, very gently, on the lips.

Her mouth opened naturally, and they kissed. His tongue, tasting of beer and cigarettes moved softly and nimbly into her mouth as her own tongue. Then, as swiftly as it had begun, Gloria pulled away. The entire episode lasted less than one minute in time. Less time than it took for him to put on his leather sandals.

"Christ, I'm sorry, Gloria. I don't know..."

"No, I'm sorry." She felt dizzy.

"I should go," he said, opening the door again.

"Yes."

Bill walked out the front door and across the front lawn to his truck as Gloria stood frozen at the door. He jumped in his truck and drove away, quickly, down Alkeld Street toward Woodward Avenue just as Troy drove up the driveway in Ted's Chevy Impala.

"We decided to call it a night early," Troy said, coming through the back door. "Is there anything to eat?"

"Eat?" Gloria said, still standing at the door.

"Yes, eat," Troy said, bending down to pet Reefer behind the ear. "It's when you put food in your mouth, chew and swallow."

"There's stew in the refrigerator from yesterday," Gloria said, continuing to look at the spot outside where Bill's truck had been parked a few minutes earlier. "It's always better the second day."

Perhaps my ancestors really are calling to me, Gloria thought. And what were they saying? It seemed they were whispering to her, *come home...*

Six

"I'm not okay, you're okay," Mrs. Wooley said.

She was pointing to a chart that she had written, once again, in chalk on the blackboard. 'You're okay, I'm not okay', was, she had said over and over, one of the worst things on her chart that anyone could possibly be. Mrs. Wooley was determined to plough this into their ten-year-old heads again and again before the school year ended.

Josh sat, still unconvinced, with his head resting on his left hand wondering if all teachers shopped at the same frumpy skirt and blouse store. He had been hearing this 'I'm okay' Transactual Analysis junk for the last nine months and, to be honest, Josh thought that Mrs. Wooley seemed obsessed with the whole TA idea, bringing up the principles in class at least once a day.

"What exciting new ideas we're going to learn!" Mrs. Wooley had said that first day of school when she stood in front of the class and held up the book *TA for Kids* before drawing a chart on the blackboard:

| I'm not OK | I'm OK |
You're OK	You're OK
I'm not OK	I'm OK
You're not OK	You're not OK

Throughout the school year, Mrs. Wooley made a point of using the TA Principle for whatever particular drama was happening in class that day. Diane Gibson steps on the class hamster and kills it? That was the perfect time to discuss how the entire class was in their judging parent state calling Diane such judging words as 'murderer', 'stupid' and 'creep'. Robbie Esposito gives Mike Fry a bloody nose at recess? It was his emotional child state that did it. Whenever something ugly happened in Class 4A, a glint of excitement crossed Mrs. Wooley's face. Another chance for her to discuss Transactual Analysis.

Josh had his doubts about Transactual Analysis from the get-go when he had tried to explain to his father this TA stuff that Miss Wooley was so gung-ho about.

"You see, there's three parts to all of us," Josh had said to his father. "You got a child, a parent, and an adult."

"Wouldn't that be nice, our own personal Trinity," his father had answered.

Then his father just smirked, shook his head and mumble something over his *Socialist Worker* about 'decadence' and finished by saying, "I think it's all horseshit, but you can decide for yourself. My only advice to you, Josh, is don't believe everything they tell you." And Josh knew exactly who his father was talking about when he said *they*. It was anyone who is in charge: teachers, politicians, bosses, foremen, churches (especially churches!). His father had even told Josh that Josh shouldn't blindly believe what his parents said either. How many fathers said that to their kids?

Like his father, Josh thought Transactual Analysis was, for the most part, a bunch of horseshit, especially all the jazz about "warm fuzzies". Warm fuzzies were what Mrs. Wooley called it when someone did or said something nice for someone else. There was a drawing of a warm fuzzy on the cover of *TA for Kids*. It had an enormous fuzzy head, a big smile, and wore a pair of sneakers. Josh thought it looked like a bargain-basement Sesame Street puppet.

Warm fuzzies had, in fact, became a type of currency in class 4A. Over the year, Mrs. Wooley would mimeograph hand-drawn pictures of the fuzzy creatures on red, yellow, and green paper and handed one out to students whenever she thought someone did or said something especially nice and warm. On their part, the students in class would exchange and trade them like baseball cards or cheap paper valentines. Josh didn't have many warm fuzzies. Not as many as he would have liked, anyway. He had once received a green one from Mrs. Wooley for letting Gary Lessing look on his math textbook during math class when Gary had forgotten his. But Josh didn't mind Gary pulling up his desk beside his at all. He liked how Gary's long eyelashes looked when he looked down at Josh's math textbook and how his long brown hair curled a bit around his ears and how he smelled like Irish Spring.

In Transactual Analysis, a cold prickly was the opposite of the warm fuzzy. Cold pricklies, according to Mrs. Wooley, had sharp spikes, angry faces with downturned eyebrows and clenched teeth. Unlike warm fuzzies, Mrs. Wooley didn't mimeograph cold pricklies and hand them out, which was a bit of a disappointment to Josh. If someone in the class called someone an 'ass', 'dick', or 'pig', Mrs. Wooley would say from her desk "Is that a cold prickly, I hear?" Josh thought if they were shamed and given a paper cold prickly, they might act a bit better next time.

Josh, for his part, did try his best not to give out any cold pricklies. Though he did, from time to time, feel completely justified in giving a cold prickly or two. Besides, how could anyone expect anything else from him when they called him 'faggot' or 'shithead'? If some kid in class tossed a cold prickly at Josh, they could expect to get one thrown back in their face, only bigger, meaner, and pricklier.

"And what's the best thing on the chart to be, Josh?" Mrs. Wooley now said, staring at him with cold blue eyes.

"I'm okay, you're okay," Josh said.

"I'm okay, you're okay! Exactly right, Josh! And I hope you all remember that when we say our goodbyes in a few weeks."

You sound like an idiot, Mrs. Wooley.

Since Josh's father had been taken to the Hamilton Psychiatric Hospital, in no way had Josh been feeling like everything was okay. In fact, if he were to plot himself on that dumb-ass chart of Mrs. Wooley's, Josh would have to make a new category that said, "I'm not okay, you're not okay, and neither is anyone or anything else in the whole fucking world". Nothing was going to be okay until his father came home. Once his father was back on Alkeld Street then *maybe* everything would be okay again. Even Josh's new puppy wasn't enough to make everything okay.

"Maybe, in the years to come, you could all give each other a warm fuzzy occasionally. Would you do that for me? Maybe, when you see each other walking down the street?" Mrs. Wooley said.

"Yes!" The entire class said. The entire class, that is, except Josh.

"I will!" Anne-Marie McCourt said with such unbridled euphoria that it gave Josh the creeps.

Anne-Marie was a skinny girl with a pinched face, messy mousy brown hair, an overbite, and glasses who had sat in front of Josh all year. Josh couldn't imagine Anne-Marie giving anyone a warm fuzzy since she had never given Josh anything but nasty looks the entire school year, even once telling him he smelled. Josh in turn called Anne-Marie an ugly piece of shit to even things out. Anne-Marie was one of five kids in the class who had been adopted. Everyone else in the McCourt family was blonde with blue eyes and then there was old Anne-Marie, all bones, eyeglasses, and buckteeth.

"And if you saw me walking down the street, would you stop and give me a big warm fuzzy too?" Mrs. Wooley continued.

"Yes!" the class said, even louder.

"Oh, yes, Miss!" Anne-Marie shouted.

I wouldn't even give you the time of day, you fruitcake.

At recess, Josh sat alone where the schoolyard asphalt met the field at Laura Secord Elementary School eating a bag of M&Ms he had bought at Boris' Little Variety on his way to school and watching the older boys play Red Rover. Josh could always tell when someone wanted to be on the other team because they pretended like they couldn't break through the Red Rover line. These boys were terrible at play-acting. Josh considered himself pretty good at play-acting. Hadn't he been acting like he wasn't in the garage the night his father cut his throat? Acting was just lying with your whole body.

Josh tossed a red M&M in his mouth and thought about the coming summer vacation. His mother was still determined to send him off to Camp Ronkewe.

"For three whole fucking weeks!" he said to himself.

Josh had just begun saying the f-word out loud more since hanging out with Shannon Perry at the fort by Red Hill Creek. Josh enjoyed the weight and acidic taste of the word *fuck* in his mouth. It was powerful. Josh also liked the way the other kids at Laura Secord Elementary looked shocked when he used it, even the older boys. Josh's father said 'fuck' all the time and Josh decided from now on, being practically eleven and smoking almost an entire pack of cigarettes a week, he was going to say it too.

He still had a couple of weeks to figure out how he would get out of the whole Cub Scout camp thing. He was not too shabby at figuring out how to get out of stuff. Once he had gotten out of sleeping over at his Aunt Sue's by giving himself a bloody nose. A *Bic* pen and a few twists up his nose and he was sleeping in his own bed on Alkeld Street. But he would need more than a bloody nose to get out of Cub Scout camp. And Josh was pretty sure his mother would just stuff his nose full of toilet paper and toss him out of the car at the camp. After all, hadn't his parents already paid the thirty dollars for the three weeks at the camp?

"Fuck camp," Josh said.

He lifted the bag of M&Ms and shook the last bits of broken loose candy shell and chocolate into his mouth, stood up, and walked toward the big green metal garbage can to toss the empty bag.

Beside the garbage can was a painted yellow line about six inches thick that ran across the asphalt and dissected the playground in two. On the opposite side was the 'girls-only side' so girls could play by themselves without being bothered by boys. The girls, however, were allowed on both sides of the yellow line, allowing them on all parts of the playground plus the field along the back of Laura Secord School, so girls had an extra hunk of schoolyard just for them. Josh thought this setup was incredibly unfair.

Josh looked around and, seeing no one looking his way, put his foot on the faded yellow line on the asphalt and then slid his foot across it. What makes *this* the girls' side anyway? Why should girls get more of the schoolyard than the boys? And most of the girls choose to play with the boys anyway. The girls' side of the playground was mostly empty, except for a handful of girls just standing around talking or playing double Dutch.

As Josh stood leaning against the red brick wall of the school with his hands behind his back waiting for the bell to signal the end of recess, Anne-Marie McCourt walked toward him and, crossing the yellow line, stood in front of Josh grinning. She was with four other girls who all stood a few feet behind her, on the other side of the yellow line.

"I saw you put your foot over the girl's line. You want to be a girl, don't you?" Anne-Marie said.

Her feet were spread apart, ready to run to the girls' side if Josh lunged at her. She doesn't need to, Josh thought, I'm sure not going to run after her.

"Leave me alone," Josh said, trying to sound as uninterested as he could.

He looked away at the boys still playing Red Rover on the field. He had heard enough of this shit, calling him a girl, from the boys at Laura Secord School and now even creeps like Anne-Marie were getting in on the act. Still, Josh refused to go to Mrs. Wooley and complain. First of all, Mrs. Wooley would probably just make a TA example out of it and, second of all, it wouldn't stop the teasing, and, finally, it would get back to his mother.

"I just wanted you to know that everyone in class thinks you're a queer too," Anne-Marie said. She laughed and ran to the girls' side of the schoolyard to where the other girls were, looking at Josh and snickering.

Josh shrugged and walked back toward where the asphalt met the grass and kicked his red ADIDAS shoe at the brown grass. Tomorrow was Saturday and he'd have two full days off before he had to come back to Laura Secord. After recess, Miss Wooley would be reading from *Prince Caspian*. She was spending more time reading during the afternoon now that the school year was coming to a close, probably to make sure that we finished that damned book before school ended. Or else the class would never know what happened to that son-of-a-bitch, Caspian, Josh thought, smiling. Well, all the class but him. Josh had read all the Chronicles of Narnia, starting with *The Lion, the Witch and the Wardrobe* that year. And, in his opinion, they had got progressively crummier as the series went on.

Across the field, all the boys playing Red Rover were now on one team with only two of the smallest boys on the other. *Game over.* Maybe tomorrow I'll play too, he thought as the bell rang. Being big for his age, he could ram through any of the grade fours or fives. Though, maybe the other boys wouldn't want him on their team and never call him over so he'd end up being left on the side with those two little loser kids. No, he wouldn't play Red Rover tomorrow or any time soon. Besides, running made his chest and side hurt and he tried to avoid it during gym class when Mrs. Wooley would put on her blue ladies' PUMA running shoes and make all of class 4A (except her) run around the school field. Josh was always last, coming in huffing and puffing. Always.

The bell rang and Josh lined up against the school with his class in the boys' line. Across from him Anne-Marie McCourt stood in the girls' line with her back to him. Her mousy hair needed a good combing, Josh thought, leaning over to her.

"You're adopted," Josh said.

"So!" Anne-Marie said quickly, spinning around facing Josh.

"Your real mother took one look at you after you were born and she said, get this thing away from me. She makes me sick."

"You are such a liar, Josh Moore!" Anne-Marie shouted.

"Not only did your real parents not want you," Josh said, lowering his voice. "I heard even your adoptive mother say she wished she'd never adopted you. She said she didn't think she'd get stuck with you. She said she never would have taken you if she knew you were going to grow up to be so stupid, ugly, and gross."

"You lie!" Anne-Marie's face turned red and twisted into an angry and hurt frown. Her bottom lip quivered.

"Sorry, but it's the truth. I overheard your mom say it to my mother during the Christmas pageant. She said it quietly and made my mother promise not to tell anyone how much she hates you."

"Liar!" Ann-Marie yelled.

"I wasn't even going to tell you, but since you're so stupid, I changed my mind. Your mom said she wanted a prettier girl and made a big mistake when they got you with your buckteeth and hog face. She said she wished she'd left you in the orphanage and she might take you back there at the end of the school year."

"That's not true!"

"No one loves you," Josh said slowly, to make each word hurt as much as possible. "And no one ever will."

Anne-Marie shook her head. "I'm telling!"

"Go ahead." Josh grinned. "Then everyone will know your mother hates you."

Anne-Marie's eyes filled with tears. *Did she really believe me*, Josh wondered? Maybe she didn't believe him completely, but she believed him a little bit. Enough to really hurt.

Now that's how you give a cold prickly.

When they had all returned to their classroom, Ann-Marie put her head down on her desk, turned her face toward the wall and cried softly as Mrs. Wooley began reading from *Prince Caspian* again.

For fifteen minutes, Mrs. Wooley read through a few pages of C.S. Lewis, stopping once or twice to walk slowly up and down the row of desks every time a black and white illustration was included on the page and each kid in class would crane his or her neck to see it. Josh didn't bother looking at the pictures; he had seen them all before. In front of him Anne-Marie, her nose still running, glanced up at the drawing of the boy Prince and then put her head back on her desk.

After she stopped reading at a rather uninteresting spot in the middle of a chapter, Mrs. Wooley slapped the paperback book closed with one hand and grinned a rather insincere teacher smile.

"Does anyone have any clipping for current events?" she asked.

Josh had almost forgotten. He raised his hand, the only one in class that did. Once nearly half the kids came to school holding a photo from the newspaper of the new American President carrying his daughter's dollhouse with the headline *Carter Moves Amy's Dollhouse into the White House*. But now, near the end of the school year, days would go by without anyone having remembered a news article for current events.

"Excellent! Come up and share it with us all, Josh," Mrs. Wooley said.

She sat down at her desk, which for some reason was at the side of the classroom and not in the front like every other teacher at Laura Secord School. Why would a teacher want to always look at her class sideways and then have to walk up to the front of the class to teach? Truth was, Josh had concluded, that Mrs. Wooley was just an out-and-out oddball.

He rose, walked to the front of the classroom, and pulled a folded piece of newsprint out of the back pocket of his jeans. He was careful not to rip it because he was planning on keeping it with the other articles he had collected about the Ragno murders. Josh had found the murder story of the killer father especially interesting, and he kept all the newspaper clippings he had gathered for months stacked in the bottom drawer of the desk in his bedroom until he could tape them all properly in a scrapbook that Josh decided he'd call "The Ragno Murders" or "When Fathers Kill."

Josh had been following the grisly story since hearing about the wife and daughter's bodies washing up on the shore of Lake Ontario. The lake was only a few blocks, walking distance, from his house on Alkeld Street and the whole Jake Ragno story was scary and fascinating and horrible all at once. And it seemed as if everyone in Hamilton was talking about the murders and the coming trial. Just yesterday, Josh's Aunt Doris blabbed on about it for over half an hour, smoking and drinking tea with Josh's mother as Josh sat on the living room floor pretending to watch television, all the while listening intently to every gruesome tidbit.

"This article is about all the evidence they have against Jake Ragno when he goes to trial in November," Josh began. "It tells most of the story about the murders and gives a timeline too. They also write about how the police searched for the body of the four-year-old son, Alan, but haven't found him yet."

Josh stopped for a bit of dramatic pause to let that set in. From her desk at the side of the classroom the teacher frowned slightly.

"The police were looking for the boy's body in the mouths of rivers and creeks around Lake Ontario, but they never found anything and now they stopped looking. The article said they did snag something or other once when they were dragging the rivers, but they lost it and weren't able to snag it again. They said it might have been the little boy, but no one is saying that for sure. But if I were the police, I would go back to that same spot and try to snag whatever it was with their hook again. That's what they use, great big hooks that stick into bodies lying at the bottom of the lake. They think that the boy was probably wrapped up the same way as his mom and sister, in garbage bags inside a Hudson Bay point blanket with the coloured stripes, and that someday soon he might wash up on shore, maybe even right here at the end of Woodward Avenue on Van Wagner's Beach. Or I guess fish could eat him and he would never be found. But the article didn't say that about the fish, I'm just guessing about that."

"Thank you, Josh," said Miss Wooley, cutting him off before he was really done. "Does anyone have any questions for Josh about his current events article?"

Gary Lessing put up his hand.

"Gary?" Josh said.

"Do you think they'll ever find the missing kid?" Gary asked.

"That's a good question. Nobody knows. Not even the police," Josh said, shrugging his shoulders.

"Do they know if the father will go to the electric chair for killing them?" another boy asked without putting up his hand.

"I hope so!" Josh said.

"No," Mrs. Wooley interrupted. "No. Canada does not have capital punishment. That means we do not execute people anymore for crimes. Not even for murder."

The entire class looked particularly morose learning this news. Josh had seen enough movies to know that killers go to the electric chair or get hanged or something equally gruesome at the end. It was how you evened things out.

"Anything else, Josh?" Mrs. Wooley asked, getting up from her chair.

"Yeah," Josh said.

Mrs. Wooley sighed and sat back down.

"The police say that when they took the little girl, Jennifer, she was eight, out of the blanket and garbage bags she was wrapped in, they could still see a purple Kool-Aid moustache on her upper lip," Josh said.

"Alright, Josh, I think that's more than enough. Thank you." She stood up again.

"Oh! And one more thing, the police found out that the knots he used to tie up his wife and daughters' hands and feet were the same kind of knot that were used in some dirty magazines Jake Ragno had hidden in his house."

"Joshua, that's enough! You can go back to your seat now," Mrs. Wooley said. She seemed surprised at how angrily she had spoken to Josh and it took a few seconds for her to compose herself again.

Josh returned to his seat even though there were still hands up and more questions that he probably could have answered with no problem at all. He knew all about the Ragno murder. Though he was relieved that Mrs. Wooley didn't try to make some Transactual Analysis argument out of the murders. What would she say? "That was some cold prickly Jake Ragno gave to his family, wasn't it, class?"

No, Josh determined, TA couldn't explain everything. Maybe TA *was* decadent, like his father said.

Whatever that meant.

The next day was Saturday. Josh had planned to simply sit in front of the TV and watch Saturday morning cartoons and lounge around until his mother would eventually tell him to get out of the house and into the fresh air for a while. Then he would either ride his bike around the neighbourhood or sneak down to the creek to see if Shannon Perry was around. Even though Josh often did as his mother told him, that was how you got through life without too many problems from parents, other times the rules his mother made were just too stupid to follow. That was why, though his mother forbade him to go to the creek or hang around Shannon, he still would. If the rules were stupid, then they should be broken. Besides, no one was the boss of me, Josh thought.

He had made himself toast with peanut butter and a cup of instant coffee for breakfast. If there were mothers on Alkeld Street who got up and made their kids breakfast (at least any kid over five years old) Josh didn't know any. Mothers were either already at work or sleeping because of shift work. And it was an awful stupid kid who couldn't at least dump Alpha-Bits in a bowl and add milk. The coffee, however, like his cussing, was a relatively new addition. He had started drinking tea when he was seven or eight and graduated to coffee earlier that year. His parents didn't care. Still, he needed two big teaspoons of sugar to make it taste any good.

Josh's new puppy, Reefer, was sleeping in the kitchen. Puppies, Josh concluded, slept far too much. And it was already evident that this dog would not really be *his* dog. The puppy seemed to prefer both his brother, Troy, and his mother over Josh, always choosing to sit by Troy or snuggle against Josh's mother's feet.

In the family pecking order, Josh was always at the bottom and now he was being pushed to the bottom again— this time by the dog. But Josh didn't really mind so much. The puppy still liked to jump on Josh's belly and face when Josh would lie on the floor, which always made Josh laugh. He had tried to take Reefer on a few walks outside, but the puppy wasn't interested in walking on a leash. Instead, Reefer would sit on the sidewalk on Alkeld Street and refuse to walk or just chew on his leash. After a few attempts, Josh lost interest in walking the puppy and left him to his brother, Troy, to walk around the neighbourhood. And since it was Troy who had been house training Reefer, first on paper and then outside, that was probably another reason the dog was closer to Troy. If Josh was dependent on someone else whenever he had to go to the toilet, then he would try to make friends with that person too.

Now Josh stretched out on the living room couch in an old T-shirt and shorts with an electric fan his mother had placed by the door blowing on him while the air conditioner in the window remained off. His mother didn't like to pay for the electricity the air conditioner would use up if only the two of them were home. As if electric fans didn't use electricity. I bet if Amy Carter was playing with her dollhouse in the White House right now it would have air-conditioning, he thought.

His mother had gone to Eastgate Mall with his aunt and Josh was alone in the house reading Jackie Collins' *The World is Full of Married Men*, a book his Aunt Doris had brought down for his mother to read but never did. The book had lots of swearing and dirty bits but, like his drinking instant coffee for breakfast, Josh' parents never stopped him from reading whatever he wanted. His father mostly read big books about politics that he would get from the library and Josh's mother didn't read much at all, though she did have a copy of *The Sensuous Woman* hidden in her bedside table. Josh had leafed through it a few times and wondered if his mother had ever taken its advice and put whipped cream on his father's wiener like it said to do in the book. He couldn't imagine her doing such a thing. However, if his mother knew exactly what was in *The World is Full of Married Men*, she might have a problem with Josh reading it. After all, he *was* still a couple of months from being eleven.

After a reading comprehension test in October showed Josh was reading at almost a high school level, Mrs. Wooley started to give Josh some books that were not the usual fourth-grade fare. First, she had lent him *The Wind in the Willows* and then, later, gave him *The Outsiders* and *A Tree Grows in Brooklyn*. However, Mrs. Wooley liked to mention each time she gave Josh a new book to read, "But you're still doing math at a fourth-grade level."

The World is Full of Married Men is a lot better than *A Tree Grows in Brooklyn*, Josh thought, putting the book down over his hard-on that, though fledging under his shorts and underwear, still impressed Josh.

Would Shannon be at the fort today? he wondered. Earlier that month Josh did steal a photograph of his mother for Shannon, a Polaroid of her opening a pair of red slippers on Christmas day, to solidify their status as fort buddies. His mother would never miss it. And in exchange, Josh decided, at some point he would sneak into the fort when Shannon wasn't around and take that last page of the magazine with the naked policeman and put it in his secret box under his captain's bed. That seemed like a fair exchange for the photo of his mother. And everything should be fair.

The summer solstice, the longest day of the year, was on Tuesday, and even though each day seemed hotter than the last, the thought of the days getting shorter again made Josh a bit sad. Summer wasn't even here yet, and already they were about to hurl away from the sun again. *If I was living here a hundred years ago, I'd be doing the sun dance now.*

Mrs. Wooley had spent a lot of time talking about Indians this year in history. She didn't tell Josh anything he didn't already know, having already read a lot about Indians at the Red Hill Library and in the encyclopedia. And since Josh listened when his father had said not to believe everything *they* told him, Josh would often double-check his teachers, especially about Indian stuff. Mrs. Wooley had taught them about tepees, totem poles, corn (which she said Indians called *maize*), and how to make Indian headdresses out of coloured construction paper. Then she made the class sit in a circle with their legs crossed like 'real Indians'. Josh raised his hand and told Mrs. Wooley that his mother and her whole family were real Indians and never sat like that.

"You don't look like an Indian," Mrs. Wooley had replied.

Josh was most intrigued by the sun dance. Mrs. Wooley had said the men of the tribe would tether themselves to a pole with sharp hooks through the skin of their chest and then dance, for hours and hours, until they finally passed out from the pain. At first, Josh thought it was more of his teacher's hogwash but discovered that the sun dance was real after he looked it up in the *Encyclopedia Britannica* in the Laura Secord School library.

The sun dance was all part of the summer solstice rejuvenation ceremony. Of course, when dingbat Wooley discussed the sun dance with Josh's class, she never mentioned anything about the summer solstice or that they did it to honour the Great Spirit. Instead, his teacher made it sound like Indians did the sun dance because they were a bunch of dopes who were foolish to believe in magic and didn't know any better back then. *I could say the same thing about your stupid Transactual Analysis, Mrs. Wooley.*

I really hope my ancestors did the sun dance, Josh thought, picking up *The World is Full of Married Men* off his crotch.

The phone rang and Josh put down his novel. His father usually called him sometime on the weekend and Josh hoped that it was him calling. Though they did not allow anyone under twelve to visit the hospital, Josh had considered just taking the bus downtown some Saturday and then, somehow, making his way up the mountain himself. He knew he could pass for twelve. His father would be happy to see him. Josh tried to imagine what his father's throat looked like now as he answered the phone.

"Hello?"

"Joshua? Is that you?" The voice dripped with molasses.

There was only one person Josh knew who had that accent. *Fuck!* If he knew it was her calling, he would have just let it ring. For a second he considered pulling out the phone cord.

"Yes, this is Josh."

"Joshua! This is Auntie Wilma. You sound like a girl on the phone, has anyone ever told you that? Hopefully, your voice changes soon. Boys should have boy voices and girls should have girl voices. It's too confusing these days as it is with men and women having the same hair and wearing unisex clothes. Is your mother there?"

"No."

"Oh, shoot! I waited until the rates were low on the weekend, and she's not even home."

"Nope," Josh said. He could almost smell the scent of decaying lilacs Aunt Wilma always smelled of.

"Hmm..."

Josh didn't like Aunt Wilma. He didn't like her syrupy southern accent and the way she purred when she spoke. He didn't think she was kind. And he really didn't like all the God stuff she continually droned on about when she was around. She was worse than Aunt Sue and Aunt Peggy put together. God was the only thing Aunt Wilma ever thought about.

"Alright, I want you to give your mother this message. Tell her I'm sorry, but Uncle Greg and I aren't... we aren't in a position to help her. Can you tell her that?"

"Is this about the six thousand dollars?" Josh asked.

"Yes."

"I'll tell her."

"And if she wants to discuss it, she can call us."

"I'll tell her that too."

"But there is one thing we *can* do. And it's for you, Joshua."

"Me?"

"Yes, I was speaking with your Uncle Greg, and we know how difficult it must be for you right now, with your father in the hospital for God knows how long and summer holidays coming up."

"It's not difficult," Josh said.

"And with your mother working all the time, we thought you could come down to Georgia when school lets out. Our church down here in Atlanta has a boy's day camp that lasts all summer long. They have Bible classes specifically for boys your age and all the other camp stuff: canoeing, swimming, archery. Greg Jr. and Jay went there when they were little, and they loved it. It makes boys all-boy. Well, I was praying about it, and God laid it on my heart, and Uncle Greg agreed."

Why the fuck does everyone want to send me to camp, Josh thought.

"No," he said.

"We are worried about you up there, Joshua. We would do it for anyone in the family who was having difficulty. And with your mother working all the time and not being around, I hear you're running around like a wild Indian up there with no supervision and no real male influence to speak of."

"I can't leave my mom right now."

"I've had two sons, Joshua, and I know that the ages of ten and eleven are critical times and if you don't… well things can go very wrong very quickly if a parent isn't careful and before you know it…"

"I could become a dope fiend?"

Josh threw that in because Aunt Wilma's son, Jay, had run away from home when he was a teenager and had gotten into drugs. Even today, Wilma didn't know where Jay was or what he was doing most of the time. Everyone in the family knew that. So that 'all-boy' camp didn't do much for Jay.

"I was going to say if you aren't careful with boys at this critical age, they could end up being one of those boys Anita Bryant is trying to stop. Or even worse, Joshua."

"No," he said again.

His mother may get him to Cub Scout camp for three weeks but if anyone thought he was going to stay with Wilma in Atlanta they were bananas. He would never go. And except by tying him up and throwing him onto an airplane, they couldn't make him.

"I was discussing Joshua from the Bible with my Sunday school class just last week, and I know it's not a coincidence. Coincidence is just another word for God doing His work. Do you remember how Joshua had the Israelites march around the walls of Jericho once a day for seven days and then on the seventh day they blew their ram's horns, and the walls of Jericho came crashing down?"

"Sure. And then the Israelites killed every man, woman, and child in Jericho. They killed everyone except one prostitute. She must have been a really good prostitute," Josh said.

Josh had never been to any stupid Sunday school, but he had checked the encyclopedia for *Joshua* and *Jericho* the last time Aunt Wilma had brought up his name and those stupid walls. Josh never understood how people could believe that crap. A ram's horn couldn't bring down a wall; a bazooka could take out some walls but a ram's horn? No way!

"I would have left Jericho alone, taken the Israelites down the road, built a new city, and just been neighbours with Jericho."

"You sound just like your father, Joshua. I'm still going to discuss you coming down here with your mother," Aunt Wilma said, sounding as if she had won the argument.

Go ahead, he thought.

"And I'll be flying up there soon to see Grandpa. He's about to meet the Lord, and I'm going to do my best to make sure he accepts Jesus before he does...."

Accept? As if she was offering Grandpa a nice cup of tea? No, more like Aunt Wilma would force Grandpa's mouth open and shove Jesus down his throat whether he liked it or not. Josh knew his Grandpa Moore, and, like Josh, he wasn't as easy to push around as others in the family were.

"Then God and I have our sights on your father. You want to be standing with the sheep when the roll is called up yonder, Joshua, not with the goats"

Josh wanted to bleat like a goat into the phone. Right then and there, Josh began rooting for his grandfather to die as much a heathen as he had lived, cussing Wilma all the way out. In fact, Josh decided, from now on, he would try and sabotage every attempt Aunt Wilma made to save any soul she cast her eye on (if he possibly could). He would align himself firmly on the side of the goats in the family. Aunt Wilma, Aunt Sue and Anita Bryant were welcome to be on the other. Who would want to be on that side anyway?

"I have to go, Joshua, this has cost me too much already. Goodbye."

Click

"*Maaaaaah!*" Josh bleated into the disconnected receiver.

He hung up the phone and went to his bedroom. In the middle of one wall over Josh's desk, taped with scotch tape, hung a watercolour his Grandpa Moore had recently painted of a pig farm, with rolling green hills, a brown barn and, in the foreground, a pigsty with one big grey sow lying on her side suckling nine pink piglets. His grandpa had told Josh when he gave him the painting that he used to walk past this farm every day on his way to school when he was a boy in England. On either side of the watercolour hung two large posters, one of David Soul leaning on the hood of a red Ford Gran Torino and the other of Bjorn Borg in white shorts and tennis shirt returning a serve, his long blond hair flying in the breeze. Also peppered on the wall, Josh had taped smaller photos of his favourite movie and TV stars like John Travolta and Shawn Cassidy that he had cut out of movie magazines and right over the head of his captain's bed hung a *Charlie's Angel's* poster with Farrah's hair taking up almost half of the space on the poster. Josh's Aunt Doris had recently taken him to see Burt Reynolds in *Smokey and the Bandit* at the Starlight drive-in and now Josh wanted to get a big poster of Burt Reynolds in his red shirt, blue jeans, and cowboy hat for the back of his bedroom door.

Interspersed between the posters and magazine photos were also a dozen or more paper cocktail placemats taped all over Josh's bedroom walls. These placemats featured colourful illustrations of every drink that restaurant served, twenty-four or more on each placemat, with a list of ingredients for each drink. Josh first started collecting these paper placemats when his Uncle Jack took his family to a fancy restaurant in Montreal. Josh became enamoured with the look, names, and colours of the different cocktails. It was like looking under Boris' candy counter. Josh quickly learned all the wonderful cocktail names like Sidecar, Alexander, Grasshopper, Pink Lady, Daiquiri, Mint Julep, Rob Roy, Angel's Kiss and Zombie. He studied each one before and after he taped them to his wall, memorizing each cocktail name and their ingredients. Josh could tell you how to make a Stinger (two parts brandy, one-part white crème de menthe), an Old Fashioned (one lump of sugar, dash of bitters, one jigger of bourbon) and at least thirty other drinks.

Now Josh's aunts and uncles and his parents' friends would all pick up paper cocktail placemats whenever they came across one for Josh to hang up on his wall with the others in his collection and with each new placemat he would compare the ingredients and rate how well the pictures of the cocktails were drawn. His favourite placemats were from Visca's Pizzeria and the Chicken Roost Restaurant. And already, at the age of almost eleven, Josh knew exactly what the first ten drinks he would order the day he turned eighteen, the legal drinking age in Ontario. His first drink would be a Harvey Wallbanger (three parts vodka, six parts orange juice, one part Galliano). Josh couldn't wait until he was old enough to walk into a bar and say, "Harvey Wallbanger, please!" Just thinking about it excited him.

Josh pulled out the frame of his captain's bed from the wall and took out his secret box hidden under his bed. It looked like everything was in there. He took out two cigarettes from a king size pack of Player's and a book of matches, returned the box under the bed, and pushed the bedframe back against the wall. Picking up his new *Tiger Beat* from his desk, Josh walked down the hall with both cigarettes dangling in his mouth. He stopped in the kitchen and grabbed a package of Pirate oatmeal peanut butter cookies from the cupboard and walked, barefoot, out the backdoor, leaving Reefer inside, watching him from behind the screen door.

He looked around, just to be safe, and then, holding the *Tiger Beat* in one hand and the cookies and matches in the other, pushed aside some tall thick weeds and squeezed into the narrow space between a neighbour's neglected picket fence and Josh's garage, walking sideways, pushing some spider webs aside, until he reached the small area ensconced between the back of the garage and the neighbours overgrown hedges and hidden from above by the limbs of his red maple tree. It was almost like *The Lion, the Witch and the Wardrobe* when the Pevensie siblings went through the magic wardrobe into Narnia.

Josh sat on a dirty faded red plastic milk crate he used as a makeshift chair with the cookies and *Tiger Beat* on his lap and lit the first of his illicit cigarettes, doing his best to inhale the smoke like Shannon and the grown-ups. His throat burned and he coughed a bit but continued to inhale with each puff from the cigarette, trying to cough less each time he held the smoke in his lungs. Wait till Shannon sees me smoke like a teenager, Josh thought, waving away the smoke. He didn't want anyone to see smoke and think his garage was on fire.

He came here often. Even through the winter, when his mother told him to go outside, he would sit on the milk crate alone and eat or smoke or sometimes read but mostly just think by himself. Once Josh had a lot more friends. When he had first moved to Alkeld Street, most of his friends had been girls. Back then no one seemed to mind that he would rather skip rope, play hide and seek, and make up plays or song and dance routines with the neighbourhood girls than play road hockey with the boys. Together he and his friends would all walk to school together, have their desks close to each other in class, and, sometimes Josh would take the girls he thought were his best friends here to his secret place behind his garage. There the girls would bring over their Barbie dolls and Josh would bring his Big Jim action figure and they'd play and laugh together until their parents called for them.

However, lately they girls all seemed to go off on their own. They told Josh to his face that they didn't want him around and often stuck to the girls' side of the playground where Josh was forbidden to go. Shannon was the first friend he had had in a long time, but they weren't really friends, Shannon just liked him around to talk to sometimes and, to be honest, Josh thought Shannon liked his mother more than him. Ever since Josh had given Shannon the Polaroid snapshot of his mother, Shannon hounded Josh with questions like what did his mother wear to bed and if she walked around the house naked and weird shit like that. Shannon, Josh thought, was probably a bit touched in the head.

When he turned nine, he had a birthday party with ten friends and eight of them were girls. The only boys there were his two older cousins. It was right after that his father took him to Cub Scouts for the first time. His father said that he had been a Cub Scout when he was Josh's age and, later, a Boy Scout before joining the army cadets and had a great time, promising that Josh would have a great time too. However, Josh did not have a great time at Cub Scouts. And he knew his father only took him there because he didn't like Josh hanging around with girls so much (on this point his father and Aunt Wilma seemed to agree). Sadly, it turned out his father didn't need to worry about Josh having so many friends who were girls. Last year, when he turned ten, Josh asked those same eight girls to come to his birthday party and all of them, *all eight of them,* said they didn't want to come. Since then, Josh concluded that not having friends wasn't as bad as people knowing you had no friends. That's what really hurt. Everyone knows there's something wrong with you if you have no friends.

Maybe he really wasn't okay.

Now his throat was burning so badly that Josh felt as if he could cough up blood, but he didn't mind so much, he had a strange feeling of pride, being well on his way to inhaling like his father and the rest of the sinning goat side of the family. Josh bent over, butted out the cigarette in the ground, and digging a small hole with a stick, buried it in case he father or mother ever came back here. He had a lot of buried cigarette butts back there. Now he was hungry. He opened the package of cookies and began eating them one at a time.

He flipped through the *Tiger Beat* reading the headlines: *David Soul and Paul Michael Glaser split! How you can get them back together!* No, Josh refused to believe that Starsky and Hutch were breaking up. And even if it were true, he certainly couldn't do anything about it. Besides, the show was a big hit. He turned the page: *The Real Reason Farrah Fawcett-Majors Cries Herself to Sleep.* She looked pretty happy in the photo, Josh thought. Again, he doubted that Farrah Fawcett-Majors actually cried herself to sleep when the woman was married to the Six Million Dollar Man. *Elton John is Looking for a Mate, Could You Rate? Sean Cassidy Tells 'What I Need from A Girl'; The Right Way to Kiss a Bay City Roller!* Josh was irritated by all the exclamation marks. And why was there always so much about Donnie and Marie? They had to be the most boring people on television.

He flipped back to the front cover with Robbie Benson. *Getting Hooked on Robbie! It's Easy and Terrific!* Josh wasn't exactly sure who Robbie Benson was (he had never seen him in anything) but he liked him immediately with his big blue eyes, pink lips, and long dark brown hair like Gary Lessing in Mrs. Wooley's class. Josh would cut out that photo of Robbie Benson and find a place on his bedroom wall to hang it. He would have to be wise about it though. He would tape the picture of Farrah Fawcett near Robbie. It seemed a boy could have as many photos of guys on his bedroom wall as he wanted as long as he had just as many photos of women taped on it too. Josh decided he would put Robbie (and Farrah) between two of his favourite paper cocktail placemats near his closet door.

It was still early, and Josh wondered what he could do. He had thought earlier about taking the bus up to see his father. He had enough of that bullshit his mother was telling him about no one under twelve being allowed to visit. He was missing his father too much. Now he would get a dull pain in his stomach whenever he thought of him. He could easily get downtown on the King Street bus but after that things were a bit more complicated. How would he get up the mountain? Josh didn't even know what the mental institution his father was in looked like. Could he just ask someone downtown to direct him to the funny farm? And what if, even if he was able to find the fucking hospital, they just wouldn't let him in for being too young like his mother said? No, if Josh was going to try and sneak up there it would take more time and planning.

He could ride his bike down to Van Wagner's Beach. Josh had read more about the Ragno murder in *The Hamilton Spectator* that morning and he had cut out an article about another woman that Ragno had been seeing before his wife disappeared. Maybe he could ride his bike to the beach and then walk along the sand, not actually to look for the boy but just to make sure nothing had washed up there on the sand. It seemed like someone had to at least *try* and look for the kid now that the Hamilton police had called off the search. All he had to do was ride down Woodward Avenue past the sewage plant and the big Gulliver's Travels Motel Restaurant billboard to Lake Ontario. It would only take about ten minutes. Of course, he wasn't allowed to go to the beach but that wouldn't stop him. He has been riding his bike down to the beach since he was nine and hasn't been caught yet.

He tossed another whole cookie in his mouth and chewed it with his mouth open. In Josh's Narnia he didn't have to eat with his mouth closed. On the other side of the hedge, he could just faintly hear his neighbours chatting about laundry on their back porch. Josh looked up at the red maple tree and tried to imagine being tethered to it with hooks through his chest. He ran his fingers over his chest and pulled at the skin. If he did the sun dance no one would think he was girly, that's for sure. It couldn't hurt as much as cutting your throat.

Aunt Wilma thought that he'd grow up queer and wear dresses. That's what she meant by that Anita Bryant crack. Josh had never wanted to wear women's clothes and had never wanted to be a girl. She was crazy. It wasn't bad enough that he was called *faggot* at school all the time, now his fucking aunt was saying it with different words. She was just as much a bully as Anne-Marie calling him a queer or those other kids at school. She just did it with an accent and a Bible in her hand.

His throat was feeling better now, so good, in fact, that Josh smoked his second cigarette just to spite Aunt Wilma and the rest of them on the sheep side. It was no problem buying his own, since he went for cigarettes all the time for his aunts, Boris would have no idea the smokes were really for him. Not that Boris would give a shit, anyway.

Josh buried the second cigarette butt, resealed the now nearly empty bag of cookies, and walked back along the side of the garage and into the house. He threw the cookies in the cupboard, grabbed a few dollars that he had hidden in his desk, and put his sneakers on. He grabbed his bicycle from the garage and drove with one hand up Alkeld Street toward Woodward Avenue. Josh's Schwinn Sting-ray bike was mostly white with a splash of candy apple red painted along the crossbar near the high-rise handlebars and had a black bucket-saddle seat. Troy had promised Josh that he would get some red paint and fix the scratch in the red paint on the crossbar, but he said that back in April and he hadn't fixed the scratch yet. There wasn't much in the world that was really Josh's alone but this bike, even with a scratch, was one of them. And for an awkward heavy kid, Josh was agile and fearless when he was on his Schwinn. It was the one of the few places Josh felt free.

He saw some kids on their bikes near Woodward Avenue and, not wanting to run into Gavin or the rest, turned on a side street and sped down the slight hill and turned onto Brampton Street without slowing down toward Woodward. There wasn't much traffic on Woodward today since it was the weekend and most of the factories were closed. Josh rode past the sewage plant and the Gulliver's Travels billboard to where the boulevard went under the highway and stopped. He could see the lake under the overpass in front of him. It smelled of fish, sewage, and the steel mills.

"That little boy is still out there somewhere," Josh said, staring at the calm blue lake. "And now they aren't even looking for him anymore."

Josh hoped that if he were ever murdered and tossed in the lake that someone, anyone, would keep looking for him for as long as it took, but, as Josh had learned during this whole Ragno case, in the grown-up world they only dole out so much time and expense looking for kids before everyone seems to raise their hands in the air and say, "Oh well, it's too bad and all, but I guess that's all we can do."

It was hot out and the sun was beating down on his head and the back of his neck. His legs were already tired from the short ride, and he knew that every pedal more would mean another pedal to get back home. A transport truck honked as it sped past Josh on its way to the highway.

Josh turned around. "Fuck it."

He headed back toward Alkeld Street, passing Munro Steel where his mother worked. It looked deserted. How could people spend their lives in a factory like that? As soon as he was old enough, he was getting out of this city. He didn't know how, but he knew it would happen. If his grandfather could come over to Canada when he was seventeen and if his father could go off to Africa when he was seventeen, then Josh could too. And he would be *seventeen* in only six years and a few months.

Josh turned onto Alkeld Street, glad to be close to home. It was too hot for a long ride. He would have another smoke behind the garage and read more before his mother got home. Maybe before dinner he would walk down to Redhill Creek and see if Shannon was at the fort. Although Shannon had said they would come up with some cool signal, they found the easiest way for him to see if Shannon was there for Josh to simply go to the edge of the train bridge and call down. If Shannon didn't respond, then Josh would usually either go home or walk along the creek by himself.

He stopped at Boris' Little Variety and, leaving his bike resting on the cement stairs, bought a Creamsicle and, because there were only two smokes left in the pack under his bed, another pack of Player's cigarettes. If Josh looked guilty about buying the smokes, Boris didn't seem to notice. Josh unwrapped his Creamsicle, put the wrapper in the garbage pail by the door, and walked out of Boris' Little Variety.

His Schwinn was gone.

Panicked, Josh looked up and down Alkeld Street, still with a Creamsicle in his mouth, and then down the side street but saw no one and no sign of his bike. He walked around the cement stairs of the variety store, hoping, praying, that maybe it had rolled away or fallen over but no— his bicycle had been stolen.

For the next hour and a half, Josh walked up and down the side streets between Brampton and Alkeld, peering down driveways looking for his bike, but he didn't see it anywhere. He wasn't even sure what he would do if he found it in someone's backyard. And the longer Josh walked, the hotter and angrier he became. He had been violated and abused by Alkeld once again. In the time it took to buy a fucking Creamsicle his world became infinitely smaller and lonelier. He felt like someone had cut off his legs.

Josh hated Alkeld Street.

As Josh walked home tears burned, ready to pour out of his eyes, but he clenched his jaw and stubbornly held them back. He wasn't going to let Alkeld Street make him cry again. Whatever they did to him. Whatever they called him. Whatever they took from him. He would not cry.

Opening his backyard gate, Josh could hear Reefer barking. His mother still wasn't home. He let Reefer out to pee and then went to his bedroom and closed the door. How was he going to tell his mother that his bike was stolen? Would she blame him? His parents had given him a chain and lock when he first got the bike two Christmases ago. He didn't even know where the fucking chain and lock were now.

Josh pulled aside the frame of his captain's bed, took out his secret box again, and sat cross-legged on top of his bed. He tossed the new pack of cigarettes in the box along with the book of matches and looked over the contents of his secret box. Everything was there: the Queen's Silver Jubilee coin; *Torso*, the paperback about the Evelyn Dick murders; the half shell of a robin's egg; and an AMWAY catalogue offering a set of novelty glasses with men whose clothes would slowly disappear when the glasses got cold. Then Josh pulled out something wrapped in white paper towel from the box. He slowly unwrapped it.

It was the jagged piece of amber glass his father had used to cut his throat.

Josh had recovered it the night that it happened. It was after the ambulance had taken his father away to the hospital and as Josh's mother was frantically calling family to tell them the horrific thing that had just happened in their garage. She hadn't noticed when Josh briefly slipped back outside to carefully pick up the shard out of a small cold puddle of his father's blood on the garage floor.

And he did it while he was watching me, Josh thought.

Josh held the piece of glass in his hand and held it up to the sunlight coming in through his bedroom window. It looked like a jewel in the sun. He had washed the blood off the glass the night it happened, wrapped it carefully in the paper towel, and put it in the secret box. This was the first time he had looked at it since that night. It was smaller than he remembered, smooth on one side, jagged on the other, and thick, like it had come from the bottom of the IPA beer bottle. Would his ancestors have used something sharp like this, maybe a sharp stone, to puncture the skin on their chest to do the sun dance?

Josh turned around the piece of glass in his hands, trying to figure out which side his father had cut himself with. Then Josh gently held the jagged side of the broken shard of glass against his own throat.

They even took my bike from me, he thought, staring at one of the paper cocktail placemats taped on his wall. Softly, in a whisper, he began reciting the ingredients of cocktails on the paper placemat. "Harvey Wallbanger. Three-parts vodka... six-parts orange juice... and one-part Galliano..."

Then Josh wrapped the piece of broken glass back up in the paper towel, placed it back gingerly in his box of secrets, and laid back on his bed as the tears began falling down the side of his face into his ears.

I'm okay, I'm okay, I'm okay, I'm okay...

July 1977

Seven

For Ted, the residuum of electroshock, a stew of medications, and countless hours talking with Dr. Shackelford were memories. And during the long monotonous days within the hospital grounds, Ted could sit for hours recollecting and reliving all the fuckups in his life. One of his biggest fuckups, as plain as the fleshy nose on his face, was joining the army when he was seventeen. Not that Ted had many options available back then; there had been a recession in the early 1960s and jobs were scarce in the factories of Hamilton. Abe had told Ted straight out that he couldn't live on Waterloo Street without bringing some money into the house. If Abe handed over his paycheque to Ted's mother every Friday like clockwork, Abe expected the Moore kids to hand their paycheques over to him with the same precision.

At the time, joining the army had made a lot of sense. Ted had enjoyed being in the Army Cadets when he was a kid. He had got a charge out of the uniform, the drills up at the Armouries on James Street with his buddies, playing drums in the marching band, and the parades. He thought that the real army would be a barrel of laughs too.

So, on the morning of his seventeenth birthday, with nothing more than his callow one hundred and fifteen pounds of flesh and a tenth-grade education, Ted made his way to the army recruitment centre and signed up for a two-year. When he returned home and told his family, his mother was concerned, Abe was elated, whereas Tessa, only fourteen at the time, had cried.

Less than two weeks later, Ted was on a bus headed nearly three hundred miles away from Hamilton to the Canadian Forces Base in Petawawa near Ottawa for basic training. For the first few months, Ted had enjoyed the discipline that the army provided, he had made some good pals and the army seemed to agree with his temperament, if not his ideals because by the time Ted had boarded that bus to Petawawa, he had already been a member of The Socialist Party of Canada for almost two years.

Ted's long relationship with the Socialist Party had begun when Ted worked two summers at National Steel Car, a freight train factory in the city's north end, during high school. Dougie Thomas, one of the union men who took Ted under his wing, told Ted he thought he was smart enough (for what, Ted wondered) but had to read more so Dougie had lent him first *Animal Farm*, and then, later, *The Road to Wigan Pier*. Ted was immediately smitten with what he read and not long after, Dougie took the fifteen-year-old Ted to his first Socialist Party of Canada meeting where, enthralled with the fiery speeches, Ted joined the party on the spot.

Ted was still a staunch socialist even after weeks in basic training in Petawawa and as he marched with his unit, he would sing a line from "L'Internationale" in his head:

> *And if those cannibals keep trying,*
> *To sacrifice us to their pride,*
> *They soon shall hear the bullets flying,*
> *We'll shoot the generals on our own side!*

The day Ted graduated from basic training all the recruits marched out on the field in front of the army brass and their wives. Ted had written home to tell Abe and his mother about the graduation and invited them up since most of the new recruits' families would make the journey from their hometowns around Ontario up to CFB Petawawa to see their sons and brothers graduate from basic training.

Ted never received a response. But, still, when seventeen-year-old Ted Moore marched out on the field that beautiful spring day in 1961, he had honestly believed his mother and Abe (and maybe even his younger siblings) would be up in the stands, cheering him on.

What a fucking sap I was!

Ted had marched onto that field with the other boys, and when the drill sergeant said, "Eyes right!" Ted searched the stands as best as he could for his family. After the graduation ceremony, he strolled over to where the other recruits and their families had gathered on the lawn near the bleachers *still* thinking that, maybe, he had missed them or that they had come late.

After boot camp, Ted was quickly off to that whole mess in the Congo as a UN Peacekeeper, robin egg blue beret and all, during the Congo Crisis. The army had given Ted a choice: the Suez or the Congo. And, at least at that time, the Congo was one of the most dangerous spots on earth. Christ, their Prime Minister, Patrice Lumumba, had just been assassinated, and Dag Hammarskjöld, the Secretary-General of the United Nations, had been killed in a suspicious plane crash there. It was as if the whole country was on the brink of civil war, and, to Ted, that meant excitement. It was an easy choice. He signed up for the Congo without hesitation. Of course, like most things in Ted Moore's life, the UN mission in the Congo didn't turn out the way he envisioned.

As a Signalman mainly working nights on the teletype machine in Léopoldville, Ted's life in Africa would consist of work, spending a few hours sleeping, and then walking, mostly alone, around the city, with its Belgian facades already crumbling onto the sidewalks below. On other days, he would stroll past the mud huts near town with his new Kodak camera, sending a roll of Kodachrome film home to his mother and Abe's house on Waterloo Street once a week. And though there were reports of Canadian UN soldiers being attacked and beaten by Congolese soldiers, Ted was young enough to think the odds were slim that he would be the first Canadian casualty in the Congo. As it turned out, except for some scuffles, with a total of 1900 Canadian soldiers that eventually went through the Congo on the UN mission, there wasn't one fatality.

However, there had almost been *one* fatality. One night, after hours of drinking at a local bar, Ted had rolled the jeep he was driving in the middle of a dirt road. He was thrown from the vehicle, nearly hitting a rubber tree, but was, except for some scrapes and bruises, uninjured in the crash. Drunk and afraid, Ted had left the jeep in the middle of the road and stumbled back to his barracks, telling his commanding officer that the jeep had been stolen in town. And when Ted finally did see death in the Congo, it would be more horrific than anything he ever imagined when he was playing soldier at the Hamilton Armouries. After that, there was no adventure in war or the army. That was when his drinking ramped up.

Not long after the incident with the jeep, Ted had to leave Léopoldville after he and two of his UN buddies, both American, were seen drinking in a whorehouse with two Congolese soldiers. Early the next morning, he was woken up by his sergeant and, with a killer hangover, was sent directly to his colonel, where Ted was told to pack his things immediately. He was being shipped out. It turned out that his two American buddies from the night before were already gone. Ted would spend his last two months in the Congo at a static signal station in Elizabethville, basically under house arrest and working straight nights. All there was for him in Elizabethville was a teletype, a bunk, and as much whiskey as he could find while his new Kodak camera gathered dust.

Ted would not do it again. If he could get a time machine back to 1961, he'd stay away from the army and scrounged for a job in Hamilton or, better yet, stay in school and maybe make it to university like Jonathan. If he had only been given half a chance. But Ted had only been back from Africa for a few months when he met Gloria at Munro Steel. And then suddenly, Ted was a stepdad himself to her two sons, all at the age of nineteen.

And that was that.

In the week since Carl died, they had left his bed empty. And his death was treated at the Hamilton Psychiatric Hospital as if Carl had simply checked out. Carl's belongings, his dirty robe, the dozens of woven baskets, and one last half-eaten bag of cheese puffs were removed the following day while Ted, Jonathan, and Rick were in the cafeteria having breakfast. When they returned to room 215W, nothing was left of Carl. And if Carl had any family, they must have wanted to keep his death quiet too. Ted had searched *The Hamilton Spectator* obituaries the days following Carl's death and found no death notice for Carl Gruber.

"Everyone deserves at least their name in the paper when they die," Ted said, sitting with Jonathan, and Rick in the hospital garden.

"They all want to sweep it under the rug," Rick said, still with some green pepper from his breakfast omelette stuck in his braces.

"It's *damnatio memoriae,* wiping a person from memory. Carl was nuts and a bit of a pig, but he was still a person," Jonathan said.

"Carl wasn't even suicidal when he came in. It wasn't until he spent hours and hours talking about his problems with Shackelford that he killed himself," Ted said

"Maybe too much talking about yourself can be hazardous to your health," Jonathan added.

"And I bet you two thought I'd be the first one to off myself," Rick said.

Yes, I did, Ted thought. But he would never say that to Rick. Ted was sorry about Carl, but he was glad that the body he had stumbled across in their room wasn't Rick.

"Guys, I know we're all a bit crazy," Ted said. "But can we three at least promise each other that we won't kill ourselves while we're at the hospital? I don't want to find another goddamn roommate dead on the floor covered with shit and a wrapped-up hospital robe twisted around their neck the next time I have to take a piss in the middle of the night. Deal?"

"You got my word," Jonathan said.

Ted and Jonathan looked over at Rick, who remained silent for a few seconds.

"All right! I promise too," Rick finally said.

"Good!" Ted said. "If any of us decide to kill ourselves, we'll do it once we get out of here and save their roommates the trauma."

"But this promise is null and void when you two go and I'm here all by myself. Then I can swan dive off the Manor House if I want to," Rick said.

"Do you want to swan dive off the Manor House, Rick?" Jonathan asked.

"Not today," Rick said, smiling. His braces caught the sunlight and flashed in Ted's eyes, and, for the first time, Ted thought it quite possible that Rick would make it out of there and see 1978, 1979, 1980, and all the rest of them.

Over that week, the three men were called, one at a time, into Shackelford's office to discuss Carl's death and, specifically, how his death was impacting them. And to ensure that none of them had the same thing on their minds since, or as Dr. Shackelford said to Ted when Ted was finally called into his office, "these things can often occur in rashes of twos and threes."

"Carl killing himself doesn't impact me much at all," Ted said. "But Carl and I weren't exactly the best of friends here. I'm sorry and all that, but to be honest... I've got too many problems of my own to give Carl too much thought."

Ted reached into the breast pocket of his shirt and pulled out his cigarettes.

"Don't you find that odd? That Carl's death doesn't affect you much when you were the one who found him?"

"Look, Carl's killing himself like that was lousy. I don't know what else you want me to say. As I said, I've got my own troubles. I'm the guy who slashed my own throat. I'm the guy who fucked up my life so badly that I'm making my wife humiliate herself to a man she hates so we won't lose our house! I'm the guy who doesn't know if I'll even have a job when I get the fuck out of here or if I'll end up in jail. So, I apologize for not brooding over Carl's suicide. I think some shrinks would find that healthy."

"It's just that many people would find discovering a man dead the way you did, a man you had shared a room with, ate with, and spoke with for almost three months, to be terribly traumatic."

"Christ! If you want to talk about traumatic, I could tell you about traumatic, doctor. I once saw a young boy, maybe fourteen or fifteen, hacked to death right in front of me by two men with machetes in the Congo back in '63. His head was split practically in two, right through his eyeball, but they kept hacking at him."

The doctor sat quietly, staring intently at Ted.

"I was driving to work with two other soldiers when it happened. We weren't sure what to do. One of the soldiers I was with yelled at them and, luckily, they ran off, leaving the boy's body in the street. We just stood over this mutilated kid, trying to figure out what to do and which gash in his flesh we should hold the one tourniquet we had in the jeep on to try and stop the bleeding. The blood was pouring out of the kid's skull and… I could see his brain. And there I am, only eighteen at the time, myself. And him making these horrible gargling noises in his throat as blood bubbled in his mouth. How long do you think it takes in Africa before flies start flying around a dead body? I'll tell you, before he's even dead. Hundreds of flies were feeding on this boy's blood before he died. Then he did die… and it took another four hours before we could get someone to pick him up. *Four hours!* The two other soldiers took the jeep to get help, and I stayed with the dead boy. I put the bloody tourniquet over his head and waited calmly like I was taught… hour after hour with that poor kid lying there on the side of the road while I did my best to swat away the swarm of flies crawling all over him."

Ted sat back in the chair and, taking a long drag on his cigarette, tried to compose himself. His face was hot, and he was sweating like Carl.

"I had my first panic attack a few months later, just before I flew home to Canada."

"That must have been horrifying, Ted. It would be very difficult for an eighteen-year-old boy to process something like that."

"Yeah, well, it's probably nothing compared to Jonathan's war stories about Vietnam. I can't even imagine the things he saw there."

"Jonathan Pressman?"

"He was in Vietnam."

"Have you ever asked Jonathan about his time in Vietnam?"

"No, but I know what it must have been like. Once you see flies eating a kid's brains, you get the idea of war. It's always the same, just different brains. It's the barbarity of society, and that's all part of the capitalist system. The ruling class produces war for a reason, and you didn't see many millionaires hacked to death in the Congo or

Vietnam, did you? No, the lower classes are always used as cannon fodder."

"Hey, Ted, let's say we go back to your time in the Congo and leave the problems with the capitalist system for another day, okay?"

"Sure! Back to the Congo, we go."

"I'm curious, Ted… what they gave you for malaria prevention when you were there?"

"Chloroquine pills every week. First, they gave me heavy-duty shots of it in the ass before I left for Africa, and once I was there, I took the pills once… maybe twice a week. I forget. I had to take it for a while when I got back to Canada too. It would give you some fucked-up dreams, but other than that, it was fine."

"And your panic attacks started in the Congo?"

"Just before I left."

"Did you know chloroquine has been known to cause depression and anxiety attacks? And it's been known to cause psychosis sometimes."

Ted was shocked. Was it possible that those stupid malaria pills were the reason he was so fucked up? Something they gave him fifteen years ago.

"But… I haven't had chloroquine in years. It wouldn't have made me depressed or anxious all these years."

"I'm just suggesting it's possible that chloroquine could have set many things in motion. That is, the chloroquine coupled with the traumatic event of the young boy you saw killed. It could be a good starting place."

"So, you're saying that me being so fucked up could all be due to you goddamn doctors?"

"Yes, it's possible that the problem may have originated with the chloroquine and subsequent medications you were prescribed."

"Jesus fucking Christ! And they also gave the Nobel Prize to the guy who invented the lobotomy. Are we about done here? All this talk about Carl and the Congo and chloroquine is making me tired."

"We're almost done, Ted. Before you go, tell me how your father is doing. Last week you told me it looked grim."

"My sisters say he has a couple of weeks. Maybe a month at

most. But since nobody has called my sister, Wilma, in Georgia to come up and save his fucking soul, there must be time. No one would dare let him die without her being around trying to push him to the arms of Jesus on his way out."

"I've told you before you can sign yourself out for a few hours to see your father, we don't have bars on the windows here. This isn't a jail."

"I know," Ted said. "Everyone keeps saying that. It still feels like one, though."

"Where did you say he was?"

"St. Joseph's."

"You could have a family member pick you up, or you could even hop on the bus right across the street, shoot down the mountain, and be at the hospital in ten minutes. I think you should go sometime this week."

"Alright, I will."

"When?"

"I don't know."

"How about you go this Saturday?"

"Okay, I'll go Saturday."

"Splendid, I'll let the nurses know."

"Great," Ted said, standing up. *And it's almost time for my medication, so lots of chances for you doctors to fuck me up even more.*

After meeting with Shackelford, Ted spent the rest of the day brooding but strangely enthusiastic; just knowing that there may be a reason for all this, or a cause of his problems, made him feel better. He filled up a can of Pepsi with what was left from another bottle of rye Doris had brought up and drank it quietly in the washroom stall, thinking that, maybe, Shackelford had found an answer to all this. He even jerked off for the first time in months while sitting on the john. Afterwards, he walked in the garden, almost euphoric in the afterglow of whiskey and his orgasm, with his Pepsi can of rye. He ran into Jonathan coming from the Manor House and sat on the same bench they had sat together with Carl only a week earlier.

"Say, Jonathan, do you think they put us together in the same room for a reason? Or do you think having two old soldiers bunking beside each other is a coincidence?"

"I don't know, Ted. I don't think they're that organized or smart around here for that."

"You're probably right. Say, were you given malaria drugs in Vietnam?"

"We were given chloroquine-primaquine-phosphate," Jonathan said with the preciseness of a pharmacist. "We took that every week we were there— and had to take it for six weeks more after I was sent home. It gave you the shits for the whole day after you took it. Then, a few months before they sent me home, they also started to give us dapsone and told us to take that the six other days of the week, then we got to have the shits every day. I stopped taking the dapsone after about a week. Why?"

"Shackelford just told me that chloroquine could cause depression and anxiety attacks. It might be where all my problems began."

"I was depressed before I ever took anything for malaria," Jonathan said, smiling. "Though panic would have been a nice diversion."

"Does Shackelford spend much time talking about your time in Vietnam?"

"Some. There isn't a lot to tell him."

Not a lot? Ted thought. Can Jonathan be serious?

Jonathan looked over the garden toward the Manor House, took off his baseball cap, and tossed it beside him between him and Ted on the bench.

"Looking back on Vietnam now, it all seems so surreal. I don't know what the hell I was thinking, going down to the States to enlist like that. It certainly wasn't ideological. I mean, it wasn't to stop the red menace or whatever they were saying at the time. I didn't care about the red menace. I just wanted excitement, I guess. I wanted to piss off my mother and father. I wanted to shoot things. And I wanted to fuck around, figuratively and literally, before starting my life, before I was trapped in a life full of tailored suits."

Ted nodded, surprised that Jonathan was finally speaking to him about Vietnam for the first time.

"I never thought I'd be sleeping next to the red menace, though!" Jonathan said with a laugh. He ran his hand through his thick black hair.

"So, I join the infantry in Buffalo, go through basic training and fly to Vietnam for this adventure and excitement, and what do I become? A fucking *REMF!* A *rear-echelon* motherfucker. That's what they called us. So, throughout the war, I worked in supplies with a nifty metal clipboard, nowhere near the front line. I left university, promised the US Army almost two years of my life, went halfway around the world to get away from Hamilton and my father's suit shop, and ended up working in… and here's the punch line, Ted… working in uniforms!"

"Uniforms?"

"Uniform supplies! Fatigues, jungle trousers, hats, helmets. I did exactly what my father did but with khaki instead of glen plaid and pinstripes. Come on, Teddy, you got to laugh at the irony of that!"

"At least you had the guts to go to Vietnam," Ted said.

"But it didn't take me long to realize that being away from the jungle was the best place to be in Vietnam. So… I kept my head down, counted uniforms in all sizes until I was sent home." Jonathan picked up his Expos cap and put it back on his head.

Across the garden, Rick walked alone through the grass in his bare feet, smoking a cigarette. Someone had finally got him into a pair of blue plaid pyjamas.

"I think Rick misses Carl," Jonathan said.

"You've got to be kidding!" Ted said.

"What was that Joni Mitchell said? That you don't know what you got until it's gone?"

Jonathan moved close to Ted on the bench, wiping his hands on the front of his pyjama bottoms.

"I'd miss you too, Teddy… if you tried again and succeeded."

"I have no plans on trying again, Jonathan. I'm now committed to being here for the duration. I promise."

"Good. I want you to know you can talk to me when we get out of here. Unless you'd rather forget about this place and everyone in it."

"Are you kidding? I'm hoping to get a hell of a discount on suits at Pressman Tailors."

"Count on it!" Jonathan said. "And someday, we can tell each other our old war stories. I don't have many Vietnam stories, having spent most of it in the storeroom, but the ones I do have are pips."

Across the garden, Rick had now laid down on his back on the grass. From time to time, his hand would move to his lips so he could take a drag off his cigarette. Ted wondered if Rick was trying to make shapes out of the few clouds in the sky like kids do.

"You really think Rick misses Carl?" Ted asked.

"I'm sure he misses having someone around he can tell to fuck off."

"Maybe we all need someone around to tell to fuck off."

"So, is Gloria coming up today, Teddy?"

"No, she'll be up tomorrow, I think. How about Lola? She will be coming up to see you today?"

"Probably not," Jonathan said. "Lola said she couldn't stand seeing me in pyjamas during the day. I told her I'd put on pants if she brought me up some clean ones like your wife does. She said maybe next week. I don't think Lola wants to look at me at all right now."

An older nurse with an old-time nurse's cap walked quickly across the garden past Ted and Jonathan toward the Manor House without saying anything as she passed. If she was there to watch them, as Carl had said, she didn't look to be taking her job too seriously.

"Have you been inside the Manor House?" Jonathan asked.

"Once to see another doctor whose office was over there and to use the washroom a few times when I didn't want to walk all the way back to the hospital john."

"They have the old asylum records going back to the 1800s in the basement," Jonathan said.

The idea of looking for his mother's asylum records briefly popped into Ted's head, but it was quickly followed with an image of a grown Josh rifling through Ted's medical records one day. That made the idea seem genuinely appalling. His mother's records were none of Ted's business.

"Did you know that there's a warren of old tunnels in the basement of the Manor House?"

"Tunnels? For real?" Ted said.

"The tunnels once connected the Manor House to the wings of the old asylum. You can still see remnants of them in the basement of the Manor House behind those old wooden doors near the washrooms."

"How do you know?"

"I took a look after using the washroom. They're old red brick tunnels, the same colour brick as the old asylum and the Manor House. You can only go about fifty feet before they're bricked up, though. Maybe they collapsed when the asylum was razed. Now they use what's left of the tunnel for storage: filing cabinets, chairs, and old freaky medical equipment that looks like something out of a horror movie with gauges and dials. I'll show you sometime."

"Tunnels, huh?' Ted said. "There's always more than meets the eye."

On Saturday after a lunch of bologna sandwiches on white bread and coffee in the hospital cafeteria, Ted showered, trimmed his beard with a pair of cuticle scissors from the nurse's desk, and put on a clean pair of blue jeans and a mustard dress shirt with the arms rolled up past his tattoo. As he signed himself out for six hours, he asked the nurse at reception to cut off his hospital bracelet, but she refused, saying it was better for him to leave it on since they would just have to make another when he came back.

And as easy as that, Ted walked out the front doors into the July midday sun a practically free man. Crossing West Fifth Street, he ripped off his hospital bracelet and tossed it in the middle of the road.

He leaned up against the bus stop pole, lit a cigarette, and ran his fingers over the scar across his throat. He had inspected it closely that morning in the bathroom mirror while trimming his beard. The black scab had finally fallen off, and it was now mostly pink except for about two inches of thickening dark red scar tissue where he had made the first and deepest cut below his Adam's apple. Dr. Shackelford had said this raised hypertrophic scar would eventually regress.

The bus stopped in front of Ted and the driver looked suspiciously at him as he dropped an adult ticket, one of two that Nurse Debbie had given him before he left, into the fare box and sat by the back door of the near-empty bus. Ted had not been on a bus since he was seventeen years old. It may be different in big cities like Montreal, Toronto, and New York, Ted thought, but in Hamilton, the only people who took the bus were either too old or too poor to drive. The bus headed down the mountain and Ted stared out the window at the city below. It was beautiful in its own way. Thousands of houses on treelined streets sprawled out from the foot of the mountain to the steel mills that hugged the bay. More and more apartment buildings and a few large office buildings had popped up in the late sixties when the city thought the good times would never end. Good times always end. Now they were in the midst of another recession. Layoffs. Unemployment. Inflation. Stagnation, The same old same old.

Ted stepped off the bus on Herkimer Street and walked toward St. Joseph's Hospital. He already decided he would only stay with the Old Man for an hour— tops. Then he'd walk the few blocks north through Gore Park to The Windsor Hotel and grab a few drinks before he had to head back up to the loony bin. Ted had over forty bucks in his pocket, collected from his wife and sisters for hospital vending machine junk, and was tempted to stop for a drink now, but if he did, he'd never get to St. Joseph's. He knew that.

Ted obtained the room number from hospital reception and took the elevator up to the third floor. The Old Man shared a room with three other men, all of them old and sickly and, seemingly, just as close to death's doorstep as his father. Ted found the Old Man in a bed beside the window, sleeping with a pained look on his face. A hospital overbed table was pushed to the side with his lunch, untouched, on a tray. Ted was relieved that his older sisters and the Old Man's wife, Helen, weren't there. He couldn't take all of them right now. He had not told anyone that he was coming.

Even having lost some weight, Walter Moore was still an imposing figure, with a full head of white hair, big brawny hands, and, even with deep lines now in his face, he remained a handsome man. Ted sat down quietly in a chair between the window and the bed and wished he could have a cigarette just as the Old Man opened his eyes and smiled.

"Hey there," the Old Man said.

"Hey," Ted said softly.

"Give me your hand, will you, Teddy?"

Ted stood up, reached out his arm, and gave the Old Man his hand. Walter took Ted's hand and using it for leverage, pushed himself into a sitting position in the bed. Then he let go.

"Teddy, you grew a beard." His voice sounded deep and sputtering; only half of what it used to be.

"It's easier than shaving in that place," Ted said, leaning over the hospital bed.

The Old Man slowly reached out and rubbed the whiskers on Ted's chin and then let his hand fall to the bed as a nurse came into the room. Her uniform was immaculately white. The nurses here looked better put together than the ones up at the nuthouse, Ted thought.

"So, another one to see you, eh, Walter?" The nurse asked.

"This is my son, Edward. We named him after my father's brother who died in the Boer War. The first Boer War," the Old Man said, smiling.

"You certainly have a lot of children, Walter, don't you? I can't keep them straight," she said as if this wasn't a Catholic hospital.

The Old Man nodded.

"Let's do try and keep it down so we don't disturb the other men," she said, looking at Ted.

Ted wanted to tell this woman, "Listen, lady, this man is a World War Two veteran, show some fucking respect! And his name is Mr. Moore, not Walter." But Ted held his tongue. At least for now.

"He didn't eat his lunch," Ted said, looking at the tray of food on the table.

"Walter is… well, he's having trouble feeding himself now, so we have to wait until someone is free to feed him. But now that his son is here…" She turned and walked out of the room.

Feed the Old Man? Christ! This had to be some kind of huge cosmic joke, Ted thought, biting his bottom lip.

"I have a little problem lifting my arms now. So… I guess I'll never feed myself an entire meal again, and Teddy… it's **goddamn** humiliating when you can't even feed yourself." He coughed, and some pink spittle flew out of his mouth onto the front of his hospital gown and on his chin.

Ted grabbed the paper napkin on the table by the food and wiped the spit from his father's face.

"You don't have to talk if it hurts your throat," Ted said softly.

"Everything hurts," the Old Man said, grinning. "Talking is one of the things that makes me feel better now."

"Are you hungry?"

"A bit… but… if you don't want to, Teddy, I can wait for Helen."

Ted rolled the table closer to the bed, pushed the tabletop over his father's chest, and began cutting up the soggy-looking meat pie with the fork.

"This looks like a real English lunch. The only thing missing is the glass of ale," Ted said. "And you eat better here than we do at the nuthouse. All I had for lunch was a shitty bologna sandwich."

Ted lifted the fork to his father's mouth and fed him a small piece of meat pie.

"That nurse looks like my teacher back in the village I grew up in," the Old Man said between chews. "She was a bit of a bitch too."

"Widecomb-in-the-Moor," Ted said, nodding while putting a forkful of carrots and peas in his father's mouth.

When Ted was young, the Old Man would tell them stories about Widecomb-in-the-Moor, his hometown near Devon, England and the historic birthplace of the Moores. He would sit in his big red chair and tell Ted and his siblings to close their eyes and imagine thatched-roofed cottages on steep green hills and winding roads like the illustration on the tin chocolate box lid they would buy at Christmas from Marks and Spencer's. Ted had never been to England (he did have to fly through Ireland on his way to the Congo), but the Old Man had painted his hometown many times in watercolour from memory over the years that Ted felt like he had been there. And one watercolour painting that the Old Man had given to Josh, now hung in Ted's house, on Josh's bedroom wall surrounded by all those paper cocktail placemats Josh collected.

"Widecomb was full of piggeries. Can you imagine an entire town that smelled of pig shit?"

Ted nodded again and put another piece of meat pie in the Old Man's mouth. Funny, Ted now thought, how his mother, Anna, never told them much about Arendal, the town she came from in Norway. All Ted knew about his mother's side was that her family had been shipbuilders for generations.

"Do you think Widecombe-in-the-Moor has changed much since you left?" Ted asked, poking at the mashed potatoes with the fork.

"Probably, everything does," the Old Man said. He cleared his throat as best as he could. "Did I ever tell you the story about the great thunderstorm of Widecombe?"

"I don't think so," Ted said.

"A couple of hundred years ago, a huge bolt of lightning hit St. Pancras, the Cathedral in our village, right in the middle of Sunday services and killed a bunch of people."

"No, you've never told me that."

"Afterwards, the people of Widecombe decided that the Devil had visited them."

His father's eyes were still a striking green, just like Ted's. *Those green eyes were the best thing the Old Man ever gave me.* Girls had always loved Ted's green eyes. And girls had loved the Old Man too— a lot of them.

Ted held up a yellow plastic cup of cold tea, and the Old Man sipped it through a straw and grinned.

"A visit by the Devil? That would explain a lot with this family."

"Oh, those clodhoppers in Widecombe still believe in pixies and demon dogs and goddamn headless horsemen too." He chuckled and began to cough again. "I'm full now, Teddy. Thanks, son."

"Do you want more tea?"

The Old Man shook his head and laid his head back on the pillow.

"I told Wilma that story about the Devil coming to Widecombe a few years ago, and she said she always knew there were demons in our family. She said she could see them all around each of us. What a loon!" His voice was sounding even rougher, and Ted tried to think of a way to allow him to stop talking for a few minutes to rest.

"Wilma has some weird ideas," Ted said. "You know, when she flies back up here, she's going to try and save your soul. All day if she has to. Then she'll probably try and save mine too. Two souls with the price of one fucking Pan Am ticket from Atlanta. You'll have to be firm with her, or she won't give you any peace."

"Maybe I don't deserve peace."

"We all deserve peace," Ted said, really meaning it.

"You know I'd kill for a butt, Teddy. I asked Peggy for one when she was here, but Sue said, 'over my dead body'. It's not going to hurt me now, for Christ's sake. I wish someone would sneak me a beer too. Or even a shot of rye. I haven't touched a drop in twenty-two years, but... every man should be able to have his last shot of rye."

"I'll come by again and bring us a mickey of rye and we'll drink it together. If they let me out again."

"My own father was a stern miserable son-of-a-bitch. He never touched alcohol and was a member of the Church of England Temperance Society for Christ's sake. And he never missed a church service at that damned cathedral on Sunday."

"Well, I guess Wilma and the rest of them came by that religious shit honestly. If your throat hurts from talking... you don't have to talk for my benefit. I'm just as happy sitting her quietly," Ted said.

"I'm going to lose my voice soon enough," the Old Man said. "What was I talking about?"

"Your son-of-a-bitch father," Ted said.

"I was the only boy out of eleven kids. My father thought the family was cursed, having had all those girls, until I was born. I was born last when my mother was forty-four. Then she dropped dead when she was forty-five."

"Probably of exhaustion," Ted said.

"My father wanted me to be a constable in the town, just like he was, and his father and grandfather had been, but after I was picked up for public drunkenness in the next village, he gave up on that and when I was seventeen, I hopped a boat to Canada. I had planned on going to Montreal for, you know, the girls and *ooh-la-la*! But I kept on going west looking for work and ended up here in Hamilton driving the streetcar. Then I met your mother and before I knew it... I had a ton of kids."

"I was seventeen when I left home too," Ted said.

"Just watch, Teddy, Josh will do the same thing. The boy has wanderlust, I can see it."

Ted nodded.

Fuck it! Ted grabbed the cigarette pack from his shirt pocket, lit one, and put it in his father's mouth. He father took a few puffs and smiled.

"Is someone smoking there!" one of the men in another bed yelled in a German accent.

"Do you ever regret it?"

"Coming to Canada?"

"Having all us kids."

"No. I don't regret having any of you. I only regret not being a better father."

"I can relate to that."

"You're a fine father, Teddy."

Ted chuckled ironically.

"Your mother came up to see me," said the Old Man, with a sad smile. "That was when I *really* knew I was dying."

"You can't smoke in here!" the voice said again.

Mom came up here? Ted was curious what they spoke about but hesitated. What business was it of his what was said between a man and his ex-wife at the end with so many years of history and eight kids? Nine if you counted Ruth.

"Your mother said she came because she had a message for me from Gabriel."

Ted winced. He took the cigarette from his father's mouth and took a drag himself.

"Funny how Mom never hears from Tessa, but Gabriel won't shut the fuck up," Ted said.

"Anna would be too afraid to call Tessa. If I didn't believe that heaven was a crock full of shit, Tessa would be the only person I'd be worried about meeting there."

"Why? You didn't do anything to Tessa."

"I left her. I left you all."

"Peggy says this family can never let anything go. She's probably right."

"I'll tell you one more story, Teddy. Then I'll let it go forever. After I heard about Abe and Tessa, I went down to Firestone and waited for Abe after his shift. I must have looked like a right fool, an old man in his sixties waiting to pummel another old man in his sixties. I almost left but when I saw him coming out of the plant with a big smile on his face holding my old grey lunchbox, I lost it. I grabbed him right there in the parking lot and kicked the shit out of him. I mean, I nearly killed him. I wanted to. I was going to. But a few of his workmates jumped on me and pulled me off him. It took four or five of them to get me off that son-of-a-bitch They wanted to call the cops, but Abe told them not to. Of course, he didn't want cops involved. I thought I broke his fucking jaw. I did knock out his dentures and stomped on them as I walked away, smashing them to bits. I only wish it had been his real teeth. That was the last time I ever saw Abe Murphy."

"I'm calling the nurse if you don't put that cigarette out," the voice yelled once again.

Ted tossed what was left of the cigarette in the cold tea.

"Is there anything else you want to ask me, Teddy? I... I may not be able to speak the next time you come. This is your last chance."

Ted shook his head. "I don't think so."

"All right... thanks for the lunch, son. And the smoke."

"I'll bring a bottle of rye with me next time..." Ted tried to say 'Dad', but the word wasn't there. Maybe next time, after they both had a drink.

The Old Man nodded slowly and closed his green eyes.

"I do have one question," Ted finally said. "What was the message Mom brought from Gabriel?"

The Old Man opened his eyes and smiled.

"A time for everything."

Ted walked along the old buildings down James Street to Gore Park. The downtown looks mummified in the goddam 1940s, Ted thought. Why didn't they have skyscrapers like Toronto? Hamilton is all stone and marble. Toronto is steel and glass. He stopped at the soot-covered statue of Queen Victoria at the foot of Gore Park. There she stood, pompous and ridiculously regal, on a pedestal with a stone lion keeping watch below her, empress over all she surveyed looking, ironically, like René Lévesque in drag. Victoria Queen and Empress, Model Wife and Mother. Of course, the old bag had never been to Hamilton. Or anywhere in Canada for that matter so what the hell did she know?

"James Joyce called her 'the flatulent old bitch' in *Ulysses*," an old drunk, sitting on a bench near the statue, said to Ted.

"Karl Marx called her Great Exposition 'an emblem of the capitalist fetishism of commodities,'" Ted replied. He wanted the drunk to know he knew stuff too for some reason.

"You sound like a commie," the drunk said, before lying back down on the bench.

"Socialist, actually," Ted said, walking away.

Ted continued down James Street to King William Street and turned toward the Windsor Hotel, stopping only once at a newsstand on King Street to buy the *Daily Racing Form*.

The Windsor Hotel, on the corner of King William and John, was one of the nastiest dives in the city and one of Ted's favourite places to drink. There was absolutely no pretention at the Windsor. On the ground floor of a decrepit three-story orange brick building with rotting wood cornice moulding along the top of the roof, the Windsor's big black door opened to an inauspicious and menacing netherworld where you could find factory workers, professionals, and housewives intermingling with bums, third-rate criminals, queers, and whores, but no one gave a shit who or what you were; people went to the Windsor to get drunk. And it was probably no coincidence that the Windsor Hotel was the last place Evelyn Dick's husband John was seen before his torso was found at the foot of the mountain thirty years ago.

The bartender, who looked grubby enough to have just walked in the backdoor from the alley behind the place, poured Ted's a small glass of draught while Ted pushed his glasses up on his nose and breathed in the familiar scent of the barroom. Booze, cigarettes, sweat, grime. He had missed it.

Ted downed the beer and ordered another with a shot of whiskey and asked the bartender to join him in the shot.

"I miss the old back bars with no women. That was where I'd always hang out. And back then, women could only get in the front bar if a man accompanied them. Seems stupid looking back on it now, but it was only a few years ago," Ted said.

"I remember," the bartender replied, pouring the two shots.

"Drunk women used to stand outside this joint waiting for some guy, any guy, willing to escort them in so they could drink. If they were going through DTs, they'd blow you in the alley before you brought them in. There's been a small river of cum swallowed behind this place. Those poor women would even buy you a beer with their dimes and nickels when you got in here. Then they'd always end up leaving with some other guy before the end of the night. That's why I preferred the back bars."

As if on cue, a middle-aged woman wearing pink slippers and a long tan raincoat came in the bar, sat on a stool two down from Ted, and ordered a small draught beer.

"Give her a shot of rye too," Ted said, feeling generous.

Ted was feeling better. This is the first time since April he didn't have to hide in the john like a criminal while having a drink. He opened the *Daily Racing Form* and looked over the long shots at Greenwood Raceway that day, handicapping as best he could in his rye-tinged head.

"And you know what?" Ted said without looking up from the paper. "There were never any problems in the back bar either. All the shit that ever happened in bars always happened up front where the women were. Anytime you got a lot of men together and only a few women there's fights. Always. But guys alone? Fuck, we're mellow, man. Have another shot with me."

The middle-aged woman wiped her mouth and began counting out change for another small draught. Ted thought for a second about buying her another shot but decided against it. *She'd never leave me alone if I did.*

The bartender filled up their shot glasses again.

"So, how's your day goin'?" the bartender asked with indifference.

"Well… just between you and me and the layer of sticky grime on the floor," Ted began, "I'm a mental patient at the Hamilton Psychiatric Hospital up on the mountain. Don't worry. I didn't escape. They gave me a few hours reprieve to see my dying father in the hospital and now I've got to get back. You see, I just sliced my throat open with a broken beer bottle a few months ago." Ted smiled, pulled down the front of his mustard shirt, and lifted his head so the bartender could get a good look at his throat.

"Have one on the house," the bartender said, pouring another shot of rye.

The woman sitting two stools down from Ted gave him a horrified look, stood, staggered past them, and exited out the front door into the light of King William Street. Ted looked down and saw that she had left one of her dirty pink slippers under her stool against the bar.

"Come the revolution, we'll all have slippers, sister!" Ted yelled.

Ted ordered another draught and, fishing in the pocket of his jeans for a dime, walked to the payphone by the men's room. It took him a second to remember the number; it had been a long time and too many volts to count.

"Dennis! How are you? It's Ted Moore… sure, right as rain… I want to put twenty-five on Con Game to win in the eighth… yeah… she's sired from Buckpasser, so I kinda feel like she's kin."

It was after ten when Ted, drunk, took the bus back up the mountain to the Hamilton Psychiatric Hospital. The nurse at reception only nodded when he walked, with a bit of a teeter, in the front door. He took a quick piss and went straight to his room in the west wing. He'd have to worry about the hospital bracelet tomorrow.

"Everything go alright?" Jonathan asked.

"Just great," Ted said, taking out his dentures and placing them on the bedside table between their beds. "Just fucking great."

"I want you to tell me again. Everything that happened, step by step," Dr. Shackelford said.

"Jesus, we've talked about this. Over and over."

"And I'd like to talk about it again, Ted. All of it. Start at the beginning for me, please."

Ted sighed and picked at one of the last bits of scab on his throat and began reciting the story again by rote, almost tuning out as he spoke.

"It started just after Christmas. I already owed the union thousands by then and my nerves were shot to hell. That's when I started seeing these little brown bugs in the kitchen cupboards. Gloria tried to tell me I was imagining them, but I didn't believe her. Then I stopped sleeping and when I did sleep, I was having wild crazy dreams."

"Like what?" the doctor asked.

"Like Josh and Gloria are zooming down the road in a car with no driver and I'm trying to catch up on foot to save them. Or I see them being chased down Alkeld Street by someone and I try to run after them to save them. Of course, I never catch up to them and would wake up screaming."

"Anxiety dreams," Dr. Shackelford said.

"And during the day while I was awake, I was gambling even more, trying to make the money back I took from the union and falling farther and farther behind. And then..."

"And then?"

"And then... the dreams changed."

"How?"

"I started to dream that I was the one driving the car or the bad guy chasing them down Alkeld Street, and they were running *away* from me. Somehow, I turned into the person I was trying to save them from. And when I was chasing them in my dream, I was carrying..."

"Yes?"

"An axe or knife."

"Did you ever catch them in your dreams?"

"No, but after that, I started to wonder if this was really in me, you know? Could I do something like that? I *was* dreaming it, for fucks sake. And I started to think that maybe I was a lunatic like Jake Ragno... and I was afraid I could hurt them the same way. So...

so I just got more and more freaked out and pretty much stopped sleeping altogether."

"And then what happened?"

"I told Gloria about my dreams, not about the axes and knives, that would have been too fucking much, you know. I just told her about how I was chasing her and Josh down. I still wasn't ready to tell her about stealing from the union yet. So, she listened to me, but the whole time she looked really alarmed. It was Gloria who told me to go to our family doctor, Doctor Heller, for help. And he put me on Thorazine right away."

"And you kept drinking."

"Yeah, I drank as much as I always did. And the anxiety got better for a while. I was sleeping, but it was like fake sleep. Like I wasn't going down as deep as I should, or I was going someplace else. Some half-way place between sleeping and being awake."

"Now, tell me about the night your cut yourself."

"Ah. Man! I can't talk about that night again! If I tell that story once more, you'll have to zap me with a million volts because I'm going to lose it. I'm not kidding, Doc!"

"Ted, I need you to tell me about that night again."

Ted sat a moment, looking out the window at the cars driving down West Fifth Street.

"Alright," he said. Bored by his own voice. "I couldn't stop losing at the track. That day I had lost even more. A huge amount, over a thousand dollars. If that fucking horse had won, I'd have paid back the union and still had money left over but... it didn't win, and I now owed the union eight thousand dollars. And... by the end of the day, I had begun to freak out completely."

"Now, take me to the garage."

"I went to the garage sometime after midnight. I had just seen something on the news about Jake Ragno and I couldn't stop thinking that I *was* crazy, and, at some point, I was going to hurt Gloria or Josh. The garage door was wide open, and it started to rain. I tried to take my mind off everything by fixing the headlight on my car, but the new bulb was fucking burnt out too. That made me really angry. Then I turned around and there's Josh standing at the garage door in his pyjamas and bare feet, shivering in the rain… just staring at me. I must have looked deranged."

"And then?"

"I wanted to protect Josh. I wanted him safe… from me and from anything I thought I was capable of. So, I cut my throat open. It seemed like the best solution at the time. In retrospect, not so much. And after they stitched me up at the hospital, they brought me here, to the Hamilton Lunatic Asylum with the electric shock and the lousy Jell-O and roommates that kill themselves. That's the whole story. Tell me that I should be locked up forever, and we'll go from there."

"No, we're not locking anybody up," Dr. Shackelford said. "In fact, I think it's almost time to send you home."

"Home?"

"Yes, in a week or so."

"Are you actually sitting there and telling me I'm cured?"

"No, you still have a way to go, but you won't need to be here much longer."

"Then, what the fuck is wrong with me if I'm not crazy?"

Dr. Shackelford leaned back in his chair. "I think you're experiencing what are called *intrusive thoughts.* Intrusive thoughts are unwanted thoughts that seem to just pop into a person's head. They can be violent or inappropriate, sometimes sexual, and are brought on by gross stress reaction and, possibly, the different medication you were given."

"Gross stress?"

"It's a sort of battle fatigue from the traumatic combat experiences during your time in the Congo; that's trauma that sticks around and doesn't go away for some reason. Perhaps it was precipitated by the malaria medication and continued, in the way of panic attacks, over the last fifteen years."

"Is there anything we can do about them?"

"Intrusive thoughts are an obsessive-compulsive disorder that can be treated, often quite well, with medication and therapy. Your alcoholism, and we'll have to discuss what we're going to do about that before you go home, probably started as just your way of coping with the anxiety of the gross stress."

"Are you saying with drugs and a good shrink I might never have another horrible thought like that again in my life?" Ted said.

"Well, a therapist can teach you how to cope with them when they do reappear. In treatment, we can teach that you don't have to obsess on unwelcome or disturbing thoughts. Instead, you can let them pass through your brain like any other of the thousand thoughts we have each day. Problems occur when you grab onto these thoughts and won't let them go. And, as you learn to stop obsessing about intrusive thoughts, they usually occur less often."

A feeling of relief almost as good as five shots of rye washed over Ted. *I'm not crazy! Not really.*

"Intrusive thoughts are more common than you might think, Ted."

"You're mean other people are walking around with thoughts popping in their heads about hurting their family?"

"And worse."

"And how do you know I won't act on these thoughts when I didn't even know."

"One of the things we look at is how these thoughts make you feel. We want to assess if they bother the person having them somehow. We look at things like… are you anxious or ashamed of the intrusive thoughts."

"Yes, I am."

"I know. That indicates that you're unlikely to act on these violent and inappropriate thoughts. I've talked to you for four months and I can see that you're not dangerous.

"Not dangerous," Ted said softly.

"Even though you aren't the model patient. You don't like rules, Ted. That's true. You've been using surreptitious medication by drinking alcohol while you've been here and smoking marijuana in the hospital garden with the rest of those mischiefs… but you are not a psychopath."

"I'll put that on a T-shirt: *Not a Psychopath*," Ted said, beaming. "I could wear it with my *World's Best Dad* baseball cap."

The doctor laughed for the first time that Ted could remember in his months there, and Ted laughed too. It felt good.

"From what I've seen, you are a loving father who would rather cut his own throat than even think about hurting his son. I explained all this to your wife earlier this week, so she knows exactly what's happening. Intrusive thoughts can be, of course, disturbing to family members. And since you now know what's going on in your head, and, with more therapy, learn that you don't need to fear these thoughts, I highly doubt you'll hurt yourself again the next time one pops into your head, no matter how bad it may be."

"You know that for sure?"

"I'm pretty confident. So… what do you say we try and get you home by the end of the week?"

"Sure," Ted answered, looking down at his brown loafers.

"You look disappointed there, Ted. What? Not ready to go home?"

"No, I am ready to go home… it's just… it's just that I'm worried about Josh,".

"Josh?"

"I'm worried that Josh will end up here in the hospital himself in fifteen or twenty years… telling you about the night he saw his father slash his own throat."

Ted was to be discharged on the first of August.

That gave him less than a week left in the nuthouse. Gloria knew he was to be discharged soon, but Ted still had not told her the exact date, instead deciding to ask a friend from work to drive him home and surprise Gloria after her day shift on Monday. And with the pull of real life occurring faster than he had anticipated, Ted began to make lists in his head of all the things that needed to be done. The shit part of it was that Josh would still be away at camp for another week after he got home.

"So, you're leaving us too?" Rick said, sitting on his hospital bed drinking a grape soda from the vending machine.

"Christ, I'm just going back to the east end of the city, Rick, not the moon."

"Will you come back and visit me sometime?"

"I think you just want me to come up to bring you cigarettes and candy."

"Yeah, that's true. But I want to see you too."

Ted tossed half a pack of cigarettes over to Rick and told him to keep them. He still had almost a full carton left.

Rick smiled. He had been smiling more and more lately. Whatever medication they were giving him was working. They had also been laying off his ECT treatments, and somehow, a really sweet kid was emerging. The world needed more kids like Rick. Ted would have to figure out a way to say that to him before he left.

Rick jumped out of his bed and walked out of the room toward the lounge. They still had not had a good rain all summer, and the city was now restricting water use. No more watering of lawns until further notice. The hospital garden had gone from lush to brown in a week. Still, one good rain and it would come back. Hopefully. But that wasn't Teds' problem anymore; in a few days, he would have to figure out how to water his east-end lawn on the sly, probably at night with the hose.

"Will you visit me and bring me candy too?" Jonathan said, smiling.

"You'll be home soon too."

"From your lips to God's ears, Teddy. Say, since you're leaving, do you want to see the tunnels under the Manor House? You might not get another chance."

"Now?"

"Yeah, now," Jonathan said, sitting up and straightening his Expos cap.

"Okay."

Together they walked down the hall, out of the hospital, and across the garden. Most of the patients were inside because of the heat, with only a few scattered around the garden smoking or with visitors. The path to the Manor House was empty, with only a lone nurse, having a cigarette on the other side of the garden with her back to them. Jonathan opened the Manor House's old heavy front door and Ted followed him down the stairs to the basement. Ted had been down there a few times to use the men's room. It was one of the quieter bathrooms to have a shit and drink rye on the sly out of a Pepsi can.

In the basement, past the restrooms, was a utility closet and just beyond that, an old wooden door with a tarnished brass door latch and a red and white sign screwed to it saying, *Authorized Personnel Only*.

A toilet flushed in the lady's washroom, and Jonathan waved at Ted to hurry as Jonathan approached the forbidden door and opened it. Ted half-expected an alarm to go off when the door creaked open. They walked in and Jonathan flipped on the light switch by the door.

Inside was what was left of the Hamilton Asylum tunnels. The dank, rounded tunnel was lined with old red brick from the last century and ran only about fifty feet before being bricked up from the floor to the top of the tunnel with newer-looking cinderblock. The tunnel was packed with filing cabinets, ancient examination tables, chipped metal tubs, and other obsolete electronic devices with menacing-looking dials and switches attached.

"We should plug some of this in, connect you to it and see what happens," Jonathan said, sitting down on the side of one of the metal tubs.

"How often have you been down here, Jonathan?"

"A few times."

"Alone?"

"Mostly alone but once with someone else."

"Doing what?

"Fucking. Right there on that old examination table."

"Get out of here! Fucking who?"

"Just a patient."

"Christ, you'd think you'd tell me," Ted said, sitting down beside Jonathan on the rusty bathtub.

"Since this is your going away party, Teddy, do you want to hear one of my Vietnam War stories? I told you I had some pips."

"Yeah, tell me one of your Vietnam War stories, Jonathan. But it better be a pip since you built it the fuck up."

"Okay, how's this? I was dishonourably discharged from the United States Army."

"Dishonourably discharged?"

"They found me messing around with another guy in the storeroom. Right in the shelves of khaki underwear."

"Is that why you're here, Jonathan?"

"That's part of it. My parents have sent me to shrinks since I was a kid; all of them trying to fix me. They never seem to be able to do it through. Maybe because a part of me doesn't think there's anything to fix. So, we all hid it pretty well after Vietnam, my folks and me, I mean. I got married like they wanted, and the elder Pressmans were thrilled when I had my first two kids. But then I was arrested in the Gore Park toilets for… you know… and that was the end of my first marriage"

"Christ, I'm sorry, Jonathan."

"I was happy, more or less, for a while after my first marriage ended. I dated some guys and even fell in love once. Can you imagine me happy? I really was. But then I had another nervous breakdown when he left me, and my folks sent me to another hospital, this time in Toronto. The doctors there had a whole new approach. They told me I had a psychosocial maladjustment and reparative therapy was the cure. Then there were months of shock treatments that make what I had in this place look like those little static shocks you get from touching the doorknob after walking on the carpet. After nineteen months there they told me I was cured and for a while I thought maybe I was. Then I met Lola and things were mostly alright for a while but once Max was born, I started again. Right back to the Gore Park washrooms and, you guessed it, I was arrested *again*. So, it was either come here or jump in front of a CN train. I chose to come here. Well, Teddy, that's the story of Jonathan Pressman. Anyway, I just wanted to tell you the truth before you left. Are you shocked?"

"It takes more than that to shock me, Jonny."

Ted had known several homosexuals before. The Socialist Party had its share. Hell, even Gloria's sister, Lydia, was gay. And his brother, Dale… well, who knows what Dale was doing. Whatever it was, Ted didn't care. Ted had other worries besides who was putting what in which hole.

"Look, Jonathan, I honestly don't give a shit if you dig guys or girls or both. I really don't. After what we've gone through together, you're probably the best friend I ever had. I've never met anyone who I could talk to who understood the army thing and the family thing and the depression thing. You're like a brother to me, Jonathan. Only more so than my brothers ever were."

"Well, maybe *this* will shock you then…" Jonathan said.

"Unlikely," Ted said, grinning. "If electric shock didn't shock me all that much, I'm not sure anything can. But you go ahead and give it your best shot, Jonathan Pressman. Shock me!"

Jonathan took off his Expos baseball cap and ran his hand through his shaggy black hair. There were tears in his eyes.

"Teddy, I think… I think I'm in love with you."

Eight

Gloria's underwear was gone.

There, on the clothesline, was a big gap where two pairs of her underwear had been hanging between her tea towels and pillowcases and, though she searched her backyard, along the fence and around the foot of the red maple tree near the garage, Gloria knew her underwear hadn't just blown away.

I should have kept a better eye on them, she thought. Her neighbour, Marie, who lived three houses down Alkeld Street, had two pairs of panties stolen from her clothesline just last week. At the time, Gloria had advised Marie to march straight over to the Perry house and make his mother pay for them. Every cent!

Gloria stood with her hands on her hips as the morning sun shone through that gap in her clothesline onto her face. *Why did he take her oldest pairs?*

She walked back up the steps of her back porch and yanked the clothesline, making the rusty rollers on either end squeak loudly with each pull, and then threw what was left of her laundry in an old yellow laundry basket. Maybe it was time to get the police involved. However, by the time Gloria had tossed the last of the wash into the basket, she had decided against it. She had a pretty good idea of how something like that would go.

"You say he took what?" the policeman would say, jotting in his black lined notebook.

"Two pairs of my underwear," Gloria would say.

"Were they new underwear?" the policeman would ask, looking at her somewhat bewildered.

"No, there were... two of my oldest pairs, actually," she would answer, mortified.

"Your oldest pairs, you say?" the policeman would reply, underlining *oldest* in his notebook.

Gloria shook her head. No, she would not call the police. She could, however, walk down Alkeld Street and speak to Janet Perry again. Gloria had confronted Janet before, twice, in fact, over the last year. All Janet could do was maybe go up to his room, root around, and then come down the stairs with an assortment of sizes and colours of ladies' underwear in her hands for Gloria to fish through.

No, Gloria did not want her old underwear back. But she was furious enough to tell Janet Perry to hand over $2.99 for each pair he had stolen. That boy had picked the wrong week to snatch her underwear! He was just lucky that Ted wasn't around. Once, one irate husband on the street had gone over to Janet's, grabbed that boy by the collar of his T-shirt, and slapped him so hard across the face that blood had spurted out of his nose while Janet stood there on her porch in her slippers and housecoat screaming. And he had only been about ten or eleven at the time, and now that he was getting older, someone, one of the husbands on Alkeld Street, was going to really hurt that boy. Many of the women in the neighbourhood were so terrified that their husbands would end up in jail for beating up a minor that they would just keep their mouths shut. Why cause problems over an old pair of underwear or two. But now Gloria had heard from Marie and other women on the street that the Perry boy was doing more than just stealing underwear.

Gloria dropped her laundry basket on her kitchen table with a smack, which startled the puppy who had been dozing off under the table.

"Why in the hell am I living in this neighbourhood full of weirdoes and screwballs anyway, Reefer?" Gloria asked, looking down at the dog.

Though she grew up in the east end, Gloria had avoided this isolated piece of east-end Hamilton, entombed between the Hamilton sewage plant, the filthy Red Hill Creek, and the steel mills most of her life, and now here she was smack-dab in the middle of it. Trapped on Alkeld Street. So why, she wondered, was she going to such extraordinary lengths to save this bloody house in this lousy part of town?

Because it's all I have.

Gloria slipped on her black work shoes and walked out her front door and down Alkeld Street the short distance to Janet Perry's house. As she walked, she grew angrier, ruminating on how he must have been watching her as she pinned her laundry to her clothesline, waiting for the moment she would turn away and walk into the house and then, bolting out, his grubby hands quickly grabbing her underpants and then running off. He was probably off somewhere now mauling them. Gloria's face turned redder as she walked faster, her hands swinging from side to side and her eyes glaring. If Ted were here, she thought, he'd say I was on the warpath. And I am.

In a neighbourhood full of ugly little houses, Janet Perry's house took the cake. Small with peeling mucus-green paint, a broken window that had been busted for years with opaque yellowing thick plastic taped over it, and an overgrown front lawn with an ancient manual lawnmower sitting rusting beside the steps leading up to the front door. If there ever was a Mr. Perry, Gloria had never seen him. Janet had lived there alone with her son before Gloria and Ted bought their bungalow on Alkeld Street three years earlier. And, like Janet Perry herself, every year, the Perry house looked more and more decrepit.

Gloria pushed the old rusty lawnmower aside, stepped over a patch of something black and oily on the cracked patio stone walkway, and climbed up the two wooden steps to the old faded and splintered wooden front porch, which creaked under Gloria's feet as she approached Janet's front door.

Gloria hit the old brown wooden door with the palm of her hand, waited a few seconds, and then hit it again harder.

"Janet? Janet, are you home?"

Gloria pushed her face against the door's diamond-shaped window and, although the glass was warped, could see Janet Perry standing, anchored, at the bottom of the stairs leading to the house's second floor. Seeing Gloria staring at her through the window, her shoulders collapsed in defeat, and she walked slowly toward the front door, doing up the top buttons of her housecoat as she slogged along the few feet toward the door.

The door opened only enough to show half of Janet's body and one eye peering out. Janet Perry was older than most mothers in the neighbourhood and looked more like a grandmother than a young boy's mother. Janet was thin with large front teeth stained yellowish-brown from nicotine that seemed to grow farther apart in her mouth each time Gloria saw her. Her greying brown hair was up in a messy lump on top of her head, and she wore a short yellow housecoat that fell to just below her knees.

"You owe me six dollars for my underwear," Gloria said. She crossed her arms, waiting for an argument. Rarely was anything achieved in the east end of Hamilton without some kind of a row, but she was determined to get six dollars out of Janet Perry if she had to shake it out of her.

Janet looked down at her bare feet and sighed, "One second," she said. She walked to the kitchen at the back of the house, returned with a small coffee can of change, and then opened the door wide enough that Gloria could see the mess of dishes and clothes in the living room.

"I have to hide my coins, or he'll take them," Janet said, wearily. She began to count out the money, first in quarters then in dimes and finally in nickels and pennies. "Five twenty-five… five thirty…"

Gloria watched silently as Janet put the coins in her hand. She was a little sickened that they seemed sticky.

"Five eighty… five ninety… five ninety-five… ninety-six… ninety-seven…"

"Janet, you've got to put a stop to this," Gloria said.

Janet nodded and then slowly looked up and down the street to see, Gloria surmised, if anyone else was watching from their own front porches. Alkeld Street was, Gloria had to agree, a nosey street.

"No, really, Janet. Did you know that boy of yours is doing more than just taking underwear now? I've heard he's starting to look through windows too."

Janet held the coffee tin close to her chest but remained silent.

"Do you understand, Janet? Women have seen him looking in their bedroom and bathroom windows. You know what they call that, don't you?"

"I'm doing my best, Mrs. Moore. I really am."

"Well..." Gloria said, tightening her grip on the sticky money in her hand, "one of these days, that boy is going to steal the wrong pair of underwear or look into the wrong window, and someone's husband is going to hurt him. Hurt him bad! He's not a little kid playing games anymore. How old is he now?"

"Thirteen. His birthday was two days ago," Janet said.

"Thirteen!" That's exactly what I'm saying, Janet. He's not a child anymore. He's a teenager, and it's just going to get worse until you get him help."

"I still have most of the cake I made for his birthday. I decorated it with white and blue icing, like the Toronto Maple Leafs, and brought it out on the front porch to cut up."

Is Janet going to offer me some of that little pervert's birthday cake? Gloria wondered. Could she be serious?

"I invited some of the neighbourhood kids who were out there on the street to come up and have a piece of birthday cake with us, but they all said no, every single one of them. I've never met a kid who didn't want birthday cake."

"Janet, are you all right?"

Janet pointed across the street at Louise Dennis' house with its red and white rosebushes and freshly painted white porch.

"Last month Mrs. Dennis made caramel apples for her son's birthday and handed them out on her porch. Every kid in the neighbourhood came running to her house to take one of her caramel apples... but none of those kids wanted any of my birthday cake. You know, I think the kids around here are a little bit afraid of me for some reason," Janet said with a weary smile, showing her brown teeth with big gaps that reminded Gloria of her clothesline.

"Look, Janet," Gloria said. "I know it's hard to raise boys by yourself. I was raising two alone when I met Ted, but I think it's time you talked to someone at Laura Secord School. Maybe they can get him some help, you know? What about his father?"

Janet said nothing.

"And if not his father… then some other man. Is there another man he looks up to, Janet? Is there an uncle or family friend or something?"

"I've tried. And tried and tried."

"Then try again," Gloria said. "It's your responsibility to get him help. When something happens— and it will, trust me, Janet, it will. You'll be the one responsible for it!"

"I gave you six dollars like you asked for. You should probably go home now." Janet said softly.

"Fine, I'm going. I just hope you get that boy some help."

"His name is Shannon. His name is not *that boy.*"

"Janet, I'm just saying—`"

"And just maybe… you should take care of the problems in your own house before getting on your high horse with other people, Mrs. Moore."

Gloria took a step back. The coins in her hand suddenly felt heavy, and she let her arm fall to her side.

"I know Shannon isn't perfect and that he has problems. No one knows that better than I do, but you're not perfect, and neither is anyone else on this street. I don't know, but I really did think that after what's happened to you and your husband, maybe you'd be a bit more understanding of other people's problems. But I guess not."

And with that, Janet Perry shut her front door. She didn't slam the door in Gloria's face; she just closed it gently, like you would on a friend who was leaving.

Gloria walked home, made herself a cup of tea using the same teabag she had used earlier that morning and got ready for work. All she wanted to do was get to Munro, sit at her machine, and turn off her brain to everything but the coils of steel in front of her. And where was Josh? She wanted to speak to him before she left for work.

Just before she had to leave for work, Gloria looked once again out the front window and finally saw Josh coming up Alkeld Street from the direction of the creek. He was wearing the same clothes he had worn yesterday, a faded dark blue T-shirt with a small tear in the collar and his blue ADIDAS shorts with three white stripes on each side. Halfway down the street he looked around, walked on to the boulevard, and wiped the bottom of his sneakers on the brown grass. He was probably down at the creek, Gloria thought. And now he's attempting to get the red dirt off his shoes, so I won't know. All three of her sons thought she was an idiot. The truth was Gloria knew practically everything that went on in her house.

As Josh picked some clay out of the bottom of his sneakers with a stick, Gloria thought just how much Josh was now resembling her. People told her, quite often, that they thought Josh looked like Ted, but that was only because they had the same light-coloured hair. The truth was, Josh looked more and more like her every day. He had the same round face, the same high cheekbones, and the same dark brown almond-shaped eyes. Josh was even starting to get round around the hips like she was. *He's looking more like me than I do.*

"I better not catch you down at the creek," Gloria yelled down the hall when Josh came in the back door.

"I wasn't!" Josh yelled back just as loudly.

Gloria was pretty sure Josh was lying about being down by Red Hill Creek, though it was possible he could have picked up that red clay on his shoes practically anywhere in that neighbourhood they lived in. And why make a big federal case out of it now. Josh was almost eleven years old, getting old enough to look after himself. Didn't he stay home alone now until she came home from working afternoon shifts. Besides, it wasn't the water dangers or slippery banks of Red Hill Creek that worried Gloria. The creek never got very deep or swift unless they had a big rain, and that certainly hasn't happened this year. What worried Gloria was that there could be some pervert holding up down there by the creek, just waiting for some blond-haired boy to happen by.

"I want to talk to you, Josh."

"Good," Josh replied. "I want to talk to you too."

He came into the living room holding a pair of scissors in his hand and fell back hard into the large chair, Ted's chair, across from her. He smelled faintly of cigarette smoke, but Gloria held back an urge to bring that up right now. He picked up the front section of *The Hamilton Spectator* and began leafing through it. He was searching for more pictures and articles about that Ragno murder, Gloria thought. Josh did that every single day, looking to cut out any articles he could find about the murder and paste them into that ghoulish scrapbook of his.

"Do you hang around that Shannon Perry behind my back?" Gloria asked.

"He's a big kid. I stay away from big kids." He turned the page of the newspaper, his eyes scanning each page before frowning.

"So, you don't ever play with him?"

"Who?" Josh asked, turning another page.

"Shannon Perry. Do you or do you not ever play with Shannon Perry?"

Josh looked up slyly over the newspaper. "You mean like outside on the street?"

"Yes. Do you ever play with Shannon Perry out on the street or anywhere else? Joshua, put down the paper for five seconds and answer me, will you? I'm asking you a serious question."

Josh slowly folded the newspaper and placed it on the floor beside the chair with the scissors on top. Then he turned to his mother, crossed his legs, and put his hands on his knees like he was at an afternoon tea party. His bare feet were dirty at the ankles from sweating in his sneakers.

"You have five seconds," he said, cocking his head to one side.

He's being a smart-ass, Gloria thought. Just like Ted. He might look like me, but *this* was all Ted.

"I asked you," Gloria said tersely, "do you ever play with that Shannon Perry boy?"

"Let's see." He looked up at the ceiling and put his index finger to his chin dramatically. "Hmm. No. No, I don't."

"Never?"

Josh put the index finger of his other hand to his chin and looked up for a second time before meeting her gaze. "No, never."

"Good."

"Well…" Josh said, picking up the newspaper. "Shannon did come over once to see Reefer this week… no, twice… he came over twice when you were at work. He was only here for maybe five or six minutes at the most. Maybe seven minutes. I didn't time it. He wasn't in the house. It was just the backyard, and we weren't really playing so it's okay."

"No, it's not okay. I want you to stay away from that Shannon Perry."

"Okay," Josh said, opening the newspaper. "I'll stay away from *that* Shannon Perry. Is that it?"

"No, that's not *it*. I want to tell you why I don't want you playing with him."

Josh put the paper down on his lap, crossed his arms, and looked squarely at Gloria.

"Because Shannon Perry is… bad. He's a bad kid."

"Is that it?"

"No, that's not it! There's something really *really* wrong with Shannon Perry. And one day soon the police are going to come and take him away."

"Because he steals ladies' underwear?" Josh said matter-of-factly. He picked up the scissors again.

"Where did you hear that? Where did you hear that he steals ladies' underwear?" she said, taken back.

"I don't know," Josh said. "Around," waving one arm in a circle over his head with the scissors in his hand.

"Well, that's exactly right. Stealing women's underwear is… well it's not a normal thing to do so… just stay away from him. And stop waving those scissors around!"

"Okay."

"Promise me."

"I said OKAY! And now it's my turn to talk to you about something."

"In a second. I'm not finished yet. I want to ask you something else. Something important." She took a breath. She had come up with a way to ask this earlier but now she couldn't remember what it was. Just ask, she said to herself. If more parents had just asked when she was young…

"Shannon Perry has never... touched you or any of your friends, has he? Or done anything strange or... well anything like that, has he?"

"Nope," Josh said, leaning back in the big chair. "He's only touched Reefer."

"I am *asking* you if Shannon Perry ever touched you in your private places.

He grinned. "You mean has Shannon ever grabbed my wang?"

"Has he?"

"Get real. He's never done anything like that. And besides, I wouldn't let anyone do that to me. Shannon only comes over sometimes to see Reefer in the backyard. We play fetch. Reefer can fetch for hours. He never gives back the stick though."

"Well, no more of that. You tell him to stay off our property or I will. I'm going to tell Troy too. I don't want that boy around here."

"Shannon has never touched Reefer's wang either. Just in case you were going to ask that next."

Gloria's face turned red. At times she wanted to slap Josh across the face so hard it would make his ears ring. No one could get her goat like he could— and so quickly. She wasn't concerned that Josh spoke his mind, that was at least boyish. It was the smart-ass stuff she really didn't like. That wasn't boyish or manly. And all three of her boys had the same smart mouth.

"I better let Reefer out to pee before I go to work," she said, getting up from the couch.

"Hey! You said I could ask you something serious too!"

"Alright what is it?" she said, turning around. Reefer walked around her in a circle and then sat at her feet. "Quickly before Reefer has an accident on my carpet."

"I'm not going to camp."

Gloria turned around and walked down the hallway toward the backdoor as Reefer scrambled to keep up at her feet.

"Please, I don't need this today. We agreed you would spend a few days to at least try it."

"No, you agreed to that. I didn't agree to anything, and I'm not going to any stupid camp!"

"You're going! If you decide you don't like it I'll come and get you, but you're going to give it a chance."

"I'm not!"

"You are!"

Gloria opened the back door and Reefer ran out toward the back of the yard to the maple tree. From the living room she could hear the fluttering sound of a newspaper being tossed across the room. And, though Gloria may have been wrong, she thought she heard Josh say, *fuck you*, clearly and harshly as the newspaper hit the living room wall.

"What did you say to me?"

"Nothing!"

"It better have been nothing!"

Her shoulders lowered in defeat. *Josh hates me.*

Reefer came running back into the house and up the stairs into the kitchen for a drink of water.

Well, considering what I'm about to do… I hate myself too.

Gloria climbed off the King Street bus and walked to the Tim Horton's coffee shop on Wellington Street and Main. Even though it was another exceedingly hot day, she wanted a small cup of tea and a few minutes to sit and calm herself down.

"What can I get you, hon?"

"Tea with milk and sugar, please." Gloria looked at the rack of fresh donuts behind the woman against the wall and then added "and a chocolate glazed donut."

Men filled the stools along the yellow laminated counter, and, not in the mood to be around any men at the moment, Gloria took her donut and white mug of tea to a small table by the corner window and sat down as some of the men at the counter turned their heads and watched her pass. She had dressed too well for this part of town, in her favourite taupe pantsuit, matching shoes, and new plum blouse. She had combed her black hair back and pinned it with a gold hairclip shaped like a butterfly. *From now on I'll always think of it as my grovelling outfit*, she thought.

She sipped her tea. It was too hot and needed time to cool a bit. A welcome delay before facing *him*. He has probably been waiting years for this day, Gloria thought. And how that son-of-a-bitch was going to enjoy this! But what could she do? She was all out of cards to play. *And it's not even my game.*

Gloria broke the donut in half and took a small bite. Stale.

She had never understood how some in Ted's family were so quick to forgive Abe. Such absolution would never have happened in her family. Gloria's brothers would have beat Abe to within an inch of his life. Not that Gloria would have wanted Ted to beat up Abe, but if Ted had given Abe one good punch in the face before Abe ran off, Gloria would have cheered. How strange it is now to think that at the time no one mentioned calling the police. No, Abe would never go to jail. Someday he would die comfortable and triumphant surrounded by weeping Murphys and probably with absolutely no regrets. What would she say to him today? Gloria had not spoken to Abe for years. She had seen him, begrudgingly, at Bonnie's first wedding and at Tessa's funeral—

No, Gloria thought, closing her eyes. *I can't think of that now. If I do, I'll never go up there.* She put down her mug of tea with a clunk.

Right then, Gloria despised Ted.

Josh was less than a year old the night it had all come out. Tessa had finally told her older sister Peggy the truth about what Abe had done to her, what he had been doing to her for years, almost from the moment he had moved in with Anna. The rest of the family had found out, one by one, via Sue, about the abuse later that night. A few hours later, Abe had run off someplace and Anna was left alone. Everyone, both Moores and Murphys, seemed shocked. Everyone but Gloria, that is.

In the years since that night, Gloria sometimes wondered, without ever saying anything to Ted, if Anna had known about what was happening to Tessa, or at least had an inkling. How could something like that be happening under her own roof for all those years without Anna at least having some suspicions? Gloria had a pretty good sixth sense for those sorts of things. She had dodged those types of men her whole life. She saw it in the way they walked, with an unsettling vigour and bounce in their step that was accentuated whenever children were around, tying their necks into knots to leer at them, always with a repugnant look on their face, half sinister and half smug, thinking no one is noticing.

But Gloria had noticed. She had her suspicions about Abe since that first Christmas on Waterloo Street, the way he plunked down the little girls on his lap like a grotesque Santa Claus in his red plaid shirt. And then the next summer, after a big Sunday family dinner at Abe and Anna's house, Gloria watched as Abe, wearing only his work pants and a white undershirt, laid on his stomach on the living room floor and made Tessa, seventeen at the time, straddle his back and squeeze the pimples and blackheads on his shoulder. The thought of it, even today, nauseated Gloria. That wasn't normal. And when Gloria got home that night and told Ted her suspicions about Abe and Tessa, what had happened? Ted had slapped her so hard across the face the blood vessels broke in her eyeball, turning the whites of her left eye blood red. That was the only time Ted had hit her.

Gloria finished the last of her tea. "If I move right now, I'll start crying," she said softly to herself. She closed her eyes and breathed in and out. It had to be done and it had to be done now, today, before July's mortgage payment came due on the fifteenth. This wasn't the first time Gloria had to swallow her pride and it certainly would not be the last. Men had knocked around her dignity, whatever was left of it, so many times before what was one more swift kick to it going to matter now? And besides, who was she, a girl from the east end, to be so grand on her high horse? Janet was right.

And what if, after all this, Abe said no? What if all this was some big ruse to make her travel all the way up here just so he could turn around and laugh in her face for revenge? Would Abe do that? Well, if he does, I'll get up and leave, she thought. Oh, why was she doing this to herself? Hadn't Ted called Abe from the hospital and set it all up? He told Ted to have her come downtown and pick up the cheque. It was all arranged. By this evening, she would have two thousand from Lydia and six thousand from Abe, enough to pay the union back in full and enough to pay their mortgage. Sonny Ferro from Ted's union was coming by tomorrow to pick up the eight-thousand-dollar cheque and then Gloria and Ted would at least have the union (and the spectre of prison) off their backs and Gloria would keep her house on Alkeld Street. And the price for all that was Abe Murphy. Abe Murphy back in their lives. Abe Murphy in her son's life.

"Enough of this," Gloria said, standing.

She brushed the few bits of chocolate donut crumbs off the front of her blouse and walked to the large ashen-coloured brick apartment building across the street. The sign in front looked old and weatherworn.

The Cordelia
Now Renting
1-2-3 Bedrooms

Sneaking through the front security door by following a lady with a shopping cart on wheels allowed Gloria to at least skip speaking to him over the apartment intercom system. She stepped into the elevator and pushed the round button for floor fourteen. That's really the thirteenth floor, Gloria thought, as the button lit up under her finger. How fitting she must go to the thirteenth floor. Of course, Abe wanted her to come crawling to him, the sadist. Why would he drive all the way down to the east end to bring the cheque to her house after she had forbidden him from ever stepping foot into it? Yes, Abe was going to enjoy this. The stale donut rolled over in her stomach as the elevator door opened, and she worried that she might throw up her tea and glazed donut on Abe's floor like Josh did at Hannah's.

Gloria knocked on Abe's door and waited. The door opened and an inviting scent of cinnamon, vanilla and lavender wafted out into the hall. Gloria wasn't softened by the alluring fragrance. *Blackbeard's house probably smelled of something like cinnamon and lavender too.*

"Who are you?" a short old woman said.

That must be Abe's wife, Gert, she thought. Though Gloria wasn't sure if they were actually married or not.

"I'm Gloria… um… Gloria Moore. I'm Ted's wife." She fabricated a smile as best as she could.

"Another Moore, eh?" Gert huffed with a scowl. "Abe said you'd be coming up here today for money."

"Yes, that's right."

"Well, then come on in." Gert pushed the door open.

"Thank you," Gloria said, following Gert into the apartment.

"Take your shoes off," Gert said, pointing to the welcome mat just inside the apartment on the scuffed parquet flooring.

Gloria bent down and pulled off her taupe leather shoes, placing them beside two pairs of black orthopaedic shoes. She stood and fastened the smile back on her face.

Gert's appearance was much the way Gloria had heard from others in the family. She was a bony old woman with a prominent osteoporosis hump, old-fashioned cat eyeglasses, and milky hazel eyes. Her white hair was so thin that Gloria could see dark red scabs and sores dotted over her greyish scalp. She was wearing a worn light-brown housedress with a too-large baby blue hand-knitted cardigan and matching knitted slippers.

"Ted comes by from time to time. Never with you, though. I've never seen you in our home before," Gert said.

"I work shifts. So… it's difficult to visit people as much as I'd like."

"Yeah, right," Gert said with a smirk. "Abe's in the toilet. You can wait in the living room for him if you want your money. Follow me."

Gloria took a deep breath and followed Gert down a dark hallway to the bright living room where large patio doors led to a balcony facing south toward the escarpment and, below, the Tim Horton's coffee shop she had just left. The room was overcrowded with dingy and faded furniture from the thirties and forties, with pieces of knitting interspersed randomly and without any colour coordination throughout the room: a green afghan lying on the back of a chair, emerald knitted pillow covers on the couch, red knitted place mats on the old walnut dining room table and knitted blue and white square coasters with a zigzag pattern on the coffee table.

"Sit there," Gert said, pointing to an armchair upholstered with large pink magnolias and gold-knitted arm covers. The old woman grunted, turned around, and went back down the hall to the kitchen.

Gloria sat and set her black leather purse on her lap. A stray spring in the back of the chair poked into her lower back as she looked around the room. The walls were covered with six sloppy-looking paintings of hunting dogs, each with a duck or some other kind of bird in their mouths. By the wall, an art deco maple china cabinet with two glass doors stood heftily with white knitted doilies on each shelf. Inside the china cabinet, which was completely devoid of any china or dishes, were small figurines of more hunting dogs and photos in silver and gold frames of all the Moores and Murphys from Wilma to Bonnie, including the only photo ever taken of Ruth. However, every one of the photos in Abe's cabinet was of Ted's siblings as children— not one of them was over the age of twelve or thirteen in the photos. It was as if Abe had embalmed the entire family as children behind cabinet glass, even Tessa. And then Gloria saw it. There on the bottom shelf was a photo in a brushed silver frame of Josh as a toddler sitting on Kevin's knee with Troy kneeling beside them in their old apartment on Barton Street. Gloria had never seen that photograph before. Where the hell did Abe Murphy get a photo of her boys? Did Ted—

"Hello, Ted's Gloria!" Abe said, walking into the room smiling. "Good, golly! I haven't seen you in years and years! You look beautiful as ever. Must be that Indian blood keeping you young!"

He was wearing a short-sleeved cream-coloured button-up shirt, black trousers pulled up over his large belly nearly to his chest, and a pair of baby blue knitted slippers that matched Gert's, slipped over a pair of black socks.

"Hello," Gloria said as warmly as she could.

Abe walked to the armchair where Gloria was sitting, leaned over, and kissed her on the cheek. Instinctively, Gloria drew away and the spring in the chair went deeper into her back. He hasn't changed much, she thought as he sat down in the middle of the rose-coloured chesterfield. He had a lot less hair, and what was left of it had turned from red to white, his pale blue eyes were even more washed-out, and he had shrunk, a couple of inches at least, since those days on Waterloo Street. But it was still, unmistakeably, and completely, Abe.

"Hot one today, huh?" Abe said, still smiling.

"Yes, it is," Gloria said.

"No need for air conditioning when you get a nice breeze up here."

All his money, and they can't afford air conditioning? Gloria thought. However, it wasn't really Abe's money at all. Any money they had stashed away was Gert's.

Gloria nodded though unconvinced that an air conditioner was unnecessary. There was a bit of a breeze, but the air was hot, dusty, and polluted by the factories and cars of the city. She preferred the cooler air near the lake by her house in the east end, even if it sometimes smelled of blue-green algae and the dead smelt that washed up on shore of Lake Ontario in the summer. Gloria would take the smell of algae blooms and dead fish any day over car fumes and factory smoke that Abe and Gert have been breathing in for years.

"I was just at your house a few months ago, but you weren't there," Abe said.

"Oh? I was probably at work."

She bit her bottom lip. Gloria had known Ted came up here to see Abe from time to time, but she had no idea that Ted allowed this monster into her house. And where exactly was Josh when Abe came down for these little visits?

"Yeah, the last time I was down at your house, I could see old Ted wasn't doing too well. I could see where he was heading as plain as the big nose on Ted's face. I came home and I said to Gerty, 'Gerty, that boy is one step away from the loony bin.' And a couple of weeks later, Bonnie calls and tells me that's exactly where he ended up." Abe chuckled and shook his head.

No, she thought this wasn't going to be quick and easy. Abe was going to play out this little torture session of his as long as he possibly could. And she had no other choice but to take it.

"Have you gone up to visit him at the hospital?" she asked. Her fingernails dug deeper into the strap of the purse.

"Nope, I don't like hospitals. But Ted did call me up from there a few times. And to be honest, he didn't sound much better than he did the last time I saw him. Nope, I don't think they'll be letting old Ted out anytime soon."

"Well, Ted's not in jail. He's there voluntarily now. He could sign himself out today if he wanted to, but he's taking the doctor's advice and staying in the hospital for a few more weeks."

"They're as loony as he is if they let him out."

From the hallway, Gert suddenly materialized without speaking and took a seat at the dining room table. She snatched some pale green yarn and knitting needles out of a stuffed grey canvas bag sitting on the table and, with a pinched face, swiftly and mechanically began knitting, her talon-like hands deftly manipulating yarn into loops and stitches as her knitting needles clicked away.

"I hope the next time I get down to your house, when this latest mess of Ted's is over, I hope you'll be there too. Family is family. That's what I always say."

There it was. Abe's six thousand dollars had strings attached. Gloria had not expected Abe to negotiate the terms right then and there. Abe's deal was straightforward: if she took his money and kept her house, then Abe would be welcome in it. And not only that, but Gloria would also have to sit there in her living room with a smile of her face and make idle chit-chat while this bastard sat in Ted's armchair and smirked at her with his coffee-stained dentures.

"Yes, I should be there. If I'm not working," Gloria said.

"We'll just have to find a time when you're not working," Abe said. "And what about Joe?"

"Joe?"

"Joe! Ted's son with you!" Abe pointed to Josh's photo behind the glass in his china cabinet.

"Josh."

Abe looked confused. "Josh what?"

"Our son's name is Josh. Not Joe."

"Ah, right! I meant to say Josh. I don't think I've seen him since he was a baby. I'd like to see more of him." Abe scratched one of his bushy white eyebrows with a long yellow fingernail. "He is my grandson, after all."

Gloria's skin crawled while a crudely painted English pointer with unnatural blue eyes looked down at her.

"Well, he's not a blood grandchild but what's that matter? You want a cup of tea, Gloria?"

"No, no thanks. I really can't stay long."

"Shift work, right?" Gert roared from the dining room table.

"Right," Gloria said.

"Just one quick cup, then," Abe said. "Gerty, go make us some tea."

Gert laid down her knitting with a snort, stood, and limped down the hallway toward the kitchen.

"You like these dog paintings? I did them all myself. They're all paint-by-numbers, all of them."

"They're nice," she lied. Paint-by-numbers. That explains why the sky was the exact shade of blue in each painting and why they looked so messy. Walter Moore painted as well, but Walter's paintings were delicate watercolours he painted from memory of his village in England or, sometimes, of the Hamilton escarpment in autumn. These things on the other hand—

"So, Ted's got himself in some trouble, eh?"

"Yes, he has," Gloria said, relieved the conversation finally moved to the cheque. "We need eight thousand dollars, or Ted will go to jail, and I'll lose the house. He took the money from the union treasury to pay gambling debts and got further and further in debt." She hoped spitting it out quickly and truthfully would lead to less questions.

"Same old Ted," he said, still grinning.

"I guess Ted thought he'd be able to pay it back when he won. Of course, he never did win. Or if he did win, he didn't win big enough."

"I told Ted years ago he shouldn't gamble. He's a loser. He always was. Nice guy but a loser."

"The union said if we pay the money back, they won't go to the police. But even if we pay it back, he'd have to resign from his union position." Gloria folded her hands on top of her purse. "I have two thousand dollars from my sister, Lydia, and we need six thousand more. And that's the whole story."

"Lydia? Is she the dyke?" he asked.

Gert returned and placed a teacup and saucer beside Gloria on the end table and then another on the coffee table in front of Abe before walking back to the dining room table and her knitting. The cup and saucer wobbled a bit as Gloria picked it up. I don't want your tea, she thought. I never asked for tea. I never asked for any of this.

"Ted's been in jail before. That was before he met you. He ended up in the drunk tank a few times after he came back from Africa. Booze and horses! That's all that boy has ever thought about in his life. Oh, that and being an agitator and communist."

"I knew about Ted being in jail. He told me all about that a long time ago," she said.

"My boys have never been in jail," Gert said without looking up from her knitting.

"He wasn't even twenty years old," Abe spat out. "Not even old enough to drink and he was in the drunk tank. I bailed him out back then too. I had to drive down to the Barton Street jail and bail him out. Not right away, though. I let him sit in there for a weekend to teach him a lesson, not that it did any good. And now…" Abe chuckled again, "I'm bailing Ted out again. See, Gerty! I told you I wasn't such a bad stepfather. No matter what that lot says."

Gert's head bobbed in agreement as she continued knitting what looked like a scarf. What, Gloria wondered, would possess someone to knit a bloody scarf on one of the hottest days of the year? She desperately wanted to take off the jacket of her pantsuit, but she refused to take off her jacket in his home.

"So, what about good old Walter Moore?" Abe asked. "Why didn't you go to him for the money? He is Ted's real father for Christ's sake." He slurped his tea.

"He can't."

"Why not?"

"He's dying." Gloria said, putting down her teacup for the last time. She wasn't going to have any more of their tea. Not one sip. She was done.

"Oh right. Bonnie said something about that. Well, I'll tell you this, even if Walter Moore wasn't dying, he still wouldn't give Ted a penny. And do you know why?"

Gloria shook her head.

"Because Walter Moore doesn't have a pot to piss in. Never did. Drove that streetcar for forty years and didn't save a penny. They'll probably have to bury him in a pauper's grave. Another goddamn Moore drunk."

"I don't think they have pauper's graves anymore," Gert said, still not looking up from her knitting.

"No, they probably bury deadbeats with my tax money, these days. No, Walter Moore pissed away every penny he ever made on booze and whores," Abe said.

"Walter quit drinking years ago," Gloria said. "Long before I even married Ted."

"And Walter gave you away at your wedding, I heard, too," he said.

"The wedding we weren't invited to," Gert yelled.

"Well, I don't have a father and Walter…" Gloria said.

"Sure, I know. Well, the guy who wasn't good enough to be invited to your wedding has already written the cheque out for you," Abe said.

He leaned over, picked up the TV Guide on the coffee table and opened it. In the middle, by the cardboard ad promising twenty records for a penny was a folded cheque.

"I made the cheque out to you. Six thousand dollars and no cents," Abe said.

"That's us!" Gert bellowed. "No sense for lending Ted Moore that money."

Abe held out his hand, making Gloria get up from her chair to take the cheque from him. The scenic cheque, with a picture of the Rocky Mountains, was signed 'Abraham Murphy' at the bottom in large girlish curlicues. Even his signature is twisted, Gloria thought. She folded the cheque and put it in the inside zippered pocket of her purse. Could she go now?

"Thank you for this," Gloria said. She then turned to Gert. "I mean thank you both very much. And don't worry, I'll send you a cheque for twenty-five dollars every month starting next month and then fifty a month once Ted gets back to work. The union job is over, but he can still go back to operating a crane at Wentworth Steel. We are going to pay you back first. Lydia said she can wait for the money."

"You know, Gloria, it would be easy for me to come by your house every month and pick up the cheque," Abe said.

"Oh, no! I don't want you to go through all that trouble. Ted could bring it up to you… or we could even mail it right to you. That would probably be the easiest way for you—for everyone," Gloria said.

"It's no trouble," he said. "It would be nice to see more of you again. And Joe too."

There it was. Gloria's final humiliation. Once a month this man will come to her house, the house he helped save, and Gloria would have to make him tea and put Josh in front of him like a piece of pound cake on a plate. No! That is never going to happen. Once she got that damned cheque cashed her only obligation to Abe was to play him back. And she would. It was impossible to forbid him from coming to the house now, but she could still make sure Josh was kept away from him. Far far away.

"More tea?" he asked.

"No," Gloria said, standing up. "No, thank you. I really must go. My shift starts at three."

"Ah, that's too bad. But we'll be seeing a lot more of each other now. And it's time to let bygones be bygones," Abe said

"Thank you again for this. I don't know what we would have done without your help." That, at least, was the truth.

"Oh, one more thing before you go, Gloria," Abe said.

"Yes?" Gloria asked.

"Gerty, get me a pen and a piece of paper so Gloria can sign an IOU."

When Gloria finally walked out of The Cordelia, she could still smell that cinnamon and lavender scent on her favourite taupe pantsuit. She would have to toss it in the washer this weekend. And the smell would probably linger in her hair until she washed it too. She would rather have Hannah's dirty scent on her than Abe's. Are they watching me walk toward the bus stop? she wondered, as she passed the Tim Horton's coffee shop. Let them watch!

And as Gloria rode on the bus back toward the east end of the city, thinking about sitting in his living room with that spring in her back, she became more indignant and more resentful with each block she travelled down Main Street. How could Ted do this to her? How could she let him do this to her? She turned her head toward the window and began to cry, wiping the tears from her cheeks with the back of her hand. Then, as the bus passed Ottawa Street, Gloria thought about how Ted's mother had miscarried Ted's twin right there on the sidewalk and suddenly a terrible thought popped into Gloria's head; something so horrible she immediately stopped crying, horrified it had come from her own mind but, still, she couldn't expel it.

God, why couldn't Anna have miscarried both babies on Ottawa Street that day?

By the last week of July, the ceiling fan above Gloria's head at Munro had still not been fixed. I'd be lucky if it was fixed before autumn, she thought, as she moved steel wire into the bin beside her. She had hoped that it would be cooler on afternoon shift, but it seemed that the factory simply held onto the heat from the morning shift, magnifying and intensifying it.

She had still gone up to see Ted religiously three times a week, even though she was still angry with him, since having to grovel to Abe. But their money worries were gone, at least for the moment. She had reimbursed Sonny his eight thousand dollars and paid her mortgage for July. Josh was finally at Cub Scout camp, though Gloria had been waiting every day since she and Doris dropped him off for a phone call from one of those camp counsellors telling her to come pick him up for some reason or other. If Josh decided to get himself out of camp, he would find some way to manoeuvre himself out. So, Gloria concluded, he must be enjoying it; or at least not hating it as much as he had thought he would. Josh had been so angry when she and Doris had dropped him off at that camp, treating Gloria like some kind of ogre, that she had cried all the way home.

It seemed Ted was right after all. Josh did need to escape from the asphalt, cracked concrete sidewalks, and factory fetor of Alkeld Street and the east end for some fresh air. Even though Josh didn't look much like it, the boy was a quarter Indian, after all. The blood of his grandmother and his Chippewa ancestors from the forests of northern Minnesota still ran through his veins. And a quarter Indian is still a lot, isn't it? But who knows, Gloria thought as she wiped the sweat from her face with a hand towel, she didn't have much love of camping or woods herself and she had twice as much Indian blood as Josh.

Gloria had another long night in front of her. Since meeting with Abe, he had plagued her dreams. The dream was always the same: Abe sat on his rose-coloured chesterfield painting another paint-by-numbers hunting dog with a bird in its mouth while Gloria sat in the armchair with the spring digging deeper and deeper into her back until it came out her stomach. Then she would suddenly realize that the bird in the hunting dog's mouth that Abe was painting was Tessa, limp, broken, and bleeding, but Gloria, impaled on the armchair, could not move…

When her shift was over, Gloria had walked more than halfway home when Bill flashed his headlights, pulled up beside her in his red pickup on Woodward Avenue, and offered her a ride home again. Her first instinct was to tell him no, but still, she climbed into his truck, welcoming not having to walk the entire way home in the dark.

"You look tired," Bill said. "You looked tired all shift. And it's hot as hell, tonight. I promise, no funny business this time."

"I already forgot all about that."

"I was afraid you wouldn't want to be friends anymore," Bill said, turning onto Alkeld Street.

"Like I said, I've already forgotten about it," Gloria said. "I have a few beers left if you'd like one. Just one, I know Alice waits for you."

"Well, maybe just one," Bill said.

Gloria had left the air conditioner on low when she went to work that afternoon and left all the doors and windows closed so the house was somewhat cool when she came home. If the neighbours are watching, let them, she thought. She wasn't about to open the door and let the cold air out, the expensive cold air, just so the Alkeld snoops would know that nothing was going on with this man in her house. She turned on the three-way lamp in the living room on high as Reefer jumped and barked again at seeing Bill.

"You are growing fast, eh, fella," Bill said, scratching the dog behind his ears.

"Could you let Reefer out the front to go to the washroom, Bill?" Gloria asked, as she walked down the hall to the kitchen.

While Bill was outside with the dog, Gloria took her nightly pill from the bottle she kept on the top of the refrigerator. The pills were a new addition to her nightly routine, given to her by Dr. Heller for her nerves earlier that month. Then Gloria grabbed two bottles of beer out of the refrigerator, opened them, and walked back down the hall to the living room. She could count on one hand the number of beers she had drank in her entire life, but she was dead on her feet, overheated after working through this bloody heat wave that never seemed to end, and she needed to cool down and relax before bed.

"Your kids around?" Bill asked. He sat down in Ted's chair by the window and lit a cigarette as Reefer laid down at his feet.

"No," Gloria said. She handed him his beer and then turned on the RCA console television and flipped through the channels until she stopped on a black and white *Alfred Hitchcock Presents* from the Buffalo station. "Troy's gone for the week to a friend's cottage up north and Josh is at Cub Scout camp."

She sat on the end of the couch closest to Bill and took a sip of her beer. Though she enjoyed the coolness of the beer, Gloria never really liked the aftertaste that came with it. Suddenly, she reached over, took Bill's cigarette out of his hand, and took a drag. She coughed a little and giggled. Gloria had never really smoked, except the occasional few drags off Ted's cigarettes, since she was a teenager.

"Smoking and drinking beer? Just who are you suddenly, Gloria Moore?" Bill said teasingly.

"Nobody." She handed the cigarette back to Bill as tears welled up in her dark brown eyes. "I'm nobody."

"Hey," Bill said. He stood up from Ted's chair and sat down beside Gloria on the couch and, putting his arm around her shoulder, pulled her close to him. "You are not a nobody."

Gloria began to cry.

"Jesus, this is so embarrassing," she said. "I don't know why I'm acting like this. I haven't been sleeping and I'm… I'm just really exhausted." Then, still wearing her blue polka-dot work bandana, she put her head on Bill's chest and sobbed, quietly.

"Don't worry about it, you've been through a lot lately," Bill said, gently rubbing her shoulder.

The two of them sat like that for a few minutes. She had missed having someone, anyone, hold her.

"You smell like Munro soap," she said, sitting up again. She took off her work bandana, folded it, wiped her eyes, and put it on an end table.

"Isabelle hated the smell of Munro soap," Bill said. "One Christmas she gave me some kind of brown soap on a rope that smelled like the backside of a beaver and asked me to take it to work and shower with it instead of the Munro soap. Now could you see me in the men's shower with all the guys with some musky-smelling bar of brown soap hanging around my neck like some kind of fucked up smelly necklace? I mean, come on. Maybe that's why she left me, the smell of the Munro pink soap." He grinned.

"Some women are never happy," Gloria said.

Bill reached over and wiped her bangs, matted against her forehead with sweat, away from her eyes.

"I feel better now," she said, pushing his hand away. "And tonight, I'll take an extra Valium before bed. So, there's something to look forward to."

She picked up her beer from the coffee table and drank as much as she could until it burned her throat. Then she covered her mouth with her hand and giggled as some beer dripped down her chin.

"I'm not a beer drinker," she said.

"I can tell."

"You want another? I have two bottles left in the fridge and I'm in the mood for another one."

"What do you usually drink, Gloria?"

"Rum and ginger ale. But I drink so rarely we never keep any rum in the house except for maybe a mickey at Christmas or New Years. You know, someone around here has to be the grown-up, Bill Hunter."

"And that's you?"

"That's always been me. My sister Lydia is the beer drinker. Doris, on the other hand, drinks rye and Pepsi but will drink anything that's around. Now Ted, he drinks rye straight and beer with his friends. Ted drinks all the time. He's probably an alcoholic. Doris is probably an alcoholic too. It seems like everyone I love is an alcoholic."

"All the best people are, I hear."

"You know what?" she asked.

"What?"

"Sometimes I think, maybe, I'll stop being the grown-up and see what happens? Like sometimes when I'm on the bus going downtown on my way to see Ted, I think about getting off at Rebecca Street, walking to the bus station, and getting on a bus going west just to see an ocean or real mountain. All I've ever seen is Hamilton Mountain— a fake mountain! Or maybe see that Nett Lake in Minnesota where my mother was born…"

"I think everyone has those thoughts. Even at the best of times," Bill said. He put his empty beer bottle down on the table.

"I'll get us another beer."

She went to the kitchen and grabbed two more beers from the refrigerator. She really didn't have food in the house to serve him if he was hungry. At least nothing that would go with beer. What went with beer anyway? She turned to go back to the living room and met Bill halfway down the hallway, just inside Josh's bedroom. He had turned on Josh's bedroom light.

"Who likes the cocktail placemats?" Bill asked.

"Oh, that's Josh's room. He collects those things for some reason. Tapes them on his wall. Don't ask me why."

"I was just seeing if you need any help."

"No, I was just seeing if there was anything to eat that I could offer you."

"Look, Gloria," Bill said, leaning against Josh's door frame. "I know you're married and that's cool. It really is. But… ah, fuck… I really want to kiss you again. Right now."

"Bill—"

"But I'm not going to do it unless you tell me I can."

"Bill, I'm sorry…"

"I lied," he said. "I'm going to kiss you again whether you tell me I can or not."

He kissed her. Gloria's mouth opened and their tongues touched. Her heart raced. He pulled her closer to him and hugged her tightly. Gloria stood, still holding the beer bottles by her side, as Bill looked into her eyes and smiled.

"God, you're beautiful," he said.
"No, I'm not beautiful. Not anymore."
"You're beautiful."

Bill took the beer bottles out of her hands, put them down on the desk just inside Josh's bedroom, and turned off the bedroom light. He touched her cheek with the back of his hand and kissed her again. The hall was dark, except for the flickering light of Alfred Hitchcock on the television in the living room, as he slowly moved his hand over Gloria's hips and up to her breasts. Getting no objection, he unbuttoned Gloria's work blouse and slipped his hands under her brassiere.

This is wrong! This isn't me! Gloria thought as Bill's lips moved down her neck to her breasts. She threw her head back and moaned as she ran her fingers through his long black hair and down his muscular back. *How much Indian blood would a child of ours have?* she wondered. Bill took off her blouse and undid her bra, letting it fall to the floor of the hallway on top of her blouse. He took her breasts in his hands and smiled.

"You're beautiful," he said again. His mouth moved toward her breasts.

Suddenly Reefer began barking. He ran past Bill and Gloria toward Josh's bedroom window and jumped up, with his front paws on the windowsill.

Gloria gasped.

There was Shannon Perry peering at her and Bill through the gap in the drapes. He must have jumped their fence and hid in the small space alongside the house under Josh's bedroom window. He stared for a second and then ran off along the side of the house.

"Oh my God, what have I done?"

The next day was Wednesday. The man on the radio said that today was going to be the hottest day of 1977... at least so far. Tomorrow could be even hotter, he had said. Gloria had gotten up early to do her laundry. She had to be downtown before noon to ensure she would be back in time to change for her afternoon shift. She made sure there was an assortment: old pairs and new pairs in assorted colours, including the pair she had been wearing the previous night. In total, Gloria put out seven pairs of her underwear on her clothesline between a few towels and pillowcases, which seemed more than fair. She looked around the perimeter of her yard and said, as if to no one, "These shouldn't take long to dry today." Then, leaving the gate unlocked and ajar, she walked up Alkeld Street to the bus stop.

When Gloria returned home from the hospital later that afternoon, she found four of the seven pairs of her underwear were gone. Slowly, her arms tired and aching, Gloria took the rest of the laundry off the clothesline and placed them delicately in her laundry basket. Four pairs should be more than sufficient payment for Shannon's silence, she thought. Then she stepped wistfully inside her house and closed the door.

Paid in full.

Nine

Camp Ronkewe had been nothing but indignity heaped upon indignity.

Looking back, Josh thought he should have tossed away the orange form they handed out to every boy after that Cub Scout meeting in early February. Most of the other boys had made paper airplanes out of them or crumpled them up into the back pocket of their uniforms or left them, forgotten, on the floor of The Good Shepherd Church basement. Instead, without even looking at it, Josh had heedlessly handed the application for Ronkewe Cub Scout camp to his father when he jumped into his father's blue Impala that evening. If Josh had known then what he knew now, he would have ripped the thing up into a million pieces and thrown it into the bushes outside the church.

The orange piece of paper sat on top of the refrigerator with the telephone and electric bills for a month or two and Josh had forgotten about it until his father announced that Josh would be going to camp for three weeks starting in mid-July. After all, Troy and Kevin had gone to Camp Ronkewe when they were his age and they had "the time of their lives".

Josh was dubious about camp from the get-go. He had done a couple of overnight camping trips to Camp Ronkewe with his Cub Scout troop, which he didn't particularly enjoy, but this? This was a whole three weeks!

Josh did enjoy camping with his family in their pop-up trailer that his father would pull behind their Impala but that was at the White Cedars Family Campground only twenty minutes away from their house, on the way to Niagara Falls. And White Cedars had a huge pool, electricity that their trailer could plug into, showers, and toilets that flushed. Camp Ronkewe was just a big field with two outhouses. Josh hated outhouses. They smelled and were full of spiders and who knew what else.

The first humiliation was the mandatory camp physical. In March, just before his father had become really ill, he had taken Josh to see Dr. Heller, their family doctor. That, Josh thought later, should have tipped him off that some weird shit was going down since through all the maladies and injuries in his short life, it was always Josh's mother who had sat in the black leather chair in Dr. Heller's examination room to watch while the doctor inspected whatever body part of Josh's needing attention. This was the first time, that Josh could remember, that his father had taken him to see Dr. Heller.

"How are you doing today, Josh?" Dr. Heller said with an English accent, coming through the examination room door.

Dr. Heller was a tall, large man with silver hair and a plump ruddy face, and jowls that reminded Josh of a cartoon bulldog. He wore a white lab coat with a stethoscope around his neck and, in his hand, he held a thick white manila file with the orange Cub Scout camp application paper-clipped to the front.

"I'm good," Josh said.

"You look pretty good to me, too. But let's take a look, anyway. Take off everything except your underwear, son," the doctor said. He tossed the manila file on the examination table and sat down on a rolling black stool.

Josh's father put his head back and rested it against the wall of the office as Josh began unlacing his sneakers.

"And what about you, Ted? How are you doing? You look tired," the doctor said, looking concerned.

"I'm working a lot of overtime, that's all. Someone has to pay the bills, you know." He gave a haggard smile.

Was he working a lot of overtime? Josh wondered, taking off his shirt. If anything, his father was home more often lately, calling in sick to his union job at Wentworth Steel every few days.

Josh took off his pants and handed them along with his shirt to his father who laid the clothes on his lap.

"Socks too, son," the doctor said.

Dr. Heller scanned through the many green, white, and yellow loose pages in the big manila file. It looked way too thick for such a young kid, Josh thought. It was as thick as *The Wind in the Willows*.

Josh pulled off his socks and stood waiting for whatever was going to happen. Whatever it was, it couldn't be that bad since his father was right there watching it all. Josh's mother had made sure that Josh had a bath and put on a new pair of underwear, right out of the plastic bag, that afternoon. Josh could still see the packaging folds in the underwear.

"Is that all me?" Josh asked, pointing to the thick file.

"No," Dr. Heller said, looking up from the file grinning. "You and your mother still share the same file, Joshua. We'll give you your own file when you get a bit older. Let's see…" Dr. Heller thumbed through more coloured pages in the file and then stopped at a white page, slightly yellowing around the edges. "It looks like we sent Joshua for a cystic fibrosis test when he was eighteen months old. He was having digestive problems, it says. Remind me what was that all about."

Josh looked at his father. No one ever told him they thought he might have had cystic fibrosis. Wasn't that what the Jerry Lewis Telethon was for? Did they find out he didn't have it?"

"Um… it turned out that all he had was a nervous stomach."

"Nervous stomach? For an eighteen-month-old?"

"Gloria and I weren't really getting along then. You had said to Gloria at the time that his stomach problems were probably because of all the hassles at home. You said it was nerves."

"You two were fighting?"

"Right," Josh's father said, getting somewhat flushed in the face, tipping Josh off that his father didn't want to talk about this, at least not with Josh there.

"Ah, that's right. I do remember that," Dr. Heller said, nodding.

"Gloria threw me out for a week. She only let me come back after I promised to cool it with all the fighting."

"No problems with his belly since then?"

Dr. Heller reached over and pushed his fingers into Josh's lower belly. Josh grimaced a bit. He was ticklish and the doctor's hands were cold.

"No," his father said. "No problems since then." He put a strand of his long sandy hair behind his right ear.

"I've filled out a few of these camp forms this month. A physical seems superfluous for ten-year-olds, if you ask me. A simple health questionnaire would be sufficient for parents to fill out. We're not sending you off to the bloody army, are we Joshua? Not yet anyways. So why waste everyone's time?" The doctor said, continuing to poke at the front and side of Josh's stomach

"Yeah, I agree," his father said.

"Still, it's good to get a look at the lad."

The doctor stopped prodding Josh's stomach and, pulling down Josh's bottom eyelids, looked in his eyes with a light and then turned him around and had Josh read the letters on a chart on the back of the examining room door.

"E V X Z…" Josh said, covering one eye.

"It's *Sesame Street* that makes him pronounce it *zee* and not *zed*. These kids watch too much American television today. They'll suck all the Canada out of these kids, watch and see. Soon they'll all be talking with an American accent, thinking ghettos are fine, and bombing Cambodia, secretly of course, is just dandy," his father said.

"Same old Ted," the doctor said, looking into Josh's ears.

"I always wondered who exactly Nixon's Secret War was a secret from," Josh's father continued, now sounding irritated. "Certainly not from the people getting the bombs dropped on them. No, it wasn't a Secret War to those people."

The doctor looked over again at Josh's father and furrowed his brows. Now he looked more concerned.

"Are you sleeping alright, Ted?"

"As much as ever, I guess. The Seconal you gave me puts me out. I just never feel like I've actually slept when I wake up in the morning. It makes me feel more like I've been slipped a mickey than had a good night's sleep." His father grinned and pushed his round glasses up the bridge of his nose.

"Do you find much difference with the new medication?"

"No, I don't."

"Still having the racing thoughts?"

"Maybe a bit less racy, but yeah, they're still there."

"See Dora on the way out and make an appointment for later this week and we'll see if we can monkey around with your medication a bit. And speaking of monkeys… can you jump up here on the examination table, Joshua."

The doctor tested Josh's reflexes and looked into his mouth and throat and even the bottom of Josh's feet.

"The special shoes have helped with the flat feet. It's a pretty good arch," the doctor said.

"Great, he'll have no problem joining up for the next world war," his father said sardonically.

Dr. Heller took the stethoscope from around his neck, put the ear tips in his ears and then placed the cold round silver end first to Josh's back and had him breathe in and out, and then he put it on Josh's chest.

"Hmm."

The doctor took off his stethoscope and looked over at Josh's father.

"Does Joshua have a heart murmur, Ted?" the doctor asked as if Josh wasn't even there.

"Murmur?" his father said, suddenly sitting up in the black leather chair. "No. I mean, not that I know of. No one ever told us that."

Murmur? Josh thought. Could that murmur maybe be his ticket out of this whole summer camp thing? He had a flash of relief. It was looking like he would be spending the summer in his own house in his own room in his own shower using his own toilet.

"Hold your breath for me, Joshua, I want to listen to your heart again."

He put the stethoscope back against Josh's chest and Josh took a deep breath and held it as the doctor, his eyes moving side to side, listen to Josh's heartbeat.

Please, let me have a heart murmur.

Finally, Dr. Heller, nodded, shaking his jowls, and took the stethoscope ear tips out of his ears.

"No, there's no heart murmur. It's just the way the lad was breathing. I think he's a bit nervous and was breathing oddly."

"Christ, that's a relief," his father said, sitting back in the chair.

"You can relax, Joshua. Nothing in here is going to hurt you. I'm not even going to give you a booster shot today," the doctor said. He put his big hand on Josh's shoulder and smiled. "Son, I examine everyone the same way, even your mother and father. I just want to make sure you're growing up healthy and strong."

"So, am I?"

"So far, I'd say you are pretty much right on schedule. Now jump on the scale for me. I want to check your weight."

Josh hopped off the examination table and stepped on the scale against the wall while Dr. Heller slid the black weights back and forth across the top until they balanced.

"Hmm," the doctor said.

Another hmm, Josh thought.

Josh, getting more nervous as the examination went on, began trembling slightly as he stood on the scale.

"Say, Ted, would you say that Joshua is overly nervous for a boy his age? There was that stomach trouble when he was a toddler, and the shallow breathing when I was checking his heart, and he's trembling now as I examined him. Anxiety can run in families."

"I'd say Josh is more… ah… sensitive than nervous."

"Ah, you think the lad's too sensitive then?"

"Well… I'd say he is. That's one of the reasons I made him join the Cub Scouts and why we're sending him to this camp this summer. If you know what I mean," his father said, not looking at Josh.

The doctor nodded again without saying anything.

Josh didn't like being called sensitive. It meant he acted like a girl. As if he were crying all the time and stuff like that. His dad and the doctor didn't know what they were talking about!

After Josh was weighed the doctor pushed on his lower stomach, just below the band of his new blue underwear when, with one quick motion and without giving Josh any notice at all, Dr. Heller pulled down Josh's underwear to his knees and gripped Josh's penis. He lifted it up, looked underneath, and examined the head and shaft. Josh, who's heart was now beating even faster, looked over at his father who was talking with the doctor about the importance of sleep like what was happening was the most normal thing ever. The doctor then quickly felt Josh's ball sack and rolled each of Josh's nuts between the thumb and index finger of his right hand, the slight pressure telegraphed to a slight pain in Josh's belly. The doctor then pulled up Josh's underwear and the new elastic waistband snapped around Josh's hips.

"All done. A healthy boy you have here, Ted." He leaned over and signed the bottom of the bright orange paper. "You can get dressed now, Joshua."

Well, that's it, Josh thought, taking his clothes back from his father. Camp fucking Ronkewe here I come.

"He does needs to lose some weight though," Dr. Heller said, and, still sitting on the black stool, he rolled a few feet over to where Josh was bent over putting on his left sock and grabbed the small roll of fat on Josh's stomach and jiggled it a bit. "See that belly?"

To Josh, having the fat on his gut jiggled in front of his father was a worse ignominy than even having his underwear pulled down and wang examined. The doctor was right though, Josh thought, pulling up his pants to his belly. *I am getting fat.*

"Yeah, we thought he was getting a bit heavy too," his father said.

"He's almost twenty pounds overweight for a boy his age. We could put him on a diet, but I wouldn't bother, not at the moment anyway. The thing I learned about overweight boys is that they usually slim down as soon as they discover girls. That should be soon. But, if he gets to be twenty-five pounds or more overweight in the next year or so we may want to think about doing something," Dr. Heller said, handing the orange form back to Josh's father.

Josh didn't know it then in March, but the indignities of Camp Ronkewe were just beginning.

*

"You're going to have so much fun, Josh!" Aunt Doris said, driving along the beach strip past the beach amusement park. Though taking the Skyway Bridge would have been a faster way to get to the camp, Aunt Doris never drove on the Skyway Bridge. She said it made her too nervous. And since Josh didn't want to get there any earlier than he had to, he didn't mind either.

"I remember going to Fresh Air Camp when I was a girl. It was a charity, I think run by the city or maybe a church, that sent poor girls to camp for a few weeks in the summer. It was right here on the beach strip. Your mom and I went for three years, and we always had so much fun! Didn't we, Gloria?"

"It was a lot of fun. It was the first time in my life I ever saw brown bread," his mother said unpersuasively.

"So, so much fun!" Aunt Doris repeated.

You're both full of shit!

"Who are you kidding, Aunt Doris! Every *single* time either of you talked about that Fresh Air Camp it always went something like 'God, I hated that Fresh Air Camp' or 'honest to God, if I knew how close I was to home, I would have run away' or 'they made me sit there hours and hours until I finished that bowl of rice pudding!'"

"I never said it was that bad," his mother said.

"And Aunt Lydia calls it Fresh Air Concentration Camp," Josh said.

Aunt Doris chuckled.

"But now, all of a sudden, Fresh Air Camp was the best thing ever! Do you think I'm stupid? Like I haven't been listening to you two all these years?"

"Alright, alright. Maybe you'll have all the fun we didn't have at Fresh Air Camp. Troy and Kevin loved Camp Ronkewe," his mother said.

"You just remember our deal," Josh said, turning away.

Josh crossed his arms and sulked. He was wearing a ridiculous navy-blue floppy canvas hat, sneakers with no socks, an old red T-shirt, and a pair of shorts that were getting too tight around his stomach. 'See that belly,' the doctor had said!

Josh didn't mind being made to go to the weekly Tuesday evening meeting of Cub Scouts at the Good Shepherd Church *too much*. The other boys in his troop were all right, for the most part, and Josh did like the songs they would sing and skits they would do, even though they always did the same old songs and skits (and they never wanted to do the new skits Josh thought up in his head), but this three weeks at camp idea was bullshit. Josh had asked around at his regular Tuesday Cub Scout meeting and it turned out that no one else in his troop was planning on going to Camp Ronkewe. No one.

"And I don't want to be gone while Dad is in the hospital."

"He might be home by the time you come home," his mother replied.

"That's even worse. I'd miss him coming home, and I want to be there when he comes home."

"Josh, I don't want you to worry about your father. Let the grown-ups worry, will you? Your father is doing just fine so just go do camp stuff and have fun, for God's sake!" his mother said.

"And don't forget what you promised me, Aunt Doris," Josh said.

"No, I won't. Are we still in Hamilton, or have we passed into Burlington?" his aunt said, checking her rear-view mirror.

"What did you promise him?" his mother asked, looking over at Aunt Doris.

"Oh, it's nothing… I just said I'd check some stuff for him."

"What stuff?" Josh's mother turned around and looked at him in the backseat.

"Aunt Doris is going to check the newspaper every day and cut out everything that's in there about the Ragno murder, so I don't miss anything for my scrapbook."

"Doris! We're trying to get him to stop obsessing about those sorts of horrible things."

"Well, he asked me," his aunt said. She tossed a cigarette butt out the window onto Beach Boulevard.

"Make sure you check the newspaper every single day. And be careful when you cut it out not to cut off any of the story at the bottom," Josh said.

"Josh, your old aunt does know how to use a pair of scissors," Aunt Doris said, lighting another cigarette.

"And I'm not obsessed," Josh said.

Twenty minutes later, they pulled off the regional road into the entrance of Camp Ronkewe, nestled into the foot of the Niagara escarpment. The dirt parking lot was full of cars, parents, and boys lugging duffle bags. A lone telephone line ran from a pole on the main road to the Big House, a large wooden building that held the office, kitchen, and mess hall, beside the parking lot. At least they have a phone, Josh thought. And it wasn't a long walk from here to Beach Boulevard if he decided to just pack up and leave. He could probably remember how to get to the Beach Amusement Park, and then it was practically a straight line to Woodward Avenue and home.

"And remember, you said if I didn't like it here, you'd come get me."

"I said you have to give it a chance. And if you don't like it after, say six or seven days you can call me and, yes, we'll come and get you."

"Six days! You said six."

"All right, six!"

"And then you'll come and get me."

"Then we will come and get you. My God, Joshua, you can be exhausting."

"I'm surprised he didn't make you write an oath in your own blood," Aunt Doris said, getting out of the car.

"And today counts as day one. Just so we understand that," he said.

Josh put his sleeping bag under his arm, grabbed his suitcase, and slammed the back door of the Cadillac with his backside harder than needed to just to register his dissatisfaction, yet again, with the whole thing. At least he didn't have to pack his stupid Cub Scout uniform. They had been told just to bring jeans, shorts, swimsuit, T-shirts, and pyjamas (they had been given a list).

"If you ask me," Aunt Doris said, taking the suitcase from Josh, "I think you are going to have a great time here with the other boys."

"Don't bet on it," Josh said.

"And wouldn't it be embarrassing to have your old aunt and mother come and pick you up after a week because you don't like it? They'll all think you're a baby!" Aunt Doris said.

"As if I care what they think. I'd never have to see any of these creeps again, anyway."

"Well, he's got me there," Aunt Doris said with a shrug.

And after six days, Josh thought, if he did call his mother and she still refused to pick him up from here then all bets were off! He would run away from Camp Ronkewe and walk home, just like his mother wanted to do at Fresh Air Camp. It wouldn't take all that long to walk home, a day at most. And he wouldn't go right back to Alkeld Street either. Maybe he would stay in Shannon's fort by Red Hill Creek for a few days just out of spite.

Josh cringed at the din of boys as they all walked or ran toward the large field where older Scouts were wrangling them into one large pack. To Josh, the sound of many boys together always sounded like... danger.

"Did you know a group of boys is called a 'blush,'" Josh said, walking towards the field.

"Blush? More like a swarm," Aunt Doris said.

Directly in front of the Big House the Camp Ronkewe field was about a hundred yards long and fifty yards wide with dense trees surrounding all three sides. Two straight lines of white pup tents had already been set up for them and ran down half the length of the field on both sides along the trees. Josh counted five tents on one side and six on the other. The patchy grass on the field was burnt to an ugly brown from the drought, making each blade hard and sharp when it scrapped against Josh's ankles. Still, even in the middle of a drought, the mountain remained mostly lush and green, towering over the south side of the camp.

A large muscular man with a thick moustache, brown friendly eyes, and short dark brown hair carrying a pressboard clipboard, walked back and forth across the parking lot shaking hands with parents, flashing a big toothy smile, and directing the boys over to the brown weedy field. Josh's mother had given the man Josh's name in the parking lot when they arrived, and he had checked it off his list with a big black marker. He wore dark blue jeans, white tennis shoes, and a khaki-brown Scout leader shirt. The shirt was regulation Scouts of Canada with bright green and yellow shoulder loops over the epaulettes, a purple and white Fleur-de-lis badge on the left side of his chest, and a small Canadian flag on the right side just above the pocket. The shirt and jeans looked like they had just been pressed and his tight jeans hugged his burly legs and rear end. Those jeans, Josh thought, were not regulation Scouts of Canada.

"That big guy must be the head honcho. You can tell by the way he walks. He's really good looking, don't you think?" Aunt Doris whispered to Josh's mother.

"Shhh," his mother said.

"I'm just saying—"

Josh studied the man. He looked a bit like Burt Reynolds in *Smokey and the Bandit*. Now Josh tried to imagine how this Cub Scout leader in tennis shoes would look in a red shirt and cowboy hat. Then Josh tried to picture him driving a Trans Am. Josh liked this smiling head honcho in tennis shoes.

More and more boys joined them on the field, all dragging large duffle or old hockey bags stuffed with their camp clothes. Josh was the only boy on the field who brought a suitcase. Already he was feeling like the odd man out, nothing new there. And this wasn't just a regular suitcase, either; it was Josh's mother's train case with a round vanity mirror attached to the inside. That mirror was, Josh had always thought, the best part about the suitcase, but now, standing in that field with his mother and aunt on either side of him, Josh was embarrassed.

"Cubs!" An older boy, a full-fledged Scout, yelled. "Line up here with your gear." He kicked at the ground with his official brown leather Boy Scout hiking and marching boot. "Right here on this imaginary line".

"It's not imaginary if we're lined up there," Josh said, rolling his eyes. "Then it's a real line; a line of *Cub Scouts*."

"Maybe," Aunt Doris said, "you should just keep stuff like that to yourself while you're here. Or you could write down all the things other people do or say that you think are stupid and tell us about it when you get home. You want to make friends while you're here, right, Josh?"

"Not particularly."

"Parents!" the full-fledged Scout yelled. "It's time to say your goodbyes! We'll see you all in three weeks!"

"Okay, Josh, we're going to go now," his mother said.

She leaned down, hugged him tightly, and kissed him on the cheek. He stood silently, looking straight ahead with his arms at his sides. He wasn't about to hug her back. If she was feeling guilty about dumping him there while his father was in the hospital, then that was just fine by him.

"Aren't you even going to say goodbye to us?" his mother asked.

"You know I'm going to miss you."

"Just go. I don't like either of you right now."

"Well, that's better than nothing, I suppose," Aunt Doris said. She opened her purse and looked for her keys.

"I hope you'll drop me a line if Dad tries to kill himself again. Or actually does it this time."

"Josh!" his mother said, looking stunned.

"And on that cheery note... we'll be hitting the road, kiddo," Aunt Doris said. She bent down and kissed him on the top of the head.

The women walked back to the parking lot, climbed back into his aunt's car, and drove back down the dirt road without him, leaving a cloud of dust behind them. Josh picked up his suitcase and stood with the other boys on the imaginary-now-real line at the end of the field.

I'll miss you too.

"Is this your first time at camp?" a short stout boy with a brush cut standing beside him asked.

"Yeah. First and last," Josh said.

"I came last year when I was nine. It's great! I love it," the kid said.

The head honcho in tennis shoes walked directly in front of the line of boys with his clipboard under his arm and stopped. He stood with his legs slightly astride, put his hands behind his back and smiled. Is this his real job? Josh wondered. His mother had told him the first day his father had driven him up to the Good Shepherd Church that he was to watch himself around the leaders and older boys. The same speech she had given him about perverts in the bushes down at Red Hill Creek. She didn't need to. He wasn't stupid. However, Josh concluded, this head honcho in tennis shoes was an all-right kind of guy, just like the Bandit. Still, that didn't mean that

Josh was going to stay more than the six days he had agreed to.

"Welcome to Camp Ronkewe, boys!" The head honcho in tennis shoes possessed the booming masculine voice of a gym teacher. "I'm Adam. I'm what you might call the captain of this here ship. I make sure everything runs smoothly for you fellas."

Strangely, Josh liked being called *fella*, No one, as far as he could remember, had ever called him that before.

"I make sure everyone has fun! I also make sure everyone follows the rules! I may be the boss around here but I'm also your buddy, so don't forget that! Just think of me as one of the guys," Adam said.

"Adam was the leader here last year too," the boy with the brush cut said. "He took us for a hike along the mountain, but I fell and got a thorn stuck in my scalp. Adam pulled it out with some needle nose pliers and put a bandage on my head; I still have the thorn in a jar at home. He can also do a wicked cannonball from the rope by the swimming hole, too."

Swimming hole? Josh looked at Adam and tried to imagine him doing a cannonball. That, Josh decided, would be something he'd want to see.

Adam yelled, "Now, I want everyone to grab a partner."

Fuck! This is always the worst, Josh thought. No one ever wanted to be his partner. And he hated having to speak to people he didn't know. Quickly, the boys who all seemed to know each other from previous years were partnering up while Josh was left looking around to see who was, like him, still alone. It's probably because I brought a suitcase! If his dad hadn't been in the hospital, he would have told Josh to pack a duffle bag and not some faggy suitcase with a mirror. His dad used to go camping all the time when he was a Scout, but his mother, being a girl, didn't know anything about Cub Scout camps or the right way to pack for them.

"Hurry up!" Adam yelled, making Josh's stomach jump. "There's a few of you still not partnered up! We know there's an even number of you."

The short guy with the brush cut had already partnered with some other kid. If Josh couldn't find a partner, Adam would think he was some kind of dink or worse.

Just then, a slim boy with grey-blue eyes, large white-pink lips like a fish, and longish blonde hair tied up in a blue and white bandana (the kind Josh's mother wore to work), came over and smiled at Josh. He wore red and white gym shorts, white socks, and a black T-shirt with an orange and white Harley Davidson emblem on the front. Yep, Josh thought, this kid looks like the kind of partner I'd get. Stupid suitcase!

"Hey! Do you want to be my partner?" The bandana kid asked.

"Yeah, sure," Josh said.

"Everyone got a partner now?" Adam yelled.

"Yes!" the boys yelled back, as Josh stayed silent.

"Good! This will be your buddy through the whole three weeks. Learn your buddy's name. He is your new best friend. Your buddy will be the boy you will go swimming with, who you will eat with, who you will go hiking with, and who you will sleep beside. You cannot change buddies. And if you come to me during your three weeks here and say 'Adam, I don't like my buddy anymore, and I want to switch,' you know what I'll tell you? I'll tell you to go jump in the lake! Got it? We all have to learn to get along!" Adam smiled again and looked up and down the row of boys. "Now tell your new buddy your name. Tell each other where you're from, how old you are, and what you like to do for fun. This is how you become buddies."

"I'm Jimmy Sullivan," the boy in the bandana chirped.

Josh nodded.

"But everyone calls me Jiffy Pop."

My partner, best friend, and best buddy who I'll swim, eat, hike, and sleep with is named *Jiffy Pop*? It sounded too stupid.

"Jiffy for short."

"Why do they call you that?" Josh asked, wrinkling up his nose.

"Well... it's because I really like Jiffy Pop and I eat a whole lot of it. So, my dad started calling me that when I was a little kid. What's your name?"

Josh considered telling him that his name was Kraft Dinner but didn't. "Josh Moore."

Jimmy grabbed Josh's hand and shook it wildly. "I've been coming here for the last two years, Josh Moore. I'm ten. My dad sends me for two sessions. That's six weeks altogether. He pays double. That's sixty dollars. I like your hat."

"I'm ten, too," Josh said. "Almost eleven. But I'm just here for three weeks. Unless I don't like it— then I'm going home in six days."

"You'll like it, Josh. You'll like it a lot."

"What's with the bandana?"

"My dad wears one. He's a biker. Everyone wears them when they ride motorcycles. It keeps bugs out of their hair. So, I wear one too."

"Your dad rides a motorcycle?"

"Yeah, he takes me on it all the time." Jiffy wore a big grin making his fish lips look even bigger. "He'll take you on it too if you want. He takes all my friends for rides. Pretty cool, eh?"

"My brother, Kevin, has a motorcycle too. But he wears a helmet when he rides, not a bandana. He takes me for rides on his too."

This was partially true. Josh's oldest brother, Kevin, did have a red motorcycle, but he had never taken Josh on it.

"Remember! I want you to tell each other what you like to do for fun! Tell each other what your favourite food is," Adam yelled.

"You go first this time," Jiffy said.

"Okay, I guess my favourite food is the hamburgers they have at the racetrack in Toronto where I go with my dad all the time. Me and my dad like betting on horses and we win a lot of money doing that."

"That's wicked! My favourite food is pizza from Mother's Pizza and Count Chocula cereal—"

"And Jiffy Pop popcorn," Josh said.

"And Jiffy Pop popcorn! And the thing I like most is riding motorcycles with my dad. I like that more than anything else."

Josh wasn't too concerned about being partnered with a weirdo like Jiffy. Though he was slightly troubled with what Jiffy would do for a partner once he left in six days. Well, five days since Josh had decided that he was counting today as one of the agreed-upon six days in their deal.

"Alright boys! Now I want each pair to join up with another pair of boys and then I want you to introduce your new buddy to them,"

Adam said. "Don't introduce yourself, introduce your buddy, and tell them a bit about him, got it?"

Josh decided to let his new buddy, Jiffy Pop, find the other boys to pair up with while Josh just stood and watched Adam tap his clipboard with his black marker. Jiffy returned with two boys who looked almost exactly alike, both with reddish-brown hair, freckles, crystal blue eyes, and wearing matching blue T-shirts with a decal of Han Solo and Chewbacca on the front.

"This is Kyle," one of the boys said. "Kyle is my twin and he's four-and-a-half minutes older than me. We're from Stoney Creek and like to go to the movies. *Star Wars* is our favourite movie."

"You're just supposed to say what I like, Shane, not what we like together," Kyle said. "Anyway, this is Shane. He's my twin. He was born four-and-a-half minutes *after* me, and he likes *Star Wars*. We've seen *Star Wars* four times. Shane likes R2D2 more than he likes C3PO"

"That's not true! I like R2D2 and C3PO the same," Shane said.

This group is getting weirder and weirder by the minute, Josh thought. Shannon was right about everyone here being creeps.

"And this is Josh," said Jiffy. "Josh is my new best friend. He likes to go to the racetrack with his dad and eat hamburgers."

"I never said that I liked R2D2 more than—"

"And this here is Jimmy," Josh said, cutting Shane off.

"That's right," Jiffy said, nodding. "My name is Jimmy, but everyone calls me..."

Josh sighed. "But everyone calls him... um... Jiffy Pop."

Kyle and Shane looked at each other, smiled, and then both covered their mouths and snickered.

"Jiffy for short."

"Jiffy Pop likes riding on his father's motorcycle, eating bowls of Count Chocula and..." Josh pushed his canvas hat higher on his head, "and wearing his mother's bandanas," Josh said, smirking.

The twins laughed loudly, and Josh laughed with them. The trick was always getting the most amount of people laughing with you, people you can make laugh rarely gave you a whack or spit at you when you walked home.

"It isn't my mother's bandana," Jiffy said. "My mother died when I was five. She had cancer here." He touched the right side of his chest.

Now Josh felt rotten. First for treating his own mother so lousily before she left and, now, for saying that bandana thing to Jiffy, who seemed like a fairly nice kid.

"And now," Adam yelled, "I want you to join another group of four boys and do the same thing. Everyone introduce everyone else! We're all becoming buddies!"

This time it was the twins who grabbed a group of four boys from farther down the field. One of the boys, a kid with curly black hair turned around, grinned, and approached Josh and Jiffy.

Josh's heart skipped a beat.

As bad as Josh thought Camp Ronkewe would be, it was about to get worse, much *much* worse.

"This is Gavin Mulligan," a taller boy said, pointing to Gavin. "He likes spaghetti, riding his bike, and kissing girls."

Josh had only seen Gavin a few times, from a distance, since the day he, Tony and Danny had surrounded him at the end of Alkeld Street. Josh didn't know he was a Cub Scout. Gavin didn't act like a Cub Scout. Or, maybe, Gavin wasn't a Cub Scout, you didn't need to be a Cub Scout to come to summer camp at Camp Ronkewe. All you had to do was be between nine and twelve years old, pass the physical, and fork over thirty dollars.

"Well, I'll be damned," Gavin said, beaming from ear to ear. "I'll go next…"

Josh held his breath. *Here we go again.*

"This fat faggot in the stupid hat here is Josh Moore. Josh likes bouncing tennis balls, having other people fight his battles… and… hmm… what else can I tell you about old Joshy? Oh, yeah! His father is in the nuthouse!"

Once every boy at Camp Ronkewe had been introduced to every other boy, they were told to pick up their gear and Josh, with his suitcase and sleeping bag, along with his 'new best buddy', Jiffy, and the twins, who shared one duffle bag, were taken across the weedy brown field, past two outhouses that made Josh's stomach turn, by Devin, one of the full-fledged Scouts, to the last tent on the south side of the field.

As they walked, Josh looked around anxiously, trying to see which of the eleven pup tents Gavin Mulligan was being led and relaxed, somewhat, when he saw Gavin standing in front of a tent on the other side of the field near the main building. Josh had simply laughed and called Gavin a liar when Gavin told the other boys that Josh's father was in the nuthouse. Josh wasn't sure if Jiffy and the twins believed Gavin or not, but he wanted to run away, right then and there.

"This is tent number nine," Scout Devin said, stopping outside the bright white tent. He stood in the same pose as Adam had with his hands behind his back and grinned. "This here is your home for the next three weeks, boys."

He's trying so hard to sound important, Josh thought, but Scout Devin still had the voice of a little kid that, if on the verge of changing, still sounded a bit girly. And Josh thought, it was a bit of a stretch to call them *boys*. Devin was only two or three years older than they were. He was around Shannon's age. Though Josh couldn't see Shannon in a Scout's uniform like this guy. Devin had short black straight hair and looked like he may have been part Chinese the way Josh was part Indian, like there was just a hint of Chinese there. And like all the other full-fledged Scouts at Camp Ronkewe, Devin was wearing his official brown Boy Scout shirt, jeans, and hiking boots. Missing on all the Scouts was their badge sash. Maybe they don't want to get it dirty? Josh thought.

"And, if you ask me, it's a beauty of a tent, too," Devin continued. "We got all new tents this year. You should have been here when I was a Cub Scout way back when. All we had were old green army-surplus tents, probably from World War Two. You boys don't know how good your generation of Cub Scouts has got it!"

Devin opened the flap of the tent and motioned for them all to go in. First Jiffy, who had done all this crap before, followed by the twins, and finally Josh.

"Nice suitcase, you got there," Devin said in his high-pitched voice, as Josh passed through the flap into the tent.

The tent was boiling hot from sitting in the sun all morning. There was just enough room for the younger boys to stand up in the middle of the tent while Devin, a few inches taller, had to hunch over a little. Josh could see that the tent was on a bit of a hill, sloping to the north. He would rather be in Shannon's fort. At least it was cooler there.

"I'm the Scout leader for your tent," Devin said, his voice failing to be authoritative. "This tent is tent number nine, like I said. Remember that number. We'll also be eating at table number nine in the cafeteria. And I'll be the one to take you around for swimming and hikes."

Maybe I'll write these guys a special song for tent number nine before I have my mom pick me up, Josh thought. *We're the boys from tent number nine. We're all fine and...* something something. He'd think about it more later.

"Okay, boys, put down your sleeping bags like this." Devin motioned a straight line with his arm up and down four times. "That way you all fit. And you can put all your bags, and your pretty suitcase, there, at the back of the tent. See? There!"

"My brother is going to sleep beside me," one of the twins said.

"I'll sleep beside you, Josh," Jiffy said.

"Okay," Josh said, unrolling his sleeping bag.

One of the twins—Josh had not yet figured out which twin was Shane and which twin was Kyle yet and didn't much care—immediately laid out his sleeping bag the wrong way near the back of the tent.

"No! I said lay the sleeping bags *this* way," Devin said.

The twin looked at Devin, studied his arm, and turned his sleeping bag around.

"That's right," Devin said.

Devin watched as the four boys laid out their sleeping bags the way he wanted and then had them all sit down.

"Are there pillows," Josh asked.

"Pillows? Do you think they had pillows during the War of 1812, kid? Do you know that boys your age were fighting in the Battle of Stoney Creek just a few miles or so from here? Do you think that they had pillows to put their little heads on at night before the battle, which by the way, Canada won?"

"No, I guess not," Josh said.

"Just roll up one of your sweaters or a pair of pants and use that for a pillow. This kid thinks he's at The Royal Connaught Hotel," Devin said, shaking his head.

"Are you sleeping with us in here too, Devin?" Josh asked.

It was going to be tight enough in tent number nine as it was and if you put Scout Devin in there with them, then they would be sleeping on top of each other. And besides, Josh thought, Devin smelled. The way Shannon and even his brother, Troy, did sometimes, some kind of funky teenage boy scent.

"No, I sleep in the Big House with the other Scouts and Adam. That's what we call the big building: The Big House."

"In a bed?" Josh asked.

"On a cot," Devin said sharply. "Only Adam gets a real bed. He has his own office with a bed. The cook, we call him Cookie, and Joy, the lady who works in the mess hall, don't sleep here at night, they go to their own homes."

"Will *you* have a pillow, Devin?" Josh asked.

"Your name's Moore, right?" Devin said, looking suspiciously at Josh.

"His name is Josh. He likes betting on horses and… something else I forgot. I'm his best buddy," Jiffy said.

"Everyone in this tent gets called by their last names," Devin said. "Everyone but me because I'm your Scout leader. This isn't a nursery school, you know. Did you boys know that Germany made kids your age fight in the army during World War Two? With real guns and hand grenades and stuff? Maybe you think they called each other Josh and Jimmy? No! They called each other by their last names."

First of all, Josh thought, German soldiers would have called each other Hans or Otto. He considered saying that to Devin but decided that, for now at least, he would take his aunt's advice and keep things like that to himself. And second of all, Josh wasn't completely convinced that this story that kids his age fought in World War Two was true. He made a mental note to ask his father when he saw him again or look it up himself in the *Encyclopedia Britannica*. But as for calling each other by their last names, that was just fine with Josh. That way he wouldn't have to call anyone Jiffy Pop.

"You're Sullivan?" Devin asked, looking at Jiffy.

"I was here at Camp Ronkewe last year, Devin, and everyone just called me Jiffy Pop. That's what everyone calls me, Jiffy Pop. Jiffy for short."

"That sounds retarded," Devin said with a sneer. "I'm calling you Sullivan and I want the rest of you to call him Sullivan too."

Jiffy lowered his head.

What an asshole! Josh thought. Right there Josh decided that he would call Jimmy 'Jiffy Pop' the entire time he was there.

"And you two are… ?" Devin said.

"Mayfield!" Kyle and Shane said in unison.

"I'm Kyle."

"I'm Shane."

Josh wondered if Scout Devin saw the problem with his naming scheme.

"You could call them Mayfield One and Mayfield Two," Josh said.

"I'll just call you both Mayfield. If I want a particular one, I'll let you know."

"Alright!" the twins said.

"We're in the first group of boys to go swimming today so get into your bathing suits and meet me in front of the Big House in ten minutes."

"Should we bring our swimming towel too?" Jiffy asked.

"Only if you want to dry off," Devin said. "Oh, wear your running shoes." He turned and walked out of the tent letting the flap close behind him.

"This is going to be fun, Josh," Jiffy said with exceptionally high enthusiasm.

Josh sat cross-legged on his sleeping bag, tossed his canvas hat to the back of the tent, and rummaged through his suitcase to find his red swim trunks with the Montreal Olympic logo on the hip. Under all his clothes, in the back pocket of a pair of jeans, he had stuffed a pack of Player's cigarettes and matches. He would have to wait until later to sneak off someplace and have one. In a day or two, once he got to know Jiffy better, he'll ask him if he wanted to join him in a smoke out in the woods. Anyone whose old man is a biker probably smokes.

"Your suitcase has a mirror!" Jiffy said.

"Yeah," Josh said, pulling out his swim trunks.

Josh and Jiffy turned away from each other and quickly changed into their swim trunks while the Mayfields went through a production of wrapping their *Star Wars* towels around themselves before pulling down their underwear. How did they ever get through the physical? Josh wondered. They were still trying to pull up their bathing suits under their towels when Josh and Jiffy hung their towels around their neck and walked in their sneakers toward the Big House where about twenty boys were already waiting. Josh looked nervously at the group of boys. Luckily, Gavin Mulligan was not among them.

"Are you going swimming with that bandana on, Jiffy?" Josh asked. Was going to sleep with it on too?

"I don't put my head under the water so it's okay," Jiffy said.

Finally, Kyle and Shane, wearing matching blue swim trunks, joined them near the Big House.

"So, tell us the truth, Josh," Jiffy said, pursing his big pink fish lips.

"What?" Josh asked.

"Is your dad really in the nuthouse? It's just that you should tell your best buddy if he is, don't you think? Like I told you about my mother being dead."

"Nah, he ain't in no nuthouse," Josh said, laughing. "He's in Montreal with my uncle. Gavin Mulligan is just a big liar. And he's had it in for me for a while now because… because I know something really bad about him that I can't talk about."

"What? Tell us!" Jiffy said.

"Yeah, tell us!" one of the Mayfields said.

"I… I can't say it. It's too bad. Like *really* bad," Josh said.

"Tell us!" a different Mayfields pleaded.

"Well…" Josh said.

The boys smiled and moved closer to Josh.

"You can't tell anyone but Gavin Mulligan steals ladies' underwear from the clotheslines in our neighbourhood."

"Why?" Jiffy asked. "Why would anyone steal ladies' underwear from clotheslines?"

"He steals them so... so he can wear them."

"Argh! Is that true?" Jiffy asked, as the Mayfields looked at Josh in horror.

"I swear to God! I was with my best friend, Shannon Perry, down by Red Hill Creek where we have a fort... well, it's really *my* fort but I let Shannon hang around since he's a pretty cool guy. Anyways, we were in our fort, which is really hidden so no one knew we were there, and we saw Gavin down by the creek wearing nothing but ladies' underwear and a brassiere and doing this weird fucking dance. Seriously, guys, stay away from Gavin."

Devin suddenly appeared, not in a swimsuit, but still wearing his Scout shirt and jeans and motioned for the four boys to follow him. They joined a few other groups of boys and their Scout leaders and walked for about fifteen minutes down a dusty dirt path with large trees and thorn bushes on either side until they came to a clearing.

"Jesus Christ!" Josh said.

This wasn't a swimming hole as much as a swamp. Even the Red Hill Creek looked better than this and it had garbage and crap from the city sewage plant flowing into it. Following Devin, Josh walked cautiously past the bulrushes and pussy willows down a path of cracked red clay up to the shit-brown stagnant water covered with floating green gunk. To one side there was a rope hanging to a tree, but it was about ten feet from the quagmire.

"Here we are, the Camp Ronkewe swimming hole! You'll be spending a lot of time here over the next three weeks," Devin yelled. His voice cracked and he cleared his throat.

"Listen up, boys!" another Scout yelled. "You have to go into the swimming hole with your sneakers on."

"Why?" one of the sixteen boys yelled back.

"Because we've had problems with boys stepping on glass and other sharp things in there. So, you got to wear sneakers. The water hole has dried up a lot this year because of the drought so... who knows what you'll find in there. Just be careful!"

A rush of boys ran into the water in their sneakers yelling and screaming. Josh's three tent mates were more apprehensive. Kyle and Shane ventured in together holding hands followed closely by Jiffy in his blue and white bandana. The boys swam as best as they could through the waist-deep water, though there was the occasional "ouch" as someone scraped their knee or hand on some sharp object at the bottom of the pond. Maybe a rusty can, Josh thought, or a broken beer bottle. Maybe Adam will have to yank it out of them with some needle nose pliers.

Josh strolled slowly around half the perimeter of the pond and then walked away. He did not fail to notice that Devin, nor any of the other full-fledged Scouts there, chose to jump into the swimming hole. Instead, they stayed on the banks of the pond, chatting with each other, only occasionally looking over at the younger boys in the swimming hole.

"Hey, Moore! Aren't you going swimming?" Devin yelled.

"I'm not going in that," Josh said, walking away.

"Suit yourself, Moore. No skin off my ass."

There will be a lot of skin off the asses of those poor guys swimming in that swamp, Josh thought. Also skin off their knees and their shins and their hands. Josh rolled out his towel and sat by the banks of the swimming hole by Derek, another kid who had refused to go into the water. Josh had met Derek during the great introduction earlier in front of the Big House. Derek had large glasses with thick lenses that magnified his eyes slightly. He was tall and thin and was wearing clothes that, because of his long arms and small torso, were both too small and too big for him.

Derek's Scout leader, Brett, had not even tried to persuade Derek into a pair of swimming trunks. Instead, Derek was wearing dark blue jeans that were a few inches off the ground but were so loose around the waist that they needed to be synched with a belt. Derek's clothes were, Josh thought, either hand me downs or his mother thought he would eventually grow into them. Derek saw Josh and held out a little purple flower with green leaves.

"What's your name again?" Derek asked.

"Josh."

"Do you know what kind of plant this is, Josh?"

"No, what is it?"

"Chicory," Derek said, twirling the plant in his fingers.

"Chicory?" Josh looked at the plant. If he were naming a pretty purple flower like that, he would not name it such an un-purple name. Chicory sounded brown to Josh.

"You must know chicory!" Derek said, rolling his eyes. "It's the stuff they put in coffee to make it taste better."

"Do you drink coffee?"

"No, but I drink tea sometimes," Derek said, He tossed the chicory aside.

"I drink coffee."

"They won't let you have coffee here, Josh. That's because Scouts Canada don't want to get sued. It's just like this business about having to go in the swimming hole with shoes on. They don't want to get sued if someone rips their foot open on glass."

"Oh!" Josh said. He hadn't thought about that.

"And if they gave you coffee and you freak out or something from the caffeine, not saying you would, well, your parents could sue them for millions."

"Hey, you're pretty smart, aren't you, Derek."

"Yeah," Derek said. "I'm probably the smartest kid here." He looked over toward the escarpment.

"Do you think that Ragno kid could be in that water, Derek?"

"Nah, his old man, unless he's a moron, would have tossed him in deep water… not some dirty pond a few feet deep."

"How old are you, Derek?"

"Eleven. How old are you?"

"Ten but I'll be eleven soon. Hey, where's your camping buddy, Derek?"

"Tommy's in there swimming with the rest of those dopes. I have no intention of getting my shoes wet."

"Is Tommy your best friend here?

"No, Tommy is a bit of an idiot, and I couldn't be best friends with an idiot."

"No, I guess not. Hey, Derek, do you want to be best friends with me? I mean, just while we're here at Camp Ronkewe?"

"No, I can't," Derek said, matter-of-factly. "I'm already best friends with Lenny, another kid in my tent. He's really smart too. Not as smart as me but he's my age. I can't be friends with a guy a whole year younger than me."

"I guess not," Josh said. He pulled a plant and held it toward Derek. "Hey Derek, you know what kind of plant this flower is?"

"That's just a buttercup."

"Oh, yeah."

"Haven't you ever seen a buttercup before?"

"I guess so. I just forgot."

"Where are you from, anyway?"

"Hamilton."

"Where in Hamilton?"

"The east end."

"Don't they have buttercups in the east end?"

"Sure they do, I just forgot."

"They say if you put a buttercup under your chin and if your chin glows yellow it means you like butter. That's a lie, of course. It's the sunlight reflecting the yellow colour of the flower onto your chin, but since everyone likes butter, everyone thinks it works. People are so stupid. I'd never live in the east end. It smells."

"Well at least it's not the north end," Josh said.

"Is it true your dad is in the nuthouse?" Derek asked.

"No, some goof from my neighbourhood is spreading rumours. My dad is in Montreal visiting my uncle for a while. I went to visit him there for a week before I came here."

Derek nodded as if Josh had convinced him, but Josh couldn't be sure. Derek was awfully smart. Josh just hoped Derek wouldn't ask any more questions about it. A smart guy could trip Josh up with questions.

From the corner of his eye Josh could see Jiffy rise slowly out of the mud hole with his black and white converse sneakers, squishing as he walked toward Josh and Derek.

"You should have come swimming, Josh! Everyone else had a buddy out there but me. No one was watching out for me. I could have drowned, and no one would know." He wiped some green slime off his arms. "We're supposed to be watching out for each other."

"I was watching from here," Josh said.

"He was watching you," Derek said as he watched a large black ant crawl over his hand. "I was watching him watching you."

"I guess that's okay then," Jiffy said. He smiled again.

"Good," Josh said. "I'm okay, you're okay."

After swimming, the boys walked back to camp, changed back into their shorts and T-shirts, and then Devin lead them into the Big House's mess hall for their first lunch at Camp Ronkewe. Josh could smell the chicken noodle soup as he walked in the door. It smelled, Josh thought, like they dumped a thousand packets of Lipton Chicken Noodle Cup-A-Soup in a big pot and added a hundred gallons of boiling water. It had the same strong chemical smell.

The mess hall in the Big House was full of boys, already eating at one of the many rectangular wooden tables placed closely together in the hall. The room was light, with large open windows below wooden rafters stretching up to the roof. It looked like the building, tables, and floor were all made from the same dark-coloured wood. At the back of the mess hall was the kitchen where Cookie, a chubby bald man with glasses, was sitting on a stool smoking a cigarette. Separating the kitchen and mess was a long counter, also made of the same dark wood, where boys were lined up for lunch. The counter had, from left to right, orange plastic trays, a stack of white plastic bowls, big piles of sliced white bread, small glasses of milk in plastic amber tumblers and, at the far end, a large cauldron of steaming soup. Behind the cauldron, a short woman in a stained dingy white apron with a pink overheated face stood dolling out soup with a ladle into the white bowls as each boy filed by. In between each boy the woman would wipe her brow with her forearm and then dip her ladle back into the caldron. That must be Joy, Josh thought, as he took his place in the queue behind Jiffy who stood behind the Mayfield twins and Devin.

"Tent number nine is getting ready to dine… on porcupine and turpentine," Josh said. He had thought of that while he was sitting by the smelly swimming hole and thought it was pretty clever. Even smart Derek probably couldn't have thought of it.

"Knock it off, Moore," Devin said without turning around.

"Chicken noodle soup is my favourite!" Jiffy said.

He and Josh picked up their trays, a bowl, and grabbed a slice of unbuttered white bread each. Jiffy's shoes, still wet, squished with each step. Poor guy. He'll have wet feet for six weeks, Josh thought.

Josh could still smell the pond scum on Jiffy. At least Jiffy didn't have hair under his arms yet so he wouldn't smell quite as bad as some of the older guys like Gavin would. And speaking of washing, where were we going to take a bath or shower? Maybe they just gave them a bar of soap and told them to go to the swimming hole.

"I like all kinds of soup. I like tomato soup, chicken and rice soup, chicken and stars soup, cream of chicken soup, vegetable beef soup. There isn't any soup I can think of that I don't like. How about you, Josh?"

Josh grabbed a tumbler of milk and placed it on his tray. He could see milk powder sticking to the side of the plastic glass where it hadn't been mixed into the water very well. He had drunk powdered milk his whole life, but his mother knew how to make it right.

"I like most soup too except mushroom soup," Josh said.

Not that Josh thought that this place would ever make mushroom soup. It looked like Camp Ronkewe relied on powdered food. But he would be there at camp for only five more days so he could certainly live with it for that short amount of time, couldn't he?

Jiffy licked his big fish lips and grinned excitedly as Joy ladled steaming soup into his bowl and then wiped her brow again. She needed a bandana like Jiffy's, Josh thought as Jiffy waited for him at the end of the counter. You don't have to wait for me, Josh thought, as Joy filled his bowl with the bright yellow steaming concoction of salt, water, and chemicals.

The two boys walked, with Jiffy leading, toward table number nine, where Devin and the twins were now sitting down to eat. They would wait for him and Jiffy. Devin had mentioned something about each table having to pray before they ate. Jesus Christ!

"After lunch," Jiffy said, turning his head back to speak to Josh, "I can show you how to tie a bandana around your head like a real biker. Then everyone will know we're camp buddies."

That's when it happened.

As Jiffy turned back around his wet shoes slipped on the buffed wooden floor and his tray fell out of his hands, tipping over. The hot bowl of yellow chicken noodle soup dumped right onto the front of Jiffy's shorts and down his bare right leg, splashing onto floor. Jiffy screamed and fell to the floor holding his leg, which was already turning bright red.

Adam ran past Josh, picked Jiffy up in his arms and carried him into the kitchen. Cookie turned on the cold water and used the spray nozzle to run cold water over Jiffy's crotch and leg and then Adam tried to take off his shorts, but Jiffy screamed even louder. Josh stood, frozen, in the same spot still holding his orange tray.

"Stop, Adam! His skin is coming off!" Cookie yelled.

Adam and Cookie quickly packed Jiffy's leg in a towel with ice and then Adam carried Jiffy to his car in the parking lot and drove him the few miles to Joseph Brant hospital.

Josh never saw Jiffy again.

After the commotion, Devin, with his cracking girly voice, tried to lead the table in some kind of prayer but Josh didn't pray. Instead, he stared down at his soup as it cooled. He couldn't eat. Later, Gavin Mulligan walked past their table and hit Josh in the back of the head with his empty tray, laughing as he passed.

Five more days, Josh thought, only five more days.

August 1977

Ten

And then Ted was home.

He had been discharged from the hospital one day earlier than expected and there had been little time for goodbyes, but he exchanged phone numbers with Jonathan and promised Rick that he would come up to visit in the coming weeks, though Shackelford had already told Jonathan that he could also expect to go home before the end of August. Rick, however, would probably be at the Hamilton Psychiatric Hospital until the end of the year. So with little notice, Ted quickly threw his things together into two large plastic *Bi-Way* bags and, on his way out, was finally given the belt to his pants back from the locked room near the nurses' station. Telling no one in his family that he was being released early, Ted had Pauly Honcharuk, a friend from work, pick him up and drive him home to Alkeld Street.

Ted walked through the front door startling Gloria, who jumped up from the couch, where she had been putting curlers in her hair, and hugged him tightly. She felt like home. The new puppy, meanwhile, took one look at Ted and ran off down the hallway and under the kitchen table.

"Some watch dog you got there," Ted said with a smile.

Later that day, Ted, was itching to get back behind the wheel of his Chevy Impala and, after telling Gloria he was running out to get dinner, went for a long drive around the east end of the city, down Barton Street, over Red Hill Creek, and past Restland Cemetery. The Old Man would be checking into Restland soon. He'll be settling in just a few rows over from Tessa. It wouldn't be long now that Wilma had arrived.

Ted briefly thought about driving up to St. Josephs to see the Old Man. He had not seen him since the day he had to feed him, never making it back up with the bottle of rye he had promised him but decided to wait a day or two to visit, when he hoped Wilma and the rest of them weren't around. Then he'd go up with that bottle he had promised the Old Man for one last drink.

Ted drove along the foot of the mountain, around Gage Park, and then past the steel mills along the bay, passing Wentworth Steel, where he would soon return to work. Right back on the cranes. Right back to booms, levers, and pedals. He stopped to pick up T-bone steaks at a butcher shop on Parkdale Avenue and then ran into the liquor store for a forty-ouncer of Canadian Club, two bottles of Niagara sparkling red wine, and that small mickey of rye for the Old Man. Ted had never shared a drink with his father.

Shackelford had given Ted the name of a new therapist that would help him with the intrusive thoughts and anxiety, but his first appointment would not be until the end of August. That was just fine with Ted. He had had just about enough talk in the last four months at the hospital to last him a lifetime, and now just knowing that his problem had a name, *intrusive thoughts*, and that other people had them and learned to deal with them made these thoughts less frightening. And, like Shackelford suggested, when an inappropriate thought now came into his head that caused him to panic, Ted would stop what he was doing and tell himself it was just a passing thought. It was nothing to be worried about. Shackelford had even suggested that Ted laugh at how ridiculous the thoughts were, but Ted was nowhere near the point of laughing at his fucked-up intrusive thoughts quite yet.

Returning home, Ted cooked the steaks on his barbeque in the backyard, sipping on glass after glass of sparkling red wine while Reefer, now seemingly comfortable with the fact that Ted was the alpha dog of the house, laid close by, dozing in the shade. It's funny that this old barbeque was one of the few things he missed while he was gone. Josh, Gloria and barbequing his own food in his own yard were the things he had missed most.

Gloria made baked potatoes, and when the steaks were done, they sat on opposite ends of the couch and ate on folding metal TV trays not saying much to each other except when she asked a few questions about the changes to his medication. Ted knew Shackelford had already talked about his intrusive thoughts to Gloria, trying to alleviate any of her remaining fears that he could go off the deep end again. But Ted didn't want to talk about all that right now; he was happy to enjoy the silence with just the sound of the Blue Jays game on the television.

As Ted cut into his steak, he wondered what Jonathan and Rick were having for dinner up at the hospital. Shepherd's pie or liver and onions, he thought, with a slight smile. Jonathan will do his best to try to talk Rick into eating the liver, but Rick will tell him to fuck off, eating only his cubed Jell-O (and probably Jonathan's Jell-O too) and then Rick would buy every Milky Way chocolate bar in the vending machine, bits of which would be stuck in his braces for the rest of the night. Someday he'd invite Rick and Jonathan down for a barbeque.

That night Gloria had gone to bed early, but she accepted Ted's advances when he stripped out of his clothes, put his glasses on the bedside table, and climbed into bed next to her two hours later. He pressed himself into her from behind and caressed her body, kissing Gloria's neck and feeling the softness of her body and the flowery aroma of her skin as his penis grew hard. She turned on her back and embraced him as he kissed her lips, gently at first, tasting the salt on her tongue and then, more forcefully, lifting her nightgown and caressed her breasts. Slowly, Ted ran his mouth down her neck, between her breasts to her stomach, and finally between her legs. He savoured her. It had been so many months. She roughly ran her fingers through his hair, and he wondered if his new beard was irritating or exciting her. Then Ted mounted her, and Gloria opened her legs wider, welcoming him.

I'm finally home.

He came quickly, thanks to his new medication, and, kissing her once more on the neck, gently pulled her nightgown back down over her hips and tenderly put the bed sheet back over her body.

"I'm going to have a quick smoke," he whispered.

He rolled out of bed, put on his glasses, and, as he walked toward the door to the hallway, he noticed two clothespins holding their green bedroom curtains tightly closed. She must have been nervous being home alone at night while I was in the hospital, Ted thought.

Ted walked naked down the hallway toward the dark living room. He was uneasy. Though the sex was great (sex was always great with Gloria), there was something off. There was a strange hesitancy in Gloria's responses, almost as if she had to take a second to convince her body to react to his touch. Perhaps it was normal after not being together for months and, because of that goddamn old medication, they had not been intimate for a couple of months even before Ted had gone into the hospital.

Gloria is still probably angry about Abe, he thought. *Of course, she was.* She just didn't want to make a hassle about it the moment he got home. She was undoubtedly worried I would fly off the handle and rush out to the garage for another shard of glass. Gloria was no shrinking violet; when she had something to say she said it. Eventually, she would give Ted an earful about how he had made her grovel to Abe for that goddamn money. He could bet on it. And how could he blame her? It *was* all his fault. It was always his fault.

Ted sat in his chair by the sofa, lit a cigarette, and gently pulled at his softening dick, still slick with cum. The air conditioner hummed beside him in the front window, and he enjoyed the cool air on his naked skin, still hot and flushed from fucking. He had been eager to finally sleep in his own bed once again but now, after all these months away from home, his bed felt strange, the way it had when he came home from Africa and began sharing a room with Dale and Andy on Waterloo Street again. The bed was the same, but he wasn't.

The day before Ted left the hospital, he and Jonathan had been sitting together on Ted's bed drinking, trying to finish what was left of Ted's bottle of rye out of Dixie Cups. The men had not spoken about what had happened in the old tunnel of the Manor House earlier that week. Instead, they were talking about getting together for dinner with their wives around Labour Day when Jonathan suddenly leaned over and gently touched Ted's knee. He placed his hand on Ted's kneecap and then moved it slowly up to his thigh, squeezing tenderly. Ted let Jonathan touch him for a few seconds to ensure he was reading the situation correctly, and to be honest, it was nice just to be touched again, but as Jonathan's hand moved even higher up Ted's brown corduroys, Ted stopped him and moved Jonathan's hand away, patting it gently as he let go.

"Sorry, Ted. Fuck! I don't know what I was thinking."

"Don't worry about it, Jonathan," Ted had said, refilling their Dixie Cups.

"I just… I just wanted to touch you before you left."

Ted put his arm around Jonathan's shoulder, and Jonathan put his head on Ted's chest and closed his eyes.

"Christ, don't you ever wash that Expos cap, brother?"

It wasn't the first pass Ted had ever received from a guy, but Ted had always been clear when it happened that he wasn't interested in messing around with men. He may have done some shit with other boys when he was a kid, but everyone did, didn't they? But to have been dishonourably discharged must have been really tough on Jonathan; that's the kind of thing that stays on your permanent record and follows you for life. One guy in basic training with Ted was tossed out for that, but they didn't catch everyone. Ted knew of two other soldiers that would hitchhike up and down the Trans-Canada Highway from Ottawa to Montreal just to get picked up by women who cruised the highway looking to pay young guys to fuck them. But the truth was, and Ted knew it, that these two boys would also take rides from guys who picked them up. He never considered those two guys queer; they were just trying to make some extra money. They had even asked Ted to join them on the Trans-Canada Highway with them once. "It's a quick way to grab some cash," one of them had said. Ted turned them down. Not his scene.

Ted did have one queer exploit. It was an impromptu threesome in his early twenties, a few years before Josh was born. He had been drinking alone at the Golden Rail on King Street after working an afternoon shift at Wentworth Steel. Getting loaded while on afternoon shift was always a challenge. You finished work at 11pm and then only had a couple of hours before last call at the bars so, if you wanted to tie one on, you had to drink quickly. That night Ted had sat in the Rail's front bar, ordered a small draught beer with a rye chaser and, quickly finishing them, ordered another two. Sitting just down from him at the bar was a woman in a blue velvet dress and, beside her, a brawny blond man who was buying the woman drinks just as quickly as she was polishing them off. Soon, Ted had shuffled down beside them and the three were talking in the chummy way soused people do at bars. The guy, Wes (Ted still remembered his name), was around Ted's age and a foreman at Dominion Metal Stamping. The woman, whose name Ted could not remember, was older than the two men by at least a decade but not homely. She had said she worked as a cocktail waitress someplace downtown and sold Avon cosmetics on the side. Ted remembered the Avon. After last call, the three of them, somehow, ended up at the woman's apartment on Mary Street and had more drinks. It had all started when Wes and the Avon lady began kissing and groping each other, in an old wingback chair they squeezed into. Ted had considered leaving, assuming she had made her choice, when Wes unzipped her blue dress and she stood, letting it fall to the floor, and then, naked, she walked over to Ted and took his hand. She then kissed Ted and lead both men to the couch where, for a while, the two men took turns kissing and fondling her breasts and ass. Soon they had all undressed and the three made their way to her single bed and, since it was a tight fit, they huddled their naked bodies close together. At some point Wes's hand had moved to Ted's thigh and Ted allowed it. It was a strange feeling having a man's fingers on his skin. Not a bad feeling—just peculiar. The booze was hitting Ted at the right time, and he luxuriated in the pleasure of four hands on his body. Through the entire episode, Wes never kissed Ted— or even tried to. Then they both fucked the woman. First Ted and then Wes. Ted had never seen another man fuck a woman before, except in blue movies, and watched, half-stoned, as Wes's dick, smaller and a shade darker than Ted's, slid in and out of the woman's vagina. It turned Ted on. And later, when Wes had slowly moved his head down to Ted's cock, Ted was ready and hard again. Ted continued to deeply kiss the woman as Wes wrapped his lips around Ted's cock and began gently sucking, perhaps so gently at first to ensure Ted didn't weird out or get violent. But Ted only moaned with pleasure and Wes seemed to take this as consent and began to give Ted one of the finest blowjobs he had ever had. He licked the head of Ted's penis, sucking out a new batch of precum that Ted had worked up, and then went deep down onto Ted's shaft. Ted could feel the head of his cock slide easily down Wes's throat, massaged by the tightening and relaxing of Wes's pharynx, and then, slip back into Wes's mouth to be sucked again as Wes raised his head. It felt amazing. Wes then licked and sucked Ted's balls for a few minutes before returning to his cock where he sucked, his blond head bobbing up and down, until Ted finally shot a load of semen, probably bigger than the one Ted had just dumped in the Avon lady, into Wes's mouth. Wes swallowed, looked up at Ted, and grinned.

"I can't believe you did that," Ted said with a smile.

Later, Ted had wondered if Wes and the Avon lady were in cahoots. A bisexual couple looking for a young guy to play a third in their sexy games. Ted never did anything like that again, but he had taken the whole escapade in stride at the time. He never felt the need to conform to some bourgeois code of ethics or moronic religious laws, anyway. The only thing he felt vaguely guilty about was fucking around on Gloria. They were living together by then, but they weren't married (and wouldn't be married until Josh was two years old). Fuck guilt! Who did he hurt? Besides, Wes gave one great blowjob. However, real gay stuff wasn't his scene. Ted could never give Jonathan what he wanted or needed— at least when it came to this. He hoped that Jonathan understood that. Ted didn't want to lose Jonathan as a friend.

Ted crushed out his cigarette in the darkness, walked into the bedroom, and climbed back into bed beside Gloria. She was sleeping soundly, perhaps at ease having a man in the house again or maybe it was her new pills. He pulled up the sheets and inhaled; they had the scent of the outdoors. She must have just done the laundry, Ted thought, as he drifted off to sleep.

The following day, Gloria was already up and dressed before Ted woke up, cheating him out of morning sex and making him worry again that she didn't want him to make love to her. She had already washed all the clothes he had brought home from the hospital, including the ones he had worn home yesterday, and had them all out drying on the clothesline. Ted made himself a cup of instant coffee, hoping it would cure his slight hangover from the Canadian Club and the sparkling red wine. He grabbed his guitar and walked barefoot out the backdoor. It would be another hot day. He sat down in a lawn chair in the middle of his backyard, in the shade under the red maple tree, while Reefer laid down and fell asleep under his chair.

"How about an oldie but a goodie, Reefer?"

Slowly, Ted started to play "Goodnight Irene" on his guitar, surprised how his fingertips, usually calloused from years of playing, had grown softer over the months since he had picked up his guitar. They hurt a bit, in a way he enjoyed, against the guitar strings. Leaning over the guitar with his long sandy hair hanging in his face, Ted tried to remember the words and how Tessa sounded as she sang along. Christ! He should have protected her. They all should have. But he was only seventeen years old when he left for the army and what could he have done for fuck's sake! And in all those years none of us, not even his older siblings, including Wilma, Jack, and Noah knew what was going on with Abe and Tessa. Well, no one but Gloria, that is. No, Gloria had figured it all out before any of them. And what did he do when she told him her suspicions about Abe?

Fuck! No wonder Gloria can't stand to look at me right now.

Ted put his guitar down on the dried grass. As he suspected, his front and back yards had gone to seed. Troy had been mowing, but no one had been watering it and his lawn was now brown with dandelions and dying clover all over it. Yes, Hamilton was under water restriction because of the drought, but once the sun went over the red maple tree that afternoon, he would do a quick watering with the hose of the front and back yards. Seeing they had not used much water for their lawn all summer, they deserve to use a bit more. Screw the City of Hamilton and their drought alert!

At some point he would have to drive over to see his mother. She had called the evening before as he was barbequing the steaks and left a message with Gloria that she was eager to see him. It was probably the longest the two of them had gone without seeing each other since Ted had been in Africa. And this month in particular, August, was always hard on his mother.

He opened his cigarette pack and took out a joint he had rolled that morning from the stash in his closet. Shackelford had told him to watch his drinking, but he didn't mention grass. Not that Ted could remember him saying, anyway. He stuck the joint in his mouth and pulled it through his lips to get it moist. Ted had never been shy about smoking pot in his own home or around the boys and they had all grown accustomed to pot smoke in the house as much as they did of his guitar playing.

Ted lit the joint, inhaled deeply, and rested his head on the back of the chair. Not a cloud in the sky. The humidity and heat mingled with the pollution from the city's smokestacks, creating a layer of brown miasma overhead. The sky was blue someplace, he thought, taking another drag off his joint and holding it in his lungs until he started to cough. This was good pot. He had bought it from Pauly Honcharuk in the spring before he lost his marbles. Ted had hidden it in an old Sanka jar in the back of his bedroom closet, not because he was worried about Gloria finding his stash, but because before Kevin moved out, he would often go through Ted's drawers, find his pot, and steal enough for a joint or two. A seed sizzled and popped as Ted took another drag. *It has a few too many seeds but other than that, it's not bad.*

"Yeah, August is always tough for Ma," he said to himself. "It's no picnic for the rest of us either."

Tessa will have been gone seven years on the eighteenth of August. They had knocked down the seedy old Colonial Hotel on Catherine Street a few years back and put up a supermarket. But even today, Ted could never stop himself from looking at the sidewalk in front of the A&P every time he drove past it. Newer hotels don't have windows that open anymore, like the Colonial did, for exactly that reason. That had all come too late for Tessa, who had killed herself by jumping out of the ninth-floor window of the Colonial Hotel in 1970.

"It sounds like she was re-enacting the trauma that happened to her with all those men," Dr. Shackelford had said, when Ted brought up her death during one of their sessions. "And trying to kill the pain of it with drugs. It's an all-too common and sad story."

They would never know why she picked that night or that hotel. Tessa didn't leave a note explaining herself before she jumped that night. All they found in her room were doodles made with a ballpoint pen on a pad of paper. She had drawn a garland of flowers: pansies, daisies, lilies of the valley, and violets with petals falling coloured in deep blue ink.

Suddenly Reefer jumped up and ran to the backyard gate. They had company.

Ted took another drag, inhaled deeply, and then stuck the burning end of the joint on his tongue to douse it.

"Who's there?" he yelled.

"It's Shannon Perry."

Shannon Perry? he thought. The little pervert kid from down the street? Why would that little bugger be at his back gate at ten in the morning?

"What do you want, Shannon?"

"I was wondering if Josh was back from camp yet."

"No, he's gone for another week."

"Okay... can I come in and see Reefer for a second, Ted?"

"Um... I guess so, sure, come on in."

Had Shannon Perry always called me by my first name, Ted wondered, putting what was left of his joint into the breast pocket of his shirt.

The boy strolled into the backyard with a big smile and Reefer jumped around at his feet like they were old friends. Like everyone in the neighbourhood, Ted knew that the kid stole women's underwear from clotheslines. It better never be his wife's underwear or Shannon would have a broken neck.

"This is a great dog, Ted." Shannon got down on his knees and rubbed the dog's belly.

"Yeah, he is," Ted said.

"I love the name Reefer, too. Josh lets me come over and play with him sometimes. Are you going to train him to be a guard dog? That's what Josh said."

"We want him to protect the house, that's for sure. From burglars and thieves and… trespassers."

"He'll be good at that, I think," the kid said with a sly grin.

What's wrong with this kid, Ted thought. Could it be that Shannon sniffed glue or did LSD or something like that? Was LSD still popular with the kids like it was in the sixties? They checked for LSD in Tessa's blood after they took her away, but only found traces of heroin, alcohol, and Valium.

"We hope so," Ted said.

"I haven't seen you around for a while, Ted."

"I've been away."

"I knew you were back, though. I saw you driving down Alkeld Street yesterday. Are you back now for good?"

"Sure. This is where I live."

"I wanted you to know that I kept an eye on Gloria while you were gone."

"You did what?"

"I'd sit on my porch at night, have a smoke or two, and wait until I saw her pass by on her way home from work. Every night that she was on afternoon shift. Right between quarter after eleven and eleven-thirty she'd walk past my house."

"You did this every night?"

"You know what, Ted? Your wife should learn how to drive. Josh and me are pretty good friends, you know, so I thought the least I could do was watch out for his mom while he was away at camp. And with you gone too…"

"That was really nice of you, Shannon. But you don't have to do that anymore now that I'm home. You understand me?"

"Sure, I understand you, Ted. Did you know Josh didn't want to go to camp at all? In fact, I can't believe they ever got him in the car.

You can't really blame him though, can you? I told him, I said, Josh that Cub Scout camp would be way too queer for me. All those guys sleeping together? No fucking way!"

"Well, his mother told him that if he didn't like it there, he could call us and we'd pick him up. He just had to give it a chance. We haven't heard from him so he's probably having a great time."

"More likely, they aren't letting him call home. I bet soon they'll call you and tell you Josh ran away."

Ted looked up and saw Gloria standing at the kitchen window, watching them with her arms folded over her chest. He was half expecting her to come out and shoo the little pervert away. She couldn't stand Shannon Perry or Shannon's mother, Janet, though, Ted thought, maybe that's because Gloria saw how very little separated the two women.

The kid picked up Reefer and sniffed him, first in his face and then the dog's belly.

"I'm going to take Reefer in the house for his nap. You'd better go home now, Shannon."

"Okay," Shannon said, putting Reefer down on the grass. "Tell Josh to come to the fort when he gets home. I'll probably be there. That's where I always am."

"Will do," Ted said.

Shannon stood up and walked toward the gate. Ted was going to have to have a talk with Josh about Shannon when he got home from camp. He had wanted Josh to hang around other neighbourhood boys but not this foul-mouthed kid. There was something more wrong with him.

"Cool scar, by the way, Ted," Shannon said, walking out of the gate.

Ted ran his fingers over the scar on his throat and then picked what was left of his joint out of his shirt pocket. For a second, he had forgotten all about the scar. Had Josh said anything to Shannon about that night?

"Wait a minute, Shannon! What fort?" Ted yelled, as the gate slammed.

Ted did not like the idea of Josh alone in some fort with Shannon Perry. Not one bit. And where exactly was this fort? I'll ask Josh about that fort when he gets home from camp, Ted thought as he relit his joint.

Ah! This was the life, at least for a while. His union job was gone, sure, fuck it, but Shackelford had given him a note to stay off work from the steel mill until after Labour Day. And maybe, just maybe, he would just stay stoned, right here in the backyard until then. He picked up his guitar and began playing "L'Internatioanle".

So, comrades, come rally,
And the last fight let us face.
The Internationale
Unites the human race...

"You are one day out of the hospital. Is it really a good idea to be smoking that junk now, Ted?" Gloria asked, coming out of the back door.

"Probably not," he said, wiping a long strand of hair out of his eyes.

"I don't want that Perry boy around here," Gloria said.

"Neither do I."

"What was he talking to you about for so long?"

"He wanted to know when Josh was coming home. And he wanted to see how our new guard dog was doing."

Ted decided it best not to tell Gloria about Shannon watching her walk home from work all summer— or about Josh and the fort.

"I don't want Josh around him either," Gloria said.

"Neither do I," he said.

"Abe called while you were having your chat with Shannon Perry. He wants to know when he can come down and pick up this month's cheque. He said he'd like us to choose a time when Josh and I would *both* be here."

"What did you tell him?"

"I told him you'd call him back later."

"You're never going to forgive me for this are you, Gloria?"

"I don't know... but even though I'm happy you're home and feeling better, Ted.... I do know that I'm not going to forgive you today."

Ted didn't move from the backyard for the next few hours.

He enjoyed being home with his own grass of his own backyard under his bare feet, even if it was brown. The puppy didn't do much except explore the perimeter of the backyard a few times and then scamper right back under Ted's chair to sleep. The way the puppy slept, curled up making soft snoring sounds, once whimpering in its sleep, reminded Ted of Rick.

I have to stop thinking about that goddamn place!

Gloria had gone grocery shopping with Doris, and by the time the sun went over the maple tree behind the garage, Ted was on his third joint, still strumming his guitar and singing "If I Had a Hammer" to the dog. Back when he had first moved in with Gloria on Barton Street, Ted had played that Peter Paul and Mary album so many times in their basement apartment that Gloria had once said she was so sick of that song that if *she* had a hammer, she'd put it through the record player.

He chuckled and then suddenly stopped.

"If Gloria were ever going to leave me, Reefer, this would be the time," Ted said. "Either that, or she'll spend the rest of her life resenting me for making her go to Abe."

Just like that fucking fur coat.

The phone rang in the kitchen and, at first, Ted ignored it. It was too nice out to have anyone ruin it. The ringing continued until, finally, Ted stood up with a grunt and, with a joint still in his mouth, walked into the house. Someone wanted to speak with him very badly and there was only one person in this family who was that relentless.

"Edward? It's Wilma. Dad just died."

Ted drove, still high, to St. Joseph's Hospital. He parked in a nearby Tim Horton's parking lot and, chewing a piece of spearmint Doublemint gum to cover up the tell-tale pot and whiskey smell, walked into the hospital with his silver flask full of rye stuffed deep into the front pocket of his pants. When the elevator doors opened on the third floor, Ted could hear Wilma's warbling soprano voice down the hall. Even in death, peace wasn't possible with Wilma around.

The hospital staff had moved the Old Man into a large private room down the hall from the ward he had shared with the three other old men. It was nice to know he was given some courtesy, if not peace, on his way out. Ted walked slowly into his father's room and stopped.

Wilma was alone, standing over him, singing "Amazing Grace." The Old Man would *have* to be dead to allow that. When Wilma saw Ted at the threshold, she smiled and began singing louder.

Yes, when this flesh and heart shall fail,
And mortal life shall cease;
I shall possess, within the veil,
A life of joy and peace.

Wilma's bouffant hair was blonder than ever and her makeup, with powder, blush, and lipstick a bright pink, maybe a bit thicker than the last time Ted had seen her. She ended the song theatrically, looking up at the hospital room ceiling like a Renaissance ecstasy painting in her pastel pink dress while holding onto the Old Man's hands. Ted just felt fortunate that she didn't feel the need to start the goddamn song over again from the beginning on his account.

"Oh, Edward!"

Wilma only began calling him by his first name since she had become a born-again Christian. Before that, she had always called him Teddy. She folded the Old Man's hands back over his chest and patted them.

"Good to see you, Wil," Ted said.

"Edward, I was *this* close." She held up her finger and thumb an inch from each other. "*This* close!"

She hugged him. A sisterly but cool hug and then stepped back and frowned. She smells the whiskey on me, Ted thought, but he didn't care. After all these years, they all knew what he smelled like. It's not like Wilma's husband, Greg, never had a drink. That son-of-a-bitch could drink all the Moores under the table, including Ted, in the old days. Hell, even Wilma could knock them back like every other east end girl in the days before Jesus got hold of her. Gin and Fresca. That was Wilma's drink. And she drank a shitload of it.

"I *so* wanted him to accept Christ," she said. She put her hand in the air and clenched her fist. "I really thought he would, Edward. I was here practically all day and all night for three days trying. And where were you all that time?"

"The loony bin," he said.

"But Dad was just too… too darn stubborn. Stubborn! Stubborn! Stubborn! Just like he was his whole gosh darn life! And now there's nothing left to do but pray for him. Pray for God's mercy."

"You go right ahead."

"Do you want to pray now? We can do it right now over Dad. We could pray for you both." She took Ted's hand and began to lead him toward the bed.

"No, I'm not praying," he said, letting go of her hand.

"Stubborn! The both of you! Maybe a little more praying would have helped keep you out of you-know-where. I'm sorry to be the one to say this, Edward, but no one who has Christ in their heart cuts their own throat. Where God is, there is no despair."

Wilma reached up and touched the scar on Ted's throat as if she was expecting to heal it with her touch. He pushed her fingers away from his neck.

"Are you sure you don't want to pray with me?"

"No,"

"Sue and Peggy and I prayed over Dad just after he stopped breathing and, call me crazy, but I think those prayers of ours helped him when he got to the gates of heaven, standing in front of the throne of the Lord. And I just sang "Amazing Grace". It was Dad's favourite hymn. He probably heard me. You know, for such a stubborn man who refused to accept Christ, he certainly did love the old hymns, didn't he?"

If the Old Man loved "Amazing Grace", then I'm a fucking monkey's uncle, Ted thought. Their father hated hymns! He liked big band music and those old bawdy English songs he'd sing around the house. What was that one he would sing about the shithouse? Ted tried to remember. "Times is Hard!" That was it! The Old Man used to sing it every morning on his way to the outhouse when Ted was a little boy.

"Where are the others?" Ted asked.

"Sue and Peggy are in the chapel. It's a Catholic chapel, but I think that's all right just this once. Though I tend to think God takes one look at all those crucifixes and only half-listens. Don't tell anyone, but I took down that crucifix that was on the wall over his hospital bed. It's in the table by the bed if anyone asks. Sue called Jack and he's driving in from Montreal this afternoon. Noah and Lynn are driving back now from Kitchener."

"And Dale?"

"I hear he flew in from Vancouver last night. He's staying at Mom's."

"So, does Mom know?"

"I'm not sure if Sue called her or not. I only called you and Jack. Ask Sue when she comes back. I don't really want Dale up here today. Seeing him at the funeral will be enough for me. I really hope you're planning on cutting your hair for the funeral, Edward."

"Where's Helen?"

"I told her I wanted to spend some time alone with Dad before they took him away. That woman was always here, with her big ears and her bad wig. Maybe if she would have left me and Dad alone for five minutes, I could have convinced him."

"She is his wife," he said.

"*Was* his wife. And can you believe that wife of his told us we should knock off the praying last night? That's what she said, 'knock off all that praying'. What sort of person tells other people to stop praying when someone is at death's door? Maybe in his heart Dad did come to Christ just before he died. He may have. And He is a merciful God."

"If you say so, Wil."

"Did Gloria tell you we offered to take Joshua for the summer?"

"You what? Why?"

"It doesn't matter now. Gloria turned down our offer. Rather rudely too, if you ask me. I told her that boy was headed for trouble, what with her working all the time and you in that hospital. So, I simply suggested that instead of letting Josh run around like a wild Indian all summer, Greg and I were more than happy to fly him to Atlanta and send him to our church's day camp."

"I wish I had heard her response to that."

"She told me not to call Joshua *that boy*. Then she said that my saying 'wild Indian' was racist. I said, how can it possibly be racist when Joshua is whiter and blonder than I am, for heaven's sake. Now if I had said that about Gloria, I could see how she would be peeved being she's half-Indian, but you'd think I called her a *half-breed* or something. When did Gloria become so darn sensitive, anyway? It seems as if positively *everyone* is too darn sensitive these days: Indians, women's libbers and especially the Black people and Mexicans around Atlanta. Suddenly everyone thinks the world owes them something. All communist ideas, if you ask me. But you know all about that, don't you?"

"Yeah, I know all about that."

"Greg and I were only thinking about that boy. You don't want your son to grow up funny like Dale, do you? We hear things down in Atlanta."

"First of all, Wilma, Gloria is right. Don't call him *that boy*, his name is Josh."

"I see you've gotten too darn sensitive too."

"And second of all, he can grow up funny or not funny or any goddamn way he wants to grow up!"

Suddenly Ted was ashamed. He had pretty much said the same thing to Gloria about Josh that Wilma was now saying to him. Isn't that why he signed Josh up for Cub Scout camp? Wasn't he also worried that Josh would grow up funny? He had told himself he was doing it for Josh. No, the truth was Ted wasn't so different from her or any other Moore. And it made him sick to his stomach to admit it.

Wilma shook her head, ignoring what Ted had said, and looked back at their father's body, which looked pretty fucking content in the bed. Probably because he didn't have to listen to her sing anymore, Ted thought.

"I just can't believe it. I was so close. I mean THIS close. I'll tell you this right now, little brother, I'm not going to wait for you to be on *your* deathbed. I'm going to get you to Christ even if I have to hogtie you and drag you to Him myself. Then after you I'll get Josh too."

"Don't hold your breath, Wil."

"Do you want to spend some time with Dad alone?"

"Oh, I don't know..."

"Are you telling me you're not going to say goodbye to your father, Edward? Stop talking like a loony tune! It's your last chance. I'll leave you alone for a few minutes. I'll be right outside in the hall."

"Okay, okay," Ted said, walking to the bed.

"Don't get freaked out but his eyes are still open," Wilma said, walking out the door.

The electric light over the Old Man's bed was turned off and the only light in the room shone in from the big hospital window. All the medical machines had been turned off and the nurse call button was wrapped around the top of the bedpost. The Old Man won't be ringing again.

"Don't worry," Ted said softly. "I'm not going to sing any hymns at you."

His father looked smaller than he ever had. Life takes up so much room in the body, Ted thought. Now there was nothing. His father's mouth was open slightly, no teeth, of course. They must have put his dentures away. That makes your face fall in. Makes you look even more dead. His eyes, green as ever, were staring up at the hospital ceiling, and he had a slight smile on his face, as if the last thing he saw was kind of funny.

Outside the window was a beautiful late summer day. The trees were still lush and green despite the drought. Funny how plants, unlike the pampered grass in his backyard, know how to get the nourishment they need. Along the escarpment, a few trees were just beginning to turn yellow and red. I hope it'll be a cold day in November when I kick off, Ted thought, not in the midst of an August heatwave. There was something so incongruous about it.

His father's arms were covered with red and purple bruises, broken blood vessels from the intravenous needles rammed into his veins over the last weeks. The panther tattoo on his right forearm he got while in the army looked smaller too. The Old Man had picked up that tattoo somewhere in his travels during the war. It was pretty good work.

Ted took the silver flask out of his front pants pocket, unscrewed it, held it up in a silent toast, and then took a sip.

"Sorry I didn't come soon enough to share a drink with you," he said. He took another swig and put the flask back in his pocket.

Ted laid his hand on his father's hand. It was cool. Not cold, but just cool, like he had fallen asleep without a blanket. His father's hands were still, even now, big and square with beautiful callouses, perfectly suited for driving buses and streetcars through the rough streets of Hamilton and for the occasional fisticuffs. "I didn't take any shit on my streetcar," he would say. But they were also the hands of a man who could paint a delicate watercolour of an English countryside or build a mahogany china cabinet. Ted's own hands were far too clumsy for such delicate work. Ted had chosen the right career when he decided to work in the steel mills.

One time, not long after Ted and Gloria had moved into their house on Alkeld Street, the Old Man had come down to help Ted build a spare bedroom in the basement for Kevin. Ted had asked Kevin before they bought that house if he planned on moving home, and Kevin had said no. Of course, a few months later, Kevin showed up at the door of their small two-bedroom bungalow with his duffel bag and record collection. So, the Old Man came down and spent a Saturday building a third bedroom in the basement with Ted. At the time, Ted had thought about how much he enjoyed working side by side with his father. In many ways, it was a day he had waited for over thirty years.

"Edward? Are you almost done?" Wilma asked from the corridor.

It was time to say goodbye. Ted had not called him anything but 'the Old Man' since he had come back into Ted's life when he was nineteen.

"Look..." Ted said quietly. "I know I wasn't the best son, not by a long shot. But you weren't the best father either, so maybe it all evened out. I don't have any hard feelings toward you anymore and that's the truth. I don't blame you for anything anymore. Everything that's fucked up in my life, I fucked up all on my own."

Then Ted started to cry. A loud sob cut through the quiet of the hospital, embarrassing him. He covered his mouth, and his face grew warm. *How fucking weird. My cry sounds exactly like my laugh.* He wiped his runny nose on the shoulder of his shirt and walked toward the door. Then Ted stopped. He turned and walked back to his father's bedside. He cleared his throat as best he could and began singing.

Please don't burn our shithouse down.
Mother has promised to pay.
Father's away on the ocean wave
And sister's in the family way.

"Ted!" Wilma hissed from the hallway, apparently forgetting that she liked to call people by their full names. "What are you doing in there? It's not funny and it's not appropriate. You hear me!"

Brother dear has gonorrhea
And times is fucking hard.
So please don't burn our shithouse down
Or we'll all have to shit in the yard.

Ted sang the verses over again louder and then once more even louder until he heard Wilma, giving up, walk quickly away down the hallway. Then he laughed harder than he had in months and touched his father's hand one more time.

"Goodbye, Dad."

Ted left Wilma and the hospital behind and, sitting in the parking lot of the Tim Horton's coffee shop, drank what was left in his flask. He felt great. Was this the closure that Shackelford had talked about? If it was then closure was fucking fantastic! He put the flask under the front seat and then drove down Main Street back toward the east end of the city. He wanted to check on his mother and see Dale. He was a little pissed off that Dale had not called him last night when he got into town. After all, he had not seen Dale in three years.

Ted crossed the Red Hill Creek, now down to a mere trickle from the drought, and turned into his mother's senior apartment off Queenstown Road. He knocked on the door and smiled when, Dale, opened the door.

"Boy, is Wilma pissed at you," Dale said, smiling. He was barefoot, wearing faded jeans and a white Rolling Stones T-shirt.

"Dale! It's good to see you!"

Ted grabbed Dale by the shoulders, pulled him close, and hugged him tightly. Then he stared at him for a second and kissed him on the lips. Fuck! He missed his little brother.

"Going by the smell, Teddy, I'd say that's Canadian Club," Dale said.

"It's a rule, Dale," Ted said, walking into the apartment." The day your father drops dead you're allowed to drink as early as you want. It's like Christmas Day that way."

"Got any more?"

"My flask's empty, kid."

"That's a hell of a scar on your throat there."

"Yeah."

"It's not as bad as I heard."

"You should have seen it in the spring. So… if Wilma told you she's pissed at me, I guess she finally got around to calling Ma?"

"Yeah, she called about twenty minutes ago. She told Ma that the Old Man died and, let me get this part exactly right… that you, Teddy, are an obscene profaner and she's ready to completely wash her hands of you."

"That sounds about right."

"Mom said she already knew he was dead; a breeze went by her or something like that when she was making her morning cup of coffee. She's at Miracle Mart across the street, getting us some eggs and bread for lunch. I'm eating her out of house and home, she said."

"You're getting chubby, Dale. It looks so good on you."

Ted wanted to grab Dale right there and hug him again. Maybe if he had hugged Tessa more often…

"Thanks, Teddy."

"So how is Ma handling it?" Ted sat at his mother's kitchen table, pulled out his cigarettes and tossed them on the table. It was the same kitchen table and chairs his mother had back on Waterloo Street.

"Looks like she's taking it in stride. I guess once you lose a child anything else is a piece of cake."

"Probably."

"And speaking of cake, you want some? She has half a pound cake on the counter. I ate the other half. I'm eating everything these days."

Like Ted, Dale looked like their father, with the big nose and green eyes and those big square hands, though Dale was blonder than Ted. Dale had also recently grown a handlebar moustache and trimmed his long hair, which was at one time, even longer than Ted's. Now Dale's hair was shorter than Ted had seen it in years. I could never give up my long hair, Ted thought, looking at Dale. *They'd have to hold me down or drug me and cut it like Delilah did to Samson.*

"Did you get up to see the Old Man before he died, Dale?"

"I went up early this morning before visiting hours. Took the bus. Thought that was fitting. Just ran in for about ten minutes and said my goodbyes to him. I could tell by the way he was breathing that he wouldn't make it through the day. But he did look… kind of happy lying there."

"I thought the same thing just now. Is Mom going to the funeral?"

"Ask her when she gets home. I wouldn't bet on it, though. She'll probably just conjure up his spirit to yell at him sometime."

"Do you think Andy and Bonnie will go?"

"Nah, I don't think so, Teddy. I sure as hell would never go to Abe's funeral, that's for fucking sure."

"Abe misses you, Dale. He tells me every time I see him."

"He only missed being able to put me down. I've never understood why you still see Abe, Teddy. Sure, I can see why Andy and Bonnie see him, he's their father, but you?"

"He was really the only father I ever knew."

"Bullshit," Dale said.

"Okay, okay, let's just drop it, then. And don't bring up Abe when you see Gloria. She's… um… finally allowed him to visit us on Alkeld Street again."

"In your house?"

"Yes."

"You've got to be kidding me! Gloria sure had a change of heart."

"Well people change, Dale. They mellow over time."

"Not Gloria! There must be a reason she's letting that son-of-a-bitch in her house," Dale said. He looked sideways at Ted and squinted his eyes from across the kitchen table.

"It's my house too, Dale."

Ted opened his cigarette pack and handed a cigarette to Dale. As Dale took it, Ted looked down at Dale's arms.

"You're looking at my track marks, aren't you, Teddy?"

Dale turned over his arms and held them out for Ted to get a better look. The marks were dark but healed. There were no more red lesions or bruising like the last time Ted had seen him. And though Dale had told Ted over the phone that he had quit heroin, Ted hadn't been really sure that he had quit until right then.

"I'm thinking of getting a tattoo over them. What do you think about a stop sign on the inside elbows of both arms. In case I ever consider using again. Or maybe a spider web. Because that's what it was like, eh? A spider web."

"How is it like a spider web, Dale?"

Dale stared at him.

"No, really, I'd like to know. Is the spider the heroin, or are you the spider and spinning these webs?" Ted asked.

"Both, I guess."

"I see."

"Hey, Teddy, you want to get a tattoo with me while I'm in town? Matching Moore brother tattoos. We could ask Jack and Noah while they're in town too."

"Sure, why not. We could ask Wilma too."

"We could get a skull or a heart or something," Dale said.

"This here is the only tattoo I'm ever going to have." Ted pointed to the tiger on his forearm.

"Have you ever noticed how much that looks like the Old Man's panther? It's even on the same arm," Dale said.

"What are you talking about, Dale? The Old Man's tattoo is a panther! Mine is a tiger. And his tattoo is on his right arm and my tiger is on the left. When I got this, I said to the guy that I'd take any goddamn thing but a panther."

"No, a tiger and a panther are pretty much the same thing. At least in tattoos."

Ted stood, cut a big slice of poundcake, and ate it over the sink. "So, any girl in your life yet, Dale?" he asked as he chewed.

"No, none to speak of."

Ted thought of asking Dale is he even liked girls like Wilma had implied but decided this was neither the time nor the place. There had been rumours about Dale being queer since he was a kid, but Ted just wanted Dale to know, like Jonathan, that Ted didn't care one way or the other if he liked guys or girls. But that would have to wait for another day, Ted thought. Maybe he'll send him a letter telling him all this when Dale is back in Vancouver. Maybe in the end, it will turn out that everyone I love is queer, Ted thought. *C'est la vie.*

"How are things with Gloria?"

"The same."

"What happened that put you in the hospital? Besides the throat thing."

"I went nuts. Depression and anxiety and a shitload of medication pushed me over the edge. And I had other problems; I owed a lot in gambling debts that I couldn't deal with."

"Ma said they gave you shock."

"They did."

"Help any?"

"At first."

"What happened with the debts?"

"I stole money from the union to cover the debts."

"Fuck off! Really? That is awesome! How much did you take?"

"Eight grand."

"Fuck off!"

"I had to. I owed all this money to some bad dudes I never should have borrowed from, and I had my mitts on this union cash and…"

"Yeah, I get it."

"But we paid it all back while I was in the hospital. Every penny."

"Where did you suddenly get the money to pay it back?"

"People."

"People?"

"Abe, alright! I got the money from Abe! And it was only a loan."

"So *that's* why Gloria is letting the bastard in your house again. So, it's like nothing ever happened. It's all forgiven now?"

"I don't need this from you, Dale, I got enough of this shit from Gloria."

"Jesus fucking Christ, Teddy! I never asked Abe Murphy for a goddamn penny! And neither did Tessa!"

"I did it to keep me out of prison, Dale. *Prison!* And, unlike you, I have kids to think about. I have to keep a roof over their goddamn heads."

"Fuck, Teddy."

Dale shook his head and Ted knew that his little brother would never respect him as much as he did five minutes ago, even half-drunk with a scar across his throat.

"I'm afraid, Dale," Ted said. "I'm afraid that Gloria will never forgive me for it."

"Gloria will forgive you."

"Yeah? How do you know?"

"If people love you, they'll forgive you."

"You sure about that?"

"I already forgave you, Teddy."

"I missed you, Dale."

"I missed you too, big brother. You were the only one in this crazy fucking family I could ever talk to. You and Tessa."

Ted cleared his throat. The booze was making him emotional, and he had to stop himself from tearing up again.

"Guess what I asked Mom to do for me last night after dinner?" Dale said.

"Christ, that could be almost anything," Ted said, grinning.

"I asked her to have a séance."

"Christ, Dale! Has everyone lost their fucking minds around here?"

"Maybe we have. Ma was thrilled to do it. She locked the door, turned out the lights, and we did it in the kitchen. She still has that old white lace séance tablecloth of hers."

"And how did it go?"

"It was fine. I used to hate them when I was a kid, especially when she tried to get in touch with grandpa. Fuck I couldn't stand that mean son-of-a-bitch when he was alive, and I certainly didn't want him like a spook in the house when he was dead."

"Who did you ask her to get in touch with?"

"Gabriel."

"Dale, have you totally lost it?"

"I thought with the Old Man dying and Ma being here all alone that she needed someone she knew and loved around her. And I thought Gabriel would be perfect for that. She always called him our guardian angel."

"Bullshit! All bullshit!"

"Maybe it is, Teddy, but it's not bullshit to Ma."

"The last time I saw the Old Man alive he told me Mom went up there to the hospital one last time to give him a message from Gabriel. So, Ma must be getting out that old séance tablecloth and calling Gabriel more than we know."

"What does it really matter if she finds some comfort in it?"

"Did you get in touch with Gabriel last night? What am I saying! Of course, you did." Ted said, crushing out his cigarette. "He never fails to make an appearance when summoned."

"Yeah, he showed up. And it seems our guardian angel has become a bit ornery in the decade or so since we've last spoken. He was a bit pissed off at everyone—especially you."

"And people wonder why I ended up in the nuthouse."

"Gabriel said, through Ma, of course."

"Of course."

"That you didn't die on Ottawa Street like he did that day for a reason. That you were here on earth to do something special, and you weren't doing it. You, my friend, were born for great things and you're fucking up."

"Yeah, I've heard that my whole life from Gabriel, the little fucker."

"Yeah, but Gabriel hasn't been so fucking pissed off before. Do you think Ma expected me to tell you? She swore me to secrecy."

"I think Ma knew full well you'd tell me, Dale. You do realize it's just her own mind trying to make sense out of her miscarriage, terrible marriage, and losing Ruth and Tessa, right? And I'm the one getting the brunt of the bullshit?"

"Yeah, I know that, but prayer is just a person's own mind too. Ma thinks she can talk to dead people, and she always will, no matter how much guff our sisters give her about it. I'm not going to give her even more guff about it. I owe her that much."

"You want her to spend the rest of her life alone in this apartment speaking with the spirits of the dead? Does that sound like a life to you, Dale?"

"There are worse ways to spend your life, Teddy. I let Ma read my tea leaves last night too."

"Well, you two went all out, didn't you? There must have been a swarm of spirits popping in and out of here floating up and down Queenston Road. And what did your tea leaves show you, Dale? A new love? A baby? A new tattoo?"

"A storm," Dale said.

"Good, we need the rain."

There was the sound of a key in the lock and Ted's mother, Anna, came into the kitchen with two paper shopping bags in her arms as Ted pulled up the collar of his shirt, as best he could, over his scar.

"Ted! Oh, Ted!" His mother placed the grocery bags on the kitchen counter and threw her arms around him. Ted could smell the familiar vanilla and jasmine scent of Shalimar. "Did you make yourself tea? Did you want me to put the kettle on? You know I really wanted to get up to the hospital to see you, Ted, but I just… couldn't," she said.

"I understand, Ma, don't worry about it."

She reached out and pulled down his shirt collar.

"My God," Anna said,

"It doesn't hurt, Ma," Ted said, gently moving her hand away.

"I already lost three children. Losing another one would kill me. I know it. Promise me you'll never do anything like that again."

"Sure, Ma, I promise."

"I mean it, Ted. They would have to bury me right next to you all the next day."

"Ma, I'm never going to do it again. I promise. The new medication worked. I'm feeling great."

Looking somewhat convinced, she smiled and took to putting away her groceries.

"Wilma will probably be calling soon with the funeral arrangements and all," Dale said.

"Did you know when I was a girl, we used to lay out our dead right in the parlour for a day or two," their mother said, sitting down at the table between them.

"That sounds like a million laughs," Ted said.

"Actually, it was quite intimate." She reached out and touched their hands. "I think that's lost today. My father would always be asked to play the piano as folks wandered in and out to pay their last respects. He'd always oblige, playing something sweet—nothing too sad but nothing too happy either. And there the body was, laid out in the parlour. Now they pick you up, cart you off, and leave you naked and alone in the mortuary freezer all night."

"Would you really prefer be rolled in right here between your china cabinet and television set?" Ted asked.

She smiled. "No, probably not. I remember one time: my cousins and I were in the house alone while my Uncle Jan was lying out in the parlour dead. The adults had all gone out someplace so there we were, four children, alone with a corpse in the house."

"What could be so important that they left a bunch of kids there with a dead body?" Ted asked.

"I honestly don't remember. We weren't mollycoddled in those days. No one was shielded from death—not that they ever could shield us! Death was all around us, for God's sake. My mother died in the flu epidemic in 1919. Every single person I knew lost someone in their family during that epidemic and this was just after millions had died in the war. No, you couldn't tell children that death would never touch them. Death touched all of us. Anyway, let me finish the story about Uncle Jan. Jan is John in Norwegian. I always thought Jan sounded nicer. I wanted to call your brother Jack, Jan, but Walter said it sounded like a girl's name. I somehow managed to get Noah's name spelled N-O-A, the Norwegian way, on his birth certificate though. No one knows that. Only me and Noah and he doesn't like it. Anyway, while us kids were in another room, we heard a loud noise from the parlour where Uncle Jan was lying out. Well of course we all screamed our heads off. No one wanted to go in the parlour to see what made that noise."

"I don't blame them," Dale said.

"But, somehow, I just plucked up all the courage I could and walked straight into that parlour. And what did I see?" she paused.

"What? What did you see?" Dale asked.

"Nothing! Uncle Jan looked exactly as he did when we had left him. To this day I have no idea what that loud noise was. But here's the interesting part of the story—"

"That loud noise coming from a corpse was pretty interesting," Ted said.

"—this was the very first time in my life that I was able to connect with the dead. While I was there in the parlour alone with Uncle Jan… he spoke to me. Just as clear as I'm talking to you now, but he was speaking directly into my mind. He said to me, 'Anna, tell everyone that old Uncle Jan says goodbye'. That was all he said. So, I told *everyone* exactly what he said to me, and do you know what people thought about me talking to the dead? Again, nothing! No one thought I was crazy or made it up or said it came from the devil or anything like that. Everyone in our family just took it in stride."

"Why do you think that was, Ma?" Dale asked.

"Because they saw I was telling the truth. Maybe because we were Lutheran and weren't so quick to judge as *some* people."

"That's some story," Ted said.

"Just don't tell Wilma that story when she comes. She hates it whenever I bring up any of my spirits. She says they're Satanic. I don't see why. Why can't you believe in God and Jesus and still believe that you can speak to the dead. Catholics pray to the dead all the time, you know. If you can pray to the dead, what's so crazy about hearing them answer back or getting a glimpse of them? Nothing."

"Well, Wilma's a Baptist and that's a long way from the Catholics."

"Wilma doesn't like Catholics," she said. "Or Lutherans or Anglicans for that matter, even though she was raised Anglican. But since she's way down in Georgia most of the time… what Wilma doesn't know won't hurt her. The last time she was here, last summer, she found a bottle of wine in my fridge and had the nerve to dump it down the drain like this was *The Lost Weekend* or something. She told me I couldn't have wine with dinner because it was a sin. So even now, an old lady like me, I have to hide wine under the damned sink behind a can of bacon grease in case Sue comes by. Sue has a direct line to Wilma and anything that happens here in Hamilton goes on the hotline straight to Atlanta, in case you didn't know. It's getting so I can't speak to anyone in this family without getting my head bit off for it."

Ted smiled at her. "You can speak to me."

"I know that. But you think my spirits and tea leaves are silly too. I know you do. And Dale here thinks it's all nonsense too… but at least he'll play along. And speaking of tea…"

She rose and began making a pot of tea using the loose-leaf tea dispenser mounted to her wall. All these years and his mother still refused to use tea bags, saying it ruined the taste of the tea. *When I leave, she'll read my tea leaves on the sly if she can*, Ted thought.

When the tea was made, his mother placed the teapot and three floral cups and saucers from her wedding china on the table.

"This was mine and Walter's wedding china. The pattern is called *Maytime*, a gift from my father and my stepmother, Sarah. They don't make china with that many different colours anymore. The big pink flower in the middle is a peony and the rest, are buttercups, violets, black-eyed susans and these ones are morning glories. Sarah said the peony was a symbol of a happy marriage, good health, and prosperity. Ha! What did she know? And have you ever noticed the small hummingbirds flying below the flowers here?"

"I wonder what the hummingbird was a symbol of," Ted said.

"I did love Walter Moore you know," she went on, pouring the tea into the teacups.

"We know, Ma," Dale said.

"I didn't love him at first, but I did, for a time. I went through a lot with Walter even before Ruth and…"

Ted lifted the teacup, leaving the saucer on the table where it was, and sipped. He never thought loose-leaf was any better than tea in bags.

"I should have used this china more when you all were young, but I was so afraid it would get broken. We only pulled it out at Christmas and Easter and the rest of the time it just sat in the china cabinet. Imagine that. I only used it twice a year for forty years. What a waste."

"It was the Old Man who bought Gloria and me our china when we got married."

"Did he?" his mother asked. "Do you know the name of the pattern?"

"No, but it has little blue flowers all around it."

"Memory Lane," Dale said, sipping his tea with one hand and holding the saucer with the other like he was drinking tea with the Queen of England (but with bare feet and track marks).

"How the hell do you know that, Dale?" Ted asked.

"I was staying with the Old Man and Helen when you and Gloria got married. I went with him when he bought it. He liked the little blue forget-me-nots. Delicate like Gloria, he said."

"Do you use your china often, Ted?" His mother poured more tea into his cup and then Dale's.

"No, probably just Thanksgiving and Christmas."

"Try and use your china more than I used mine, Ted. Did I ever tell you two that it was my stepmother, Sarah, who really liked Walter Moore? I'm sure if she could have, she would have married him herself."

"I really hated your stepmother, Ma," Dale said.

"I was fond of Walter Moore, and, at the time, that seemed like more than enough to marry him and, to be honest, there weren't that many men beating down my door. And Sarah had said to me, 'Anna with those big Norwegian hands, feet, and ass of yours, you're going to be an old maid if you let Walter Moore slip through your fingers.' So, we got married. Of course, I never thought in a million years that I'd be pregnant every minute of my life from then on. A body just can't take being constantly pregnant like I seemed to be. That's why I miscarried so much. I had a miscarriage for practically every baby I had. You thought it was only Gabriel, didn't you? But if I had known that Walter Moore drank so much, I never would have married him."

"We all inherited that Moore addictive personality," said Dale. "Even the ones who don't drink a drop. The addiction just comes out in different ways, like with the religion obsession. Jesus might as well be Canadian Club to Wilma and Sue."

"The Old Man stopped drinking years ago," Ted said, suddenly wishing he had had that last drink with him.

"Well, that's all fine and dandy, boys," their mother said. "But even so, there are mistakes that can't be easily wiped up like you would with spilled milk and a paper towel. Look at Ruth. How can you fix that mistake? You can't, can you?"

"One thing I've learned since I got clean is that if we all demanded our pound of flesh from everyone who hurt us… we'd all be ripped to shreds," Dale said.

"I know there'd be nothing left of me," Ted said.

Anna looked toward the window. "The day we buried my father it was raining," she said. "I was in a car with Abe and my stepmother following the hearse. At that point Walter Moore had been out of my life for, my God, at least fifteen years and, of course, he didn't come to my father's funeral… but as we were driving away from the funeral home, I saw Walter there. He was standing alone on the sidewalk in the rain, in a suit and overcoat, wearing a poppy, and saluting my father's hearse as it drove by. A soldier from World War Two, soaked to the bone, showing his respects to a fellow soldier from World War One who had once been his father-in-law. That was, strangely enough, the only time I cried during my father's funeral. I don't think anybody else noticed Walter being there but me. It had been such a long time but, right then, I remembered why I once loved Walter."

If Ted had been alone, he probably would have started crying again right then. That was, perhaps, the kindest story he had ever heard about his father. When I go, Ted thought, I hope someone could remember a story as kind as that to tell about me.

"You know, I really wish I could have come up to see you at the hospital, Ted," his mother said. "I tried once. I made it to Kresge's downtown but couldn't go any farther. I just could not go back there. You have no idea what it was like to be put in there back then."

"It's okay, Ma."

"But I was happy you were getting help, all the same. Maybe, just maybe, if I had gotten Tessa some help after… after we found out… things might have been different, but she just plain refused."

"Ma…" Dale said.

"You don't know this, but I was hurt that way too... for years by Sarah's brother when I was a girl and... and eventually I was able to move on. I honestly thought that Tessa could do the same thing but... she didn't."

"She couldn't," Dale said.

No one could have imagined that it would end on a sidewalk outside the Colonial Hotel on Catherine Street.

"I just hope Walter died in peace. That's probably the best thing any of us can hope for." She looked down sadly at her empty teacup sitting on the saucer in front of her on the table, gently touching the big pink peony with her finger.

"Ma," Ted said. "If you want to read my tea leaves... go ahead."

His mother smiled, gently touched Ted's arm again, and reached for her reading glasses.

That night when Ted went to bed, he and Gloria didn't make love. Instead, he let her sleep and later, after 2am, he crawled into bed beside her. She had taken an extra Valium that Dr. Heller had prescribed for her while Ted was in the hospital. The Old Man's death had hit her hard. They briefly discussed picking up Josh from camp but ultimately decided against it; they would tell him about his grandfather when they picked him up in a week. By then the funeral will be over, Wilma would have returned to Atlanta, and life should be back to normal. Why drag him away from camp, where he seemed to be enjoying himself, into a house of mourning.

The next morning when Ted woke up, he found Gloria carefully dusting each piece of their Memory Lane china and then putting it back, lovingly, into their china cabinet. Still tired, he made himself some instant coffee and went down to the basement with the newspaper, he had grown tired of the endless summer sun and wanted to sit in the cool darkness for a time. He turned on the television, lit a cigarette, and was thinking about how nice it was going to be not having to step foot inside another fucking hospital for a long time when the phone rang.

"Is this Mr. Moore?"

"Yes?"

"Mr. Moore, this is Adam Heichman. I'm the head counsellor at Camp Ronkewe... I'm calling to let you know we had to take your son to Joseph Brant Hospital in Burlington early this morning... The doctors want you to come right away... They may have to perform emergency surgery..."

Eleven

Christmas 1964 was the first time Gloria met them. She and Ted had only been together a few months at that point, but Ted had asked her, quite earnestly and sweetly, to meet his family on Christmas Day, and Gloria agreed. She would have to meet them all eventually, after all.

"They're a little high-strung," he had said with a chuckle. "I've taken exactly two girls home to meet my family since I came back from the Congo and both of them dropped me like a hot potato right after meeting them."

Ted was rebelling against the army brush cut he had worn for two years, and his hair was longer than most of the men at Munro Steel. Everyone in the plant called it *beatnik hair*. Gloria had known Ted was attracted to her, sneaking looks at her behind the Buddy Holly glasses he wore in those days, whenever he passed her machine on the shop floor, sporting a shy boyish grin. Even in Gloria's silly kerchief and work clothes, Ted still liked what he saw, and Gloria felt flattered by the attention. They flirted for months. It was all in good fun to start. She was in her early twenties with two kids, was newly divorced and, until Ted, she had never dated any of the men at Munro. Gloria never wanted stories told about her in the men's locker room or out on the loading dock like those stories she knew were told about some of the girls. As it turned out, Ted never really asked her out on a date at all.

The first time Gloria and Ted went out together they were part of a group of ten or twelve who, after marching in the Labour Day parade, headed to the Golden Rail for a few drinks. Gloria wasn't even going to go but Miriam had talked her into it. All Gloria could remember about that evening at the Golden Rail now was laughing. Ted had been so funny and charming but also damned sexy in a tan jacket, white shirt, tight black slacks, and leather ankle boots that zipped up on the side. You'd think he was dressed for a night on the town instead of a Labour Day parade. And those green eyes of his! They never seemed to leave her except when he would suddenly look away whenever Gloria returned his gaze. It made Gloria tremble. After they had all left the bar, Ted drove Gloria home to her apartment on Barton Street where she stretched three pork chops between the four of them and, once Kevin and Troy had gone to bed, she took Ted into her bedroom.

By Christmas 1964 they were a new family. She, Ted, and her boys had hung up four stockings, watched *Mr. Magoo's Christmas Carol* on television, and before the boys went to bed, Ted had played *Silent Night* on his guitar. Watching her boys at Ted's feet, looking up at him like he was their favourite person in the world while he played guitar that Christmas Eve, may have been the moment she fell completely in love with him. In the morning, Kevin and Troy had more toys under the tree than they ever had before. With Gloria and Ted both working at Munro Steel, it had been her first really flush Christmas in years. Ted had moved in by then, though not officially, as his mail was still being delivered to Abe and Anna's house on Waterloo Street. No one at Munro Steel knew they were living together then either, not even Miriam (or if Miriam ever suspected, she stayed silent). After that first Christmas dinner, Gloria, who wasn't much of a drinker, let Ted make her a rum and ginger ale to steel herself against what lay ahead. Then she and Ted dropped Kevin and Troy off at Doris and Ken's house and headed to Waterloo Street to meet Ted's family.

"What are they going to think of a divorced woman with two kids living with their son?" she asked him, only half-jokingly.

"They know you were married before… and that you have a couple of kids. I told them weeks ago," he said, turning onto Waterloo Street.

"What did they say about that?"

"Nothing."

"They're going to size me up to see if I'm good enough for you."

"Gloria, my family is hardly the measuring rod for the better families in Hamilton. I'll let you in on a few of *their* secrets sometime."

Ted smiled, glanced over at her with those green eyes, and touched her cheek with the back of his hand. That calmed her stomach and comforted her. From the get-go his touch always made her feel better.

"So, Abe is your stepfather?" She wanted to make sure she had the name correct.

"Pretty much."

Gloria knew what that meant. Her own mother had never married the man she had lived with after Gloria's father ran off either. There were a lot of women in Hamilton who had resorted to simply taking a man's name without ever being married. It just wasn't easy to get a divorce back in the forties as it was when Gloria divorced. And in those days, women often never knew where their husbands went when they walked out the door for good. They just disappeared. Her own father had vanished when Gloria was four years old, never to be seen again.

Ted pulled his powder blue Chevy Biscayne up to a small two-story house covered with grey vinyl siding. On the iron railing leading up the stairs, large Christmas lights flashed cheerfully, if somewhat too incessantly, as if needing neighbours to know it was the most jovial house on the street. The white glow of the picture window framed a tableau reminiscent of most East End Hamilton houses: an artificial Christmas tree, this one with fake white globs of Styrofoam snow on the branches, covered with mismatched ornaments, and a few strings of lights blinking more slowly than the lights on the outside railing. Behind the tree, a few shadows moved back and forth across the room. Ted hopped out of the car as Gloria pulled up the collar of her brown fox coat and waited for him to open her door (he still did that in those days). He took her arm, helped her out of the car, and they walked arm-in-arm up the pathway to the house as Gloria looked up at the two windows on the second story and wondered if one of those rooms had been Ted's.

"When will I get to meet your real father?"

"Let's save the Old Man for some other time. Maybe Easter." He swung open the door almost hitting a little girl about five years old, dressed in a Christmassy red velvet dress and white leotards with no shoes.

"It's Uncle Teddy," the little girl yelled, before doing a pirouette and running out of the living room into the hall.

A combination of nutmeg, cigarette smoke, mingling perfumes, beer—and the heat!—struck Gloria as if she had been smacked in the face with a warm, damp, holiday tea towel that had been used to clean up spills all Christmas Day. Suddenly, kids appeared from everywhere running toward Ted. He must be the favourite uncle, she had thought. And that was a very good sign. She began trying to count the children scattered about when a short stocky woman emerged from the hallway wearing a matronly, but pretty, black dress and a red waist apron with green lace tied around her hips. She had salt and pepper hair, leaning more toward salt, with a fair complexion and deep lines carved into her face. The woman came toward them smiling, and Gloria assumed the woman was about to hug her, but she abruptly stopped and folded her arms over her chest.

"Hello! Hello!" she said, in a faint Scandinavian accent.

"Merry Christmas, Ma." Ted leaned over and kissed his mother on the cheek below a spot of rouge that Gloria thought was quite nice and cheerful and complemented the woman's light complexion.

"Merry Christmas! And this must be the famous Gloria."

"Yeah, this is Gloria," Ted said. He handed over a gift-wrapped box of Pot of Gold chocolates to his mother that Gloria had bought and wrapped earlier that week.

"Hello, Mrs.... um..." Ted's mother's name vanished from Gloria's brain. "It's so nice to meet you."

"Oh, call me Anna."

"Nice to meet you, Anna."

"Oh, what a pretty fur coat you have there. You can leave your shoes here by the door then I'll introduce you to everyone."

Gloria saw the pile of shoes by the door and begrudgingly took off her new black pumps. Gloria never made women take off their shoes at her house. After all, shoes were a part of a woman's outfit.

Anna turned to one of the children standing by the door and handed him the gift-wrapped chocolates.

"Christopher, go put this under the tree for Nana."

The boy took the chocolates, shook them too hard, and then tossed them under the tree with several other similar-looking packages. Across the room, a phonograph was playing a scratchy Perry Como Christmas record.

"You want something to drink, Glo?" Ted asked.

"Not right now, thank you."

"Well, I'm getting a beer," he said, and disappeared down the hallway.

The living room was inviting, with wallpaper sporting large white magnolia blossoms on a red background and a carpet of rose-pink and well-kept furniture. A few slapdash paintings of hunting dogs hung on the walls around the room.

"We've all been waiting to meet you," Anna said, guiding Gloria through the small living room to a brown chesterfield directly across from the Christmas tree. On one end of the chesterfield a thin teenage girl with her sandy blonde hair in a flip at the shoulders and wearing a crushed blue velvet dress and black nylons was sitting with her legs and arms crossed, looking as if she wanted to take up as little space as possible. On the other side, two little boys, around six or seven, dressed alike in red shirts and clip-on black bow ties were sitting looking bored.

"This is Tessa, Ted's younger sister," Anna said, nodding toward the girl. "Tessa is short for Esther. Esther was my mother's name. Tessa just turned… what is it, Tessa?"

"Sixteen," Tessa said.

"She just turned sweet sixteen. You'd think I'd remember that," Anna said. "Tessa comes after Ted and Dale and before Andy and

Bonnie. My God, sometimes I can't even believe I had that many babies. This is Ted's girlfriend, Gloria."

"Hello, Tessa," Gloria said.

"Hello. I love your fur coat, Gloria," Tessa said.

"Move it, you two," Anna said to the two little boys. "Let your Uncle Teddy and Gloria sit down."

The boys begrudgingly gave up their seats and joined three more children sitting on the floor eating potato chips out of a large green Tupperware bowl on the coffee table. Beside it, a candy dish of green and white hard ribbon candy was left untouched.

"Thank you," Gloria said to the boys.

Gloria sat down, unbuttoned her fur coat, and pulled her arms out, leaving it behind her on the couch. She could feel beads of perspiration on her forehead as, one by one, Anna pointed across the room at various men and women, all with the same green eyes and fine sandy-brown hair as Ted and rhymed off names. All the women seemed to have the same matching beehive hairdos. They must go to the same hairdresser, she thought.

"And let's see… Ted's brothers Jack and Noah are in the basement playing air hockey with the boys and Ted's baby sister, Bonnie. You'll meet them later," Anna said.

Ted returned to the living room with a bottle of IPA beer in his hand and a mouthful of something he must have grabbed off the kitchen table. He smiled and sat down on the chesterfield with a thump of hominess between Gloria and Tessa. He had dumped his coat somewhere along the way.

"Meet everyone?" he asked.

"Well…"

"I'm in the middle of introducing her to everyone, Mr. Bossy. Drink your beer and hush up," Anna said.

"You should put that on a pillow: *Drink your beer and hush up*. It's the Moore family motto," a short portly man with an Irish accent said, walking proudly into the living room. He had an upturned nose, flaming red hair with a receding hairline, and wore a red plaid shirt, grey pants, and brown leather opera slippers.

"That's Abe," said Anna with a smile. "Abe's my husband."

"Hello," Gloria said. She waved at Abe from across the room.

"Abe, this is Ted's Gloria," Anna said.

"Ted's Gloria! I like that!" Ted said, putting his arm around her.

"Well, hello there, Ted's Gloria!" Abe said, picking up the little girl in red velvet. He sat down in an armchair and put the little girl on his lap. "You didn't bring your sons along, eh, Gloria?"

"No, Kevin and Troy are at my sisters showing their cousins their new toys."

"Ah, that's too bad, too bad," Abe said. The little girl in red velvet squirmed until he put her back down on the floor.

"Maybe next time I can bring them along," Gloria said.

"And see what you can do about getting Ted to the barber before New Year. He's looking more and more like a goddamn girl," Abe said.

"I like Ted's hair," Gloria said.

"So do I," Tessa agreed.

"Abe is Andy and Bonnie's father. I'll get you a scorecard later," Ted whispered in Gloria's ear.

"I think I've got it figured out."

"And Tessa here is my favourite sister," Ted said, putting his other arm around Tessa's shoulder.

"And you're my favourite brother, Teddy."

"She's only saying that because Dale isn't here right now," said Ted with a grin.

"No, you've always been my favourite brother and you know it."

"Yeah, you're right, I am pretty great."

"Just promise me you won't ever leave and go to Africa or anywhere else too far away again."

"I promise I will *never* leave you again, Tessa," Ted said. He reached for a piece of hard ribbon candy on the coffee table. "Where is Dale, anyway?"

"Out."

"I'll have to introduce you to my younger brother, Dale, some other time. He and I shared a bedroom until I joined the army. Dale is… the nice sensitive one."

Most of that Christmas night in 1964 with Ted's family was a blur to Gloria now except for what happened at the end of the night. Gloria had already managed to get Ted to find his coat and was about to say her goodbyes when Anna, who had spent most of the evening in the kitchen, entered the living room and asked Gloria to join her and Ted's sisters in the kitchen for a cup of tea.

"Maybe we should wait and do that some other time. Gloria and I have to pick up Kevin and Troy at her sister's place," Ted said.

"So soon? A cup of tea won't take any more than ten or fifteen minutes, for heaven's sake!" Anna said.

"You don't really have a choice," Ted's chubby thirteen-year-old half-sister, Bonnie Murphy, said.

"That might be a bit much for her first time here," Ted said.

"What's this all about?" Gloria asked, turning to Ted.

"I do tea readings," Anna said. "It's a tradition in our family for all the ladies to have their tea leaves read by me on holidays. I've been doing it since I was a little girl. My mother taught me before she died. And if I do say so myself, I'm pretty good at it. I am rarely wrong when it comes to tea."

"Oh, I don't know…" Gloria shook her head. "I don't like that sort of thing."

"It's a family tradition," Bonnie said. She grabbed a handful of potato chips from the Tupperware bowl on the coffee table and jammed them into her mouth, leaving salt and chip crumbs on the front of her red pinafore dress and around the corners of her mouth, where her once-pink-frosted lipstick was now smeared with grease and holiday chocolate into a dusty rose. Gloria could see that Bonnie was Abe's daughter. Both Bonnie and fourteen-year-old Andy had the same upturned Irish nose, square chin, and wild red hair like Abe. Hair colour was a clear demarcation between Murphy and Moore.

"Oh, please come, Gloria. It's something just for the girls and you're one of us girls now," Ted's older sister Peggy said with genuine enthusiasm.

"At least for tonight," Sue, yet another Moore sister said, standing near the hallway. Sue wore a matching brown skirt and pleated maternity top and held a cigarette in one hand and a whiskey and water in one other. Probably due in a couple of months, Gloria thought.

"Please, come, Gloria," Tessa said.

"Oh… why not?" Gloria said, standing up from the chesterfield.

She left her coat on the couch and walked, along with the other women, Sue, Peggy, Bonnie, Jack's first wife, Abbey, and Tessa following, down the hallway to a small square kitchen with baby blue walls and black and white checkerboard vinyl flooring. On the black laminate countertop, what was left of a Christmas turkey laid on a platter waiting to be chopped up for leftovers or Boxing Day turkey sandwiches. Anna directed Gloria to one of the chairs around the kitchen table and Gloria took a seat between Tessa and Peggy as Anna placed a plate of sliced fruitcake with white almond icing in the middle of the table.

"Let's just get this over with. I told the Old Man we'd stop by before we went home," Sue said, swirling her whiskey and water in her hand.

"We visited the Old Man this afternoon," Peggy said. "Has Ted taken you to see our father, Walter, yet, Gloria?"

"No, not yet."

"My dad was more of a father to Ted than Walter Moore ever was," Bonnie offered with the smirk of someone who thought they were on the winning team.

"Bonnie Murphy, if you open your fat mouth about my father again," Sue pointed her cigarette at Bonnie from across the table, "I'll smack your face so goddamn hard that it will hit the kitchen wall and slide down to the floor."

"Mom!"

"That's enough from all of you! What will Gloria think of us?" Anna said with an embarrassed smile. "Let's just do this tea reading and have some fun."

"Wilma says tea reading is Satanic," Bonnie said. "The last time she was up here she said when you do tea readings, you're practically inviting the devil into your house every time. 'Why not just toss out the welcome mat for Satan,' she said."

"Then it's a good thing Wilma is not in my kitchen at the moment, isn't it?" Anna replied.

"Wilma is our oldest sister," Tessa said to Gloria. "She lives down in Georgia."

Of all Ted's siblings, Tessa looked the most like Ted, Gloria thought. She had been spared the large Moore nose, but Tessa had the same crooked smile and slightly sad green eyes as Ted. Already, that first Christmas, Gloria was putting two and two together.

"Wilma married an American and moved down to the States years ago," Sue said. "She has two little boys now and became a big-time Baptist, if you can believe it. A lot of those Americans in the south are Baptists. God knows why anyone would want to be a Baptist. They don't have any fun." Sue chuckled, sipped her drink, and lit another cigarette.

"The rest of us are Church of England," Peggy said. She reached over and took an unfiltered Cameo menthol cigarette out of Sue's cigarette pack.

"The Murphys are Church of Ireland," Bonnie said. "Peggy and Sue always like to forget that we're part of this family too."

"It's the same bloody thing, dumbbell. It's Anglicanism in Ireland," Sue retorted.

"Actually, I was raised Anglican too," Gloria said.

Though, Gloria thought, perhaps *raised* wasn't the right word. However, her father was indeed Anglican, he had married Gloria's mother at an Anglican church in Fort Francis and did send Gloria off to St. James the Apostle Anglican church in the east end for Sunday school when she was a child. She and her siblings had gone every Sunday until her father left. After that they never went to Sunday school again. Gloria decided against telling the gaggle of ladies at the table that she had also been married in an Anglican church the first time around.

"You're Anglican?" Ted's sister-in-law, Abbey, said with astonishment "But Ted said you were an Indian. I didn't know there were Indians in the Church of England."

"Well, they let us in," Gloria replied.

"You're Indian? How wonderful. That must be where you get your beautiful skin and hair," Tessa said.

"Are you a full-blooded Indian?" Sue asked. "You don't look quite like a full-blooded Indian. I mean, you're brown like an Indian, but you have more white man features, you know what I mean?" She flicked her menthol cigarette ash into the ashtray in the middle of the table near the sliced fruitcake.

"I'm half Indian… on my mother's side."

"Oh, you're *half* Indian," Abbey repeated, as if it all made sense to her now.

"When we drove down to Georgia to see Wilma last summer," Bonnie said, "we went to her giant church and when they asked for people to come down to the front and be saved, I stood right up, I felt I had a calling, but Daddy told me to sit down. I still might become a Baptist like Wilma someday. That religion is so… exciting and dramatic. Like me!"

Sue rolled her eyes and took a long drag on her cigarette.

"Gloria, you're first," Anna announced, putting the bone china teapot, decorated with big pink peonies and other colourful flowers, in the middle of the table.

Anna placed a matching teacup and saucer first in front of Gloria and then in front of each woman seated around the table. Gloria breathed in deeply, picked up the cup, and sipped the orange-brown bitter liquid.

"I'm sorry, Mrs… Anna, but I don't think I can drink anymore of that," Gloria said, after managing only about half the cup. She began picking a few stray tea leaves off her tongue as daintily as she possibly could.

"Not enough, drink more!" Bonnie said.

"Oh, that's more than enough," Anna said, picking up Gloria's cup and saucer. She turned the teacup upside down and dumped the contents onto the saucer with a clink. Some tea spilled onto the table, which Anna quickly sopped up with a yellow tea towel before turning back to the clump of tea leaves on the saucer.

"Now this is interesting," Anna said. "Do you see this, Gloria?" She pointed her thick index finger at the middle of the saucer. "Here's a heart! Plain as the nose on my face!"

Anna looked around the table as if to incite confirmation from the women. Tessa and Peggy nodded while Bonnie, already looking bored, shrugged her shoulders and picked some icing off a slice of Christmas cake.

"A heart is one of the best things you can find in the leaves," Anna said, scrutinizing the soggy leaves. "That means love is coming your way, Gloria."

"Well, that's exciting," Gloria said, somewhat embarrassed.

"Maybe a wedding, even," Anna said. She looked up from the tea leaves and smiled at Gloria. "Everyone wants to get a heart in their leaves. You know I don't think I've seen a heart show up in the leaves for years and years."

Gloria nodded. She hoped that was the end of it and Anna would turn her attention to one of the other women sitting around the table.

"I think the last time I saw a heart was with Sue's tea maybe five years ago. And I don't have to tell you how that turned out, do I?" Anna continued.

Gloria nodded her head in agreement even though Gloria had no idea how it turned out with Sue since Gloria didn't know Sue or her story at all. Except that, like Ted, Sue seemed to like her rye.

"I love getting hearts," Tessa said, looking over the leaves to see Gloria's heart. "I haven't got a heart in… well forever."

Bonnie licked icing off her fingers. "I got a heart the last time we did this at Thanksgiving."

"No, you did not," Sue said.

"And here's a mushroom," Anna said, turning back to Gloria's leaves. Her Norwegian accent seemed to get stronger as the tea reading went on. "Yes, that most definitely is a mushroom. Now that's something you don't see every day. A mushroom means… a baby is in your future."

Gloria looked down at the wet leaves in the saucer. It didn't look like a mushroom to Gloria as much as a partially erect penis. Which, Gloria supposed, could also mean a baby.

"Oh, wait!" Anna said. "One more thing! This triangle right here in the middle of the saucer means something unexpected is going to happen to you. Do you see that triangle there, Gloria?" Anna held the saucer right under Gloria's nose.

Gloria nodded.

It looks more like an iceberg to me.

*

Hell had frozen over, Gloria thought. She stood alone in her kitchen on Alkeld Street, fuming. She knew exactly how this was going to go. She had gone up to The Cordelia, sat in his living room, and invited him to her home. Now she would have to live through this production number every damned month.

From the kitchen window she watched Josh in the backyard tossing a rubber ball to Reefer. Josh had only been home from Cub Scout camp for a week, eight days early, saying he would throw himself down the mountain if he were ever sent back. She entrusted that damned camp with her son and how did it end up? With Josh in the hospital. And Gloria knew bloody well that there was more to the story than either Josh or Ted was telling her. However, the bottom line was this: no matter what, Gloria would never force Josh back to camp. If Ted thought Josh was too girly, like that sister of his kept saying, then that's just too bad! Maybe Josh would be gay like Lydia or Bill's brother in Toronto. So what! If Josh had been born here two hundred years ago, he would be a medicine man or a teller of stories or something like that. That's what Bill had said.

Ted shouted from the living room, "They're here!"

Gloria took the cheque that she had already written to Abe off the top of the refrigerator and wondered who 'they' were. Did he bring that wife of his down here, too?

"Did you hear me? They're here!"

"I heard you."

"Gloria," Ted said, walking into the kitchen, "I know this isn't the best solution but just remember that he did help us out of a pickle. And we did tell him that he could come down and visit us from time to time."

"I know what I told him. I was there."

Calling what they were in a *pickle* was too cutesy for Gloria. There was nothing cute about what had happened to them. They will be obligated to that man for years. She put the kettle on the stove, screwed a smile on her face again, and walked with resignation up the hallway as Abe Murphy came through her front door like he owned the place. He wore black pants, black leather shoes with white socks, and another short-sleeved white shirt with the top few buttons undone, showing the low neck of his undershirt. In his arms he carried a gift: a knitted orange and black afghan. No doubt knitted by Gert, Gloria thought.

"It's us!" Bonnie Murphy sang, entering the house behind him. She wore an old yellow T-shirt and a pair of tight faded denim jeans. Her face, glistening with sweat, was pink with blotches of crimson.

Damn it! No one had told Gloria that Bonnie was coming too. But why shouldn't she want to witness Gloria's humiliation too? Anything goes at their house now. We're selling indulgences for a few dollars on Alkeld Street.

Abe smiled. "Just us old-timers." He kicked off his shoes, handed the afghan to Gloria, shuffled to Ted's chair by the couch, and picked up the newspapers on the seat before sitting down. The afghan smelled of lavender.

"*The Daily Racing Form* and *Socialist Worker*, huh? Same old Ted." Abe sat down in Ted's chair, stretched out his short legs, and crossed his feet at the ankles. The smug look on his face reminded Gloria of Christmas 1964.

"Yeah, same old me," said Ted.

"Could I get anyone a cup of tea," Gloria asked.

"Tea?" Bonnie scowled. "It's too hot for tea! Do you have a Tab? I'm doing Atkins now. I don't want to be up on stage with this extra twenty pounds." With a grunt, Bonnie sat on the floor by Abe's feet.

"More like fifty," Abe said.

"Tab?" Gloria said. "No, we have Pepsi, cream soda, and red Kool-Aid."

"Nothing diet?"

"No, sorry."

"I'll have a cream soda then," Bonnie said. "I deserve a little cheat since I exercised along with Ed Allen's TV show today and I really haven't *officially* started Atkins yet. I still have to buy the book. I'm in jeans and baggy shirts this summer but next year I'll be in halter-tops and shorts. Is that air conditioner of yours even working? It's so hot in here."

Gloria went into the kitchen and, leaning up against the sink, stared out the kitchen window. If she could drive, she would get in the car and ride as far away as she could. She knew having Abe in her house would upset her but never thought it would be this difficult. Her heart pounded. I hate him, she thought. And here he is in my house!

Gloria served Ted and Abe their tea in the living room but didn't make any for herself. If nothing else, she refused to drink tea with him again. It may have been a small act of defiance, but it was all she could do right then and then. Gloria may have shared tea with people she wasn't fond of, but she wouldn't do it with someone she hated. She may have fallen far but she wasn't about to fall *that* far.

"I was having lunch at Dad's today, and I said, right out of the blue, 'Hey, why don't we go see Ted and Gloria. We haven't seen them in such a long time,'" Bonnie said.

"Uh huh," replied Gloria.

"That scar on your throat isn't as bad as I heard," said Abe.

"Nah, it's not so bad," Ted said, scratching his throat.

Abe chuckled. "I heard you fell throat first on a piece of glass."

"That's right, I fell throat first on a piece of glass."

The room got quiet. If I had a cup of tea in my hand I'd throw it in Abe's face, Gloria thought. She was sitting on the end of the couch, as far away as possible from Abe while still being in the same room.

"Well, I for one have some great news," Bonnie said. "You know how everyone always said that I should be a singer?"

No, Gloria thought. She had never heard anyone say Bonnie Murphy should sing. In fact, no one in Ted's family could really sing worth a damn, though they all desperately wanted to, for some reason.

"So, one day I was in church and… let me try to explain this right."

Jesus! I can tell this is going to be a long story, Gloria thought.

"It was like God started talking to me during the third hymn. There we were singing "When the Roll is called up Yonder", and you know how I can really sing that one." Bonnie lifted her head and began singing, "Oh when the roll is called up yon-der I'll be there!"

Ted said, "We got the idea!"

"I'll tell you what happened," Abe said. "This one comes to me last month and gives me this whole spiel about how God wanted her to sing. Like God doesn't have anything better to do than talk to her. I should know by now that every time someone comes to visit it's to get money out of me."

"That's a lie!" Bonnie said.

"All I know about this singing baloney of hers is that it's costing me almost two thousand dollars."

"It'll be worth it. Anyway, there I was singing "When the Roll is called up Yonder". She began singing the song again.

"Knock it off, will you!" Abe yelled. "It's enough I'm paying for that crap! That doesn't mean I have to listen to it too!"

"Anyway, as I was singing, I was hit by this feeling. And by now I know when the Lord is speaking to me. His word comes to me like a whisper."

"I guess that's better than a two-by-four," Ted said.

"And the Lord said to me, 'Go sing, Bonnie. Sing my song. Sing for me!'"

"That's louder than a whisper… but softer than a two-by-four," Ted said.

"And if Wilma can sing in the choir down in that gigantic church of hers in Georgia, I can certainly do the same thing at these tiny Baptist churches we have around here. We need more music in our churches, as far as I'm concerned, and I'm the gal who can really rattle those rafters—"

"Where's your boy, Gloria?" Abe asked.

"—I want to go to the Canadian Gospel Music Convention in Ottawa next spring—"

"You can pay for that yourself."

"By that time, I have *got* to have my own record. I've looked into it, and I think I can get all the equipment I need plus the record made for a song. Could you imagine how many records I could sell at a Gospel music convention? And I could travel to different churches with Ray, and I'd do a number or two for them. Can you see it? I'd have a tape of pre-recorded music and a speaker and microphone. That's all I'd need! Well, that and the voice God gave me. Then every Sunday I'll hit a different Baptist or Gospel church. I could go all around Hamilton and even to Toronto. I could sell records and tapes at each one and then... well... I'd be set for life. A big gospel star! Maybe even television. Who knows? Even Jim and Tammy Baker had to start somewhere."

The woman is delusional, Gloria thought. Ted's whole family is delusional, living in a fantasy world. If it wasn't Ted's socialist utopia or his sisters' eyes on heaven it was Anna's tea leaves. Not one of them was looking at the here and now except Gloria and maybe Abe. And being in some kind of coalition of realists with that bastard made her angrier still.

"This singing idea she's got in her head will just end up flushing more of my money down the toilet," Abe said. "And right after I gave her a thousand dollars for that goddamn wedding of hers. She's bleeding me dry! And remember what she served for dinner at that wedding of hers? The second wedding I paid for, mind you."

"We didn't make it to the wedding," Ted said.

"Well, I did, and I still don't know what she spent that thousand dollars on but it sure as hell wasn't on the food, that's for sure. Gerty said it was the cheapest wedding she had ever been to."

"I didn't send anyone home hungry, did I?" Bonnie said. "And who doesn't love Kentucky Fried Chicken? Besides I spent most of the money on flowers. Oh, the flowers were *gorgeous*. White and yellow, mostly, with some pink tossed in. Flowers aren't cheap. The sad thing was, you two missed Dad giving me away."

"I keep giving her away, but she keeps coming back," Abe said, laughing. "I told her this was the last time I'd do it. Two's the limit. Am I right Gloria?"

"Two is certainly my limit," Gloria said.

"I won't be getting married again," Bonnie said. "Hey, Gloria, I can feel my blood sugar getting a little low. I'm starting to get a little dizzy. The doctor said I'm hypoglycaemic, did I tell you that? I need to eat small meals throughout the day, or I can pass out. Could I have a peanut butter and jam sandwich or something before I keel over?"

Bonnie got up, not without some struggle, without waiting for an answer and, yanking up her jeans, walked down the hall to the kitchen.

"Help yourself," Gloria said.

"Where's your boy?" Abe repeated.

"Um… I think he's outside playing someplace," Gloria said.

"He was just in the backyard," Ted said.

"I think he might have left," Gloria answered. "With that Perry boy. Probably down to Red Hill Creek. Have you seen the creek lately? It's like a small trickle with this drought."

"I see Josh in the backyard!" Bonnie yelled through a mouthful of food from the kitchen. "Boy, he's getting fat! Looks like he could use Atkins too!"

Damn.

Bonnie came back into the living room with two peanut butter and jam sandwiches on a paper towel and fell back onto the floor with a thump. "I said Josh is in the backyard."

"I'll go see if he's still there," Gloria said.

She was determined to try to get Josh away from the house until Abe left. She had planned to tell him to run off and play somewhere, anywhere, but Abe had arrived too early. But Ted had followed her down the hallway.

"I don't like this any more than you do, Glo, but we promised him when we took his money that we'd make peace," Ted whispered as they stood in the kitchen. "It's time to make peace. It's time to heal… for everyone's sake."

"Sure, let's serve our son up on a silver platter to Abe."

"We aren't serving up our son to anyone. We're just letting Abe meet Josh… and showing that in this house, at least, we believe in forgiveness."

"You go right ahead and forgive all you want."

"I'd kill Abe before I'd let him ever hurt Josh. You know that. Please trust me and believe that I know what I'm doing. He's never going to be around him alone."

"Did you say that to Tessa too?"

"Jesus Christ, Gloria."

"I can't stand looking at him."

"Abe didn't push Tessa out that window."

"Yes, he did. Just as much as if he was in that hotel room with her. And for some reason, you can't see it."

Ted turned around and walked to the back screen door. "Josh! Come inside the house for a few minutes. I want you to meet someone."

"Right now?" Josh asked.

"Yes, just for a few minutes. Leave Reefer outside!"

"Alright," he said, tossing the ball to Reefer.

Gloria followed Ted back into the living room, and they took their seats on opposite ends of the couch.

"Where's Josh?" Abe asked again. He fidgeted in his seat and peered down the hall. "I hope he's here."

Gloria saw red.

"He's coming," Ted said.

"I already have a gig singing!" Bonnie said. "Did I tell you that? I called up my old music teacher, Mr. Hanley, who I know is now the principal at Laura Secord School, and I told him how great it would be for me to be the soloist for their Christmas pageant in December."

"How did you track down your old music teacher?" Ted asked.

"I used the phonebook! I just looked him up and there he was. It wasn't hard at all."

"You called a teacher you haven't seen in twenty years at home to ask if you could sing in a Christmas pageant four months from now?" Ted asked.

"Three times!" she said. "The first two times he said he'd have to think about it. The third time I called he wasn't home, so I tried to convince his wife what a great idea it would be. I forget her name."

"That's nervy," Gloria said.

"Hey, it's the squeaky wheel that gets the grease! So *finally*, he said I could do a couple of Christmas songs if it fits in with the pageant, but it will. But he doesn't know I'm planning on doing more than just a Christmas a song." She shoved the last of her second sandwich in her mouth.

"A Peggy Lee medley?" Ted asked.

"No!" she said through a mouthful of Skippy Peanut Butter. "I said to myself it would be wrong to leave Christ in that manger like a lot of Christians do at Christmas time. He needs to be put on that cross dying for our sins. That's where He belongs. So, I'm going to do one real hymn along with "The First Noel" or "O Holy Night". I'm not sure which one I'm going to do yet; I'm thinking either "It's Still the Blood" or "Saved by the Blood" or "Nothing but the Blood". You know, one of those hymns with blood in the title. I want everyone at Laura Secord to know about Christ's blood and our redemption from sin."

"That should go over well," Ted said. "Nothing says Christmas like 'Nothing but the Blood.'"

"Like I said, I'm not leaving Christ in the manger, but you'll find out for yourself since Josh goes to Laura Secord. You'll be there to hear me!"

Lucky us, Gloria thought. Parents heading to school to hear "Jingle Bells" will hear Bonnie Murphy screech out some godawful tune about a bloody cross. She rubbed her temples with her fingertips; her head was pounding, and the pain radiated down her neck.

The back screen door opened and shut with a slam and Josh came hesitantly into the living room. Gloria knew Josh wasn't that fond of his Aunt Bonnie much as it was.

"Hello, son!" said Abe.

"Josh, do you remember Abe? My stepfather?"

"Hi," Josh said.

"This is your grandfather," Bonnie said.

"Well..." Gloria replied.

"I hate when the Moores tell their kids to call Dad *Abe*. It's disrespectful," Bonnie said.

"Sure, I remember him," Josh said. "He was married to Grandma after Grandpa and Grandma got divorced. Now Grandma and him are divorced too. It's not so hard to understand."

"You mean after your dear sweet Grandpa, Walter Moore, left your grandma high and dry," Bonnie said.

"Bonnie," Gloria said. "I'll tell you this once. Don't you ever say one bad word about Walter Moore in this house, you understand? He hasn't even been gone two weeks yet. And I loved him like a real father... and so did Josh. It was his grandfather."

Why did that horrible man have to bring that girl with him, Gloria wondered. Though Bonnie wasn't a girl anymore. She was almost thirty, though she acted like a ten-year-old. Gloria might have to have this man in her house for the time being, but she didn't have to hear this crap about Walter when he was still warm in his grave.

"You're getting chubby, Josh! Looks like you could use the Atkins Diet too," Bonnie said, picking some white bread out of her front teeth with her fingernail.

"That's what Doctor Heller said at my physical," Josh said.

"Josh is just fine the way he is, Bonnie," Gloria said.

"Come here, Josh," Abe said, sitting forward. "Let me get a good look at you and see how much you've grown. You know I wasn't able to see you for a long time."

Josh walked slowly over to the old man and stopped a few feet away. Gloria smiled. Her boy had good instincts.

Abe put out his hand, grabbed Josh's arm, and pulled him close. Gloria moved to the edge of her seat. She wanted to vomit.

"How old are you now?" Abe ran his hand with the long yellow nails through Josh's blond hair.

"Ten," Josh said, taking a step back. "Almost eleven."

"Ten!" Abe shook his head. "You know, when I was eight years old, I had to leave my home in Belfast and was shipped to Canada where they put me to work on a tobacco farm. That's what they did to orphans like me in Ireland, they packed them up and sent them here to Canada to work on family farms. Oh, they promised us that good families would adopt us, and they said we'd all go to school here and have real loving parents. Ha! You know how I was treated? Like a slave. You should have seen my fingers when I was your age, black from the tobacco I had to pick. At sixteen I took off and never looked back."

"That must have been crummy for you," Josh said, backing farther away from the old man.

Abe grinned. "You can call me *Papa* if you want, son."

"No, thanks." Josh turned toward Gloria. "Can I go back outside now? I don't like leaving Reefer out there alone since my bike was stolen."

"Yes, you can."

When her unwanted guests had finally left, Ted went down to the basement to watch television while Gloria stood again in her kitchen window watching Josh in the backyard. Her stomach hurt again. Someday she will search for goldthread along the foot of the mountain and make goldthread tea just as her mother did. As Josh laid on the grass and let the puppy jump on his belly, Gloria tried to imagine him playing with Alice and Corey up on the Six Nations Reserve. Maybe her ancestors were calling to her. But what are they saying?

"I just don't see why you have to be the one to do it?" Ted said. He sat in his armchair in the living room, reading the Saturday newspaper while Josh laid on his stomach watching cartoons.

"I told you months ago that I'm helping with the Munro float for the Labour Day parade," Gloria said. "I told you when you were in the hospital, and I told you again last week before Abe came for his cheque."

"Christ, a Labour Day float takes five goddamn minutes to do. You put up a sign on the fucking truck and a few streamers, and you're done."

"They're expecting me and I'm going." She had spent the entire morning arguing with Ted and now she was finished. She didn't like all this bickering in front of Josh, who was, undoubtably, soaking up everything they were saying.

"They can't put streamers on a truck without you?"

"Over the years, you've worked on a dozen Wentworth Steel floats for Labour Day parades, Ted. You know it doesn't take five minutes. You have spent days and days decorating them."

Since Ted came home from the hospital, he seemed jealous of the time she spent at work— or anyplace that she wasn't with him. Last year he didn't mind one bit when she worked on the Munro float. However, a year ago he was up to his neck in his own problems. And, as much as Gloria hated to admit it, Ted was beginning to act peculiar again. He wasn't sleeping well and was spending most days in the basement watching television alone. At least he wasn't seeing bugs again.

At least he's hasn't mentioned bugs to me.

"And if we do go on strike this week, we'll lead the parade," Gloria said.

"Why?" Josh asked, without looking away from the television.

"Because the union that's on strike in Hamilton always leads the Labour Day parade. I told you that last year," Ted said.

"Geeze, I forgot. Take it easy," Josh snapped. "Are you going on strike, Mom?"

"I hope not."

"You'll go on strike," Ted said. "You've got a pigheaded bunch there. But after a couple of months on strike, you watch, the whole lot of you will end up taking the dime they're offering you now plus a couple of pennies more. This isn't a year for big contracts. Maybe in three years you can grab them by the nuts."

"Yeah, grab them by the nuts in 1980," Josh said.

A strike would be the worst possible thing that could happen to them right now, Gloria thought. The employees at the plant had already voted down the company's first offer and the vote on Monday was to vote on their 'final' offer. If they turned that down, they were on strike. Word on the shop floor was that everyone was going to turn down the extra dime Munro was tossing at them like scraps in front of dogs. But Gloria had learned, after almost fifteen years at Munro, that you can never believe what people say on the shop floor. The vote was secret, and these people had mortgages and rent to pay.

"Go make your float." Ted tossed the sports section of *The Hamilton Spectator* aside and went down the stairs to the basement followed by Reefer.

"I'm going to hang around outside," Josh said. He slipped on his sneakers, walked out the back door, and, grabbing his new bicycle from the garage, drove off toward the end of Alkeld Street.

Gloria didn't even bother telling him not to hang around Shannon Perry or go down to Red Hill Creek. Since Josh had been home from camp, he seemed... meaner and angrier. If Ted wasn't acting so angry himself, she would demand to know what exactly happened at that Cub Scout camp. Maybe it was better not to know.

She had hoped that getting Josh a new bicycle would make him a bit more cheerful. Luckily Doris had given Gloria a hundred dollars and driven her to Sears to pick up the yellow bike that Josh had chosen from the catalogue. Doris had secretly taken it from her monthly house budget. "Ken can eat hamburger instead of steak for a few weeks," Doris had said. For that, Gloria was grateful. She certainly couldn't afford the extravagance of a new bike right now, not with a strike looming and Ted still on sick leave.

Since it didn't look like Ted was going to drive her to Munro to work on the Labour Day float, Gloria put on her work shoes and walked down Alkeld Street toward Woodward Avenue. It was humid. In her purse she carried a compact umbrella and a rain bonnet, ready for the really good rain that had threatened all summer but never happened. However, she had heard on the radio that morning that this could be the day for that big thunderstorm to finally hit.

She looked behind her a few times as she walked down Alkeld thinking that perhaps Ted would drive up from behind her in his blue Impala and offer to take her the rest of the way down Woodward to Munro. No luck there, it seemed. As she passed the Perry house, she saw Shannon sitting on the porch smoking a cigarette with his dirty bare feet up on the railing. She pretended she didn't notice him.

Since it was Saturday, there wasn't much traffic on Woodward Avenue and as she approached Munro, Gloria could smell Lake Ontario: the malodorous mix of late summer algae and dead fish coupled with the funk of the sewage plant beside the lake. It was the unmistakable aroma of August in East End Hamilton. *And I humiliated myself to Abe Murphy so we could stay here.*

A cool breeze cut through the humidity in the air, the kind Gloria had not felt since April, and gave her the slightest of goosebumps down her brown arms. The heat wave was finally ending.

She did not tell Ted that Bill would be working on the float with her today. Gloria had not been alone with Bill since the night Shannon had spied on them through Josh's bedroom window. During her shifts, Bill would smile as he walked past her machine, or come by when the girls were eating their lunch outside, but the two of them were never alone. Gloria wasn't even sure how it ever got so far that night. The simple explanation was that she was lonely and sad. And Bill Hunter was there. The truth was that she was infatuated with Bill. She was intrigued with his strong body, long black hair, and handsome smile. Most of all, she was captivated by his beautiful brown Native skin that looked and felt so much like her own. Bill had removed some of the confusion about her identity that she had carried throughout her life. Gloria came closest to understanding exactly who and what she was when she was with Bill. And to be honest, the day that Abe came to her home, sat on her furniture, and touched Josh's hair, Gloria had hated Ted so much that she would have packed up herself and Josh and gone to Bill's on the Six Nations if Bill had asked her that day. And what if Bill asked her now?

Gloria walked up the Munro parking lot, empty except for Bill's truck and a few other cars, to the warehouse at the back of the plant. Even though there was a strike vote looming (or maybe because of it), the company had let the union use the warehouse this weekend to make up the float, which was just one of their old flatbed trucks decorated with hundreds of orange and yellow streamers hanging off the truck bed to the road, some paper flowers, and a big white sign tied to the front.

The bay doors were open, but Gloria didn't see anybody around, though someone had started taping streamers around the truck. Gloria went to the ladies' room, rolled up toilet paper around her hand, and soaked up the perspiration that had gathered in her armpits and down the small of her back. Then, tossing the damp paper in the garbage bin, she rolled up some more to wipe the sweat between her breasts.

She came out of the ladies' room and saw the shop steward, Sylvia Reid, a small red-haired woman in her fifties, standing by the truck. Sylvia had worked at Munro Steel since she had come from Scotland twenty years earlier. She was loud and liked to think she was the one who really ran things at the factory. For the last ten years, she had run unopposed in her union position. Even the men at Munro chose not to go up against Sylvia. Still, Sylvia's position and her ability to wrangle for votes did not translate into affection. Most people grumbled about her laziness, how little she actually did at Munro, and what a filthy mouth she had (for a woman). Gloria thought that no one would say a word about any of that if Sylvia were a man. Gloria had not seen Sylvia in a few weeks since Sylvia was only around during the day shift— if you could find her.

"Glad you made it, Gloria!" Sylvia said with a deep voice only decades of smoking could create. "So, fucking typical that half a dozen people said that they'd help decorate this goddamn float, and only three people show up! Ah, well, fuck it! What do you think of the float so far?"

"It looks fine," Gloria said.

"How's Ted?"

"Oh, you know, he's fine. Itching to get back to work at Wentworth."

"Good to hear it! I knew he'd bounce back. Even when he worked here, I knew he was a strange one with that Beatles' haircut and all, but he's a good egg."

"Do you think Munro will still let us use the truck if we go on strike? Can Bill just cross the picket line and just drive it away to the parade?" Gloria asked.

"No, they won't! So, *if* we do go on strike Monday, we'll march without the fucking truck. Right in front of the parade, of course."

Gloria wondered why Sylvia's accent had not lessoned after twenty years in Canada.

"And all this work on the float will be for nothing?" Gloria asked.

"Yep," Sylvia said. "But that's life in the big city."

"Hamilton Glass is on strike too. Who decides which of us will lead the parade?" Bill asked, walking in from the storeroom at the back of the warehouse with a banner rolled up under his arm. He wore the cut-off shorts he had gone swimming in the day Gloria went up to the reserve and the same short-sleeved blue velour shirt.

"I think a steel mill takes precedence over a stupid bottle factory!" Sylvia said. "And the Aluminum Brick and Glassworkers are *nothing* compared to Steelworkers!"

"There's a lot more Hamilton Glass workers than there are of us. This isn't a very big mill compared to Stelco, Dofasco, or Wentworth," Bill said.

"I *said* that we'll be marching first if we're on strike! And you can take that to the fucking bank, Bill Hunter!"

"Whatever you say, boss," Bill said, chuckling.

Bill unrolled the banner, SOLIDARITY FOREVER—UNITED STEEL WORKERS LOCAL 1551, and gave it a shake. A family of earwigs scurried out of the unfurled banner in ten different directions over the warehouse floor.

"AAAAH!" Sylvia screamed, running away from the insects.

Gloria tried not to laugh as Sylvia tried to regain her composure and her air of superiority while holding her chest and searching the floor for earwigs.

"How long has Munro had this old banner?" Bill asked.

"Since the fifties, at least," Sylvia said.

"Looks pretty lousy. Did someone run over it with the truck last year?" Bill said.

Sylvia apprehensively picked up the end of the banner, looking worried that more bugs might rush out at her.

"Yeah, this does look like shit," Sylvia said. "We should have a new one made next year. Someone remind me next spring about it, and I'll allocate some money for it. I can't be expected to remember bullshit fucking nonsense stuff like banners and streamers when I have important things on my mind. For Christ's sake! We might be on fucking strike next week."

"I think the banner will do for one more year," Gloria said. "No one gets too close to it anyway."

Sylvia turned and walked to the ladies' room.

"We're not going on strike," Bill said. "Trust me; we'll take the extra ten cents and the heat breaks."

Gloria had only been on strike once. That was back in '66 and, though they could get through the five-week strike with little difficulty then, she didn't want to live through another strike again—not now. In 1966 she had Ted's paycheque to rely on. Ted had just started his job as a crane operator at Wentworth Steel and was making good money, much more than when he worked with Gloria at Munro. Ted's job was one of the highest paid non-office jobs at Wentworth Steel. However, losing five weeks of her pay today would be disastrous. Strike pay would be almost nothing. And Gloria would never go back to Abe again. *Never!* She would jump off the Skyway Bridge before she asked Abe for another penny.

"So, how are you doing?" Bill asked, pulling at some stray white threads from his cut-off jeans.

Gloria shook her head and bit her bottom lip.

If I start talking about it now, I'll start crying.

Bill reached out and touched her shoulder. She imagined his body under his velour shirt, how he looked in his wet cut-offs jumping into the pool surrounded by children who adored him. It was far too easy to imagine herself living in that house on the Six Nations with Alice, Corey, and Josh, cleaning his work clothes and fixing his meals. She saw herself barefoot, walking on the land and feeling like she belonged there, maybe even having another child or two. It wasn't too late for her. *But why all this foolish fantasizing like a schoolgirl?* Bill had never said anything of the kind to her. His wife had just left him. And what about Ted? Was all this fantasy nonsense only occurring now because Ted had been ill?

"I want to talk to you," Bill said, still gently touching her shoulder.

There was a clap of thunder that made Gloria jump. When was the last time Gloria had heard thunder like that? April? She looked out the warehouse pod doors and saw dark storm clouds coming in over the mountain. Within seconds the rain began. Large raindrops slapped the dusty road and disappeared into the sharp brown grass on the lawn around the plant.

"Fuck! The windows of my car are open!" Sylvia yelled, running out of the ladies' room and into the parking lot. When she came back into the warehouse, soaked to the skin, Gloria could see a bit of red hair dye running down the side of her face. She must have just had her hair coloured, Gloria thought, feeling a strong pang of sympathy for her.

The three finished decorating the truck as the rain continued throughout the afternoon. When they were done, Gloria thought the old flatbed truck looked pretty good, as good as any other float that would be in the parade. As Sylvia locked up the plant, Gloria walked out the side door, stood under the awning, and tied her plastic rain bonnet around her head.

"I'll drive you home," Bill said, coming up behind her. He took his truck keys out of the front pocket of his cut-offs. "And we can talk about... us."

Us?

Gloria nodded.

Bill slammed down the warehouse garage bay door and double-checked that the door was locked.

As they were about to run for Bill's pickup truck, Gloria saw the headlights of a blue Chevy Impala flash and moved toward them.

Ted had come to pick her up.

"We can... um... talk on Labour Day," Gloria said. Then she ran through the rain to the Impala and got in the front seat with Ted.

"Sorry," Ted said, looking down at the gearshift. "I should have driven you."

"That's alright, Ted, you're here now."

"They say there's more rain on the way."

"Well, we need it. We need it, badly."

When they returned home to Alkeld Street, Josh was not there. Josh was not a baby but, still, Gloria didn't want him out in this storm, especially if it was going to get worse. That's how colds get started, she thought, by getting wet. And Josh already had pneumonia twice; his lungs weren't the best. Now she was getting worried.

Gloria was standing at the window looking down Alkeld Street toward Red Hill Creek for Josh when a lime-green Ford Meteor drove up and stopped in front of their house.

"I don't believe it."

It was Hannah. She opened the door of her Meteor, pulled herself out of the driver's seat, and rushed, as well as Hannah could rush, toward the front door with her black patent leather purse in her hand.

"Well look what the flood washed in," Ted said.

"Ted, go help her up the stairs!"

"Why? She didn't help me." He walked past Gloria and down the basement steps.

Gloria went out the front door in her bare feet and took Hannah's hand as she struggled to walk across the front lawn and up the stairs of the porch in the pouring rain.

"Hannah! You shouldn't have come out on a day like this!"

"I know it! I know it! It's the first time I've driven in months, and it turns into a hurricane. Just my luck!" Hannah said, forcing a smile.

Gloria rushed to the washroom and grabbed a bath towel from the linen closet.

"Don't bother taking off your shoes, Hannah," she said, handing Hannah the towel. "Just sit down here in Ted's chair. Do you want a cup of tea to warm up?"

"No, I can't stay. I just wanted to give you this." Hannah opened her purse and pulled out a cheque. "Here," she said, handing it to Gloria.

Eight thousand dollars.

"This way, you don't have to borrow two thousand from Lydia. I know she's not made of money either. I'm sorry it took so long. Doris was right. Family *is* family."

Gloria held the cheque in her hand and started to cry.

"Stop that, Gloria," Hannah said, patting her face with the towel. "I'm just sorry it took so long. I was being… spiteful. I can be such a big fat spiteful person! I was sitting at home alone all summer thinking about how horrible I was to you. Probably because I'm so miserable myself right now that, maybe, I wanted everyone else to be miserable too, and… well, it's been bothering me for weeks. We're family. Family does for each other, right?"

"Thank you, Hannah. I'll pay you back a little each week, I promise."

"Take your time. I'll probably be dead soon anyway. And then who will I leave it to anyway? Not to George, that's for sure." She chuckled.

Gloria reached out and hugged Hannah.

"Hannah, please sit down and let me make you a cup of tea."

"No, no, no," Hannah said, opening the front door. "Red Hill Creek is flooding. It's broken its banks and rising fast. I'm afraid that Barton Street will be flooded if I wait any longer and, if it does, I'll have to drive around the whole city to get home."

"Then I'll come down and see you after Labour Day," Gloria said.

Gloria helped Hannah down the front steps and back to her car. Then ran back to the porch and waved as Hannah drove away.

She didn't even notice she was now soaked through to the skin. All Gloria felt was relief.

I can pay back Abe the six thousand dollars, she thought. She would send him a cheque—registered mail—after going to the bank next week. And she would ask for the IOU she signed back. Maybe she would burn it in the barbeque. Still, the damage was done, they had let Abe off the hook, and he was back in their lives. For God's sake, he had even touched Josh's hair. But he could never lord the money over her now. And whenever Abe came down to her house on Alkeld Street, it would be by Gloria's rules.

Wait! Gloria suddenly thought. Red Hill Creek is flooding!

Where's Josh?

Twelve

The sound of a bell ringing from the Big House woke Josh from a deep sleep the day after Jiffy left. Josh's grey sweatshirt, rolled up in a ball, made a more comfortable pillow than he had imagined. The tent was already getting warm in the morning sun, and the back of Josh's flannel pyjama shirt was damp from sweat. Josh had spent the night before sulking, sitting quietly around the campfire while the mob of other boys sang dumb camp songs and fought over the few bags of stale marshmallows to roast on the fire. According to the deal he had made with his mother, he could call her in four days, and she would come and get him.

He kicked off his sleeping bag and scratched two mosquito bites on his right ankle as the bell rang again. Beside him, the Mayfield twins were stuffed into one sleeping bag, facing each other, still sleeping. Kyle must have climbed in with Shane sometime during the night. Josh thought they were fine as tent mates went, but the twins had talked for a good hour before going to sleep— about their cat, their mother, about *Star Wars*, mostly about *Star Wars*. Josh had wanted to tell them to shut up but didn't. With Jiffy gone, Josh was outnumbered in that tent.

"Are you three deaf?" Scout Devin shouted, raising the flap of the tent.

The twins woke up with a start, staring wide-eyed at Devin while trying to sit up in the sleeping bag.

"That's the bell! I told you yesterday that when you hear that bell in the morning you get up! You get dressed! And you make your way to the Big House. You capiche?" Devin shouted.

"Devin is Jiffy... I mean, is Sullivan coming back today?" Josh asked, unbuttoning his damp pyjama shirt.

"He won't be back *this* year," Devin said. "The kid's ended up with second and third-degree burns on his leg. The klutz."

Josh felt terrible. If Jiffy hadn't been looking back at him while he was walking, he wouldn't have dropped the stupid bowl of soup. He was Josh's buddy, after all. *I'm a horrible buddy.*

"Since you were his buddy, you can pack up all of Sullivan's gear after breakfast, Moore. Just shove all that moron's crap in his duffle bag and throw it outside the tent. Adam will make sure it gets to his mom and dad," Devin said.

"He only has a dad," Josh said.

"Who cares? Now you three finish getting dressed, grab your toothbrushes and towels, and meet up with all the other Cub Scouts in front of the Big House. Now!"

"Will I get a new buddy?" Josh asked.

He hoped he could go solo for the rest of his time here. He couldn't tell Devin that he was leaving in four days, and there was no reason to be paired up with someone new for such a short time.

"You three can be buddies from here on. Now move it!"

Josh and the twins quickly dressed and made their way to the Big House with their towels and toothbrushes. What was Devin's problem? Josh thought, approaching the Big House. They weren't late at all. They weren't the first to arrive after the bell, but they sure weren't the last. And he and the twins waited over twenty minutes until all the campers finally emptied from their tents and made their way to the Big House. Josh kept an eye out for Gavin Mulligan, one of the last boys to arrive, just in case. Josh had sat as far away from Gavin at the campfire as he possibly could the night before but did notice Gavin grabbed two stale marshmallows from the package when they were told they could only have one a piece to roast.

Finally, Adam came out from his office at the back of the Big House, followed by three full-fledged Scouts, each carefully carrying a large oval metal pail full of water. Adam looked as ironed and pressed as he did the day before and Josh wondered if Adam had an ironing board in his office and if he spent each morning standing in his underwear ironing his clothes. Josh grinned.

"Okay, fellas," Adam yelled. "As you all know, a Scout is clean in thought and word and deed and body. Now I may not be able to do a heck of a lot about your dirty thoughts, but I can do something about your dirty bodies."

Adam laughed loudly, and most of the boys laughed along with him. Josh remained silent.

"I want all of you to strip down to the waist and line up behind one of these three pails of warm soapy water. Wash your face, chest, underarms, and necks with the washcloth beside the pail and, after drying off with your towels, I want you to brush your teeth with the toothpaste provided at the end of the table, then walk to the bushes alongside the parking lot and brush your teeth there and spit there, and only there in the bushes! We'll do this every morning."

He's got to be kidding, Josh thought as Adam walked back toward his office.

There was no way he would touch anyone else's dirty water, never mind putting it on his face! Josh stood in line behind the twins for a while and then, when he thought no one was looking, walked toward the toothpaste at the end of the table while pretending to dry his neck with his towel.

"Moore!" Devin yelled.

"Yeah?" Josh said nonchalantly.

"Did you wash your face and neck?"

"No," Josh answered.

"You have to clean yourself. Get back here in line and clean yourself first."

"No," Josh repeated. "Not there."

"It's okay, Josh. The water is just a little grey," one of the twins said, drying his face.

"I'm not touching that water," Josh said, crossing his arms.

"Moore, I'm not telling you again! Wash yourself, or we'll get Adam! And you don't want me to get Adam!" Devin shouted.

"Get Adam," Josh said softly.

Suddenly he realized that this might be his early ticket out of Camp Ronkewe. Not following the rules would surely get him tossed out, wouldn't it? And it wasn't breaking his deal with his mother about waiting six days.

"What's up with you?" super smart Derek said, walking up to Josh.

"There's is nothing up with me, Derek."

"Don't you know that it's scientifically proven that germs cannot live in warm soapy water? And you're holding up breakfast for everyone."

Devin walked to the back of the Big House, and, after a few minutes, Adam reappeared. He was carrying a cup of coffee in a white mug and did not look happy. Josh steeled himself and clenched his jaw.

"So, what's this about you not wanting to wash yourself, Moore?" Adam said. "Did you not just hear me say a Scout is clean in thought and word and deed *and body*? I didn't make that up, Moore. That's not an Adam rule. That comes straight down from the founder of the Boy Scouts, Lord Baden-Powell. Now would Baden-Powell steer you wrong, Moore?"

Adam grinned and put his hand on Josh's shoulder, and Josh felt somewhat comforted.

"I don't want to wash in dirty water, Adam. I don't like it and I… I can't do it. Please don't make me," Josh said.

Adam took his hand off Josh's shoulder.

"He refused to go swimming with the other guys at the swimming hole yesterday too," Devin said.

"Oh yeah?" Adam said, looking down at Josh suspiciously.

"He doesn't like water, Adam!" Gavin yelled from the bushes with a mouthful of toothpaste.

"What do you think, fellas," Adam said, turning toward the group of boys and smiling. "Should I have the Scouts wash Moore? We've had to do that before with grubby little boys who didn't want to wash themselves like men. And, trust me, Moore, you wouldn't like it if we washed you." He bent down close to Josh's face. "You *really* wouldn't like it one bit."

Three Scouts, including Devin, came up and stood behind Adam grinning with their arms crossed over their chests.

Josh took the towel off his neck, put it on the burnt grass, and then placed his blue toothbrush on top. He took a step back, widened his stance slightly, and clenched his fists in a guarded position. He didn't raise his fists, not quite yet, but he was ready. Another Scout whispered into Devin's ear and smiled. Josh had learned on Alkeld Street that, though he couldn't win if *all* the older boys pounced on him, he would hurt a few of them before he was taken down. And sometimes, just hurting them on your way down is better than nothing.

"Try it," Josh said defiantly.

Adam stared at Josh. He's sizing me up, Josh thought, so he held Adam's gaze without blinking.

"Fine! If you don't want to wash, Moore, that's up to you. I don't think your parents will be too happy when they have to drive you home at the end of three weeks with their windows open, but, hey, it's up to you."

Josh slowly put his fists down. Did he just win? This all seemed way too easy. Nothing was ever that easy when it came to boys. Josh didn't trust Devin or the other Scouts, who were still looking sideways at him with slightly dangerous grins.

No, this wasn't over.

"However, tough guy..." Adam continued. "Even if you don't want to wash like a man, you still have to brush your teeth. And on that point, I won't take no for an answer. Do we understand each other, Moore?"

"Okay," Josh said.

"But! You aren't getting away scot-free, my grubby little friend. I'm putting you, Josh Moore, in charge of emptying and cleaning the wash pails once everyone is finished washing in the morning. While we're eating breakfast, you empty the pails, scrub them in the kitchen sink with soap, and set them out to dry in the sun. And *then* you can eat breakfast, you understand?"

Josh nodded in agreement, took the crinkled-up toothpaste tube from the end of the picnic table, and walked to the brushes to brush his teeth. It would only be for four more days, he thought.

The next few days at Camp Ronkewe were broken up with daily trips to the water hole where Josh would wait on the perimeter sitting alone (since even Derek had stopped talking to him) until the boys were done wading, a few hikes along the base of the escarpment, some soccer in the weedy field that Josh chose to forgo to read The Legend of Sleepy Hollow in his sweltering tent with the flap open, sneaking away to the trees for a smoke, and the nightly campfire where the stupid camp songs were getting tiresome. Josh did his best to stay away from Gavin Mulligan, but it seemed that Gavin had already forgotten about Josh, having easily made lots of new friends at Camp Ronkewe.

Over this time Josh did not use the outhouse, choosing instead to piss in the trees behind the tent and holding off taking a shit until the fourth day after lunch when the boys were on a hike. Adam's car, a long white Thunderbird, was gone from the parking lot, and since Josh didn't have a buddy to keep an eye on him, the twins never cared where he was, Josh pretty much had his run of the place, so he took the chance to sneak into the back of the Big House and into Adam's office to use his private washroom.

Josh could hear Joy washing powdered eggs off the breakfast plates in the kitchen as he quietly opened the door. He walked past Adam's small clumsy-looking wooden table with logs crisscrossed for feet and four wooden chairs, and his single bed covered with a khaki bedspread and sporting a big fluffy pillow with a bright white pillowcase. Against the wall by the window were a metal filing cabinet and a desk with some papers and a black phone on it, the first phone Josh had seen since coming to Camp Ronkewe. That's what I'll use to call home tomorrow, Josh thought. He walked into Adam's washroom and locked the door with a click. Tomorrow was day five.

Everything in the bathroom was white and sparkled like a commercial for Comet cleanser. Even the toilet brush beside the toilet gleamed. Adam had his own shower stall with a shower curtain. No dirty pail of water for him. Josh deeply inhaled the strong scent of ammonia as he lifted the white plastic toilet seat. The water was blue and smelled better than the flowers Derek had shoved in Josh's face their first day at camp. Josh sat down and he could feel the grit of some Comet left on the seat and his bowels relaxed and released.

He reached for the toilet paper. It was light pink and quilted and smelled like lady's perfume. Mom never bought such fancy toilet paper, Josh thought as another heavy turd of digested powered food, fell from him. Even my shit smells like powered chicken soup, Josh thought. He flushed to toilet and walked out of the washroom.

He gasped.

Adam was sitting in a chair at the table with his arms crossed waiting for him.

"Just what the hell were you doing in my washroom, Moore?"

"Um… I had to… and since I thought no one was around… that no one would care if I used the flush toilet."

Adam stretched out his leg and kicked another of the wooden chairs away from the folding table. "Sit down."

Josh sat and, just to antagonise Adam, slowly crossed his legs at the ankles.

"Dammit, you're frustrating, Moore!"

"Sorry," Josh said, not meaning it.

"But you aren't the first frustrating boy that came through here." He pulled a pack of cigarettes out of the pocket of his pressed Scout leader shirt and, lighting one, blew smoke across the table towards Josh. "We usually run into one, sometimes two, every summer. And my job here is to make you and other frustrating boys like you… less frustrating. Less frustrating to your parents, to your teachers, to everyone."

In Transactional Analysis terms, Adam is saying that *Camp Ronkewe is okay and I'm not okay*, Josh thought.

"Now listen, you have to get over this bullcrap about washing in water that's a little dirty or using the outhouses. It's… sissy stuff! Besides, we have those outhouses emptied and cleaned once a week. In fact, the honey truck comes tomorrow to clean them. They're clean as a whistle.

"How often is your washroom cleaned?"

"Now, if I let all the boys in this camp use my washroom it would be chaos around here, see? And if all the other boys here, forty-four of them, can man-up and deal with dirty water and outhouses, so can you."

"It's forty-three since Jiffy got second and third-degree burns," Josh said.

"My toilet is off limits."

"Alright."

"Now get out of here."

Josh got up, pushed his chair back where it had been, and walked toward the door. Suddenly, Adam leaped forward in his chair, grabbed Josh's right arm hard, twisted it, and yanked Josh toward him.

"If you ever come in my office again you will regret it, Moore," Adam said through gritted teeth.

He let go of Josh's arm and shoved him backwards toward the door. That night, after the campfire and songs, when Josh changed into his pyjamas, he found a huge purple bruise on his upper arm where Adam had grabbed him. It was sore to the touch.

"Asshole," Josh said.

Tomorrow Josh would tell Adam that he wanted to use the phone in his office to call his mother. Then, an hour later, at most, she and Aunt Doris would come and get him. He only had to get through one more night.

They pounced the next morning.

Josh had slept well that night, knowing that soon he would call his mother and tell her to pick him up. He had fulfilled his side of the bargain and was sure his mother would fulfill hers. Josh had packed up most of his clothes in his suitcase the night before: his swim trunks that had never gotten wet, his dirty socks that he had only worn at night around the fire, two clean pairs of pants, some shorts, and a rain jacket he never needed.

He had been somewhere between dreaming and awake, enjoying the sun warming the morning dampness from the tent and anticipating the Big House bell. Pleased that the bell had not yet rung, he turned over and was surprised to see the twins missing. Only their empty sleeping bags were there in a heap on the floor of the tent. Deciding they had gone to the outhouse together, Josh closed his eyes and dozed off back to sleep.

They grabbed him by the arms first, yanking him out of his sleeping bag. They dragged him out of the tent and onto the hard ground outside where most of the Cub Scouts were already dressed, standing in a semi-circle around his tent. Josh's eyes, tried to adjust to the bright morning sun and, through his half-closed eyes, he could see that it was Scouts Devin and Brett pulling him across the field as most of the campers laughed and cheered.

"Get the fuck off me!"

He was able to escape from Devin and Brett's grip and fought back as best he could, but then two more Scouts, Tommy and Dean, sprang on him, each grabbing one of Josh's limbs and lifting him off the ground.

"Cripes, he's heavy," Tommy said.

They carried him toward the Big House, letting his ass drag on the ground, which pulled the pyjama bottoms off his butt as they made their way past the row of tents down the length of the field. The entire way, Josh fought back, trying to kick his legs, and twisting his body in an attempt to break the older boy's grip, but the Scouts, young teenagers, were too strong.

"Let me go!"

"You're gonna learn what happens to boys that won't wash," Devin said, holding tight to Josh's right arm.

Josh kept kicking, hoping to free one leg so he could kick one of the Scouts hard, right in the face. Anything to stop them.

"Look at his fat ass!" Gavin Mulligan yelled from nearby. Then he came up on Josh's left side carrying one of the marshmallow roasting sticks with the sharp fire-charred end and, started whipping Josh with the stick, leaving black soot marks and bits of last night's melted marshmallow on Josh's hips.

The Scouts dropped Josh near the Big House in front of the picnic tables but instead of three washbasins on the tables, today there were three tin buckets of water, a jug of pink Palmolive, and two white toilet brushes.

"I'm telling Adam!"

"Go ahead and tell him," Devin said with a sneer. "He's right over there."

Over by the tree, Adam stood smoking a cigarette and sipping coffee.

Josh pulled his pyjama bottoms back up over his butt and lifted his hands in front of him, palms up, hoping they would stop. His hands trembled. He backed away, not sure where he would go, but the other boys, led by Gavin encircled him from behind. He was trapped.

"Alright," Josh said. "I'll wash myself like you want."

"Too late," Brett said.

"Leave me alone!"

He couldn't fight them all. His only hope was that someone might feel sorry for him and help him. Then he saw Joy, the soup lady, standing to the side of the picnic table with her arms crossed. She looked irritated, as if she just wanted to get her Palmolive soap back and start breakfast. No, she wasn't going to help him.

Whatever happens, I won't cry!

Devin and Tommy jumped on Josh and yanked his pyjama top over his head. It snagged around his throat for a few seconds and pushed against his windpipe. He struggled to breathe until Devin, finally, pulled the pyjama shirt so hard he ripped off the top button and it went over Josh's head. Josh tried to push the larger boys off him, punching at them, once hitting Tommy hard on the side of his face. But then Devin tackled Josh and he fell onto his back, knocking the wind out of him as Devin grabbed Josh's pyjama bottoms at his ankles and yanked them off with one quick motion.

"A flag," Devin yelled. He held Josh's bottoms over his head and waved them as the other Scouts held Josh down, naked, on the brown grass and weeds.

"Stop it! Get off me and give me my pyjamas back!"

Devin tossed the pyjama bottoms aside, picked up the plastic bottle of Palmolive off the picnic table, and pointed it at Josh as he stood over him.

"Alright, let him go."

The Scouts let go of Josh and moved aside as Devin squeezed the plastic soap bottle and pink soap shot out of the bottle in thick ribbons, hitting Josh in the face and stomach. Soap burned Josh's eyes. He tried to wipe the soap out of his eyes but only rubbed it in deeper. Then someone, probably Devin, threw one of the buckets of freezing water into Josh face. Coughing and blinded, Josh tried to stand up but was pushed down, hitting the side of his face on the ground, and piercing his bottom lip with his front teeth. He tasted blood mixed with soap in his mouth. He turned on his side and curling into a ball, covering his genitals with his hands.

Don't cry, he told himself. Don't cry. But it was no use. The soap in his eyes mixed with humiliation and the pain in his lip was too much and he began to sob.

Another pail of cold water was thrown onto Josh's chest as Devin and Tommy began scrubbing Josh's naked body with the two toilet brushes. The brushes, made of wire with hard plastic bristles, scraped through Josh's hair, across his face and over his cut bleeding lip. Josh winced with the pain and placed his hands over his face to protect his eyes and lip as the Scouts roughly scrubbed his belly, under his arms and down his legs as the laughing, hooting, and hollering continued from the boys gathered around them. A brush scraped down Josh's neck and chest while another ripped aggressively over the sensitive skin of his penis and scrotum making Josh groan in pain. He turned onto his stomach and placed his hands over the back of his head, but the brushes continued to move brutally down his neck and back, jabbing into his sides and over his butt.

"Okay, that's enough," Adam suddenly yelled. "Everyone back to your tents. Breakfast in ten minutes."

Josh lay, still on his stomach, on the ground gagging and choking on the soapy water as Devin threw the last pail of cold water on the back of Josh's head and dropped it on the ground with a clank beside Josh's head.

Josh rolled over onto his knees and, trying to stand, slipped in the wet grass onto his back into the muddy soapy water, hitting the back on his head on the ground. And then, wiping the soap out of his eyes, he carefully stood up and walked slowly to where his pyjama bottoms were lying, wet and dirty in the mud, by the picnic table while soapy water, tears and blood dripped down his chin, He picked up the pyjama bottoms up and, turning the wad of wet fabric around in his hands, tried to find the hole to put his leg in.

"Sorry about that, son," Adam said, walking over with one of the large white towels from his bathroom. He took Josh's wet pyjama bottoms away and wiped the soap, mud, and blood from Josh's face with the towel before wrapping it, almost lovingly, around Josh's shoulders. "But like I told you, Moore, if you weren't going to clean yourself like a man then we were going to have to do it for you!" Adam chuckled to himself and messed up Josh's hair like they were the best of friends.

Josh touched his swollen lip; it was twice its normal size. His head was all messed up. It was like he wasn't even sure what had happened had really happened. It was as if he left his body at some point and was just now returning to it.

"It was all in good fun," Adam said.

Adam walked Josh to the back of the Big House, into his office, and then to his white polished bathroom. Josh stood silently by the sink with a blank look on his face as Adam turned on the shower.

"Here you go. Hop in my shower and rinse yourself off, you still have some mud and soap on your back. Devin's gone to your tent to get you some clean clothes; he'll be back in a minute."

Josh watched the clean clear water stream out of the showerhead as Adam walked past him out of the bathroom.

"And wash your mouth, Moore. It looks like you accidentally hit yourself in the face when they were washing you."

Adam shut the bathroom door behind him. It clicked shut. Josh dropped the towel from his shoulders, walked into the shower stall, and began to sob. He spit blood onto the bottom of the shower and watched it swirl around and around until it finally went down the drain. It wasn't just his cut lip. He was sore everywhere. There were red scratches, scrapes and welts forming over his belly, arms, and legs. Even his private parts were red and scratched.

Maybe they're right, Josh thought. Maybe they're all right: Adam, Devin, Gavin, Anne-Marie, and the rest. Maybe there is something wrong with me. Maybe... maybe I do deserve this.

Soon Adam came into the bathroom with a pair of Josh's underwear, the shorts he came to camp in, and a clean T-shirt that

Devin had grabbed from Josh's packed suitcase. He placed Josh's clothes on the side of the sink.

"Here's your clothes, son. I hope you learned your lesson about a Scout always being clean." Then he turned, left the bathroom door ajar, and went back to his office.

Josh turned off the shower, dried off with a new clean white towel hanging on the towel rack and dressed.

Fuck that!

He pulled his T-shirt over his head. There's nothing wrong with me! I didn't deserve any of this. There's something wrong with *them*. All of them. And from here on in, he decided, no matter what they did to him, he wouldn't cry again at Camp Ronkewe.

Adam was sitting at his desk writing something on a piece of yellow paper when Josh walked toward him. "Don't be late for breakfast." Adam did not look up from his paper.

"I want to call my mother," Josh said calmly.

"Sorry. No phone calls home except in emergencies. And a fat lip isn't an emergency."

"My mom said I could call her after five days if I wanted to go home, it was our bargain, and I want to go home."

Adam sized him up again. "I didn't agree to that bargain."

"I don't like it here. And… and my dad won't like what you just did to me today, Adam."

"What I did?"

"What you all did to me."

"Looked like you and a few of the fellas were just roughhousing to me. In fact, Tommy has a swollen eye from where you just punched him in the face. I'm thinking that Tommy's dad probably won't like hearing that a bully like you punched his son either."

"Let me call home!"

Adam sat back in his old wooden swivel chair and grinned. "I told you: we get at least one boy like you every summer. And I told you that I'm a pro at making frustrating boys like you less frustrating. And that's what I'm going to do. Trust me, after three weeks at Camp Ronkewe your mother and father are going to be thanking me. One day you'll thank me too. Trust me."

"Let me call home! Please!"

"No."

"Yes!"

"I'm not fooling around with you anymore! Get this through your goddamn head! You aren't going home. But what you are going to do is clean yourself every fucking morning at those washbasins like every other boy in this goddamn camp! You're going to play soccer and baseball and swim in the swimming hole and hike along the mountain and you're going to shit in the outhouse! And if you don't, then the same thing that happened to you today is going to happen again and again and again—but each time it'll be worse. You'll have more than a fat lip when we're done with you, Moore. I'm going to turn you from a little queer into a real boy if I have to break your neck to do it! And that's it! Now, get the fuck out of here."

Josh walked out of the office.

"No, Adam, that's not it."

That afternoon they were serving chicken noodle soup again in the mess hall. Josh could smell that same chemical smell as the day that Jiffy was burned. Josh stood in line behind the twins with his orange tray and watched as Joy ladled out bowl after bowl of the bright yellow concoction to the Cub Scouts. She didn't seem to recognize Josh as the naked kid being scrubbed in the field when she ladled out the steaming soup into his white bowl. Maybe she didn't recognize me without my pyjamas around my ankles and a toilet brush in my ass, Josh thought.

"Careful, it's hot," Joy said grumpily, wiping sweat from her forehead with her forearm.

"No shit."

Josh walked away and grabbed a glass of powdered milk. They probably make her say that now to every boy she ladles that yellow crap out to since Jiffy got burned.

That's it!

Adam had said no phone calls home except in emergencies. This boiling powdered soup here could be my one-way ticket out of here, Josh thought. It certainly was for Jiffy. It would hurt, that's for sure. Josh remembered how Jiffy had screamed when the bowl of soup spilled on him, but it would all be over in one quick second. Just one quick motion and it would be goodbye, Camp Ronkewe, for good—if Josh had the guts to do it.

Josh walked through the tables in the mess hall toward table number nine. Across the room he could see Gavin looking at him and laughing with all the other boys at his table. *All I have to do is tip the tray and let the hot soup splash onto my leg just like Jiffy did*, Josh thought, passing table number three. *All it would take is one quick movement to overturn the tray then, like Jiffy, Adam and Cookie would quickly put cold water and ice on his leg and, after a quick trip to the hospital, he would be back on Alkeld Street in time for dinner.*

As he passed table number five, Josh tried to think of the best place to spill the hot soup on himself. As he sat down to eat? No, then it would all end up in his lap and he didn't want to burn his dick and balls like Jiffy did; they'd been through enough today as it was. It would be best to let the soup spill on just one of his legs, maybe the right thigh, then it would drip down his calf and turn his whole leg red. Josh held his tray tighter with his hands, the steaming yellow soup splashed a bit against the sides of the bowl, as if it was ready to help him by jumping out onto his leg. *All right, as soon as I get to the table, I'll do it.*

As he approached table nine, Devin and the twins had already prayed and started eating without him. Devin was carefully taking small spoonfuls of soup from the side of his bowl while the twins were both leaned over, blowing incessantly on their bowls. Josh held his breath.

On the count of five.
Five. Four. Three.
Two...
One.

He couldn't do it. He was too afraid of the pain. Poor Jiffy had screamed like Josh had never heard anyone scream before. And what if Josh lost some skin like Jiffy did. Does skin grow back? Could it scar? Besides, Adam, who now hated his guts, may just let him suffer without even getting him ice or taking him to the hospital. Even more defeated, Josh walked to his place at table number nine.

"You smell better today, Moore, I wonder why?" Devin said, snickering.

Josh bit down on his swollen lip, put his glass of milk on the table, and, looking Devin squarely in the eye, Josh slowly tipped his plastic tray forward, and his steaming bowl of yellow chicken soup slid down his plastic tray with a swoosh, and dropped with a wet thud onto Devin's lap.

The twins stopped blowing on their soup and their crystal blue eyes bugged out in horror as full-fledged Scout Devin let out an ear-piercing scream.

He sounds even more like a girl when he screams, Josh thought, calmly sitting down and taking a sip of his powdered milk.

That night, as Josh sat around the campfire, he thought up a plan to get out of Camp Ronkewe. And this plan didn't include burning himself with boiling soup— or anyone else. The soup he had spilled on Devin's lap, maybe because he was wearing denim jeans, or maybe they had stopped making the soup so hot after Jiffy was burned, hadn't really hurt Devin much at all. Except for some blistering on his inner thighs (he had an icepack Adam had given him between his legs most of the day), Devin had been back at table number nine that evening for a dinner of boiled hotdogs and, lucky for Josh, the twins had told Adam that the whole thing had been an accident, since they had seen Josh 'trip' as he had walked by their table. Still, Josh was certain that Adam knew it wasn't an accident.

Now he had a new plan to get out of Camp Ronkewe. No, there was no hot soup involved this time. Josh stuffed a marshmallow in his mouth. The only thing he needed was a little time.

On his eleventh day at Camp Ronkewe, Adam drove Josh, who was bent over, writhing and screaming in pain, to Joseph Brant Hospital. Barely able to walk, it felt like his stomach was about to explode all over the interior of Adam's white thunderbird. When they arrived at the ER, it didn't take long before a doctor took Josh into a small room in Emergency and pushed down on his Josh's belly and shook his head.

"When was the last time you pooped?" the doctor asked.

"Can't remember."

It had been a moment of genius when Josh had come up with his scheme to get out of Camp Ronkewe. If Adam and the rest of the full-fledged Scouts were going to boss him around and try to control every aspect of his life for three weeks, telling Josh what to eat, where to sleep, when to play, where to wash, and even where to go to the toilet, then Josh decided that he was going to control one of the few things he could: his shit.

"I didn't want to use the outhouse like they were making me and, since Adam wouldn't let me use the flush toilet in the Big House, I just stopped going."

"Ah," the doctor said nonchalantly, making Josh think he had heard that story a thousand times before.

"And Adam wouldn't let me call my mom to pick me up after five days and take me home, which was our deal when I went there, so I just… held it all in."

"Joshua, do you do that often? Hold in your poop to get your own way or when you're upset or… for any reason?" the doctor asked.

The doctor had dark friendly eyes, black curly hair, and wire frame round glasses just like Josh's father wore. He looked intently at Josh when he asked questions, treating Josh like he was a real person. Not like Doctor Heller, who spoke mostly to Josh's father when he had examined Josh, the way a vet would examine Reefer. Josh could tell that this doctor actually *saw* him.

"No, this was the first time I ever tried it," Josh said honestly.

"I don't want you to do that again, Joshua" the doctor said, suddenly looking very serious. "You can damage your insides by holding it in. The next time that you're troubled, like you were at this camp, I want you to go to an adult and tell them."

"I won't do it again."

"Do you think you could use a toilet here?"

"I don't know," Josh said.

Slowly, hunched over, Josh walked to the toilet in the Emergency Room. He sat and, with the doctor just outside the stall door, tried to poop. But now he really couldn't go at all.

"You're impacted now," the doctor said. "We're going to have to give you an enema, Joshua. It's just a little water to flush you out and once it's all over you'll feel a lot better."

The enema at Joseph Brant Hospital was the last indignity Josh had to suffer through for Camp Ronkewe.

When it was all over, Josh finally had a long hard bowel movement and, finally, the pain in his stomach went away. Lying in a hospital bed with a real pillow and a curtain around him, Josh smiled. Even though the Emergency Room was crowded and noisy, it was almost like having his own room again. On the other side of the curtain, a few beds away, Josh could hear the doctor first chatting with a nurse and then Josh heard Adam's voice.

"Where are his parents?" the doctor asked.

"I called them," Adam said. "Someone is on their way here to get him."

They think I can't hear them, Josh thought, straining to hear over the weird beeps and occasional moans of the emergency room.

"I can't let him go back to your camp. He's going to need to rest for a couple of days with soft foods," the doctor said.

Josh loved that doctor.

"That's just fine with us. That's one weird kid you got in there. He gives all the other boys the creeps and no one in the camp likes him one bit. I had thought, probably too optimistically, that I could help him out. Teach him how to man-up a bit. I put in a lot of time and effort trying to be his buddy and get him involved with the other Cub Scouts, but this kid is a lost cause."

"A lost cause at ten?" The doctor said.

Almost eleven, Josh thought.

"Is that even normal? Not that this kid is very normal but, you know, a kid stopping himself from taking a dump because he wanted his own way so badly?"

Josh strained to hear but couldn't hear what the doctor said at that point. He wanted to know himself if he went a bit overboard with this whole idea to get out of camp.

"I've never heard of anything like that in my life, and I've been around Cubs and Scouts since I was one myself. How can anyone, especially a kid, just stop shitting like that?" Adam asked.

"My guess is that the boy must have been quite motivated to get out of your camp."

"He must be quite nuts, if you ask me. He refused to wash and wouldn't play or swim with the other boys. I had no idea he wasn't shitting. I can't keep track of when forty boys shit and when they don't. I thought his appendix was going to burst or something by the way he was acting on the drive here. And then it turns out all he needed to do was take a crap. I'll tell you this, Doc, if he were my kid, I'd kick his ass so hard he'd never shit again."

"Well, he's doing well enough to go home now. Are you going to wait with him until his parents come?"

No! Josh thought. Just get in your ugly white car and go back to Camp Ronkewe where you belong, Adam.

"I don't want to see the little goon again. I'll wait in the waiting room for his parents. Then I'll tell them what a problem he was and the trouble he's been to me and the other boys at camp. We tried to stop it, but he was his own worst enemy. You know he even gave one kid a black eye."

Josh folded his arms behind his head and looked up to the ceiling. *Fuck them!* Either his mother would call his Aunt Doris or, if Troy were home, he would drive his mother here to get him and take him home. He would be home for dinner. After eleven days of sleeping on the ground with a sweatshirt for a pillow, Josh soon dozed off.

"Josh, wake up."

Josh opened his eyes and saw a man with glasses, a scruffy beard and a light-pink scar across his throat standing over his bed looking down at him.

"Dad!" Josh bolted upright and threw his arms around his father's neck. Finally, everything seemed like it would be okay.

"I came home earlier this week. I was going to surprise you when I picked you up at camp next week, but you decided to surprise us all, didn't you?" he said, smiling.

"I'm not going back there," Josh said.

"Turns out they weren't too thrilled at the possibility of having you back at their camp anytime soon either."

"Is Adam gone?"

"Yep, back to Camp Rack-and-Ruin or whatever the hell it's called."

"Good," Josh said.

"They're going to discharge you now that I'm here so we shouldn't have to wait long," his father said, sitting down in the chair beside the hospital bed.

Josh decided he liked his father's new beard. He almost looked like a completely new person. A lot better than the weeks leading up to his going into the hospital. He just seemed like he was... there.

"I want you to listen to me, Josh, you can't ever do that again. Holding everything in like that. It can mess you up."

"The doctor already told me that."

"And he's right. Promise me you won't ever do that again."

"I won't. I just didn't want to use the outhouse or wash in dirty water. I asked them to let me call home after my fifth day, but they wouldn't let me."

"Adam told me in the waiting room that some of the other boys razzed you about not washing yourself and you got in a fight with some of them. He said you gave a Scout a black eye."

"It wasn't like that! They jumped on me in the morning and dragged me out of the tent. All of them! That's when I gave that big kid the black eye. Then they pulled my pyjamas off, squirted soap at me, and then scrubbed me with toilet brushes. And then they threw buckets of cold water in my face and between my legs and laughed when I fell down and cut my lip. The... *fuckers!*"

"Josh, listen to me. That kind of stuff is just what boys do. Guys goof around like that all the time. They yank each other's pants down. They piss in the woods. They fart and spit. It's just... guy stuff."

"But I don't like it."

His father reached over and put his hand on his shoulder. "You have to get over this fear of guy stuff."

"I'm not afraid of anything."

"When I was around your age, I went swimming in Red Hill Creek with my buddies and they stole my clothes and left me there naked. I had to steal washing off someone's clothesline. I came home in a pair of men's work pants ten sizes too big. And when I see those guys today, we laugh about it. That sort of goofball stuff made us better friends. That's how you get to be one of the guys; one of the gang."

"I don't want to be one of the gang."

"Yes, you do."

Josh began to cry. *He's just like Aunt Wilma and Adam and the rest of them. He thinks there's something wrong with me.* His stomach still hurt a bit and his bum hole was burning from the water they shot up there and the log-sized turd he passed. And now here he was seeing his dad for the first time in over three months, and they were fighting.

"Alright, let's just forget it all for now. I'm just… trying to make it easier for you to… get through life. But maybe that's just not you." His father smiled, reached over, and mussed up Josh's hair. "Jesus, you do need a bath, kid!"

Josh laughed and wiped his nose with the collar of his T-shirt.

"But I'd like you to do something for me, Josh."

"What?"

"I want you to promise me you won't tell Mom about what they did to you with the soap and water. I mean *never* tell her," his father said.

"Why not?"

"Because your mom is a girl and girls don't understand that kind of stuff. Only boys understand that kind of joking around, okay?"

Josh studied the scar across his throat. It did look kind of cool, just like Shannon said it would.

"Okay, I promise."

"And don't tell her you stopped going to the bathroom on purpose to get out of camp, either. That would just worry her too. Let's just tell her… that you were constipated from the food they were feeding you. We'll keep the rest between us."

"Okay, I won't tell her that either."

"And Josh…"

"Yeah, Dad?"

"I really missed you."

It's funny, Josh thought, how what started as one of the worse days in his life had turned into one of the best. His father looked and acted just like he did before he got sick and, except for the scar, looked even better. Josh hoped that his father would barbeque when they got home. After that, maybe Josh would go down to the creek and look for Shannon. He hoped the fort looked as good as it did before he left eleven days ago.

"Hey, Dad?"
"Yeah?"
"Did you see the dog?"
"Sure did."
"He's a great dog, isn't he, Dad?"
"Sure is."
"Dad?"
"Yeah?"
"Did you know my bike was stolen?"
"Yeah, your mom told me. We'll get you a new one as soon as we can. And a good lock so it doesn't happen again."
"Hey, Dad?
"Uh-huh?"
"I'm never going back to Cub Scouts on Tuesday nights again."
"No. I think we're all done with that."
"Dad?"
"Yeah?"
"Are you all better now?"
"Right as rain, Joshua. Right... as... rain."

During Josh's time at Camp Ronkewe, a new grisly crime had elbowed Jake Ragno off the front page of *The Hamilton Spectator;* a young shoeshine boy in downtown Toronto had been raped and murdered by three men who then left his body on the roof of a seedy massage parlour. It was a dangerous time to be a kid, Josh thought. First it was Alan Ragno, killed here in Hamilton by his own father, out there at the bottom of Lake Ontario someplace, and now it was this poor shoeshine kid in Toronto. The shoeshine boy had only been a year and half older than Josh and, since the newspaper had been reporting daily on every horrible new detail since his body was found, Josh's mother had become even more anxious about Josh taking off alone on his new yellow and black Raleigh chopper bicycle. Where are you going? When will you be back? Stay away from the creek! Fat chance, Josh would think as he rode away down Alkeld Street. If he could give a full-fledge Scout one doozy of a black eye he could take care of himself.

The morning after he returned from camp, his father sat him down and told him that his Grandpa Moore had died two days earlier while Josh was at camp. Josh cried and taped his obituary from *The Hamilton Spectator* on his bedroom wall between his grandfather's watercolour pig farm painting and a paper cocktail placemat from The Trocadero Restaurant. Now he only had one grandparent left. He wasn't going to count Abe, who wasn't really a grandfather at all. That Friday, he went to his Grandpa Moore's funeral. It was the first time that Josh had been to a funeral, since this was the first time anyone he knew had died, but, like his father, Josh didn't cry during the funeral the way his mother and others did. He was more interested in the strange rituals that accompanied death: the music, the eulogy and even where people sat in the church seemed to be governed by certain set rules. Josh did enjoy how, during the funeral procession to Restland Cemetery, that his father could drive right though the red lights and other cars seemed to wait patiently.

After the burial, the family went to the local Legion Hall for the wake. Josh decided that the wake was the best part of the funeral, since there was food and desserts, even if he had to see his father's sisters. At the wake people had stopped crying and were laughing, remembering funny stories about his grandpa. That's what the whole funeral should be like, Josh thought. As he stood at the food table putting a ham and cheese sandwich on white bread made by the Legion's Ladies Auxiliary on a paper plate, Aunt Wilma sidled up to him and snatched an egg salad sandwich from the food table.

"Where's your father, Joshua?"

Josh pointed to the bar at the back of the legion hall where his father was standing, having a beer with Josh's Uncle Jack and Uncle Noah. At a table near the bar, Josh's mother was picking at her potato salad with a plastic fork and chatting with Uncle Jack's third wife, Becky.

"Oh, I should have guessed your father would be at the bar," Aunt Wilma said. "You really should have come to Atlanta for the summer, Joshua. I heard that the boy's camp at our church had their best year ever."

Aunt Wilma wore a black dress and her hair looked poofier than ever. She raised her Styrofoam cup of coffee to her pink lips, sipped, and then made a face like it was the worst coffee she ever had.

"I've had enough camp to last me a lifetime," Josh said.

"And you'd be a lot safer down in Georgia than you are around here at the moment. I suppose you heard about that poor shoeshine boy in Toronto. Murdered by that gang of homosexuals! If this were Georgia we wouldn't wait for any courts or greasy lawyers to get them off on some technicality, we'd just hang them from the nearest tree. And we shouldn't stop at just those three murderers either. I think it's time we exterminate the lot of them! Every pervert on God's green earth."

"Those three men are the scum of the earth." Uncle Dale said, walking up behind Aunt Wilma.

"Oh, Dale! You scared me!" Aunt Wilma said, putting her hand over her chest. "Yes, they are. Nice to see the two of us actually agree on something."

"And I think they should be tossed into jail for the rest of their lives for what they did to that child, Wilma. We should throw away the key!"

"I'd like to see them fried for what they did but, of course, Canada decided an eye for an eye is passé or something. They are just lucky they aren't in Georgia."

"But you're dead wrong to blame every gay person on God's green earth for the horrific act of these monsters. You can't blame all gay people for what these three assholes did any more than you can blame all heterosexuals for what Abe Murphy did to Tessa."

"How dare you bring up Tessa to me today, Dale!"

"I don't remember you saying we should exterminate all the straight people on God's green earth after we found out about Abe,"

Uncle Dale said. He popped a whole butter tart into his mouth and grabbed another.

"It's not the same thing at all."

"It's exactly the same thing," Dale said through a mouthful of butter tart.

Aunt Wilma got up and walked away muttering something about washing her hands of Dale, choosing to sit at a friendlier table across the room with Aunt Susan and Aunt Peggy where, Josh thought, she would have less trouble intimidating others.

What did Abe do to Aunt Tessa? Josh wondered. He didn't want to ask Uncle Dale right there. Josh knew that his Aunt Tessa died when he was a little kid. He could still kind of remember her, but that was all. More secrets! The longer Josh was around this family the more he knew they were all up to their fucking necks in dirty secrets.

"How's my favourite nephew?" Uncle Dale said.

"I'm alright, I guess."

"Funerals can suck, eh?"

"They're not so bad," Josh said.

Uncle Dale was dressed in blue jeans, a familiar-looking and overly black jacket, white shirt, and no tie.

"Is that Dad's jacket?"

"And his shirt," Uncle Dale said. "It's a bit big on me, though. I've always worn his hand-me-downs and, I guess, I still am." He chuckled, piled more butter tarts on his paper plate, and motioned with his head for Josh to follow.

Josh picked up his plate and followed his uncle to an empty table away from the rest of the family near the emergency exit.

"Your dad told me you had some problems at Cub Scout camp this summer. He said they ambushed you and… hurt you."

Josh's face turned red. The whole incident was so fucking embarrassing. Josh didn't want to talk about it and was irritated that his father had told his Uncle Dale about it. It was like his pants were being pulled down all over again. Now his Uncle Dale probably thought Josh was weird too; a creepy kid who could never get along with other boys. One by one everyone was finding out he was some kind of a freak. Even Aunt Wilma was probably over there telling the rest of the family he was a weirdo. Probably telling them she thinks I'll end up in the funny farm too someday, he thought.

"Yeah... the other boys at camp... they didn't like me. And the counsellors wouldn't let me go home, either. Then the whole lot of them got kind of mean and... it was okay... really... it was all just guy stuff. Dad says I shouldn't get too upset about guy stuff."

"Fuck that!" Uncle Dale said so loudly that Josh's aunts turned around and gave him the same dirty look. "Sorry, Josh, but your dad is wrong on this one! He told me what they did to you and that isn't *guy stuff*, kid. They attacked you! It's nothing but plain old bullying!"

"That's what I thought too. But sometimes you get bullied so much that you forget that's what it is. It becomes... normal somehow."

Aunt Wilma stood, marched over, and stood across the table in front of Uncle Dale.

"If you can't control your language you'll be asked to leave, Dale," Aunt Wilma said in her fake Georgia accent, looking stern. "I don't know if you think you're back in Vancouver with your own set of... *friends*, but right now you are at your father's funeral with godly people. Maybe you have forgotten what godly people are like, having been living in garbage for so long. Have some respect here. I won't warn you again."

"And remember, Josh," Uncle Dale said, looking Aunt Wilma in the eye. "Bullies can come in all shapes and sizes. Bullies can even come with pink lipstick and dyed-blonde bouffant hair."

Then his uncle threw another butter tart in his mouth and grinned as Aunt Wilma stormed off to another room with both Aunt Sue and Aunt Peggy jumping up from their table to run after her.

That's when Josh decided he loved wakes.

For the remaining days of his summer vacation, Josh stayed away from home as much as possible. Since the funeral, his father had spent most of his time down in the basement, watching television, coming out only in the evenings to water the front and back yards. His father had not mentioned anything to Josh about seeing him in the garage the night he cut his throat and Josh decided that there must be an unspoken contract between the two of them that they were just going to forget the whole horrible nightmare forever and Josh was more than happy to bury the memory of that night deep inside himself where it would, he hoped, one day dim and vanish completely. Perhaps his father really didn't remember Josh was there. After all, he had been sick enough to slash his own throat that night. And what the hell did it matter to anyone now, anyway? Josh would carry the memory himself until they buried *him* at Restland Cemetery too.

Then one Tuesday in mid-August, Elvis Presley died.

The news of the "King of Rock and Roll" scrolled along the bottom of the TV screen while Josh was watching a *Spider-Man* cartoon. His mother gasped and that weekend his Aunt Doris came over and the two sisters listened to him croon "Hound Dog" and "Love Me Tender" on their 8-track in the living room and talk about how young he was to die and that poor little daughter he left behind. Josh left them to their grief and nostalgia and headed to his sanctuary behind the garage to read *Tiger Beat* and smoke a cigarette he had stolen from his father's Player's pack. Josh wasn't sure if he believed in God, but he liked the idea of his grandpa and Elvis arriving in heaven at the same time.

Most days, Josh rode around the Alkeld neighbourhood on his new bike and killed time until dinner. He'd ride to the school or across the train tracks on Woodward Avenue to Edmund Park, or down to the lake. His new yellow Raleigh chopper was a cool high-rise, with the front tire smaller than the back to resemble a motorcycle and the word *CHOPPER* was written in bold black capital letters across the down tube. It had a black banana seat and a foot-long sissy bar, which Josh thought was a much more practical height than Gavin's four-foot one. Josh was almost pleased that his old Schwinn was stolen. He also did his best to avoid Gavin Mulligan, seeing him with Tony Sheehan and Danny Jacovitch only a few times throughout August and spoke to him only once.

"I bet you liked that toilet brush in your ass, didn't you? Didn't you, fag boy?" Gavin Mulligan had said one day when Josh was unlocking his bike from the railing at the Little Variety Store.

"Fuck you, Gavin Mulligan," Josh replied before riding away.

It's true. Bullies did come in all shapes and sizes. Next time, Josh thought as he drove off down Alkeld Street, that he would have to come up with something better to say back to Gavin than just 'fuck off'. On the bright side, Gavin and his friends would be off to Red Hill Junior High School come September and Josh would have a full year without them. And maybe by the time Josh reached Junior High he would be as big or even bigger than them. Josh's grandmother was Norwegian and had once told him that he had Viking blood in him and could easily grow to be six and a half feet tall or more in size. Unlikely, Josh thought, since no Moore man was more than five nine or ten. But still, it *could* happen.

Josh also spent some days at the fort with Shannon Perry. But now the whole thing was getting boring. Red Hill Creek was down to only half the size it was at the beginning of summer because of the drought and Shannon's fort was starting to get old too. The only thing to do was sit on the hard ground and smoke cigarettes or look at the same naked pictures of women while Shannon talked about Josh's mother. Josh didn't like Shannon going on about his mother one bit. Still, the fort was somewhere to go that was away from the house and he was still Shannon's fort buddy. That wasn't something you could just forget about.

The week before Labour Day, Josh was ready for the new school year to start. This year he would have Mr. Tanner with the groovy moustache, and they would finally be given ink pens. No more pencils like babies! Josh had already been shopping with his mother for new school clothes for grade five and had been a bit distressed when he was now in size Husky. As if *Husky* was a size? Dr. Heller and Aunt Bonnie were right, he was fat. When school finally started, he would try and lose some weight then surprise everyone at Christmas when they saw how much weight he lost.

Today, Josh was gloomy. *I'm not okay and you're not okay.* His parents were fighting again about some stupid Labour Day parade float his mother was working on and Josh left the house, having had enough. This was the first day all summer that Josh had worn a jacket. There was a chill in the air and over the mountain dark clouds were gathering. Was it finally going to fucking rain? If he was lucky the stupid parade next week would be rained out too. Josh's father would expect him to either march with him along the Wentworth Steel float or sit on the Munro float and wave like an idiot. Some float! It was really just a stupid semi-trailer truck they hung some shitty crepe paper around. Josh's father had Josh in the parade since he could walk— even before that. His father had told Josh that he had carried him on his shoulders during the Labour Day parade when he was a toddler. Josh just thought that was weird.

With nowhere else to go, Josh drove his bike down Woodward Avenue to Broadridge Avenue and past the Church of the Good Shepherd and over Red Hill Creek. Crossing Nash Road, he entered the front gates of Restland Cemetery and, following the gravel road, finally stopped and leaned his new bike on his grandpa's gravestone.

Walter George Moore
1904-1977

They still had not put the sod over the dirt they had laid over his grandfather. Josh had been going to visit his grandfather's grave every few days since the funeral earlier in August. He missed him. His grandpa had once told Josh that the two of them would visit his hometown of Widecombe-in-the-Moor in England together someday, but now, if Josh ever wanted to see the cathedral the Devil visited, he would have to go by himself.

"Mom was right, Grandpa. You'll be looking at that boot factory for all eternity," Josh said, looking toward Barton Street.

And then the rain hit.

Josh put the hood of his jacket over his head, grabbed his bike, and rode to one of the maintenance buildings in the middle of the cemetery. He stood in the doorway, waiting for the rain to stop, but it seemed only to rain harder. Still, he didn't want to go home so he decided to take a ride down Nash to the train tracks and then follow them to the train bridge to see if, like Shannon had said, the fort was waterproof. And even if it wasn't, his jacket was.

Josh drove his bike carefully through the pouring rain, trying not to wipe out in one of the puddles down Nash. He passed the boot factory and the old roller rink heading toward the railroad crossing and then turned left onto the CN train tracks, riding the few hundred yards to the train bridge over Red Hill Creek and stopped. He stood, sitting on his bike with his legs astride above the creek looking down. The creek had risen. It had not risen a lot, but it had definitely risen some. Josh was glad to see it, finally, look more like a real creek again. He chained his bike to the "Danger, Trespassing on Railway Property Is Illegal" sign along the tracks at the top of the embankment and carefully leaned over the bridge.

"Shannon! Are you down there, Shannon? It's Josh!"

There was no answer. The rain was now coming down in sheets and, wanting to get out of the rain, Josh carefully walked down the muddy path on the south side of the bridge, to the creek. It was going to be a bit of a hassle getting the mud out of these sneakers before going home, he thought. He walked to the bridge and shouted into the stone tunnel under the bridge for Shannon but again there was no answer. Josh had never gone into Shannon's fort without him being there. That had been one of Shannon's rules since the beginning but, since it was raining, Josh decided that he wouldn't mind. Not that Josh had any intention of telling Shannon. Watching his step, he walked under the bridge. The water was higher than Josh had ever seen it and he had to walk close to the wall to avoid stepping into the creek, which was running brisker than it had all summer.

Josh pulled aside the branches of thorn bushes hiding the fort and crawled in. It was actually pretty dry in there, being wedged between the bridge and the foot of the hill. He took off the hood of his jacket and sat on the old piece of carpet, hugging his cold bare legs trying to warm up. Maybe I should start a small fire just outside the fort, he thought. He looked through the coffee cans that Shannon had hidden for matches but did not find anything but ladies' underwear and nudie magazines, so Josh abandoned the idea of the fire. It was time to start carrying his own lighter in case this ever happened again. All smokers should carry a lighter anyway.

The sound of rain and wind in the trees was soothing. He had forgotten raindrops sounded lovely as they hit the leaves, bridge, and red clay. And the creek was beginning to have the wonderful swirling babbling sound it had before the summer drought. Josh flipped through the Hustler Magazine, now somewhat worn and fading, with the naked cop on the last page and wished he had a cigarette as a train rumbled above him. It was a long freight train on its way toward Buffalo. In the rain, the train whistle sounded as if it was being blown right beside him in the fort. Those whistles, irritating when he had first moved to Alkeld Street, would now lull him to sleep in his bed late at night. He yawned.

Suddenly, water began flooding into the fort. Josh quickly scurried out through the bushes and saw that the creek had risen all the way to the fort at the foot of the hill. There was no way Josh could walk under the train bridge to the other side now. The creek was at least waist high under the bridge, flowing strong and swiftly toward the lake. He had to get up the side of the hill now! And he had to do it going through the impenetrable north side of the bridge with the thorn bushes and no footpath.

Holy fuck!

Panicking, Josh tried to scramble up the hill, which was now just a cliff of red mud, and he quickly slid back down the muck toward the creek. The raging water had now swept most of the fort away, and appeared to be growing higher by the second, swirling with red-brown eddies and whitecaps. He grabbed one of the thorn bushes near the foot of the hill to prevent himself from falling backwards into the water. He winced as they pierced the skin on his hands and, after catching his breath, he pulled himself a few feet up the hill by slowly grabbing another thorny bush above him as best he could.

"Help me," Josh squeaked out.

Idiot! Nobody is going to hear you out here, he thought. You're going to have to do this yourself. Slowly and painfully, he pulled himself up the hill. About halfway up, one of his sneakers came off and was swallowed up in the red muck. If he fell now, he would be swept away to the lake and end up just like that Ragno boy, except he would have done it to himself.

And what if the water rises faster than I can climb?

Josh tried to move up the hill but lost his footing again and fell backwards into a huge thorn bush that stopped his fall but tore into his scalp, back, and legs. He reached out and grabbed on to the root of a tree growing in the side of the hill. I can't do this, he thought. I'm going to be swept out into Lake Ontario. And they'll never find me.

Someone yelled, "Josh!"

Josh looked up and saw Shannon Perry, soaking wet, looking down at him from the train bridge.

"Shannon, help me!"

"Hold on!"

Shannon carefully climbed down the side of the embankment, holding onto tree branches with each step and ignoring the thorn bushes as they scraped at his skin, until he reached Josh. He grabbed Josh by the front of his shirt.

"Grab the tree branch! Now take a step… now another! Good, that's it!"

Slowly, with Shannon still holding onto the collar of Josh's shirt, the two boys made their way up the muddy hill to the top where Josh collapsed onto the train track as the rain pounded over him, washing away the red mud covering his body. He thought for a second that he might cry but didn't. He had cried enough this summer.

"Thank you," he said as the rain fell on his face.

"That's why I told you not to come down here if it was raining hard," Shannon said, sitting on the polished silver rail of the railroad track. They were both wet, muddy, and bleeding from their hands and legs.

"How did you know I was here?"

"I wanted to see how my fort was doing in the rain and I saw your new bike locked to the sign pole. Good thing I did." He stood and looked down, over the bridge, at the creek below where his fort had been. "Fuck! That was a great fort! And all my cool shit was down there too. Now it's all gone."

"Not all of it," Josh said as he pulled out a pair of ladies' underwear from the pocket of his jacket. "When it flooded, I grabbed what I could for you. Sorry, I got some mud on them."

Shannon smiled and took the grubby underwear from Josh.

"You know what, Josh Moore? You turned out to be a pretty good fort buddy. Maybe we'll even rebuild the fort next summer."

When Josh got home, his mother read him the riot act. There was no way Josh could lie his way out of this (though he considered it) and fessed up about being down at Red Hill Creek when the rain started. However, Josh didn't tell her anything about the fort, Shannon, the underwear, or about nearly drowning. All he told his mother was that he was on the bank of the creek when the rain started, had lost his shoe in the mud, and scraped his hands, legs, and scalp on the thorn bushes getting back up the hill. Just as Josh didn't tell his mother about what really happened at Camp Ronkewe, he decided that since his mother was a girl, she wouldn't understand about what happened at Red Hill Creek that day.

"It was an old shoe anyway," he said.

"Get undressed and take a shower while I soak those clothes in the laundry tub. Then I'll put some Polysporin on those scrapes. And no more creek! Ever!"

He went to his room and, as he began undressing, took the folded last page of the Hustler Magazine with the hairy naked policeman out of his back pocket. It was a bit wet but was otherwise in as good shape as it had been in the fort. At least I got this, he thought as he got out his secret box from under his captain's bed and placed the dirty picture between the pages of the Amway catalogue. He finished getting undressed to his underwear then walked down the hall to the bathroom to take a shower, looking at the scrapes, scratches and puncture marks made by the thorn bushes over his body. There would probably be some small scars.

This has been one lousy fucking summer!

Labour Day, 1977

Thirteen

i

Ted had been to the Ironworker's Union Hall once before. It had been for a buddy's wedding reception back in 1964. That wedding had been one of the first times he had taken Gloria out. His friend's marriage didn't last more than a year, but it wasn't a total loss since he had taken some great photographs of Gloria with his camera in Gage Park that day.

Christ, Gloria was beautiful.

Ted had not told Gloria where he was going when he left. It wasn't anyone's business but his own. One day he would tell her that he had finally taken Dr. Shackelford's suggestion but AA just wasn't for him. Though Ted's drinking was one thing that Gloria rarely nagged him about, his gambling was another matter entirely.

Ted turned his Chevy down Waterloo Street. He would occasionally drive past the old house, surprised how it looked smaller and sadder with each passing year. Maybe that was because he was feeling smaller and sadder himself. He stopped the car and looked up at his old bedroom window on the right side of the house that he shared with Jack, Noah, Dale, and Andy, at different times, through the years. The window on the left had been Wilma, Sue, and Peggy's room and, much later, Bonnie's. In the back of the house, across from Abe and Ted's mother's bedroom, was Tessa's room. Originally just a storage room above the kitchen, Tessa's room was the smallest in the house. Ours was never a happy house, he thought, driving away. Hopefully whoever is living there now is happier than we were.

Before Ted left the mental hospital, Dr. Shackelford had suggested, quite strongly, that Ted at least *try* one of these meetings to see if it 'spoke to him'. Ted had promised Shackelford that he would attend one, but he had been avoiding it for the entire month he'd been home. Nonetheless, that morning he had finally acquiesced and looked up the number for Alcoholics Anonymous in the phone book after having woken up with one of the worst hangovers of his life and feeling so anxious that he had thought that he might be having a heart attack. It took his own medication, a joint, and two of Gloria's valiums to get him to relax enough to even dial the number.

Ted had stopped sleeping in his bed with Gloria most nights, choosing instead to sleep on the old couch in the basement, telling himself it was because he didn't want to wake her in the night with his tossing and turning. During the day, he sat alone in the basement with the curtains drawn watching sports or old movies on television or playing songs like "Goodnight Irene" and "Ain't No Sunshine When She's Gone" on his guitar. But now playing guitar just made Ted even more depressed. And he hated the way Gloria looked at him when she thought he wasn't looking. She thought he was about to go off the deep end again. And she was still pissed off with him about Abe, even though they had paid him off completely, including a bit of interest, with the money that Hannah had given Gloria. If she were a drink on one of those paper cocktail placemats on Josh's wall, the way she looked at him would be two parts pity and one part anger: *The Gloria cocktail*.

Ted had gone up to the psychiatric hospital twice during August to visit Rick, taking him up cigarettes and candy and sitting with him in the garden. Ted had been thrilled that Rick was looking better each time he saw him; he was now acting more like a kid and less like a sad middle-aged man. Rick had even started some kind of a budding romance with one of the girls from the east wing that the doctors and nurses, though closely watching, were not entirely discouraging. The last time Ted was up there, Rick said he was even looking forward to finally getting his braces off. Jonathan had been sent home from the Hamilton Psychiatric Hospital two weeks after Ted but the two of them had spoken only once since then. Ted had called and left Jonathan messages a few times, but Jonathan never called him back, so, Ted had concluded, either Jonathan's wife, Lola, wasn't giving Jonathan the messages or Jonathan had decided that he didn't want anything to do with his old crazy hospital friends. And that was Jonathan's prerogative. Maybe Jonathan, like Rick, was doing great, getting back into life up there in the west end of the city.

Ted wasn't doing as well.

Though the intrusive thoughts were pretty much bearable right now (as he continued to use the techniques that Dr. Shackelford had taught him to let those thoughts flow over and through him), since they had buried the Old Man, Ted could feel that he was beginning to fall into a slight depression and his anxiety attacks were increasing. The only place he could battle the anxiety was in the dark quiet basement alone. He was still betting on the horses and, though he had fallen a few hundred dollars into debt at one point, was able to hit a long shot and clear his debts for now. He would have told his new psychiatrist all about it, but his new doctor had cancelled their first appointment and rescheduled for mid-September. *By that time, I might be certifiably nuts again.*

Arriving downtown at the union hall, Ted parked the car in the lot behind the building and, after a moment when he considered driving away, turned off his car. This was the first time in months he had the heat on in his Chevy. Ever since that heavy rain last week it was as if someone had flipped some gigantic switch somewhere, turning summer to autumn. Today the high temperature was only in the mid-sixties in Hamilton and tonight it could drop into the forties. Soon it would be winter again. Still, the weatherman on the local news said it would be a pleasant sunny day tomorrow for the Labour Day parade. They always had good weather for the Labour Day parade. If Ted believed in God, he would say God was a socialist too.

The cigarette smoke hung heavy in the air when Ted walked through the front doors of the union hall. The room was large, large enough for a union meeting, New Year's dance, or wedding reception. It looked to be set up for a church service with rows of wooden chairs facing a podium in front. Placed around the room were white cardboard signs with black writing with trite sayings.

First Things First, Let Go and Let God and *Easy Does It.* Ted hated sloganism. Sloganism destroyed dissent.

Less than half of the chairs in the hall were filled. That makes sense, Ted thought. Who would come here on a Sunday night? If you had to choose, wouldn't you go to an AA meeting on a Wednesday or something? At the back of the room was a table with a few thick blue books and pamphlets scattered on it with titles like *Are You an Alcoholic? Take a Quiz!* Easy answers to a complicated question. No, he would not be perusing the pamphlets or taking their quiz tonight. And where were all the women? He knew enough women who were drunks to know there should be at least *some* women at a meeting of alcoholics. *Maybe women are better at handling it.*

He skipped the suspicious looking coffee urn with a mountain of white Styrofoam cups and, standing alone on the north side of the room, lit a cigarette. I should have stopped at Tim Horton's and grabbed a coffee on the way, he thought. About half of the people there had brought their own coffee. Maybe he would stop at the Tim Horton's coffee shop on Wellington and Main on his way home. Ted's eyes darted across the room to see if there was anyone there he knew. Ted knew a lot of people in this town and a lot of them drank.

"Nope, no one I know," he said to himself with relief.

Then, in quick succession, five men, each with big goofy grins, seemingly catching the scent of fresh meat, made a beeline to Ted to introduce themselves.

"First time?"

"Welcome!"

"Do you live in Hamilton?"

"Married?"

"Kids?"

"Have a coffee!"

"Our coffee is renowned in AA circles!"

Ted shook their hands and told them his first name and not much else. Like fucking Moonies, he thought as he politely extricated himself from the five men and took a seat at the end of the back row. He placed a tin ashtray on the seat beside him to prevent anyone from sitting down right beside him and checked the distance between himself and the exit again.

One rotund balding man with a cigarette hanging from his mouth moved the tin ashtray and sat down in the chair right next to Ted. He made Ted's flesh creep. Once at the Tivoli theatre during the 3D skin flick, *What the Swedish Butler Saw,* in a practically empty theatre, some guy had come over and sat down right beside Ted and yanked out his cock. Ted had just rolled his eyes under his red and blue 3D cardboard glasses, got up, and moved to another seat across the theatre. That guy at the Tivoli knew not to follow but Ted wasn't sure about this guy beside him now.

"I remember my first time," the man said.

The man suddenly noticed the scar on Ted's neck with a look of shock and then, quickly, his eyes darted back up to Ted's eyes and he grinned, unconvincingly.

"Uh huh," Ted said.

"Hard coming through the doors, eh?"

"Not as much as I thought," Ted said.

That was true. The question really wasn't if he had a drinking problem or even whether he was an alcoholic. The question was whether he was going to do anything about it. And the answer was probably 'no', he wasn't. Maybe someday he would tackle this, but not right now.

"Okay, let's begin," a man shouted over the din from the front of the room.

He's got the face of an old drunk, Ted thought, crossing his legs. Only booze can give you a big red face like that.

"For those of you who are new, anyone who is going to speak tonight has already been asked so don't worry. Nobody is going to ask you to speak tonight. So just relax and enjoy the meeting," the man said.

Ted lasted about halfway through his first AA meeting.

As some poor guy, not much older than Rick, was telling the roomful of people some sob story about driving his station wagon into the front porch of his mother's house, Ted quietly got up and left the union hall as the rotund guy looked on with disappointment, like his fishing line broke bringing in a Chinook salmon. Ted walked toward the parking lot and chuckled as he imagined how Abe would have reacted if Ted had driven his car into the front porch of that old house on Waterloo Street. He'd probably still be making payment to the old son-of-a-bitch.

Checking his watch, Ted hopped into his Impala and drove straight to the liquor store nearby on Main Street and bought a 40-ounce bottle of Canadian Club. He had just made it before the store closed.

"First things first," he said with a smirk.

Sitting in the liquor store parking lot, he unscrewed the cap, took a few swigs, and lit a cigarette. He placed the bottle beside him on the passenger seat and drove west, down King Street and past the bright flashing white and gold lights of Diamond Jim's Tavern. Ted had been inside Diamond Jim's a week earlier when he picked up some cash winnings from a local bookie. The red leather half-moon booth seats were tattered, ripped, and grubby and the old stage was now gone. It looked more like the Windsor Hotel today. It was hard to believe that it was the same place Ted used to go for a classy night out when he was young. Now Diamond Jim's was, like most of that area of King Street, a dive. He tried to remember what singing group he had once seen at Diamond Jim's with Gloria but couldn't recall who it was. Was it The Temptations? Gloria would remember. She never forgot a goddam thing.

Ted knew Jonathan's address. Jonathan had given it to him the day Ted left the hospital. Jonathan and his family lived on Blackwood Crescent in the Ainslie Wood neighbourhood in west Hamilton near McMaster University. Blackwood Crescent was about as far from the east end of the city that you could possibly get and still be within the borders of Hamilton.

It wasn't hard to find.

Jonathan's house was a red-brown brick split-level bungalow with an attached garage, the sort of house that Ted had always coveted, with a long driveway and a large blue spruce in the front yard. Unlike Alkeld Street, it looked like every house on Blackwood Crescent complimented the others in style and colour. Behind the houses, the rising escarpment gave the neighbourhood a bucolic feel, giving the

TO REFRAIN FROM EMBRACING

impression of being much farther from the steel mills than it actually was. Every lawn on Blackwood Crescent looked immaculate. Every lawn, that is— except Jonathan's, which was badly in need of mowing.

There was a flickering light, probably the television, but the rest of Jonathan's house was dark. Ted looked at the clock on the dashboard of his Impala. *9:25pm*. That's not too late to drop in on someone, he thought. And, after all, he did have a bottle of Canadian Club whiskey and he really wanted to see Jonathan. He had no one to talk to for weeks and needed, not some heavy discussion, but just to sit and shoot the breeze with someone who understood what he had been through. What he was *going* through.

Ted parked on the street in front of the house and walked up the driveway with the bottle of whiskey in his hand. He climbed up the front porch steps and saw that the front door was slightly ajar. Inside, the television was on but there was no one in the dishevelled living room. Ted knocked on the open door.

"Hello?" he said, pushing the door open wider.

There was no answer. Ted sniffed the air nervously. Images of Carl sitting at the side of his bed with his robe wrapped around his neck came to his mind, but he quickly pushed them aside. Jonathan is not Carl, he said to himself.

"Jonathan? It's Ted! Ted Moore from… from the hospital."

Ted walked slowly into the house. All the windows in the front room were also open and it was as cold inside Jonathan's house as it was outside. He turned on a lamp by the black leather sofa and called Jonathan's name again as he walked down the dark hallway searching for a light switch. He opened the first door he came to and, turning on the light switch, found a child's bedroom, painted bright blue, with an empty crib in the corner. All four drawers of the white dresser were open with only a few clothes remaining in them. The floor was scattered with some baby clothes and a few toys.

Ted turned and moved to a second closed door across the hall and, taking hold of the doorknob, stopped, letting his hand fall to his side. Still holding the bottle of Canadian Club in his hand, Ted unscrewed the cap and took two large mouthfuls. He closed his eyes for a second, bracing himself, and then turned the doorknob and slowly opened the door. If this was going to be like Carl, this time he was ready for it.

Ted turned the light on by the door and saw Jonathan lying in a double bed on his side facing away toward the window, wearing only a pair of khaki military boxer underwear. The bed was stripped, and a yellow sheet and two pillows were lying in a pile on the floor by the door. The one window in the room was wide open and the curtains were gently waving in the breeze. Like the child's room, the dresser drawers were open with clothes tossed on the floor along with Jonathan's Expos ball cap. Ted walked to the bed and touched Jonathan's upper arm. It was cold.

"Jonathan?"

Jonathan slowly turned around, looked up at Ted, and then turned away, back toward the window. His body trembled in the cool breeze.

"Jonathan? It's Ted."

Jonathan said nothing. Ted put down the bottle of whiskey on the bedside table and scanned the room for empty pill bottles but didn't see any. This wasn't an overdose. No, this was something else.

"Do you think I'm going to let you check out on me, Jonathan Pressman? If you do... then you'd better fucking think again!"

Ted shut the window, closed the curtains, and picked up a quilted orange bedspread that was lying on the floor between the bed and the window and threw it over Jonathan. Then Ted took off his jacket and tossed it aside on the floor by Jonathan's Expos cap.

"You hear me, Pressman?" Ted said loudly, unbuttoning his shirt. "You'd better think again." He stripped off his dress shirt and white T-shirt and threw them in a pile of clothes by the bed. Once more he reached for the whiskey bottle and drank, breathing heavily between each big burning swig. Ted then placed the bottle back down on the bedside table and climbed into the bed. He wrapped his arms around Jonathan and held him closely under the bedspread, pressing his naked torso against Jonathan's freezing back while rubbing his arms and legs with his hands to warm up his cold skin.

"You've got to come back, Jonathan."

Ted rested his face against the back of Jonathan's head, letting his breath warm the nape of Jonathan's neck.

"You hear me, Jonny? I promised you that I wouldn't check out and if I can't give up then neither can you! You've got to come back and deal with all this shit like the rest of us… even if it's just to mow your goddamn lawn."

Into the early hours, Ted laid there in the bed, holding Jonathan in his arms, singing Leonard Cohen and Kris Kristofferson songs softly into Jonathan's ear and trying to coax him back into some kind of coherent state. Yet Jonathan remained silent. If I can't reach him by morning, Ted thought, then I'll call Shackelford. Maybe the best thing for Jonathan right now would be for him to go back to Room 215W. Just for a couple of months.

It was almost dawn when Ted got an idea. He would try one more thing.

"Jonathan, I want you to listen to me. You told me back in the hospital that you thought you loved me… and, in a way, I love you too. You're one of the best friends I've ever had, and I can't take losing another person like this. So, if you really do, Jonathan… really do love me, I mean… then I want you to talk to me right now. Please!"

Jonathan's breathing quickened and he began to sob.

Thank fucking Christ! Ted thought, holding Jonathan even tighter.

"Lola left me," Jonathan said softly.

"I know."

"She took Max and went back to her parents in Winnipeg."

"We can deal with that."

"I've lost pretty much everything."

"You've got more than you think."

"Did I miss Labour Day, Ted?"

"No, it's tomorrow… well… today."

"Are you marching in the parade?"

"I always march."

"Then storming the Winter Palace?"

"I'm a socialist, Jonathan, not a communist."

"Teddy?"

"Yeah?"

"Thank you."

Ted continued to hold Jonathan in his arms until the two men both finally fell asleep as the sun came up.

ii

Gloria did not wait up for Ted.

Years of living with him had taught her that much, but when she woke up early on Labour Day to discover Ted had not come home, she became frantic. She didn't want to call up his friends looking for him, not so much because they might think she was a shrew for hunting him down, but because she knew that, even after this stint in the hospital, Ted still wasn't well. Not really. The only person she did call (quietly in the basement as not to worry Josh who was still sleeping) was Doris, who calmly told her that it was a holiday weekend and Ted was most likely drinking into the early hours someplace with one of his good-for-nothing union friends. Still, Gloria worried.

Then, just after eight in the morning, Ted called to say he had gone to Jonathan Pressman's with a bottle of whiskey, had gotten drunk, and passed out on Jonathan's couch. It turned out that Jonathan's wife had left him and taken their little boy to Winnipeg. Ted said he would meet her at the parade that afternoon.

Even if, someday, I were to leave Ted, I would never take Josh so far away as Winnipeg, she thought. A boy still needed his father. Her first husband still saw Kevin and Troy, albeit very rarely. Whatever Ted's flaws were, he was a good father. Better than most on Alkeld Street, that was for sure. He stepped up to the plate with Kevin and

Troy too. And now they were so much like him it was almost hard to believe he wasn't their biological father. And considering where Ted had come from and what he had gone through, he could have turned out a lot worse.

Gloria had sent Hannah the nicest thank-you card she could find from the Hallmark store after Hannah had given her that cheque. And for the rest of her life, she resolved never to let anyone, including Doris, say rude things or make fun of Hannah. It was thanks to Hannah that Abe would never come down to pick up another cheque. And when he did return to Alkeld Street, Gloria would decide if she (or Josh) would be there. Soon, Gloria knew, she would have to tell Josh about Abe. But how do you tell a ten-year-old to be careful of his step-grandfather? For now, it seemed sufficient to simply keep her eyes peeled like one of those mama bears who watches their cubs from the trees, letting them roam freely but ready to pounce if they fall into danger.

Nevertheless, she couldn't help thinking how much better it would have been for everyone had Hannah just lent her the money back at the beginning of the summer when Gloria had first gone up to her apartment on Queenston Road. Though such thoughts made Gloria feel ungrateful.

The hero of the story often comes late.

The one bright spot was that her union had voted to accept Munro's final contract and, like Bill had said, took the ten cents and heat breaks. There was some bickering around just how hot the shop had to be for the one ten-minute heat break to commence, but the union and company finally settled on 92 degrees or hotter in the middle of the shop floor. Of course, this week it was freezing out, so it didn't matter.

Gloria got dressed in a pair of tan slacks, a pink knit sweater, and a blue jacket for the parade and, while waiting for Doris to drive her downtown, wiped a wet cloth over her refrigerator to remove the fingerprints and smudges from her boys. How do they get fingerprints all over everything?

She walked to the living room and saw Josh outside, speaking with Shannon Perry on the sidewalk.

"Josh, come inside. We're leaving soon." She stood, waiting for him at the door.

"Where ya going?" Shannon asked him.

"Some stupid parade *she's* making me march in."

Josh turned and walked sluggishly up the front steps and into the house as if he were going to the gallows instead of a parade.

"I already told you, Josh, that this is the very last year I'll ask you to march with us in the parade," Gloria said.

"Ask me? I don't remember you asking me anything. You just told me I was going to march with you and that it would be a million laughs. Just like that stupid Cub Scout camp. I have no say in anything."

"Well, I'm sorry, but you've always enjoyed the parade and I thought you'd want me to sign you up again. If you don't want to do it again, there's a bunch of kids that are waiting to take your place on the float next year."

"Good!"

Even with all his complaining, Gloria would still miss him if he really didn't march in the parade next year. It had once been such a special occasion for their family. It always filled her with pride to see all her men take part, Josh sitting on the Munro float while Troy and Kevin marched along with Ted and the Wentworth Steel float. Gloria's first unofficial date with Ted had been on a Labour Day all those years ago, and it had been the first night the two of them had spent together. She had always considered Labour Day to be *their* holiday. The Moore-family holiday.

Now that was ending too.

"And why are you still hanging around with Shannon Perry when I specifically told you not to?"

"I forgot you told me not to," he said.

"You forgot?"

"Yeah, like you forgot that I didn't want to march in this stupid parade today."

"Josh..."

"And Dad forgot to come home last night."

Feeling defeated and on the verge of tears, Gloria went to the kitchen, reached to the top of the refrigerator, and grabbed the bottle of Valium. She took one and, after a few seconds, another.

"She's here!" Josh yelled from the living room, making Gloria jump.

She followed Josh to Doris' Cadillac and sat down in the passenger's seat as Josh hopped in the back. Doris wore red jeans, a purple paisley blouse, and a denim jacket. Where would Doris even have found red jeans?

"Christ, it's cold today!" her sister said. "It would be nice to find a happy medium somewhere between freezing cold and boiling hot. We had to put our heat on last night. So, you guys ready to march?"

"Are you going to watch the whole stupid parade, Aunt Doris?"

"I'll watch you guys and your Uncle Ken march but then I'll probably go. Labour Day parades aren't the most exciting things on earth."

"No, I suppose they aren't, are they?" Gloria said. "Especially for kids."

Josh crossed his arms. "But you keep dragging me to them year after year."

"How's the tummy, Josh?" Doris asked as they drove down Alkeld Street.

"The tummy? The tummy is fine."

Josh put his hand out the window and waved to Shannon. He was sitting on his porch with his dirty feet up on the railing smoking as they drove past. Gloria looked the other way, pretending not to notice.

"I think they should have let you call home from that camp if you were that sick," Doris said. "I would have given them a piece of my mind if my kid ended up in the hospital unable to take a shit."

"Me too," Josh said.

"Did your mother tell you I cut out all the Ragno stories I could find for you while you were at camp but they kind of stopped reporting on it after that shoeshine boy was found murdered in Toronto. Now the newspaper is full of only that story every single day. I guess we'll have to wait for the next horrible murder for the shoeshine boy to be knocked off the front page."

"Ragno's trial starts in November," Josh said. "There should be a lot of articles in the paper when it starts. I might need another scrapbook. I'm calling it, Ragno: the Murdering Father."

"It's a holiday. Can we please talk about something else?" Gloria asked, looking over at her sister.

"It's Labour Day," Josh said. "It's not like it's a *real* holiday."

"Maybe you get your constipation problem from me," Doris continued. "I've had a problem with constipation since I was a little girl. Now I eat a big bowl of All Bran and drink a glass of prune juice daily, which keeps me running like clockwork. Seriously, you can set your clock by when I head to the toilet to poop. It's every morning at nine-twenty."

"Well, Josh is fine now." Gloria hoped to steer the conversation away from murderers, bowels, and toilets.

"No, there's nothing worse than working hard for a poop."

"Doris, please."

"Josh, did you know that when I was a little girl, your grandmother gave your mom and me some old Indian remedy made from flower roots when we had trouble with our tummies? It was called goldthread tea. It tasted awful, but it worked like a charm for tummy trouble! Didn't it, Glo?"

"Stop saying tummy," Josh said. "I call it my *gut*. Not my *tummy*. Not my *belly*. My *gut*! I turn eleven in a few weeks for God's sake. And I'm not drinking any crappy-tasting Indian root tea to make my *gut* feel better."

"I don't remember anyone asking you to," Gloria said.

"No one asked me if I wanted to march in the parade, but here I am about to march."

"Will you give me a break today?" Gloria said.

"Not want to march? But you always loved marching in the Labour Day parade."

"Well, I don't love it anymore! And another thing, I'm not sitting on the back of that stupid truck with the stupid streamers with all the stupid little kids waving like a stupid idiot again this year. I'll march on the road with you and the grown-ups."

"Fine," Gloria said. "Just don't ask me halfway through to tell Bill to stop the float so you can sit on the truck because you got tired because I won't do it."

"Who's Bill?" Josh asked.

"You know Bill. He's driving the truck."

"No, I don't know anybody named Bill."

"Bill is the man we bought Reefer from. He's bringing along his little boy, Corey, to sit on the Munro float too. You remember Bill and Corey, Josh, I know you do."

"Nope."

Josh just wanted to fight with her today. He had been in a bad mood since coming home from camp. He blames me for sending him there, leaving him there, and Gloria thought, he blames me for Ted not doing well. *Women get it from every goddam side!*

"You remember Bill. He's an Indian man who lives up on the Six Nations Reservation. Last year, you met him and his kids at the Munro Christmas party."

"Oh, sure, I remember Bill the Indian."

"Don't call him that."

"Then what do you want me to call him?"

"Call him Bill. And another thing, don't ask him a lot of embarrassing questions about being an Indian when you meet him either. It's rude."

"I don't want to meet anybody. And I don't feel like having to be around some kid as young as Corey. Corey is only about five or six and he's one of those kids that likes to run all over the place. During the Christmas party all he did was run through the hall and keep trying to jump on Santa Claus' lap. Even Santa had to tell him to get lost."

"Wow, aren't you a little ray of sunshine today, Josh," Doris said.

There wasn't much traffic, and they quickly drove through the city down King Street, passing Diamond Jim's Tavern, which looked even worse than the last time she had seen it.

"I saw The Platters there once," Gloria said, more to herself than anyone.

"I love The Platters!" Doris said. "Why didn't you invite me too?"

"Oh, that was years ago."

"Diamond Jim's was something in those days. Now it's a dump. They never looked after it or put any money into it. It's falling apart," Doris said.

Doris parked the car on King William near The Windsor Hotel and the three walked down James Street toward the armoury. More and more shops were closing on James Street, leaving just boarded-up empty storefronts. Pressman Tailors was closed for the holiday, but Gloria still looked in the window, past the suit jackets on headless half-mannequins, to see if anyone, maybe Jonathan or Ted, was in the shop. But it was dark and empty.

When they arrived at the armoury, Doris left them to find a good spot on James Street to watch the parade. That shouldn't be hard, Gloria thought, since there were always so many more people marching in the Labour Day parade than watching it. In the armoury, the unions were lining up with Hamilton Glass, still on strike, poised to lead the parade. Gloria wondered if Sylvia would have been able to bump them out of the lead if Munro really had gone on strike. Sylvia talked a good game, but she was all mouth and little else.

Gloria and Josh walked toward the Munro float, covered with orange and yellow streamers and the SOLIDARITY FOREVER—UNITED STEEL WORKERS LOCAL 1551 banner. We really do need a new banner, Gloria thought.

"I have to piss," Josh said.

"You have to watch your mouth," Gloria replied.

"Why? I learned that word at camp. You wanted me to learn to speak more like a boy, didn't you?"

Gloria sighed. "Okay, go to the men's room. I'll be over there at the Munro float," she said, pointing toward the truck. "You see it?"

"I see it. I'm not blind."

He took off toward the men's toilet near the back of the armoury. Gloria never liked Josh going off to public washrooms by himself but, either out of resignation or the Valium she took earlier, she decided not to worry about it. He was getting old enough to look after himself. In fact, she would tell him he could go down to Red Hill Creek to explore if he wanted now, even though he had been going there for years.

At the Munro float, Sylvia and Miriam were already sitting on the two Muskoka pine deck chairs placed in the middle of the flatbed truck. Four men Gloria worked with were also sitting on the side of the truck with their legs hanging off the side, waiting for the parade to begin. In the cab of the truck Gloria could see Bill with Corey in the passenger seat. Seeing her, Bill said something to Corey, stepped out of the truck, and walked nonchalantly toward Gloria with a Tim Horton's coffee cup in his hand.

"We didn't get a chance to talk," he said. He stood a foot away and, looking straight ahead at the crowd in the armoury, sipped on his coffee.

"Josh is in the men's room," she said. "And Ted is probably around here someplace with the Wentworth Steel float. It's not a good time."

"We could wait forever waiting for a good time."

Gloria looked around the armoury for the Wentworth float. It was usually one of the largest and most elaborately decorated.

"I'm not sure what's going on between us, Gloria."

"Me neither... I never," she said softly. "What happened at my house was the first time I..."

"I believe you."

"Daddy! Are you coming back!" Corey yelled from the truck.

"One second, Corey!"

"It's all so mixed-up right now," Gloria said. She continued to scan the armoury for Ted while watching the men's room door for Josh. What was taking him so long?

"What is it you want, Gloria?" Bill said.

"What do I want?" How many people had asked her that question in her entire life? Certainly not many, that's for sure. So few, in fact, Gloria could not remember the last time someone asked her what she wanted. She choked back tears. Panicking, she rooted in her purse for a Kleenex and finding nothing but her work kerchief, used that to wipe her eyes.

"What do you want?"

She wanted Bill. At least that was what she wanted right at that moment. That was the truth, but what exactly did that mean? Did she just want to be away from the stresses and pain of that summer?

She was attracted to Bill, that was true, but how much of this really had to do with him? What if Bill Hunter was like one of those mannequins in Pressman Tailors, just... wearing all her dreams of better things? If they moved forward, people would get hurt: Ted, Josh, and Troy.

"I'm too confused to know what I want right now," she said.

"Okay, fair enough. But let me tell you where I am right now, and the rest will be up to you," Bill said.

Josh came out of the men's room and looked toward the Munro float. Gloria waved, and he rolled his eyes and slowly walked over toward her. "I like you, Gloria. You know that, eh? We could have a pretty good shot at a pretty good life up on Six Nations if it gets that far. Like I said before, I'm not much into spirits and such, but I think your ancestors, our ancestors, may be calling you home. To my home."

"Calling me home?"

"Just think about it."

"I will," she said faintly.

"Walk along the driver's side door and talk to me when the parade starts," Bill said. "I have more to say."

"Daaaaaddy!" Corey yelled again, trying to open the truck door.

"I'm coming," Bill yelled, walking back toward the truck. "Stay in the truck until I get there!"

Josh walked up beside Gloria and crossed his arms. "When does this stupid thing start?"

iii

Josh sat in one of the bathroom stalls in the men's room of the armoury taking a few drags off the cigarette that Shannon had given him earlier that morning. He had almost learned to inhale now and enjoyed the burning feeling of smoke when it came out of his nose.
Fucking stupid Labour Day.
His father had not come home the night before. He had heard his mother on the phone with his Aunt Doris that morning when she thought he couldn't hear her. It was all happening just like it did the last time his father went nuts. But this time, Josh wasn't going to be surprised or hurt. If that took resignation on his part, then that was fine. Fuck everything and everybody. And why was his mother still bitching about Shannon? One day he'd tell his mother that Shannon saved his life at the creek and that would fix her wagon.
Josh took another drag of his cigarette, tossed the butt into the toilet, and listened to it sizzle before standing up and pissing into the toilet bowl. His mother was probably wondering why he's been in the toilet so long and he wouldn't put it past her to come bursting into the men's room to make sure he wasn't being held captive by some pervert or something.
He put the new lighter he had just bought into his pocket and, walking out of the restroom, saw his mother talking to Bill the Indian. Bill was a few inches taller than Josh's father and had long

black hair parted down the middle of his head that fell down past his shoulders. It was about as long as Josh's father's but looked more modern. Bill was wearing a pair of jeans, tighter than his father ever wore, brown loafers, and a tight navy-blue T-shirt that hugged his chest and showed off the beginnings of a paunch at his midriff.

Seeing Josh, his mother moved a step away from Bill and waved. Bill walked toward the Munro truck and helped a little boy in white pants, a denim jacket, sneakers, and holding a box of Lucky Elephant pink candy popcorn out of the passenger side of the truck. That must be Corey, Josh thought.

"Josh, you remember Bill and his boy, Corey," his mother said.

"Yeah, you have a daughter around my age too, don't you?" Josh asked.

"That's right!" Bill grinned. "My daughter, Alice, is right around your age, Josh. She decided she'd rather hang out with her friends today."

Lucky her, Josh thought. He looked at Bill's nipples sticking out from under the tight shirt. What did his mother think of such a thing?

"Corey, do you remember Josh from the Christmas party?"

"I don't know," Corey said absent-mindlessly, handing the box of popcorn to his father.

"You don't want anymore?"

"No. Not right now. Later."

As they stood in the middle of the armoury, Josh looked at Bill, Corey, and his mother. They were all pretty much the same colour. If this were an episode of *Sesame Street*, they would sing that "One of These Things is Not Like the Other" song, and it would be Josh who'd be the thing that didn't belong. And if having the lightest skin wasn't enough, his blond hair was another thing that set him apart from the others, who all had shiny black hair.

If you're brown hang around.

Now, Josh thought, if Mrs. Wooley were to suddenly appear here as they walked along James Street, she would probably tell Josh (and anyone else within earshot) that black hair was okay and blond hair was okay and both were just fine and dandy. However, Josh thought, if

Mrs. Wooley *did* suddenly appear here on James Street and give him that "I'm okay and you're okay" crap right now, he would tell her to fuck right off. Josh didn't feel okay and, to be honest, Josh wasn't all that crazy about his mother being here with Bill while Josh's blond-haired father was somewhere with the Wentworth workers.

"So, you're a full-blooded Indian, eh?" Josh said, looking up at Bill.

"Joshua!" his mother snapped. "You know you don't ask people questions like that."

"Why? You and Aunt Doris are always talking about being half Indian and how your mother was a full-blooded Indian."

"That's okay," Bill said. "I don't like talking too much about blood, but I am Indian. A Mohawk."

"Okay..." Josh really wanted to know if Bill was a full-blooded Indian.

"I'm Indian, just like your mom is Indian."

"My mom is only *half* Indian. And I'm only a quarter, and a quarter isn't so much. That's why I'm not brown like all of you guys."

"I don't hold much stock in fractions when it comes to people. You learn about fractions yet, Josh?"

"Yeah, I hate them. Kids at school, and sometimes even the teachers, say I can't be a real Indian because I have blonde hair. And that's true. There's no blonde-haired Indians on TV. And I'm Norwegian and English too."

"You know what I think? It doesn't matter what those teachers and other dumbass kids think. What do *you* think? Tell me, do you think you're an Indian? Do you feel inside that you're Indian like your mother and me?"

Josh thought for a second. There *was* something there, but he wasn't quite sure he could describe it. He knew he was part Indian and could always feel that deep inside him. And if he had been born with black hair and darker skin like Troy and Kevin, he'd probably feel it even more.

"Yes, I'm Indian too. Some."

"Then forget the fractions." Bill put his hand on Josh's shoulder and squeezed. Josh's father always did that too.

"And I'm Indian too," Corey said.

"You sure are!" Bill said.

Corey grabbed the box of pink candy popcorn out of Bill's hand and put more in his mouth. A few kernels missed his mouth and fell to the armoury floor.

"Don't let anyone tell you that you're not Indian again, Josh. And if they do, tell them to go to hell. Or send them to me, and I'll tell them."

"I want to ride on the truck," Corey said.

"I never saw a kid love trucks as much as this one," Bill said.

Corey grinned at Josh with pink popcorn kernels in his teeth. "My dad drives trucks. One day I will too."

"Trucks? Sure, trucks can be cool," Josh said.

"I want to drive big, long trucks like that one." Corey pointed to the Munro float. "Are you riding on the truck too?"

"No, I'm too old to ride on the truck. I'm walking along the side this year."

"I was hoping you'd sit on the truck and keep an eye on Corey," his mother said. "But that's all right if you don't want to."

"Sitting on the truck is for babies," Josh said.

Josh had spent the last four years sitting on a stupid milk crate on the Munro float, waving like a moron to people along James Street, but he had demanded to walk this year more out of spite than really wanting to walk the distance of the whole parade.

"Don't force the kid if he doesn't want to ride on the float," Bill said.

"Ride on the truck with me," Corey said, putting his little sticky brown hand in Josh's.

Josh had once wanted a younger brother but knew now it would never happen. "Well… I guess I could sit on the truck with him."

"Good man!" Bill said.

"But I'm not waving like a goof," Josh said.

"No waving. Got it." Bill smiled. "How about after the parade, we all go out for something to eat? Someplace with paper cocktail placemats."

How did Bill know that? Josh wondered. Either his mother told Bill that he collected paper cocktail placemats, or Bill had been in his room. Is that possible?

Someone yelled, "All right, folks, listen up! We're about to start the parade! Hamilton Glass, get ready!"

They walked to the float and Bill lifted Josh and then Corey, still holding his box of pink candy popcorn, on top of the old flatbed truck, which was trying, unconvincedly, to look cheery with stupid construction paper flowers and hundreds of crepe paper party streamers hanging around the flat bed down to the ground. Josh and Corey sat beside each other on orange milk crates, like the one Josh had behind his garage, near the truck's rear end. There was a total of six kids and four adults on the float with Josh being, of course, the oldest kid. The children all sat on milk crates while his mom's friends, Miriam and Sylvia, sat on big wooden chairs in the middle of the flatbed. Four other men, who already looked drunk, sat with their legs hanging over the side of the truck. Along the sides, Josh counted over fifty people, Munro employees and their families, marching along with the float. He knew a bunch of them. The same old faces he saw at every summer picnic at Gage Park and the lame Munro Christmas party. Ten minutes later, they were driving slowly down James Street waving like fools.

Josh looked at his mother. She was walking up front, beside the cab, speaking with Bill as he drove.

"Is your mom here at the parade too, Corey?"

"My mom ran off with Mike. Now she lives in Nova Scotia," Corey said indifferently.

"That sucks," Josh said, feeling sorry for the little kid. It must be rough having your mother run off.

"She sends us letters sometimes."

"I guess letters are better than nothing."

"She's going to have a baby now, but he's only going to be my half-brother. You know what a half-brother is?"

Josh nodded. "Yeah, I know what that is."

The truck continued down James Street to King Street and turned east as Miriam and Sylvia waved and blew kisses to the people on the street like they were queens. School starts tomorrow, Josh thought. He had a new set of pencil crayons and a new plaid pencil case. He was all set for when they gave him his first ink pen.

He was ready for school to start again even though he would have to see people like Ann-Marie McCourt and her gang again, telling him he was crazy or queer or whatever. If only he could look and act more normal.

At least there would be no more fucking *TA for Kids* this year. He'd sort of miss the warm fuzzies though. His new teacher, Mr. Tanner, will be his first male teacher. What would that be like? A man teacher? If he expected Josh to call him *sir*, he was dreaming. Josh would never call anyone *sir*. Nonetheless, Josh did like Mr. Tanner. He had that moustache and looked a bit like Burt Reynolds. He was looking forward to having a teacher that looked like the Bandit. Suddenly Josh was feeling more optimistic than he had in some time. Who knows? Maybe it would be a great year.

"Happy Labour Day!" Josh yelled.

"Happy Labour Day!" Corey repeated.

The sun peeked out from behind a building on King Street as Josh waved at the people standing along King Street. The man in the top hat on the giant red Diamond Jim's sign seemed to be pointing the big diamond on the end of his black cane right at them. If I were old enough, I'd go there after the parade and have a pina coloda, Josh thought. Three parts pineapple juice. One-part white rum. One-part coconut cream...

Josh did not notice when Corey dropped his box of pink candy popcorn, spilling the pink kernels around his feet or when he had stood up from the plastic milk crate to collect his popcorn. Corey had only taken one step when Josh turned around and saw the little boy's right sneaker get caught in the cheap orange crepe paper.

Corey tripped.

He tumbled off the side of the flatbed truck and slipped below the orange streamers under the back wheels of the truck.

Josh opened his mouth to scream out Corey's name but couldn't make a sound.

May 1978

EPILOGUE

"Breathe," Gloria said softly.

This morning, Ted mentioned that he saw bugs in her china cabinet. After that, Gloria took out every piece of her Memory Lane bone china and then checked all the shelves looking for any sign of bugs. She didn't find a thing.

My God, I can't go through this again.

Ted had been getting progressively worse for months, but since his friend Jonathan had sold his house and moved out to Winnipeg to be closer to his wife and son, Ted had become despondent. When Jonathan was here, the two of them seemed able to help each other out through their bouts of depression, two old soldiers who seemed to understand each other and their problems. Then Jonathan was gone. Now Ted was alone, spending all day in the basement, having been fired from Wentworth Steel after not showing up for work for weeks. He had just refused to go. Even the union couldn't save his job this time. After he was let go, he suddenly became vehemently anti-union, even sending a long rambling note to the Socialist Party of Canada explaining why he had been wrong to support them all these years and was leaving the party for good. He had also put his guitar out on the curb with the garbage one night. It was like living with a stranger.

Ted's sister Wilma had called from Georgia last week to say she had caught wind that Ted was in the middle of another nervous breakdown, and she planned on coming up to Hamilton to help out. Yes, things were so bad with Ted that Wilma was coming up. Even Ted's mother, Anna, had called Gloria to say she had spoken to Gabriel, and he wanted Gloria to know not to lose hope. She had thanked Anna for passing on the message from Gabriel and then went into her bedroom and cried for an hour.

She sat down on the sofa, sipped from her teacup, and scratched Reefer behind the ear. He was almost full-grown and now preferred staying upstairs with her rather than being in the basement with Ted. Well, if she had to start taking the bus back up the mountain to the Psychiatric Hospital again, this time, she was determined to go up only once a week. Ted would have to deal with that. Who knows, maybe she would have to go through this with Ted every few years. *Until I die or he dies.*

"For better or worse, they say, right, Reefer?"

Gloria ran her fingers through her hair. She needed her summer perm, but they didn't have the money. She would have to rely on curlers until next Christmas. Maybe things would be better then. She was on afternoon shift again today and, with the windows of the plant open, there should be a nice breeze by the time the sun went down. Luckily, this May wasn't as warm as last year. She hoped she wouldn't have to endure another hot summer like that again. One in a lifetime is enough.

There had been word on the shop floor that Munro would close for good but thank God that didn't happen. Not yet anyway. If she was to lose her job at Munro, she had no idea how they would survive this time. If Ted would only pull himself together and find a job. Crane operators could find work anywhere in Hamilton. If only…

Bill didn't speak to her much at work anymore. He had taken some time off after Corey had fallen off the Munro Labour Day parade float and when he did finally return, he was on a different shift (Gloria assumed he had requested to be moved off the same shift as her since it was so awkward being around each other now). Corey must have had his own guardian angel looking over him that day. If he had fallen headfirst, Bill's truck could easily have gone over his chest or head. As it was, the back wheels went over his right lower leg, breaking some bones, but with some rods and pins, Corey Hunter kept his leg. Little boys, the doctor had told Bill, were quite resilient. Corey would be fine. He was back to school by the end of November and would probably even outgrow the slight limp. Thank God! How could Bill have lived with himself if he had killed that child?

Just after New Year's 1978, Bill married his neighbour Michelle at Brantford City Hall. Michelle had spent most of the fall nursing Corey, even doing his school lessons with him. Bill was lucky to have someone like Michelle, Gloria thought. And now Michelle and Bill were expecting, too.

"She won't be wearing bikinis this summer, Reefer."

During the parade, just before Corey's fall, Gloria had told Bill that she had finally decided what she wanted. Well, *wanted* wasn't exactly the right word. Gloria had decided what she *needed* to do. She had gotten carried away, and although she and Bill could stay friends, she was staying with her husband. She still does not regret that decision. Ted needed her. She was now their only source of income, and things were tight. Gloria could still send at least *something* to Hannah every week, even though Hannah had told Gloria over and over that she could wait until Ted was working again, but God only knew how long it would be before Ted found another job. He never left the basement now except to drive to the liquor store, pay off a bookie, or to Restland to wash Walter and Tessa's gravestones. Gloria looked at the clock to figure out when she could take her next Valium. Dr. Heller prescribed one pill two to four times a day, depending on her anxiety.

There had been a few other changes on Alkeld Street. Shannon Perry had been sent to a group home for young offenders in February after he was caught looking into Louise Dennis' bathroom window. Now Janet Perry keeps to herself more than ever, still living in her old house that gets older and dumpier every month. Gloria knew she would eventually see Shannon again. He'll be back on Alkeld someday. Where else would he go? He will probably go back to his mother's home again and again throughout his whole life, between stays in jail. There's just no good in that boy, she thought. She had tried to persuade Janet to get him some help when there was still time, but…

After Corey's accident, Josh had stopped talking for over two months. His new teacher, Mr. Tanner, and Laura Secord School had been very understanding, helping find Josh a child psychiatrist who diagnosed it as hysterical mutism. Gloria had never heard of such a thing. That had been the worst time for her, not knowing if Josh would ever speak again, but by Christmas, Josh began speaking again as if nothing had ever happened. Just like her old friend Carole had. He has gained quite a bit of weight over the last few months, though, and Gloria wondered if the two things were somehow connected. She would have to ask Dr. Heller during her next appointment.

Since Jake Ragno was convicted of murder earlier that year, Josh seemed to have forgotten all about the Ragno family, putting the scrapbooks under his bed for safekeeping with the box of things he thought she knew nothing about. She would have been relieved, except that he was now still cutting out articles about that shoeshine boy killed in Toronto, gluing all of them into a new scrapbook he wrote, "Shoeshine Boy Murder," on the front of. It disturbed Gloria more than when he was obsessed with Jake Ragno.

They never did find that little Ragno boy, she thought with a shiver.

But other than that, Josh seemed fine. He spent too much time alone, and it didn't seem like he had any friends at school; all the girls he used to hang around with had abandoned him since their interests had changed to boys. Now Josh stayed in his room alone too much, not even riding his new bike anymore. Gloria tried to tell him to go outside, but he preferred to listen to his records and read. So now, she had her son alone in his room and her husband alone in the basement. Maybe loneliness was the real Moore curse, she thought. But Josh would find his way once he gets to Red Hill Junior High next September. She had to believe that.

Gloria took another sip of her tea. She had been having stomach trouble since the fall, and this goldthread tea seemed to help, just as it did when she was a girl and her mother had made her drink it while she gently rubbed Gloria's stomach and sang her traditional Indian songs. Now every few weeks, Gloria would take the Parkdale bus from Alkeld Street to the foot of the mountain with an old wicker basket and search for goldthread. This year she, Doris, and Lydia were planning on going to a real powwow near Brantford. Was it possible for her to regain, even a little bit, of what she and her family had lost? She closed her eyes and held the warm yellow tea to her chest. Her ancestors had been speaking to her all along. She had just not been listening.

"But I'm listening now."

Gloria stood up. It was time for work.

About the Author

Jeffrey Luscombe, was born and raised in Hamilton, Ontario, Canada. He holds a BA and MA in English from the University of Toronto and attended the renowned Humber College School for Writers where he was mentored by writers Nino Ricci and Lauren B. Davis. Jeffrey has had his fiction published in *Chelsea Station, Zeugma Literary Journal*, and *Filling Station Magazine*. In 2010 he had two stories shortlisted for the Prism International Fiction Prize. In 2013 he was shortlisted for the Kerry Schooley Award by the Hamilton Arts Council for his debut novel, *Shirts and Skins*. Jeffrey has also contributed articles, photographs, interviews, opinions, essays, and reviews to several newspapers and magazines in Canada and The United States including *The Globe and Mail*. He currently lives in Toronto with his husband, Sean. *To Refrain From Embracing* is his second novel.

Printed in the USA
CPSIA information can be obtained
at www.ICGtesting.com
LVHW091227170724
785577LV00004B/49

9 781590 217481